Cabel kicked open
the bedroom door

He stood rooted to the spot. "Sweet Jesus," he breathed reverently.

Maggie was more startlingly beautiful than he'd remembered. A riot of fiery curls fell over one shoulder, parting over her pale breast.

Maggie trembled as the fierce heat of his eyes raked over her body. Neither of them moved for what seemed an eternity. Then he started slowly toward her.

Her lips shaped a protest, but no sound emerged.

Driven by a strange compulsion he neither sought nor understood, Cabe entered the room, each step bringing an increase to the throbbing pressure in his loins. This was but a dream—a dream that had grown all too familiar.

How many times had he pictured her like this, her hair unbound, spilling over her milk-white breasts, the sweet curve of her waist an irresistible invitation?

Dear Reader:

Harlequin offers you historical romances with a difference: novels with all the passion and excitement of a five-hundred page historical in three hundred pages, stories that focus on people—a hero and heroine you really care about, who take you back and make you part of their time.

This summer we'll be publishing books by some of your favorite authors. We have a new book by Bronwyn Williams entitled *Dandelion*. It continues the story of Kinnahauk and Bridget and their grandson, Cabel. Brooke Hastings makes her historical debut with *So Sweet a Sin*, a gripping story of passion and treachery in the years leading up to the American Revolution. *Seize the Fire* is an exciting new Western by Patricia Potter. Caryn Cameron's latest, *Silver Swords*, is an adventurous tale of piracy set in Florida in the early 1800s. You won't want to miss these or any of the other exciting selections coming soon from Harlequin Historicals.

We appreciate your comments and suggestions. Our goal is to publish the kinds of books you want to read. So please keep your letters coming. You can write to us at the address below.

Karen Solem
Editorial Director
Harlequin Historicals
P.O. Box 7372
Grand Central Station
New York, New York 10017

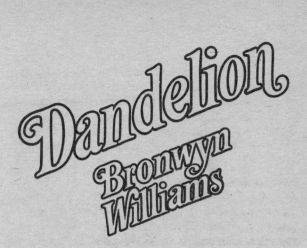

Harlequin Books

TORONTO • NEW YORK • LONDON
AMSTERDAM • PARIS • SYDNEY • HAMBURG
STOCKHOLM • ATHENS • TOKYO • MILAN

Harlequin Historical first edition June 1989

ISBN 0-373-28623-6

Books by Bronwyn Williams

Harlequin Historical

White Witch #3
Dandelion #23

BRONWYN WILLIAMS

is the pen name used by two sisters, Dixie Browning and Mary Williams. Dixie Browning wrote over forty contemporary romances for Silhouette Books before joining her sister to write their first historical. A former painter and art teacher, Browning divides her time between her home in Winston-Salem and North Carolina's Hatteras Island.

Mary Williams is married to an officer in the Coast Guard and has lived in such diverse places as Hawaii, Oklahoma and Connecticut. The mother of three grown children, she now lives on Hatteras Island, where both sisters grew up.

For Rebecca Mary Stevens Burrus,
our mother,

And for Mary Elks, Hatorask Indian,
who in 1788 sold a tract of land
on Hatteras Banks to Nathan Midyett.

Chapter One

Cape Hatteras, 1718

Cabe didn't know whether to laugh or to cry. If it weren't for the feeling of disappointment—not to mention the persistent need in his groin—it might be funny. In sharp contrast to Lettie's height and robust build, her new husband, George, had a spare figure with narrow, sloping shoulders, a pale, hairless face and a noggin as smooth as a goose egg. Poor George was going to need a right powerful tonic, he told himself as he turned off onto Water Street—that is if he thought to keep up with Lettie's vigorous appetite. Unless she'd changed considerably since the last time he'd visited her neat one-room cabin, Cabel Rawson's ex-mistress could milk a man plumb dry before he even got shed of his boots.

A gibbous moon rode high in the sky as he turned in to the One Eyed Cat, a noisy public house that served as drinking place, wenching stall and debating forum. It was crowded, as usual, its low-ceilinged rooms smoke-filled and unbearably warm in the late May evening. The reek of rum and overheated, underwashed bodies was a palpable force, and Cabe, more accustomed to the clean air of the open seas, grimaced with disgust.

Ignoring several invitations, he made his way to the taproom. He would be no fit companion this night, even though he knew most of those present by face, if not by name. They were seamen and their tarts, for the most part, with one or two local politicians thrown in for good measure. Those were a breed he avoided at all costs. Any seaman seen drinking with a politician in this year of 1718 was looked on with suspicion by his mates—usually with just cause.

Sweat formed on Cabe's brow, and he wiped it away with the sleeve of his shirt—one of the linen shirts Lettie had sewn for him in happier days. Thinking of Lettie brought back the bitter taste of disappointment, and he called for rum. Tossing a copper onto the bar, he gazed around him in distaste for the tavern, the present company and all to do with Bath Towne. If it weren't for the fact that the customs officer, the warehouses, and thus the cargoes to be shipped, were here, he would give this town a wide berth. But business was business, and at least the Carolina ports didn't tax a man out of existence, as did the ones in Virginia.

He comforted himself with the thought that the *Bridget* was already loaded and cleared for the Indies, ready to sail on flood tide. With a fair wind downriver, they could cross the sound and hit the tide right on the other end, as well as avoiding a layover when she stopped off at Hatteras to pick up the rest of his crew.

Thank God it was Pa's turn to stay at home and look after the youngers. Both men chafed at being housebound, taking it by turns, and Cabe had stayed behind on the last run. But not even the thought of the journey ahead could mend his dark mood. Dammit, it was a long haul out to the Indies, and he had an itch that needed scratching!

As the laughter seemed to grow louder, Cabe's mood deteriorated further. Why in hell did the woman have to pick this particular time to marry? Couldn't she have waited until after he'd come and gone? What was it about being "respectable" that drove a woman to such desperate lengths?

Cabe lifted the tankard and swallowed. The rum was watered, and that only added to his frustration. He told himself that he might even have married her himself if she'd had a bit of patience.

But then his conscience—that small inner voice his grandfather had called the Voice That Speaks Silently—whispered that he would never have married sweet Lettie, no matter how long she'd waited. He was not a man to be tied down, and Lettie was not the sort of woman to take on a ready-made family consisting of a cantankerous old man, a strapping lad of seventeen, an ornery eight-year-old and an infant not yet weaned.

All right, so he would never have married her. Even so, she shouldn't have left him high and dry with no warning—without giving him time to search for another compatible woman; someone clean, mature enough to know how to please a man, but not of a mind to tie him down. Cabe considered himself a reasonable man. He would never expect a mistress of his to confine her favors to a man who was at sea more often than he was ashore. However, he insisted on her having the good sense not to risk lying with every randy seaman with the price of a tumble in his purse.

Feeling a light pressure on his thigh, Cabe glanced down. His eyes lifted to the owner of the pudgy hand that seemed to have set a course up his trouser leg, bound for his restless crotch. Like Lettie, she was a big wench. His first glance suggested a similar comeliness of form and feature. But then she smiled, and the resemblance ended. She had rotten teeth and bold, tired eyes.

The straying hand slipped back to his knee, and she looked him over, from his oiled jackboots to his neatly clubbed black hair.

"Ye're a big, bold devil, ain't ye?" She threw back her plump shoulders, flaunting ample charms that threatened to bounce free from the low-cut neckline of her dirty bodice. "Flora can handle a big brute like you any night of the week. You'll go to sleep wi' a smile on your face, I can promise you that, I can." She punctuated the statement with a flick of her skirt for added enticement.

Not for a moment did Cabe doubt her words. His expressionless gaze moved slowly down to her fleshy ankle and then up again, to the necklace of grime that circled her throat. He considered the long voyage ahead, briefly envisioning her soft round body and the quick relief it promised.

And then he swore softly. The thought was unappetising, even in his condition. Disgruntled, he tossed down the last of his watered rum and headed for the door, ignoring the invitations from several other women and a few of his mates. He was no fit company for man nor beast tonight.

To the southwest, the stars were covered with an iridescent skin of clouds, but the moon was still high enough to light his way back to the waterfront. The tide would still be too low to risk the shoals at the mouth of the river, for even now he could see a length of barnacled piling exposed as he stepped up onto the weathered plank wharf.

Beneath his feet, a hundred rats scurried around in the dank world of mud and refuse. An elderly whore sidled up to him, and he ignored her. They were thick as weeds on the docks, coming out at night like the moths and the mosquitoes. His step quickened as he approached the far end, where the *Bridget* was moored.

For the first time since he'd walked in on Lettie and her bridegroom unannounced, Cabe's spirits began to lift. She was a fine ship and a stout one. Dark-hulled, her furled sails gleaming palely in the moonlight, she was larger and considerably newer than Pa's old sloop, the *Eliza Lea*.

His spirits sounded again. Unless they found some woman willing to take on the care of the youngers, leaving the two of them free to work both ships instead of taking turns, they'd likely lose the new schooner before the year was out.

He stepped around two men who blocked his way. They were haggling loudly over the price of a whore, who cheerfully egged them on. Neither man was sober enough to unlace his trousers, much less take his penny's worth of pleasure. While Cabe had never considered himself overly fastidious, at least he was blessed with enough common sense not to seek relief from among the women who serviced every ship that cleared customs. He had troubles enough without inviting more.

Ten paces farther along, he spied a member of his own crew relieving himself over the *Bridget*'s rail. The man glanced up at his approach. Giving himself a shake, he adjusted his trousers and flipped a salute. "Evenin', Cabe. Figgered you'd be moored tight to Miss Lettie's bedstead till time come to cast off."

Cabe cursed the fact that aboard ship, a man couldn't blow his nose without the whole damned crew knowing it. "Stow it, Amos, or you'll be swimming home in your own piss."

"Anything you say, Cap'n. Seein's you're back early, though, I'll just mosey on down to the Cat and have myself a dram or two."

"Just be sure the lot of you're back before the tide turns." He watched the old man leap nimbly ashore and head toward the tavern, regretting his sharp tongue. It wasn't Amos's fault Lettie had left him high and dry. On the other hand, by the time the crew boarded for the outward run, they'd likely all have heard the gossip. He might as well let them know right off that he'd deck the first man who cracked wise over his mistress's defection.

For several minutes after he boarded his schooner, Cabe leaned against the rail and stared unseeingly at the activity on the far end of the wharf. Whores hawked their wares in varying tones, depending on their degree of desperation. It was a rough time for women, many of them having been left fatherless or widowed by the war. The lucky ones found husbands, the rest did what they could to earn their way. God knows, they provided a needed service, but at what risk? He'd known of men who'd caught the pox from dipping their wicks unwisely, and then spread the same sickness to their own women. God knows how many men these women serviced—and how many of those men had visited ports so depraved that a healthy whore was a rarity.

A crewman from a lugger out of Boston sauntered by, and a woman emerged from the shadow of the warehouse. Cabe had not even known she was there. He looked on with no real interest as she waylaid her mark and commenced her pitch in a voice too soft to carry.

The seaman listened, shook his head, and went on his way, and the woman slipped back into the shadows. It occurred to Cabe when he caught a glimpse of her face that she should never have left them in the first place. He'd heard it said that all cats look alike in the dark, but some looked distinctly better that way.

Another man strolled past, and once more the doxy attempted to lure him with her soft-voiced plea. From his vantage place in the shadow of the aft cabin, Cabe listened, for some reason finding himself curious about the woman. He was unable to make out more than a few words. "Do you—?" he heard her ask.

Evidently, the seaman didn't. "No, sorry, lass. Maybe another time."

She approached a few more men, with the same results, each time stepping back into the shadows, her back stiff and her tousled head unbowed. He'd give her this, Cabe decided with reluctant admiration—she was no quitter.

He knew the exact moment she noticed him. She studied him for several moments before moving closer to the edge of the wharf. To his amazement, Cabe found himself wondering how she summed up what she saw. He was nothing to set a maiden's heart aflame. On the other hand, he seldom sent children screaming to hide in their mother's skirts. An average man, he reckoned himself to be. Neither better nor worse than most.

"Sir?" she said in a timorous voice.

He could see her better now, and what he saw disturbed him for reasons he couldn't begin to fathom. Once more he felt a stirring in his loins. He swore under his breath. *Damn* Lettie for leaving him in this shape! "Are you talking to me?"

"Yes, Captain. I, uh . . ."

She cleared her throat and then went on in that infernal whisper that got on his nerves more each time he heard it. Everything about her got on his nerves! She was obviously not very good at what she was doing. Never would be, if tonight's example was anything to go by. There wasn't enough meat on her bones to bait a hook, much less lure a fish. The only thing she had in common with the rest of her sisterhood was her lack of cleanliness. Even from here he could see a streak of dirt where the neck of her gown dipped low on her shoulder. In the dim light he couldn't tell much about her coloring, but whatever its shade, her hair was likely infested with all manner of vermin. It looked as if it hadn't been groomed in years. Cabe could not abide slovenliness in a woman. Lettie, for all her faults, had been fastidious.

Without actually intending to, he barked at her. "Speak up, girl! If you've something to say, then say it—unless you're ashamed to."

She stood some eight feet away, teetering on the edge of the wharf as if she were toying with the idea of taking a moonlight swim.

He wouldn't recommend it. The whole waterfront reeked of refuse, both human and animal. Amos wasn't the only one who used the waterway as his own personal chamber pot. "Well?" he challenged when she seemed unable or unwilling to respond.

"Yes. That is, I wudder if..." Her voice seemed to lose its momentum, but then she braced herself, lifting her chin as if she were bloody royalty. "I was wuddering if you would be deedidd sub body to—" She pressed a hand to her nose, which unfortunately resembled a mashed turnip. Then she shook her head, her frail shoulders sagging.

Dammit, the wretched little mort was beginning to get under his skin. And that irritated him even more. She was nothing more than a dockside tart, Cabe told himself—dirtier than some, skinner than most—and hell, she couldn't even speak clearly!

Still, she was a woman. No matter what his other faults, Cabe had never intentionally hurt a woman in all his twenty-five years. "Sorry, girl. I'm not interested."

"But I thought—that is, I'd hoped..."

He swore impatiently. Digging into his trousers, he came up with a couple of coppers and tossed them toward where she stood. One fell through a crack and splashed softly below, the other coming to rest against her boot. "Here. Go buy yourself something to eat. If you'll take a word of advice, you'll leave the waterfront to those more experienced at looking out for themselves. Whether you think so or not, you've been damned lucky tonight."

Not that he thought for a minute she would heed his advice. Unwilling to watch her try and fail with the next man to come along—or worse, try and succeed—Cabe ducked into the nearby cabin. It was stifling hot, as he'd known it would be. Besides, he was far too restless to be confined. And he had to escape before he did something he'd regret on the morrow—and perhaps for a long time after that.

Peering up from the darkened hatchway, he waited only until he saw her move on, and then he leaped up the remaining two steps and onto the deck again, where he began to pace. He stripped off his shirt and flung it aside, allowing the night air to dry the sweat on his back.

Thus he found relief from the heat, but none at all from a more pressing discomfort. The gentle lapping of water on the hull became a sensual sound, and he cursed softly, knowing that he would get no rest before they sailed.

Maggie McNair stared at his broad back each time he took another turn around the deck. Were all men so peculiar? She'd thought he had kind eyes, but then, what did she know of kindness? At least he hadn't come after her with a cane, which set him apart from the two men she'd run away from.

The trouble was, she hadn't run far enough. Not yet at least. And she was having no luck at all in finding a ship bound for Charles Towne. For all she knew, her brother Gideon might no longer be in Charles Towne—she hadn't heard from him in more than a year. But she had to go somewhere. She could hardly keep on running forever. So far, she hadn't managed to get more than a few miles away from the farm.

All she needed was a ship that would offer her free passage in exchange for her services as a cook. You'd think she was asking for passage to the moon for all the luck she'd had. How could she have known that all ships carried their own cooks? Or that most all the vessels sailing from Bath were outward bound by way of Ocracoke Inlet, which lay far north of her destination?

She simply *had* to be gone from here by morning, if it meant stealing a rowboat and setting out alone. Come daylight, Zion would turn the town upside down looking for her, and if he found her, he would be well within the law to drag her back to the farm, where he'd force her to marry his half-witted son. If she didn't die of sheer horror, she could look forward to a lifetime of doing the work of three women and two mules, with a daily beating thrown in for good measure.

Maggie lifted her chin in a gesture her mother would have recognized had she still been alive. She'd remarked on it often enough—the McNair stubbornness.

Satan's willfulness, according to Zion.

Two sailors strolled past, smoking pipes, and she struggled to draw in a deep draft. Her father had smoked a pipe. Maggie remembered little about the man who had died so long ago, but whenever she caught a whiff of tobacco, it stirred dim memories of the last real happiness any of the McNairs had known.

Unfortunately her poor nose was unequal to the task. Nimrod, that wretched clod, had bashed it so hard it was probably broken. She could hardly breathe, much less smell. She couldn't even sound her words properly, a discovery she'd made the first time she'd approached a sailor to ask if he were bound for Charles Towne. He'd looked at her as if she'd lost her wits and hurried on his way, shaking his head.

At least she'd managed to rinse off the worst of the blood when she'd passed the horse trough, although there was not much she could do about the grime and sweat from her day in the cornfield. Once aboard ship, she would change into her clean gown. It would never do to turn up on her aunt's doorstep looking like something the wolves had fought over.

As for her hair, it was beyond help by now. There hadn't been time to find her comb, and what with the dampness, it was all snarled, like an unraveled length of curly red rope.

She waved away a swarm of mosquitoes and slapped the one that evaded her. It was impossible to breathe through her nose, yet breathing through her mouth was hazardous when the pesky things were so thick a body fair choked on them. She wished she hadn't lost her bonnet. At least she could've fanned herself with the brim.

Oh, it was hot for May! And she was hungry. And thirsty. And—No! Not even to herself would she admit that she was frightened, for she'd finally escaped, hadn't she? Or had she?

"Do't thi'k about it, Baggie," she told herself, and then she swore with equal clumsiness. How was a body supposed to talk with a nose swole as big as a pumpkin?

Dear Lord, just let me get away from this place, and I'll never complain about my nose or my hair or not having a pair of drawers to my name again. I promise.

Maggie was a keeper of promises. And though she'd taken more than her share of punishment since her father had been killed in the Tuscarora Indian Wars, leaving her mother with eight-year-old Maggie and ten-year-old Gideon to raise, she was not a complainer.

One of the forty-odd widows, many with orphaned children, who had descended on Bath Towne after the war, Jane McNair had been grateful when the widowed Zion Johnston, a respectable planter—a man of substance, according to his own account—had offered for her.

Both Maggie and Gideon had hated the dour Zion on sight. It had been mutual. The man had taken one look at Maggie's fiery red hair and pale green eyes, and at Gid's birthmarked cheek, and his ice-gray eyes had hardened.

Nor had they ever thawed in all the years since.

Maggie's real father, Seth McNair, had been a seaman, a red-haired Scotsman who grew dimmer in her memory each year. He'd come home only often enough to leave his wife with child, and Jane had lost three babes to miscarriage, and one to fever before he was a week old. But for all that, only hunger and desperation could have driven a gentle creature like Jane McNair to commit herself to marrying a man she hardly knew.

Zion's "substance" had been in the form of land, great fields of corn and tobacco that required backbreaking labor, and none to accomplish it save Maggie, Gideon and Jane. Zion's own son, Nimrod, was more hindrance than help. Still, the hardship was nothing new. Maggie had worked since she was big enough to card yarn and pull weeds. After her father had come home that last time, only to get himself killed by a stray arrow in the last days of the war, she had known little but hard work and an empty belly.

By going to live on a farm, they had hoped at least, for an end to the everlasting hunger, but their hopes were soon dashed. Many were the nights they'd gone to bed with little food, for Nimrod ate enough for three, and Zion was too stingy to waste on his own table what he could sell at market. According to Gid, the old man was so tight he only sat on half a chair—a comment which had been overheard and repeated by Nimrod, resulting in another whipping with Zion's razor strop for poor Gid.

Zion had never warmed to his new family, nor had Nimrod. An overgrown child whose mind had been scarred by an early bout of fever, he had compensated by developing the cunning of a weasel. Neither Gid nor Maggie had known a moment's peace since coming to live on the farm, but Gid, at least, had eventually escaped. Zion had finally driven him away with his unrelenting cruelty. As if it were Gid's fault that he'd been born with a blazing mark on his right cheek. Even with the mark he was beautiful, with bright gold hair and eyes so blue they made the sky seem pale in comparison.

But Zion had seen only the birthmark. The mark of Satan, he'd called it, plain as day for all to see. And Maggie's pale green eyes and unruly red hair, hair that no amount of combing could tame, were strokes of the same devil's brush.

"No mortal has eyes of that ungodly coloration," the old man had informed her at her first transgression. "Satan signs his handiwork, and it be up to all God-fearing men to seek it out before it spreads its evil!"

By the time she'd reached the age of eighteen, Maggie had been sought out more times than she cared to remember. That day's beating had been brought on by nothing more wicked than taking a moment out from chopping weeds in the cornfield to weave a wreath of honeysuckle for her mother's grave. It had hurt so to see that shallow mound of raw earth. Poor Jane had had little enough in this life—a small wreath of wildflowers was not much to ask.

If only she hadn't fallen ill with that awful wasting disease so soon after marrying Zion. She'd been too weak to keep up with the backbreaking work and too weak to escape. Gideon had taken it as long as he could before leaving. He'd vowed to come back for them as soon as he found his Uncle Will in Charles Towne, but he'd been only a boy when he'd left.

Maggie had been thankful he'd escaped, even though it had meant more work for her, caring for her mother and working in the fields as well as in the house. Gid had a quick temper and a streak of rebelliousness that would have landed him in serious trouble had he stayed on.

She prided herself that she'd done a good job of standing between her mother and her stepfather. Zion had no patience with illness, and Nimrod took his cue from his father. Both of them were out of the house most of the time, leaving Maggie to tend her mother and do all the cooking and scrubbing, the spinning, weaving, sewing, candle-making, soap-making, preserving, drying and smoking of food for the winter months. So long as she kept the near cornfield free of weeds and didn't dawdle about smelling wildflowers or watching the bluebirds teach their young to fly, she'd been spared all but the occasional caning until recently.

Meanwhile that great oaf Nimrod would be lolling about in the shade of the barn, or fishing in Adam's Creek, with never a harsh word from his father.

Gradually it occurred to Maggie that there were no longer any people to be seen on the docks. The few pine torches lighted to keep thieves from the warehouses had burned out, and all the ships were dark. Had she fallen asleep? She was so weary, it was possible.

Stirring herself from her cramped hidey-hole, she rose, dusted down her skirt and stepped out of the shadows. The ship nearest her, a two-master, was utterly still, with no sign of crew nor the young captain with the kind eyes and the short temper.

She owed him a copper. Even now it nestled deep in her apron pocket—the first coin of her own she'd ever possessed. With a grin composed largely of sheer bravado, she considered waking him to ask if a copper would pay her fare to wherever he was bound.

Gathering up a quilt that was rolled around her few possessions, Maggie made her way as silently as possible in the clumsy boots that had once been Gid's. Taking care to stay in the shadows, she slipped aboard the dark-hulled schooner, knowing neither its name nor its destination. It was enough to know that she was finally outward bound, for she'd distinctly heard a mention of sailing on the tide.

She would go wherever it took her, for she was past caring at this point. With no comb and no bonnet, she'd be a sorry sight indeed when she landed, but any amount of embarrassment was better than staying on to marry that lout. The pain in her back had lessened to a dull, throbbing ache, one with which she was all too familiar. But it, too, would ease in time.

From a source beyond her ken, Maggie dredged up a glimmer of optimism. In a few days, she told herself—a week, at most—her bruises would have faded, the pain been forgotten, and the swelling in her nose would have gone down so that she didn't sound quite so much like a pig snorting at the trough.

Any day now she would discover someone who was just waiting for a woman of her particular talents. In all modesty she could lay claim to being industrious and honest. She could hitch up a team of oxen and work a field all day, and then turn to baking a pigeon pie fit to tempt an angel. And while she'd never been more than fair to middling when it came to spinning, she was a good hand with a needle.

Meanwhile all she had to do was find herself a hiding place where she could rest and collect her strength while she journeyed toward freedom and the bright new future that awaited her.

Chapter Two

She was going to die. Buried alive in a hot, smelly tomb with the whole ocean crashing down on her, with deafening bolts of lightning striking all about her, knowing that at any moment she would either drown or be crushed under mountains of cargo, Maggie prayed earnestly for the quickest and most merciful death.

She whispered her goodbyes to her mother, her father and to Gideon, wherever he was. Then she lurched to her knees and vomited into the bilge again.

The moment the hatch had slammed shut over her head, she had begun to have doubts. For what seemed hours she'd complacently rested her poor blistered feet while she considered her future. Finding Gideon was her first priority, of course, but that might take time. Meanwhile she would have to support herself.

Once the euphoria of having safely escaped had begun to fade, she'd come to certain conclusions. Throwing herself on the mercy of an aunt and uncle she'd never even met held little appeal. In truth, she didn't much care for the notion of being beholden to her brother, who might have a wife and family of his own by now. Gideon had made his way in the world. Surely she could do no less.

For the first few hours it had been pleasant enough, although her back had ached abominably from Zion's last beating. Still, tucked away among all the barrels, bales and bundles, she'd felt safe enough, with a slice of moonlight directly overhead and the soothing sound of water lapping against the hull.

Eventually exhaustion had overcome her and she'd dozed off thinking of her mother, of Gid, of cool, tart cider and tasty pigeon pie with wild onions and hot Java pepper...

Sweat trickled onto the raw welts on her back and she stirred restlessly in her sleep. In her unguarded condition, the past slipped into the present, and she was back on the farm dribbling a trickle of water over her shoulders to ease the fire. With the startling clarity of a dream, she heard the voice she had come to hate and fear.

"Them oxen been unharnessed yet, Nimrod?"

"I had to feed up, Paw. Maggie didn't do it like she was s'posed to," came Nimrod's whining reply.

"Lazy slut. Wash yourself, boy, you're muddier'n the hog wallow. I'll see to the beasts myself."

Maggie yanked at her sleeves, unfastening the lacings that held them to her bodice. A lazy slut, was she? The day after her own mother was laid to rest, and he'd kept her in the cornfield since sunup? And now she was a *lazy slut*?

Standing behind the blanket that partitioned off her few square feet of space, Maggie flexed her back, deliberately worsening the pain as if to show that nothing Zion could do would keep her from leaving this hateful place and taking with her everything that had ever belonged to a McNair.

She began easing the tight bodice, long since outgrown, from her shoulders—the coarse cotton had already stuck to her skin in some places. Finally it fell about her hips, and for one delicious moment she allowed the air to flow over her damp body. Oh, to have time to slip down to the creek wearing naught but her shift, to let the cool water glide over her body, soothing her wounds, to drift for hours, with no one to see her, no one to call her away...

Suddenly the door slammed. A current of air stirred her curtain, and before she could cover herself, it was snatched aside. Nimrod stood stock-still, his red-rimmed eyes widening as they caught sight of her bare breasts. "Corr-r, Maggie, them's pretty! Kin I touch one?"

"Out! This very minute, Nimrod, or I swear I'll flay the hide off your miserable carcass!" Maggie tugged at her gown, but it resisted her efforts, sticking to her damp skin as she attempted to pull it back up.

"I'm old enough to touch one, Mag. I'll be seventeen come July. Pa says a man's old enough to take a woman to wife when he's seventeen, and I'm gonna ask 'im for *you*." He grinned foolishly, as if inviting her to share a secret.

Maggie shuddered. It was unworthy to feel such revulsion for one of the Lord's more unfortunate creatures, but she couldn't help it. Nimrod had been bad enough when they were children. Now that they were older he was truly frightening, his strength greater even than that of his massive father.

She managed to get her gown in place. "Go fetch in a few sticks of split pine if you want hot bread for supper, Nimrod. The fire's gone plumb out, and your pa'll be coming in hungry before long."

"No he won't. He set out to unharness Jonah and Belem, but he stopped off to look at the old chicken run. He's a-gonna tear it down and build a new one on your ma's grave, 'cause he says as long's he can't plow there no more, he might as well get some use out of her some way. Pa says she was too puny to do him much good in—"

"Out!" Maggie screamed, hurling a candlestick at him. It caught him squarely in the face. Too outraged for once to be wary, she bent over to sweep up the pail of water beside her pallet, and Nimrod caught her about the hips.

"You hurt me," he exclaimed plaintively.

"I'll do worse than that if you don't let me go," she threatened, struggling against his overpowering strength.

"I like it when you wiggle your bottom against me like that, Mag. It makes me feel all—"

With one furious effort, Maggie broke free. Panting, she whirled to confront her tormentor. Marry *Nimrod*? She'd sooner feed her own flesh to the crows. How could that hateful old man even dream she would go along with any such plan?

"Once we's married, Mag, I kin sleep in your bed instead of in the barn. You seen what that red rooster done to that old speckled hen, didn't you? I'm a-gonna do it to you, Mag. Pa said I could. He said a woman had to—"

"If you think for one minute I'm going to let you climb onto my back and pluck the feathers out of my neck, you're trailing your wing before the wrong hen, Nimrod Johnston. No man alive will ever do that to me!"

"Pa'll give me anything I want, and I already told him I want you."

"Then you can just go back and tell him different, because I'm not ever going to let any man treat me the way your pa treated my mother!"

"They was churched."

"Well, I'm not churched to any man, so you can just tell your pa to cook his own meals and slop his own pigs from now on!" Maggie knew it was foolish to let herself get so exercized. Try as she would to be suitably meek, Nimrod invariably got her dander up. What if she said something to provoke him? Suddenly she was frightened of what he could do to her.

Nimrod's cloudy gray eyes took on a crafty look. "You think I'm dumb, but I know something you don't. I know what men does to women, Mag. Want me to show you?"

Before she could back away, he lunged for her, one hand going to her breast, the other grabbing her by the hair so that she couldn't move without snatching herself bald. She felt his thick, wet lips being mashed against her own and she gagged. Clawing frantically at him, she tried to pry him away, but it was no use. For all his youth, Nimrod had the strength of an ox.

And then, with a final vicious twist, his hand left her hair and began groping beneath her skirt.

Blind with panic, Maggie kicked out, her iron-hard boot catching him on the shin. Cursing, he doubled over, but before she could escape, he reared up and smashed his fist into her face.

Blood gushed into her mouth and down over her breasts, splattering her torn gown. She hardly even noticed the pain, but Nimrod seemed momentarily startled by the abundance of blood.

It was all the advantage she needed. Ducking around him, Maggie fled out the door and down the path toward the woodlot, praying she wouldn't run into Zion on the way.

Nimrod was right behind her, but for once his size worked against him. Maggie knew every tree in the forest, every berry patch and every tangle of honeysuckle—at least all those Zion hadn't burned out. Breathless with fear, she managed to lead Nimrod into the midst of a blackberry thicket, and while he was blundering about, trying to free himself from the vicious canes, she darted back the way she'd come, slipping into the house.

There was no time to waste looking for the trinkets her father had given her mother—barely enough to snatch her mother's marriage quilt from the chest. Oh, piety! Her other shift was still out on the bushes where she'd left it to dry!

Did she dare take the time to fetch it?

No. Even if it took that thickheaded oaf all night to find his way out of the brambles, Zion would be coming in any moment. One shift would have to be enough.

But she would need her bonnet. No decent woman would— and with summer coming on—

Oh, where was it *hiding*? She'd worn it to the field that morning, and she didn't recall taking it off—unless it had fallen off when Zion grabbed her arm and swung her around to cane her.

She heard a booted foot on the back stoop and froze, her lungs constricted painfully.

Zion.

Snatching her clean gown down from the peg on the wall, she wrapped it in the quilt and pushed it through the window, wriggling after it with no thought to the parts that scraped on the narrow frame. She'd been climbing out that window since she'd first come to live with the Johnstons, but it had been a few years since she'd tried it. She'd filled out a bit since then.

She was gathering up her few belongings when she heard Zion roar her name. As if she weren't dead tired, as if every bone in her body weren't bruised and aching, she sailed over the rough ground, down the rutted cart track, thankful that the moon had not yet risen.

An hour later, she was wishing it had. Swamp rimmed the narrow track to Bath Towne on one side, shadowy forest on the other. Driven by thoughts of Zion and Nimrod on her heels, of slavering beasts that came out at night to hunt, and the great, slithery serpents that inhabited the lowlands, Maggie ran until she could run no more, stumbling again and again on the hardened mud ruts. Panic pounded along her veins, blinding her to all reason.

She had to get away. Zion would kill her if he caught her now, and Nimrod—

Dear God, it didn't bear thinking about!

Not until she was forced to slow down did she realize that her feet were blistered, the blisters long since broken. Either her boots were too large or her feet were too small. Gid had outgrown the things years ago and passed them on to her, but she'd never managed to grow into them. Now they were stiff from years of slogging through muddy fields. But they were all she had, for her mother's foot had been even smaller than her own.

Mama—Gideon... Oh, please!

Maggie mumbled something about shoes and canes, and wished that whoever kept shaking her and screaming in her ear would go away. She fought her way to consciousness, wondering why she was being rocked in this enormous cradle, and why her mother couldn't sing to her instead of shrieking fit to wake the dead.

A surge of nausea struck her and she sat up, realizing that she was no longer racing tearfully over a rough, pitch-dark cart track. She'd escaped, only to find herself trapped in a prison of another sort. Fighting down nausea and panic, she told herself it was only a small thunderstorm. The screams that had awakened her were no more than wind howling in the rigging. As for the creakings and groanings all around her, she had no way of determining their source. It was black as pitch!

Footsteps sounded overhead. Her eyes widened in the darkness. If she cried out, she might be rescued. On the other hand, she might be taken back to Bath Towne and delivered into Zion's hands again. Was it worth the risk? She could be certain of only one thing—if she went back, it would be forever. Zion would see that she never had another chance to escape.

The footsteps crossed overhead and paused, and Maggie felt her way back into a niche between two hogsheads. She couldn't take the chance, not until she was certain they'd come too far to turn back.

She soon discovered the source of all the creaking and groaning. With every slow roll of the storm-tossed hull, the ropes and battens that held the varied cargo secure gave just enough so that the whole load swayed outward and then back.

Dear Lord, what had she stumbled into? The moment she heard the footsteps recede overhead, she scuttled out from between the hogsheads. If those flimsy barriers gave way, she would be crushed instantly! Using her hands, she began a cautious inventory of her surroundings, having seen little enough in the thin slice of moonlight that had filtered down into the hold before the hatch cover had been slammed shut overhead.

The first thing she discovered was that she, along with the cargo, seemed to be on some sort of platform, surrounded by foul smelling water that sloshed over the edges at every roll. And the rolls were growing steeper and more frequent as the intensity of the winds increased.

They were sinking.

As hot as it was, Maggie began to shiver. Her empty belly heaved as they commenced another sickening roll. With a low groan, she collapsed onto her side, feet awash, skirts trailing unheeded in the bilge. She was going to be sick again.

If only they would stop this infernal motion! If she could just breathe a bit of fresh air into her lungs. In the dank and oppressive atmosphere, surrounded by kegs of pickled pork and bully beef, by hogsheads of tobacco and bale upon bale of hides, the stench was enough to get through even her poor battered nose. In close quarters and immense quantities, tobacco was no longer a pleasant reminder of a distant memory.

The more the ship rolled, the more Maggie's belly revolted. And the sicker she became, the more nauseating grew the smell of all those stinking hides. There was no end to it, no help for it. No matter what she did, she was doomed.

By now she'd lost all track of time. All she knew was that she'd retched until her sides ached and her throat was raw, and been flung against every hard surface in the hold until she was one enormous bruise. She was soaked with bilge water from head to toe, and the warm, putrid stuff seemed to be getting deeper by the minute.

The bow lifted slowly, hovered for a sickening eternity and then slammed down with bone-jarring suddenness. Maggie was flung against the ladder. Instinctively she grabbed hold of the splintery contraption and hung on, little more than half-conscious.

It was then that she felt it. The cold water. From overhead. It was trickling down onto her face.

Oh, Lord, they truly were sinking, she thought miserably. *Dear Father in heaven, I'm right sorry if I offended you by kicking Nimrod, but you'll have to admit he was not your finest piece of work. Please look after Mama, and Papa, if he's up there. And while you're at it, you might glance down here somewhere and keep an eye on Gid.*

On the verge of adding a few promises and perhaps a modest request or two, she felt another torrent strike her uplifted face. The seas were breaking over the deck! Any moment now they would come crashing in on her head, and she wouldn't stand a chance.

She had to get out of there. She hadn't endured years of cruelty from that old heathen, years of torture from his wicked son, just to lie down and die without a whimper.

Clawing her way up the ladder, she began pounding on the hatch cover with one fist while she clung to the upright with the other. Her limbs were so weak they threatened to give way, but stark terror lent her strength to hammer and shove and scream until her voice was no more than a rasp.

At first it was only a sliver of light, but it was enough to give her courage. Bracing her backside in the opening between two rungs, Maggie shoved with both fists until the heavy cover began to give. A handbreadth, then two. And then almost an arm's length all at once! Nausea and terror forgotten, she poked her head above deck and began edging up the ladder until she could support herself with her arms on the raised hatch rail.

"Jubilatiod!" she whispered. She would have laughed for joy, except that her abused throat seemed capable of emitting no more than a few squeaks.

They weren't sinking after all—it was only rain! Glorious, beautiful fresh water, falling out of the sky. Only the occasional wave washed across the deck, and now that she could see again, nothing seemed quite so terrible.

Opening her mouth, Maggie lapped up raindrops and felt them pepper her skin, bringing blessed relief from the heat, from the dizziness, from all those hours of being thrown about in the bowels of this seagoing cockleshell. With any luck at all, it would even wash away the stench of the bilge.

High overhead the wind shrieked through the rigging, its voice diminished now. Wet canvas snapped all about her, but the retorts no longer sounded like gunfire. Before her very eyes, the storm rumbled fitfully out to sea, trailing its cloak of darkness behind it.

With trembling fingers, Maggie lifted the tangle of sodden curls from her neck, allowing the rain to shower down on her back. As salt from the bilge and her own sweat leached into the raw welts once more, she winced, but soon the coolness eased the sting, and she lifted her face to the sky, closed her eyes and opened her mouth again.

"What the bloody hell! Who brought you aboard?"

Her hair was torn from her fingers, nearly torn from her scalp, by a ruthless hand. Maggie felt her neck stretched to the limit when she tried to turn and confront her attacker.

"Ow! Get your rotted, filthy ha'ds off by hair!"

The rotten, filthy hands left her hair, only to force their way under her arms. She was dragged roughly out of the hatch opening, with no regard whatsoever for her knees or her shins, which scraped painfully over the sharp edges. The man spun her around to face him, demanding once more to know who had brought her aboard.

To think she'd once considered those eyes kindly. They were the color of polished brass, and every bit as hard. But aside from that, she could make out little or nothing. Her own eyes had yet to recover fully from hours spent in total darkness.

However, some things were quite clear: he was taller than she by a head, and she was a full inch or two over five feet. He was broad of shoulder, dark of complexion, and at the moment, he was mad as a hornet for no reason she could fathom.

"If you had a graid of se'se," she snapped, hampered by her swollen nose and her raw throat, "You'd be od your dees givi'g tha'gs that you're still od your feet! We albost sa'k, you dough!"

"Who brought you aboard my ship? I'll have his damned—"

"There's dough deed to curse."

"There's *every* need to curse! I don't allow wh—women aboard my ship, and my crew damned well knows it! They're nothing but trouble. Any man who can't keep his pants laced up long enough to get across the sound has no business working the deck of any ship, and when I find out who it was, he can damned well start walking. From here!"

Maggie was swaying on her feet, it all being too much for her. As if seasickness and fear of drowning weren't enough to bear, now she had to try and explain herself to this hatchet-faced man, and she couldn't even talk! Knowing that appearances were hardly in her favor at the moment, she stretched herself as tall as she could manage. Ignoring his bone-crushing grip on her upper arm, she rasped, "By dabe is Baggie McDair. I should like to dough precisely *where* I ab, a'd *who* you are, a'd—a'd *why* you fi'd it decessary to break by arb. I'b hardly likely to rud away, you dough."

Cabel blinked in surprise. What the devil had he fished up out of the depths of the hold?

He allowed his gaze to move slowly over the half-drowned trollop, taking in her hair, her pinched little face with the unfortunate nose, and her sodden garment. If she was wearing a single undergarment, it must be every bit as threadbare and wet as her gown, for he could see the outline of her most intimate secrets. Those tiny hardened points poking out the front of her skimpy bodice hadn't got that way from passion, though. At least he didn't think the sight of him had inspired any such reaction.

To his acute discomfort, the very thought of her skimpy charms, as unappealing as they were, had an immediate effect on his body.

Godamighty! This was the last thing he needed.

After several long moments of silence, during which he did his best to force his mind into less dangerous channels, the redhead spoke again. Her voice—somewhere between a croak and a whisper, and with some sort of an impediment to boot— was difficult, but not quite impossible to understand.

"Well? I'b waiti'g. I believe you owe be ad expladatiod?"

Cabe's mouth fell open. Belatedly he snapped it shut. He'd been right about one thing last night—she was no quitter. The wretched little harlot didn't even know when she was licked. "The hell you say," he drawled, amusement leavening his anger.

"Do you have to swear with every other breath? There's eduff filth id this world without your addi'g to it."

He shook his head in disbelief. A whore who was offended by plain talking? How the bloody hell had he managed to saddle himself with this—this—female?

He asked as much. "How the bloody hell—" At the lowering of a pair of red-gold brows over the strangest pair of eyes he'd ever come across, he filled his lungs with air and tried once more. "Why in God's name did you pick my ship? If you hoped to make your fortune by servicing my crew on the outward journey, then you can just forget it. Put a woman like you aboard a ship, and she'll founder before she even makes the inlet."

"You do't like wibbed." It was a statement, not a question.

"I don't like— Dammit, I didn't say that! It's just that, well, it just don't do for a man to start thinking with his cod when he's aboard ship. It—it ain't safe!"

She looked as if she were going to argue with him, but instead she sighed, sagging so that he instinctively tightened his grip on her arm. Poor little mite looked like something the gulls had picked over and left.

Poor little mite! Was he going soft in the head? It wasn't the first time one of his men had smuggled a woman aboard, but few of them had tried it twice. He'd threatened to geld the whole damned crew, knowing that such threats were hardly taken seriously by men who'd known him all his life.

Hell, he'd had Lettie aboard more than once. A man got hungry after a long haul, and in his cups, any one of them might've fallen asleep and forgotten to hustle his bit of skirt ashore after he'd taken his pleasure of her.

But discipline was discipline, dammit, and they all knew his feelings on the matter of whores.

Amos? No, rum was his weakness, not women. Young Douglas was fixing to get married as soon as he could throw a hawser onto a preacher and hold him long enough to get the deed done. Polly would stretch his hide on the net shed if she thought he'd been lifting skirt. And the rest were already wed.

Which left Matt. His own brother, damn his wild, rapscallion ways. The lad was old enough to, but dammit, he was *still* too young!

"It was Matthew, wasn't it?"

"What was Batthew?" Maggie scarcely cared. She was too weak to stand, too proud to collapse.

Cabel shook her, only to feel a tinge of guilt when she fell to her knees. The little tramp was nothing but skin and bones. Ugly skin and bones at that! He couldn't say much for his brother's wisdom in picking up a woman from the docks, and even less for his taste. But then, his own taste had never run to redheads. Particularly dirty, underfed ones with pale pinched faces, big staring eyes, and noses that resembled potatoes.

"Come on," he muttered. Half dragging, half carrying her, he hustled her aft to his cabin, not wanting to have to deal with any questions from his crew until he'd had time to think of how to handle the matter. At her querying look, he said gruffly, "I don't have time now to waste on you."

Maggie stumbled after him, wondering dazedly if he meant to heave her over the side. No time to waste on her *now*, he'd said. Did that mean he was going to waste time on her later? Or had she better take a deep breath and prepare to start swimming?

Fine. That was perfectly all right with her. She wouldn't even have to hold her nose, besides which, she'd much prefer to take her chances with the creatures of the sea rather than trust herself to the tender mercies of this yellow-eyed bully. He made even Zion seem a kindly old soul.

Rain filtered through her lashes, blurring her vision. A trickle ran down her cheek, following the groove that had been a dimple when she'd had enough flesh on her bones to plump out her cheeks. It puddled in the corner of her mouth, and she licked at it greedily, realizing that she'd been perishing of thirst all the while she'd been tossed about in that dank hellhole.

"By thi'gs," she protested suddenly, digging in the heels of her boots. "I left all by thi'gs dowd there."

He ignored her, and she had no choice but to follow him. By then they were approaching what appeared to be a small cabin near the stern. When her captor opened the door, Maggie looked around her curiously. If this were to be her new prison, she would gladly accept her sentence. There was even a bed! A real bed, with feathers and not corn shucks—and fine holland sheets! And a washbowl and ewer, and two tiny windows with real glass.

The man released her without a word. He wiped his hands down the front of his shirt as if to cleanse himself of her touch. Maggie, dredging up one last shred of the McNair pride, looked her captor over with all the haughty disdain she'd once seen Governor Eden's wife bestow on drunken old Monty One Foot. "If you would be so ki'd as to fetch by thi'gs, I should like to cha'ge idto sobethi'g dry."

"You brought along your *baggage*? What the hell was the boy thinking of? He's old enough to know that your sort can be had in any port for a penny a tumble!" So saying, he left her there, slamming the door and securing it tightly behind him.

As if she would willingly have escaped from such a paradise.

At the smooth click of the latch outside, Maggie's indignation collapsed like the hollow thing it was. She sat down on the edge of the bunk, covering her nose with her hands as if warming it would somehow make breathing and speaking easier. It was the final indignity, trying to make herself understood by someone who obviously didn't want to be bothered with her at all.

And then she jumped up again, suddenly conscious of her filthy wet skirt on his pristine bedding. If only she could think clearly. It was as if her brain was connected directly to her wretched nose! Old yellow-eyes seemed to think she'd come aboard at the invitation of someone called Matthew. Since that seemed to be what he held against her, she would just have to explain to him that . . .

Explain what? How could she explain anything at all without going into the whole thing, and she wasn't about to do that. Not with a stranger. Not even with a friend—if she'd had one.

Restlessly she began to pace. And then she began to examine her surroundings more closely. The cabin was small, scarcely larger than her own curtained-off corner of the Johnston house, but there the resemblance ended. The furnishings! Ah, those were as fine as ever a body could wish for, all rich wood and gleaming brass. They were sturdy, and plainly made, yet handsomer than anything she'd ever seen.

And the feather bed. If she were cleaner, if she had the courage, she would sink into its heavenly depths and not come up again for a year! However, rest could come when she'd earned it. First she had to set about correcting the impression that some innocent sailor had offered her free passage aboard his ship. Maggie had been taught from childhood to bear responsibility for her own actions; she might not have money, but she had her pride.

But pride was much easier to maintain when one was clean and dry and neatly groomed. How long had he been gone? Surely long enough to fetch her things if he were of a mind to. Which must mean that he planned to leave her here, wet and bedraggled, so that he could lord it over her with his fine cabin and his fine, dry clothing.

She sat on the edge of a cherrywood chair, half fearful of his return, half hopeful. She hated suspense, and besides, she had a more pressing need now. Dark spots were dancing before her eyes, and her belly was rumbling louder than the thunderstorm. If she didn't soon get a bite to eat, she'd be a poor match for a day-old chick, much less for a seagoing tyrant who blistered the air with curses every time he opened his hard-lipped mouth.

Her gaze wandered idly about the cabin, coming to rest on a finely made chest, and she wondered what was inside. Gold? Clothing, more likely, for there was no press in the room. It would be locked, of course.

It was not.

Well, surely it could do no harm to look. It wasn't everyday a body got to see such fine shirts, and drawers that were nicer than anything she had ever owned. And two pairs of hose, both dyed a rich shade of indigo and soft as a cloud. His sort would never have blisters on his feet from wearing poorly made hose that had been mended until they were lumpy and misshapen. Or doing without.

Her gown was beginning to dry, and in drying, it stuck to her back again. Maggie wriggled her shoulders unconsciously as she gazed longingly down at the finely stiched garments in the chest. Besides the hose, there were two pairs of drawers, scarcely mended at all, and three linen shirts. The man must be wealthy as a lord!

How could anyone so blessed begrudge her the use of a single shirt after denying her the comfort of her own things? Or a pair of his fine hose to warm her cold feet, for the air had grown chill after the passing of the storm, and she was soaked to the skin.

According to Zion, a wicked thought was the same as a wicked deed. Maggie decided that since she had already sinned, she may as well have the benefit of her wickedness. Moving swiftly before her gown could stick any tighter to her back, she began easing it off, letting it puddle along with her wet shift around her feet. She had no drawers. She'd owned only one pair, and her mother's need had been greater than her own. Since then, there'd been neither time to weave nor money to buy cloth.

She stepped out of her boots, hating the slimy feel of wet leather against her bare skin. It took but a moment to slip a pair of the finely knit hose over her white, shriveled feet and pull them up over her limbs. They were miles too large, but heavenly warm!

She eased her arms into the sleeves of a soft linen shirt, marveling at the closeness of the weave. The captain's wife was clever with a loom and a needle, she would give her that—although why such a clever woman would tie herself to a hard-faced man with the disposition of a water moccasin, she could not have said.

There was a small mirror on the wall above the washbowl, with a razor strop hanging beside it. Standing on tiptoe, Maggie could just see the top of her head. She was attempting to comb through the mass of snarls with her fingers when she heard a click, a squeak, and a familiar oath behind her. Slowly she came down off her tiptoes.

Turn around, she commanded herself. Confront the scoundrel and show him that you aren't afraid! After all, she'd done nothing to be ashamed of, nothing he hadn't brought on himself with his disdainful treatment, she reminded herself.

But no matter how bold the command of her mind, Maggie's body simply refused to obey.

Cabel halted just inside the cabin, his eyes narrowed against the dim light from the two small portholes. Damned if he wasn't beginning to understand what the boy had seen in the saucy little wench. From the stern, wearing nothing but a pair of his best hose that trailed a good six inches off the tip of each foot, and one of the shirts Lettie had made him that all but swallowed her down to her knees, she was a right fetching sight. Her face might not be much to look at, but her knees were neatly turned, with the swell of her calves tapering sweetly down to incredibly delicate ankles.

And her skin. God knows, there was one thing to be said for redheads the world over. If they didn't freckle, why then their skin was as smooth and fair as the richest cream. Which was almost enough to entice a man to run the gamut of their fiery tempers.

He rammed his hands into his pockets, angered to discover that his body was reacting with uncomfortable enthusiasm to the woman he'd spurned back in Bath. He'd just come from accusing Matt of spiriting her aboard—the boy had denied it, of course. Cabel had threatened to leave him behind with Pa to help with the youngers instead of taking him along on the Indies run.

And now, bedamned if he wasn't shamed by his own weakness.

"Would you like a pair of my trousers, or were those not to your liking?" he asked in a deceptively mild tone. His gaze had not wandered far from the twin pink cushions that glowed faintly through the tail of the thin white shirt.

The man's sarcasm wasn't lost on Maggie. She shifted nervously, steeling herself to face him. Why hadn't she had the good sense to wait a bit longer before prying into his private possessions? Thou shalt not covet, the Lord said. First she'd looked, then she'd coveted, and then she'd helped herself. "I'b sorry. I thought you were't cobing back, a'd I was cold."

"Cold! In the middle of summer?"

"It's odly Bay," she whispered.

The quick thinning of his lips suggested that he hadn't come back to discuss the weather. "Couldn't you find a worthier market for your wares? Matthew's hardly more than a lad."

Her wares? Had he mistook her for a peddler? Selling what, pray tell? And who was this Matthew he kept on about? Sooner or later, Maggie knew she would have to set the record straight, but not when she could scarcely speak. It would be difficult enough to sort out all her supposed wrong-doings without that added drawback.

But before she could decide what to do, he was behind her, his hand clamped down on her shoulder in a grip that fair buckled her knees. "Answer me, woman! Were you thinking of making your fortune aboard my ship?" His fingers bit into a fresh bruise, and Maggie moaned softly under her breath. "My brother might not be man enough to look out for himself where women like you are concerned, but I'm more than a match for you. Let's see what you've baited your hook with."

Pushing against her chin with his knuckles, he angled her head toward the light. "Your pretty face? No." If he was aware of the anguish that showed in her eyes, he chose to ignore it. Normally far too kind to refer to a lack of beauty, Cabe had been pushed beyond the boundaries of decency. He told himself that frustration, untimely lust and the resulting guilt had twisted the judgment of stronger men than he. "Then you must be hiding something under that shirt of mine. Shall we see? Perhaps you'll make your fortune yet, woman."

"Please." Maggie wrapped her fingers around his wrist, her eyes pleading with him not to shame her so. "You're bistaked."

As he pried the fingers of her other hand from the shirt she clutched together, his smile was not a pleasant thing to behold. "Am I? Then you were brought aboard against your will, is that what you want me to believe?"

Maggie shook her head, unable to speak.

"Then you just happened to wander into my cargo hold for a bit of a rest after a long night's work and fell asleep?" Another finger was pried loose. With hard palms, he smoothed the lapels wider over the faint swell of her breasts.

Cabel's breathing grew harsh. She was too young to be living this sort of life. It disturbed him. What disturbed him even more was the fact that he cared. Knowing that what he was doing was wrong—that the time had come and gone to sate his bodily hungers—he was still unable to let her go. Compelled by something in her eyes, he continued to ease the flimsy shirt apart, to lay bare her vulnerable flesh.

She was nothing to look at, and yet there was something about her. "Did you run away? Is that it?" While he waited for her reply, his hands grew still on the lapels of her shirt. *His* shirt. Sewn for him by Lettie, now respectably married. The shirt was so thin he could see the faint shadow of her nipples. She might be young, she might be homely, but she was definitely a woman, and he was reacting like one of the wild stallions that roamed the island on scenting a strange mare.

"Dammit, answer me!"

Suddenly Maggie had taken all she could take. "Yes!" she screamed hoarsely. "I rad away! Is that what you wa'ted to hear? Well, you've heard it, so dow let be alode!"

Lowering his head, Cabe looked directly into her eyes—strange eyes, paler and clearer than green eyes had any right to be. "From the life you were leading?"

Miserably she nodded, dropping her gaze to the broad expanse of chest that rose like a wall before her. She felt like beating her fists against it; she felt like leaning her head against it, closing her eyes and sleeping until this nightmare ended.

His fingers tightened, and the sound of torn linen was loud in the quiet cabin. "From one man? Or did you grow tired of what you were doing? Were you so inept that you were starving to death? I watched you try and fail a dozen times, remember?" Hating what he was doing, he was driven to go on.

Maggie had taken all she could bear. Wrenching herself from his grasp, she flung herself onto the bunk and pulled the sheet up to her chin. Light from the starboard porthole slanted across her face, hurting her eyes, and had she but known it, emphasizing the lumpy swelling that was her nose. "Just put be ashore, that's all I ask of you. Gib be a cha'ce to get by thi'gs a'd you cad put be dowd adywhere. I'll bake my owd way frob there."

Cabe considered the matter. They were anchored off Hatteras, and already some of the crew were arriving. He'd sailed the inland leg with no more than eight men, but it took twice that number for the outward journey. Dammit, he'd wanted her gone before they showed up, but that had been too much to hope for. A woman aboard a ship was pure trouble—even one who looked like this.

Especially one who looked like this, a mocking voice whispered in his ear. Plain or not, there was something about her...

"All right, I'll fetch your bags while you get ready to go ashore. You won't find much custom here. I'd set out for a busier port first chance. You'll do better there."

Maggie sagged with relief. She was deeply shocked at the strange feelings that had swept over her, setting them down to an aftermath of seasickness—or perhaps hunger and thirst. The odd tingling sensation, the funny weakness. She'd never felt anything like it, nor did she hope to again.

"There's just by quilt with by good gowd folded idside," she told him. Watching him stride from the room, the tops of his high boots making a soft swishing sound as they brushed against his thighs, she let out a long, shuddering breath. Thank goodness she would soon have seen the last of him. These past two days and nights had seen her more shamed than she'd ever been in all her near eighteen years!

He was back almost before she could brace herself for his return, holding out her mother's marriage quilt and her best gown. Both were soaking wet. She stood clutching the shirt around her and took them both from his hand, staggering under the weight of the wet quilt.

He took it from her and folded it into a neat bundle. "Dress yourself," he said gruffly. "I don't have all day, the tide's near ready to turn."

Maggie eyed the limp gray rag with distaste. It would feel no better than the one she had taken off, but at least it was cleaner. And the bodice didn't strain over her chest so much.

Seconds passed, marked by the gentle roll of the ship. "Well? What are you waiting for?"

"For you to leave."

Feet braced apart, Cabel moved easily with the motion of the deck. "I'm not leaving you here to go through my cabin and line your pockets with whatever strikes your fancy."

Maggie came to an instant boil. "There, I just dew you'd be thi'ki'g that! You thi'k I'b do bore thad a thief!"

"I think you're considerably more than a thief, but I don't want any light-fingered doxy pawing through my things, either."

"Why you—you—I would *dever*—!" Maggie protested in a furious squeak, her whole body trembling with indignation.

"That's not my shirt you're wearing? Those are not my best woolen hose you helped yourself to the minute my back was turned?"

Maggie had no ready answer. Her shoulders slumped, and she reached for the quilt and dragged it around her shoulders, preparing to change under it's cover. But the heavy weight of it slid to the deck. "Oh, piety," she whispered, tears stinging her eyes.

"All right, I'll turn my back," Cabel said gruffly. That was a new one—a modest whore! "But don't waste any time. I want you off my ship as soon as possible, and no mistake. Understand?"

She understood, all right. If there was one thing she understood, it was when to stay and when to run. This was no time to stay. Hopping on first one foot and then the other, she yanked off the hose and rolled them into a neat bundle. He would probably burn everything she'd touched the moment she left his stinking old ship, but that was his affair.

Next came the shirt. Soft as it was, it had already stuck in one or two places, and not even for his lordship would she yank it off willy-nilly, skin and all.

"Aren't you done yet?" Cabe demanded impatiently. He could hear the sounds of the crew settling in, laughing and yelling back and forth as they stowed their gear in the fo'c'sle. Dammit, he wanted her gone!

"I'b hurryi'g as fast as I cad!" Maggie muttered, struggling to tug her wet gown down over her arms. The skirt was twisted around her head, leaving her completely bare from the neck down, and that was the moment Cabe chose to turn around.

His eyes widened at the sight of the angry stripes that covered her thin back, from the soft swell of her buttocks to her shoulders, which were barely covered by the coarse gray skirt. There were old scars visible between fresh abrasions, and yellowing bruises as well as much newer ones.

The last lingering traces of desire fled as he stared at the shocking spectacle. He, who had never even flogged a man in the line of duty, though he'd fought his share of tavern brawls, felt his stomach heave at the evidence of such raw brutality.

Quickly he turned away. It was none of his business. She said she'd run away. He'd half suspected her of having turned out some poor devil's pockets while he lay sated in her bed, but perhaps she'd had another reason for running.

It was none of his business, he reminded himself again. The sooner she was off his ship, the better. "For God's sake, aren't you done yet?" he snarled.

"You do't have to swear at be, I'b fidished. A'd I assure you, sir, you're do bore a'xious to be rid of be thad I ab to see the last of you."

Chapter Three

Seldom had Maggie felt so embarrassed as she did now, sitting in the small open boat, with the crew of the *Bridget* hanging over the rail, offering a wealth of good-natured advice while the captain rowed her toward shore.

"Amos! Get on the bilge pump," roared Cabel. "I want 'er dry as a bone by the time I get back!"

"I'll be coming 'round to see you soon's we get back, Missy," called out the toothless, grinning sailor. "You gussy up some, an' we'll go a-steppin'."

Maggie's face burned. She gripped the wet, folded quilt and wished she dared pull it over her head. One quick look at the man at the oars told her he liked the situation no better than she. With each stroke, his powerful muscles roped with tension, sweat beading on his deeply tanned brow. His generous mouth, which had softened a bit while he'd been attempting to reclaim the shirt she'd borrowed from him, was set once more in a grim line.

"Don't go a-runnin' off with no sweet-talking Ocracoker," cried a youth from halfway up the foremast. "I'll be back afore ye can skin a cat!"

Amid a chorus of hoots and catcalls, Cabe swore softly under his breath. Damned inconvenience, that's what it was, getting his men all stirred up just when they were about to get underway, wasting his time when he had a hundred things that needed his attention.

"Aye, she's a couthy one, ain't she?" The voice drifted across the water, clearly audible over the squeak and rattle of the oarlocks. "Pity about her nose. Kinda puts me in mind o' the snout on John Burrus's old boar."

Maggie buried her face in her hands. She hadn't cried for her mother. She had never once cried when Zion had lit into her with his cane. She hadn't even cried when that great hulking oaf, Nimrod, had run his filthy hands over her body and then bashed in her nose, but suddenly, she felt dangerously close to tears.

"Try the widow Gaskins," the man said curtly as he guided the launch toward a weathered wharf with the deft angling of a blade. "Follow the road, turn right, first house you come to. She'll give you a bed until you can make arrangements to get away. Bound to be a boat sailing up the coast in a day or so. Ask at the boat yard. Jeremiah'll fix it up for you."

Turn to the right, ask at the boat yard—Maggie tried to store away the information, but her head was reeling, partly from the rough crossing, but mostly, she feared, from a lack of sustenance. It was hardly the first time her belly had rubbed her backbone. Like as not, it wouldn't be the last.

Drawing in a deep breath, she forced herself to smile. Confound your enemies with kindness, her mother had always said. Perhaps her enemy had already confounded her. From the way her head was drifting off, someone had certainly addled her wits. What a fine impression she would make on the widow Something-or-other when and if she found her. Somehow she must convince the woman to take her in for a day or so, at least until she regained enough strength to be on her way.

"Would you please tell be where we are?"

He waited so long, his square jaw dead set against her, that she thought he wasn't going to reply. "The Northern Carolina sandbanks. Yonder's Hatteras, but I warn you, it's no fine town like Bath or Edenton—you'll find sparse pickings there. If you take my advice you'll set out for Virginia on the first ship headed north. Your kind fares better in a big port town. Now out you go."

The northern sandbanks! Good Lord, that was nowhere near Charles Towne! "Oh, but you do't uddersta'd, I was bou'd for Charles Towd."

"I don't haul passengers, even the paying kind." He steadied the longboat against a piling and waited for her to clamber up.

Maggie eyed the distance balefully. If she could throw a leg over the back of an ornery old mule, she could probably manage to mount the wharf, but it would not be a graceful act, and she'd as soon not have an audience. The oaf! He could hardly wait to be rid of her, nor did he intend to soil his hands on her again.

Well, she could hardly wait to be rid of him, either. Leading with her chin, she rose to her full height. Unfortunately the combination of light-headedness and an unstable boat were too much for her. Dropping her quilt, she threw out her arms for balance and would have toppled over the side in another instant.

Moving so fast she'd not even known what he was about, he grabbed her, his hands biting into her back. In agony at the fresh assault on her bruises, Maggie crumpled against him. She must have made some sort of sound, for he released her almost instantly, but the damage was done. She bit her lip against the pain.

"Sorry," the man uttered.

"It's dothi'g," she managed to gasp. He could have no way of knowing that even the gentlest touch on her back was torture.

"I'd advise you to be more careful of your, ah, business associates in the future."

Her business associates? Would that she could find one! The man talked in riddles. However, to be fair, the fault was probably her own. With this dratted swollen nose of hers, she probably hadn't made herself clear. Hadn't even tried, in fact.

Two men sauntered over to peer down into the boat, one grinning broadly, both looking extremely curious. "Brought me sweet fer me birthday anniversary, Cabe? Ye're a day late, but I thank 'ee kindly all the same."

Cabe glared at the toothless jokester. "If you think Bessie'll let you keep her, you can have her with my blessing, Silas. Otherwise, send her on to Emma Gaskins."

The man called Silas laughed, while the younger one took Maggie's hands and hoisted her up to the wharf. Steadying herself on a weathered piling, she turned in time to see the broad back of the man who had dumped her so unceremoniously ashore. As hateful as he'd been, she was somehow stung that he'd dismissed her without so much as a backward glance.

Chin jutting, she turned quickly away.

So. Here she was, all ready to commence her new life. Smoothing her gown, she shifted the rolled quilt to her other arm and smiled as brightly as if she were accustomed to landing in an all but deserted place among rough-looking strangers. "I believe you were to direct be to the widow Gaskids' house?" she prompted.

"Don't mind my funnin', Missy. Just havin' a go at young Cabe there. He don't let up on hisself near enough, poor boy. Afeared of losing his *Bridget*. Reckon in his boots, I wouldn't neither." Taking her by the arm, the old man led her to a sandy cart track that cut through a thicket of scrub oaks. "Just follow on down the road, bear right at the burnt stump, and it's the first house ye come to. Plank across the ditch'll give some, but she's sound enough. She'll carry yer freight, all right."

Hearing the creak of oars clearly in the still morning air, Maggie hastened to follow instructions. Gabe—was that what the old man had called him? Gabe, short for Gabriel? Well, whoever he was, he was certainly no angel! A yellow-eyed devil was more like it. He'd have been a match for Zion himself. His Bridget could have him, and with her blessing!

She would have welcomed Zion's cane at the moment. Her legs felt distinctly wobbly. In fact, her whole body still rocked as if she were back in the middle of the sound in a raging storm. So much for her saltwater heritage. She had once dreamed of going to sea with her father, her mother and Gideon, seeing all the parts of the world she had only heard about. She'd never have made it past the mouth of the river.

Stumbling along the sandy rutted track, Maggie ignored the hunger pangs that gnawed at her innards and the light drizzle that soaked through her gown. The agony of her raw blisters had eased to a dull ache, which was easy to ignore in light of all she had to consider.

What if the widow Gaskins refused to take her in? Where would she go from there? The man called Gabriel had mentioned a boat yard and someone named Jeremiah. Once she had time to gather her wits and put herself to rights again, she must set about getting away from this desolate place. What could a body find to do in a place like this? She'd seen sign of horses and oxen, but it certainly didn't appear to be farm country. There'd been scarcely any rooftops to be seen, and not a single woman.

As she neared a narrow swaybacked plank set across a rush-lined ditch, Maggie heard a croak and a splash, followed immediately by another, louder splash. Edging cautiously out onto the makeshift bridge, she marveled briefly at the size of the bullfrogs. Halfway along the swaying plank bridge, she became aware of a commotion in the water.

"Mm-maa-ma!"

That was no frog! It sounded more like...a lamb?

"Mama!"

Dear Lord, it was a child! Steadying herself on the stake that braced the center of the span, Maggie peered over her shoulder in time to see a tiny gray fist disappear under the surface. Without a second thought, she leaped into the creek, quilt and all, and began slogging through waist-deep water and knee-deep mud toward the small figure struggling to keep his face above the surface. "Ha'g od, I'b cobing! Keep your dose up!"

Moments later she had the wriggling scrap of humanity in her arms. He was still fighting her, his mud-streaked face wild with fright. "Stop that! How do you expect be to lift you ashore if you wo't let go by leg?"

"Becky Mary!" someone screamed from nearby, and Maggie spun around, the child clinging to her like a leech.

They both went under. Maggie's quilt floated free, the gown and shift she had so carefully tucked away in its folds settling slowly to the bottom without a trace, the water being thick with the mud their brief struggle had churned up.

"Becky Mary, you come here this minute! Oh, I'm so sorry, your lovely things are all wet—your gown, your hair..."

Blinking the brackish sludge from her eyes, Maggie looked around, realizing for the first time that she was not alone. Evidently the child's mother had shown up a moment too late.

"If you can pry her loose, I'll take her from you," the young woman said. "I saw where your things sank. I'll help you fish them out once I've tied this wicked girl down so that she can't budge.''

Maggie managed to get the child to where her mother could grab her small muddy arms and drag her up the bank, scolding with every breath. Then she began feeling around the sticky bottom for her things. The water was unpleasantly warm, and she tried not to think of all the slimy creatures it could be hiding in its murky depths.

"No, farther out toward the middle. Now back a bit, in line with that water bush.''

Following the instructions, Maggie located her quilt, which was all but unrecognizable under a layer of black slime. By the time she had rescued that, her ruined shift and her other gown, she had lost her boots in the sticky mud.

Tears threatened, and she wiped them away with a furious swipe of a muddy forearm. Blast! She could have howled with discouragement. For a ha'penny, she would lie right down in this stupid, miserable ditch and let the waters close right over her head. She'd detested those boots—they had all but ruined her feet, even with her lumpy hose and a corn shuck rolled into each toe—but they were the only boots she owned.

Besides, they had belonged to Gideon. Now even those were gone, and her mother's marriage quilt was ruined, and she was up to her knees in foul-smelling muck, and—

"I don't know how to thank you, Miss, uh, Ma'am. This wicked little mite loves frogs above all else. Many's the time I've fished her out of the rain barrel, until I finally got Jere to put a lid on it. Actually, it was a good day's work, because we don't have near as many wiggle worms now, and hardly any frogs at all.''

Hanging onto the mud-covered child with one hand, the young woman with the dark auburn hair and the snapping brown eyes covered her mouth with her other hand. "Oh, but will you listen to me, going on like a fish crow, and you not even out of the ditch yet. Here, let me take your things.'' And in the same breath, "Becky Mary, don't eat that mud fiddler, he's dead!''

Sagging with discouragement, Maggie tossed her sodden belongings onto the bank and wrapped a bundle of rushes around one hand, after first testing their roots. Having lived around water all her life, it was not the first time she'd been in this position. It was simply the first time she had lacked the will, much less the strength, to haul herself ashore. At least her nose seemed to have opened up a bit. She could breathe. Perhaps she could even talk without snorting.

"Oh, my, they're all ruined, aren't they? Here, let me—oh, you're already up? Oh, my, just look at you! Were you on your way to see Emma Gaskins? You're not in the family way, are you? My glory, I do hope you didn't pop a gusset, but leastways, you don't look very far along. Where'd you come from, anyway? Ain't often we see strange womenfolk around here. Menfolk come and go, what with the boats and all, but I don't ever recollect..."

Didn't the woman ever pause for breath? Maggie lay on the ditch bank, panting from her exertions, and stared balefully up at the woman who was no more than a few years older than she, at most.

"Where's your man, still aboard his boat? Men and their boats, I do declare, marry a seagoing man, I always say, and you're as good as a widow the day you wed."

Maggie nodded, her eyes closed as she slowly brought her breathing under control. And then she shook her head hastily as the woman asked *which* boat. Gabriel's boat, she might have said, but it hardly seemed worth the effort. Nor could he be described as "her man"—not by the wildest stretch of imagination!

A gentle hand began stroking the hair off her brow, and she opened her eyes and looked up into a lightly freckled face gone soft with concern. "I'm truly sorry. I do yammer on, don't I? Always did. No cure for it, far's I can tell. But there, you're not interested in me and my troubles. Let me help you up to Miss Emma's house. She's not at home right now. Rachel was due last week, and John must've sent for her, 'cause I saw her go up the road with her bundle while I was putting out my wash. That's when this child of mine got away from me. I declare, she's fast as a greased green snake. Becky Mary, where did you—come back here this minute!"

Maggie sat up. She didn't know Emma from John or Rachel. "Do you think I might have a sup of something to drink?"

"Lor', child, of course you can!"

Somehow, without Maggie's quite knowing how it came about, she found herself in Sara Rawson's kitchen, gobbling down cold pone bread while she waited for water to boil for tea. It wasn't real English tea, Sara explained apologetically, for the stuff was too dear for any but the rich to drink, what with the Crown taxes and all.

As if Maggie had been accustomed to anything more than homegrown tea. She hadn't tasted China leaf since she was six years old.

"We do have coffee. There's that to be said for a seaman—he can keep a woman in nice things, though I'd just as leave have chicory or dandelion, myself. Still, there's nothing like hot yaupon tea when you've had a set-to. I cure it myself, with ballast stones Jedd give me when I married Jeremiah."

Jeremiah. That was one of the names mentioned by Captain Gabriel. But which one? Before she could ask, Sara was off and running again.

"You'd better strip off that gown you're wearing and let me see if I can soak the worst of the mud out of it while you wait for the kettle to boil. If you don't, it'll stink like dead fish when it dries."

Maggie peeled the skirt away from her thigh. It felt cold and slimy. Her best gown! Still, she was reluctant to strip down again without so much as a shift underneath. She should've taken the time to fetch her clean one off the bush before she'd left the farm. "I'm afraid I don't have much on underneath."

Denying Sara was like denying a plague of locusts. She simply ignored the objections. "I'll dip up a tub of water while you step out of your things. Don't mind the floor, I ain't scrubbed it today anyway. I'd give you a mite of privacy, but the baby's asleep in the other room. We have two, you know," she added proudly. "But don't worry, my man won't be home until dinnertime, and Isaac's off goodness knows where. I do declare, that boy is . . ."

The soft scolding voice poured over her like a gentle rain, running off just as quickly. Maggie was in a quandary. Her modesty had been affronted so many times lately, she would almost rather stay as she was, than undress before another stranger.

Besides, she didn't think she could bear for anyone to see the marks of Zion's latest caning. It was bad enough to carry his mark, without having the world know of her shame.

"Oh, my sakes, you're shivering, aren't you? Let me get you something to wrap up in before you catch your death of cold." So saying, her hostess bustled away, to return a moment later with a coarse cotton bed sheet, soft with wear and neatly mended, patch on patch.

Maggie clutched it gratefully. She was chilled to the bone, despite the steamy weather, having lived in wet garments almost constantly for what seemed an eternity. "I hate to muddy your nice clean sheet."

"Oh, fie! I told you, Rawsons was good at providing for their womenfolk. Never a one sails out of here that he don't bring back a bolt of cloth or a nice new kettle or some such. Don't know what I was thinking about, not to offer in the first place. I've been so busy lately, what with Jedd's brood and mine, it's a wonder I haven't nursed the corn bread and served up the babies for dinner!"

"I can't think why you're being so kind to me," Maggie murmured.

"You can't? Then you must've jarred your noggin when you sailed off Emma's footbridge after Becky Mary, in which case, I'm more beholden to you than ever. Tea's made. You set by the fire there, while I put these things to soaking. Cold water'll get most of it out, then we'll boil your clothes up with my best lye soap. But if the quilt's filled with wool...well, ne'ermind, we'll just soak it and hang it out for a few days. I vow the stink'll blow away directly."

Exhausted by the constant flow of words, Maggie sipped the strong green tea, allowing its restorative warmth to seep through her. It was what she needed at the moment. "I don't suppose you know of anyone sailing for Charles Towne anytime soon?" she asked after a while.

"From here? Why would a body want to do that? Bankers has more cargo than they can haul right across the sound, and a fine inlet just down the banks a ways past Ocracoke."

Maggie nodded, unequal to the task of explaining about Gid and why she was seeking him. After so long, she was beginning to wonder if she'd ever find him again. With a bit of encouragement, she would simply take root where she was.

"You got folks down to Charles Towne?"

"I'm not sure." Maggie sipped her tea, her brows puckered thoughtfully. "My mother's brother married a woman who lives there. I've never actually met either one of them, but I thought it might be a good place to start hunting for what little family I have left."

"A body do need family, don't they?" Sara's face softened. She was a soft woman, small, nicely rounded, with a snap in her eyes and a quick way of moving. Maggie was beginning to believe she also had a tongue that was hinged on both ends.

"You've not got a man a-waiting for you, have you?" Sara continued.

Sighing, Maggie shook her head.

"How come you landed here when you was bound for Charles Towne?"

"It was dark . . ."

"You stowed away, didn't you?"

Tugging the bedsheet closer around her, Maggie buried her face in the fragrant steam from her blue-and-white patterned teacup. "After my mother died, my stepfather—I needed to get away, that's all. But passage takes money, and all I had was a copper someone gave me just before I left."

"Money's scarce. Most folks trades for what they need, or make do without it."

"I was willing to trade my labor for passage, only I couldn't find anyone going my way."

"Looks like you come pretty far on a copper." Sara's cheeks creased in a wide smile.

"I did that, right enough. I lost the blooming thing right off. It's somewhere in a cargo hold, sloshing around in the bilge."

Laughing outright, Sara shook her head. "If you was down in the hold when those squalls went a-ripsnorting through last night, you must've left more'n a copper down there. Either that or you've got a stronger belly than most. No wonder you're looking puny."

From the next room came the sound of a fretful wail, and both women looked around. "Wet and hungry. I know that song," Sara said as she hurried from the kitchen.

A moment later she was back with a plump, red-faced infant. "You met my eldest, Becky Mary. This is Charity Ann. She's got four teeth and another just coming in, and I can tell you, dinner takes the starch plumb out of me, especially when I have another one about the same age to feed, as well."

"You mean a twin?"

"I mean my husband's infant brother."

With the squalling baby on one hip, Sara stirred molasses into a bowl of scalded cornmeal, covered it and set it aside, and then settled down to attend to more pressing business. The noise abated instantly, and fascinated, Maggie watched the tiny fists kneading the full, blue-veined breasts. With her clothes in a washtub and her quilt in a heap outside the back door where she'd dropped it, she could hardly take her leave, even if she knew where to go.

"Jeremiah's mother—that's my husband, Jeremiah Rawson—"

The boat builder. She was almost sure of it. Maggie stored that nugget of information away in her head as Sara's soft voice droned on. Perhaps through Sara she could prevail on Jeremiah to get her aboard the first vessel headed for the southern Carolinas.

"—as I was saying, Jeremiah's mother died a week after little Eli was born, and me with a brand new babe of my own. Of course I stepped in, because poor Jedd was a dead loss. Lor', that old man fair worshiped that woman of his, after near twenty-eight years together. He was real broke up when she died."

Warm, full of pone bread and tea, Maggie had a tendency to nod off. She might not have landed in the place where she'd set off for, but at least she was safe. Once she'd caught her breath, she would begin making plans for the next few days. Meanwhile she would just as soon sit and let Sara lull both her and Charity Ann with her soft, ceaseless prattle.

"Tried my best to look after both households, but I can tell you, there's times when I can hardly drag myself to bed of a night. At first I kept Eli here for feeding him in the night, but I had Jedd and all the rest of the boys underfoot whenever they were in port, and me with only these two small rooms for the four of us. Now Eli stays home, and Jedd or one of the boys looks after him, and I go over there to nurse him. Jedd bought a cow, but I've not had time to mess with weaning the poor mite, and Jedd's scared to death he'll starve less'n I go over four, five times a day. If he wakes in the night, they give him a sugar tit."

She clicked her tongue, and Maggie's eyes widened as she fought to stay awake. "Best I can do," Sara went on. "A body can't work night and day, feeding two growing young'uns and looking after a passel o' men as well. Eat like food was going out of style, they do, and not a one of 'em can cook a lick. Anne spoiled her boys, from Jeremiah right on down, though I do believe Matt was always her favorite. But then along come Isaac, and a few years later, Eli. Poor thing, she was just plumb wore out."

She shook her head, shifted the babe on her lap and offered her the other side without missing a lick. "I'll not say a word against Jedd. He's done the best he could, but if ever a man was born to the water, it's Jedd Rawson. They take turn and turn about staying home, but it fair sticks in his craw to be nurse-maidin', knowing his boys is outward bound and him back home a-boiling napkins and chasing after that limb o' Satan, Isaac."

On and on the gentle voice droned. Maggie didn't even bother to listen, to try and keep up with who belonged to whom. There was nothing she could do. Besides, she had her own future to sort out.

"All the same, I do wish I could find some decent woman willing to take on a household with five menfolk, and the youngest still in his cradle. If Matt would settle down—but then, he's only a boy himself, still a mite wild for husband-ing..."

Suddenly Maggie was wide awake. *Some woman willing to take on a household of men, including a baby?* "A house-keeper, you mean?"

"Angel o' mercy's more like it. Jedd's a fine man, as kind-hearted as ever a body could be, but he's only a man, and youngers needs a woman." Sara cast a speculative look at her sheet-clad guest.

"How many children did you say there were?" Maggie asked, wishing now she had paid more attention.

"Children? Well, some's grown, and the grown ones wouldn't be a bother, what with two ships to keep running between the main and the Indies Islands. Jedd and the two middle boys handle that. My Jeremiah's the oldest. He's a boat builder. Built me this house before we were married. Jedd and Anne had five boys in all, with Matt in the middle and Isaac only three years older than my Becky Mary. And then there's baby Eli, the darlin'est boy in the world. Hardly a peep out of him, poor sprout, and him spending hours lying in the hammock Jeremiah rigged for him out under the cedars, just awaiting for someone to come along and give it a shove and set it to rocking."

Sara studied Maggie from the corner of her large, acorn-brown eyes. Seeing the speculative look, Maggie began to shake her head. She was no fool. She had just escaped one such situation—an old man, reputed to be a pillar of the community, and his motherless son.

"Did I tell you that Jere's been promising to take me and the children with him on a journey to Boston as soon as Jedd finds someone to look after Isaac and Eli? I've never been off the island in all my born days, less'n you count Ocracoke," she added rather wistfully.

Maggie thought for a few moments. She would just as soon not have to set foot aboard anything larger than a rowboat for a few weeks. Looking after an infant and an eight-year-old would be a pleasure, and if the men in the family were sailors, like her father had been, why then, they'd scarce be a bother. "Just the two youngest, you say?"

Sara's face brightened, the lines of tiredness not quite so much in evidence. "I expect you'd have to do a fair mite of washing, for I've let some of it slide. And the mending, too. Cabel's got him a woman somewhere on the mainland who keeps him in fine stitching—I just wish he'd marry her and bring her home with him, but he's too canny to get himself caught when the women will do for him free. Jedd's hard enough on shirts, but Matt busts out of his clothes faster than I can sew 'em up. And you'll want to lay by food once the garden starts coming in heavy. There's corned mullet aplenty, and Jedd keeps a few hens for eggs, and—"

"Sara, please...I haven't said I'll do it. Besides, he might not want me."

"Not want you!" Sara's eyebrows peaked in surprise. "Why, after the way you sailed off that bridge after Becky Mary, we're already beholden to you. Not many people would jump into a ditch full of cottonmouths without a second thought."

Maggie felt the tea and pone bread threaten to return on her. When she found her voice again, she said, "Well, perhaps just until you get back from Boston, then. That is, if Mr. Rawson is willing to trust me with his children."

Chapter Four

Cabel sat at his desk, cargo manifests spread before him, and stared blankly at the slanting sunlight that swayed back and forth across the floor. The weather had held fair all week once they'd cleared the banks, but he had learned to expect surprises this time of year, especially as they neared the warmer latitudes.

Surprises. Shaking his head, he felt his fingers curling into a fist, which he pounded gently on the rimmed cherrywood surface. He'd had enough surprises to last him for a while. The little redheaded strumpet with the great green eyes and the lumpy nose had been a distinctly unwelcome surprise, one that had affected his whole crew.

One by one he'd taken them aside a second time, trying to discover if any one of them had had a hand in bringing her aboard. In the end he'd been bound to conclude that she'd stowed away, for he knew his crew. Naturally all would drink. Some would game and some would wench. But none would lie. Island men all, they were at home aboard both the *Bridget* and the *Eliza Lea*, sailing with either Jedd or himself. It was a flexible arrangement that suited all concerned, and neither Jedd nor Cabe had ever been forced to lock a crew up in port, as was the common practice, to assure that there would be men enough for the return voyage.

Cabe ran a hand through his thick black hair, disturbing its neatly bound symmetry. The month of May was more than half done. Aside from the short runs up the coast with lumber, they'd counted on at least three more voyages this season hauling meat, hides, tobacco and grain out, and sugar, rum and molasses in. But there'd be little sugar left in the islands after mid-June, for the planters were in the habit of shipping a crop as soon as it was out of the field to take advantage of first market prices abroad. After that, there was too great a risk of hurricanes.

"Damn it all!" he swore softly in frustration. They were getting farther behind each day. A year ago, when they'd purchased the *Bridget*, they had counted on running both vessels together, doubling their capacity and increasing their range with the smaller sloop and the larger schooner. By using Ocracoke Inlet instead of the deeper ones to the north, they avoided Virginia's Crown taxes, and could thus undersell their northern competitors—although lately they'd run an increasingly higher risk of encountering pirates along the banks.

But then Anne had died. Everything had changed after that. Jedd, Jeremiah and Matthew had grieved heavily and openly, as was their nature, and then prepared to get on with their lives. They'd forgotten to take into account Isaac and the infant, who had been named Eli Dozier Burrus Rawson, for all his scrawny size.

It was then that they'd discovered that not a woman on the island had time enough to come into their home and look after them, not even Emma Gaskins, who serviced birthings, dyings, and all manner of injuries.

Isaac, dark like Cabe, but without Cabe's lighter eyes, had turned inward in his grief. Where once he'd been an imp of the devil, into more mischief than even Matt had been at that age, he'd grown quiet and withdrawn, allowing none of them to comfort him.

Cabe grieved for the boy, for he, too, had known a closeness of spirit with his mother that he had never shared with his father, for all else they had in common. Anne had been Cabe's link with his grandfather, Kinnahauk, the last chief of the Hatorask tribe. Both his grandparents had left the island soon after their daughter had died, to join the Hatorask on the mainland. Cabe thought perhaps they had gone in search of their son, his uncle Stormwalker, to tell him of his sister's death.

Cabe was proud of his Hatorask heritage. It burned in him like a fever. It was Kinnahauk's blood, he was certain, that made him feel things a body had no business feeling, think thoughts that no white man would admit to thinking. There were times when he could hear voices in the wind, and he told himself it was the spirit of his ancestors, knowing all the while that it was only the live oak branches rubbing together, or the wind whistling through the shrouds.

Perhaps he was daft. For all he found being white a far more comfortable life, he could never deny the darker side of him.

A slant of sunlight struck his desk, the rich red color of the wood reminding him again of the woman who had called herself Maggie McNair. Even matted and wet, her hair had glowed with the same depth of color.

The planes of his face hardened as he stared at the bed where she'd rested. The mirror she'd strained to see. The chest she had rifled to steal one of his shirts. The woman was worse than tar on a boot heel! No matter how much he tried to get rid of her, she stuck. Thank God he'd discovered her before he'd cleared the inlet and headed for the islands, or there was no telling what he'd have done by now. As dirty, homely and bedraggled as she'd been, she'd already begun to work a spell on him before he'd dumped her out on the wharf.

The bile rose in his throat as he remembered that brief glimpse of her battered back. Something twisted painfully inside him, and he told himself that any man who would treat a woman that way, no matter what she'd done, deserved to be drawn and quartered.

Maggie surveyed her new domain with cautious pride. Truly, the tide did seem to have turned in her favor, but she'd wait and see before she settled in. Jedd Rawson had intimidated her at first. Though handsome for a man of his age, he was rough-hewn. With his gray-streaked beard and bushy brows, he'd looked fierce enough, but she'd gradually come to see that he was simply out of his element. She suspected he was even a bit lonely, for all his five sons.

She'd learned that of the three women he'd brought into his home since his wife had died, not a one of them had stuck. The first, a widow near his own age, had tangled with Isaac and walked out the first day. The second, a woman from the north banks who had come with her trunk and all her belongings, had lasted almost a week before she, too, had given up. Next he'd tried a neighbor's fourteen-year-old daughter, hoping that she, at least, would have the wit and energy to keep up with a babe and a small lad, but she'd been worse than useless, spending all her time flirting with the middle son.

"Women are strange and difficult creatures, Mistress Mc-Nair. I admire them mightily, but if I live to be a turtle's age, I'll never understand 'em. My Anne, rest her soul, was as fine and gentle a creature as ever walked the banks. I married her when she was naught but thirteen years old, and never once come to regret it, but I've yet to fathom her ways. The Lord must understand 'em. He was the one that put 'em together. I reckon He just don't intend for mortal man to know all His secrets."

It was his eyes she liked best of all, Maggie decided. A body could tell a lot about a person by studying his eyes. Cap'n Jedd's were the blue-gray color of the pale violets that bloomed back on the farm—or had until Zion had plowed them under. There was kindness there, and humor, something she'd not seen for many a day. He struck her as a proud man, yet a gentle one.

Still, Maggie wasn't ready to give her trust too quickly. She knew to her sorrow that a person's looks could be deceiving. All of Bath Towne had considered Zion Johnston a fine, upstanding man. If anyone had told the townspeople of the way he'd treated his second wife and her children, they'd have sworn it was all a pack of lies.

And there was the man, Gabriel. While there'd been scarce enough light on the docks to see by the night she'd run away, she'd thought to herself that he had gentle eyes, and hoped he would come to her aid.

Too late she'd learned that hopefulness was like reflections on the water. It made a body see things all wrong, things that weren't even there.

Having stayed only long enough to nurse the baby after introducing Maggie into Cap'n Jedd's household, Sara had handed Eli over to Maggie, instructing her on how to hold him and how to raise his wind. Promising to be back before dark to feed him again, she had taken her leave.

It was the baby Eli who finally won Maggie over. While her mind was still troubling over whether to go or stay, the feel of his warm body in her arms, the sight of his grave face, his tiny features and his great wondering eyes tugged at her heart. She tried to resist, not wanting to set down roots only to have to tear them up again. A body needed to be careful not to put down roots in bitter soil. How did she know if she could thrive in this place? It was scarcely more than a sandbar stuck out in the middle of the ocean.

But then Eli smiled at her, showing two pearly nubs on his bottom gum, and she was lost. Jedd, his eyes dancing with something that looked suspiciously like satisfaction, mumbled something about fetching Isaac in from the water and left her alone with the infant, to cuddle and croon to her heart's content.

By suppertime Maggie had still seen nothing of the eight-year-old. In gruff apology, Jedd explained that the boy was inclined to roam, and more than likely he had taken his flat down the creek to Jeremiah's house. "He'll come around, Missy. He's a good lad, only quieter than most. Solitary since his Ma passed, but then it don't hurt for a boy to learn to be on his own some."

Maggie was not unaware of the question in Jedd's voice and in his eyes, but she was not yet ready to commit herself. For all she knew, Isaac could be another Nimrod. She was fairly certain the old man would treat her well, for in spite of her experience, common sense told her that not all men were cut from the same bolt of cloth.

Still, Maggie was a keeper of promises. She could not afford to give her word lightly. Sensing Sara's disappointment, she'd told them only that she would stay on for a few days.

Now she shifted the baby on her knee, rubbing her chin over the fine dark fuzz on his head. "He's a fine boy, even if he is a mite damp."

"He ain't been washed down lately. I'd a mind to do it afore I bedded him down for the night."

It was obvious that this man was about as comfortable caring for a baby as she had been crossing the sound in a storm. And though the babe wasn't her own, she was sorely tempted to stay and look after him. At least until she felt more like setting foot on another ship to go in search of Gideon.

Maggie knew she needed time for her back to heal, time for the swelling around her nose to go down so that she could breathe through it without squeaking, though both her back and her nose were improving every day. She needed time to repair her gown so that Gideon would not be shamed by her appearance when they finally met. It was bad enough that she had neither shoes nor bonnet.

Under Jedd's awkward guidance, she clumsily fitted the coarse cotton padding around the baby's bottom and then settled him in his cradle, rocking it gently while Jedd tiptoed heavily from the room. She tried humming, discovered that with her swollen nose, it was impossible, and la-la-la'd softly until Eli's eyes closed.

As soon as she tiptoed back into the kitchen, Jedd offered to show her over the house. It was a fine house, larger than most. Built of tightly fitted logs covered with cypress shingles, it was floored with pine and raised off the ground so that storm tides could pass underneath. There were even holes bored through the floors in each room so that it would not float off its foundation, which Maggie considered a clever idea once it was explained to her.

"Three rooms," she marveled. "Why I never heard of such!"

"My wife fancied a house with rooms to it," he said with a touching blend of pride and modesty. "The babe's been sleeping with me in the front room. Jeremiah has his own house, and the other two has the back room when they're in, with Isaac in the trundle."

Peering into the neat bedroom, Maggie was reminded again of the man called Gabriel, for reasons she was at a loss to explain. She made up her mind to ask Sara about him the next time she saw her.

The tour completed, Jedd disappeared again. It struck her that he was not unlike a small boy himself, finding one excuse after another to go outside and play.

"You'll be a-wanting to get your sea legs under you," he told her. "I'd best go bail out the skiffs. They'll be up to the gun'les after all them squalls we been having."

Maggie wandered alone through the house, noting the fine feather beds on even the narrow trundle. Goose down, for she'd been shown the feather barrels out in the net shed. There must be wildfowl aplenty in the fall, for both barrels had been full.

There was a great heap of mending waiting for needle and thread. Boys were ever hard on clothes, as she well remembered from Gideon's younger days. Holding up a pair of trousers, she saw that it had been cut down from a larger pair—ones that had probably belonged to the middle son. Matthew? Yes, Matthew. She was beginning to get the straight of the Rawson brood.

Then there was Sara's husband, Jeremiah, who was the eldest, and another one besides. Where did he fit in? What had Jedd called him, Cabel? Strange name. She didn't recall hearing it before.

Before he'd gone out that last time, Jedd had mentioned hopefully that he and Isaac were accustomed to taking an evening meal about dark. He'd shown her the outdoor oven, which was far larger than Zion's had been, and the cool room, which was built of openwork, high off the ground under a stand of cedars to catch any hint of breeze. There she'd found hams and pickled pork, bacon and salt fish, eggs and a bowl of thick clabber. In the kitchen were barrels of flour, cornmeal and hominy, and more molasses than she'd seen in a year's time at Zion's house. Which told her that the Rawson males had a taste for sweets.

There were chickens aplenty—some laid, some set, some crowed, and a few just scratched, according to Jedd. She inspected the cow shed and introduced herself to the swayback cow she would be expected to milk twice a day.

She lingered longest at a sunny patch, protected from fowl as well as browsing deer by a netting fence, where fresh new greens grew in neatly raised rows. Onion tops were already yellowing, bean vines were blooming, and soon there'd be pumpkins, squash and gourds for drying.

But what delighted her most were the wildflowers left to bloom unmolested around the borders. There were sweet-smelling honeysuckle vines, and small white starlike blossoms, some tiny purple things, and scores of small, sunny-faced dandelions.

The more she saw of Jedd Rawson's snug homestead, the more inclined she felt to linger. If Gid had indeed gone to sea with Uncle Will, then where would she have lived, even if she'd found him? With Uncle Will's wife? All she knew of the woman was that she was the widow of a wealthy ship owner who didn't take kindly to having her second husband's ragtag relatives sullying her fine house.

As the sun began to layer the western sky with bands of coral and gold, Maggie tried out a slab of bacon and sizzled tender young greens in the fat, then poured a gourd full of water into the pot and set it to boil while she went back outside to cut off a few slices of ham. She brought in the clabber, as well, for with a topping of molasses, it would serve as a sweet. That done, she scalded enough cornmeal for dumplings to add to the greens.

And then she waited. As kind as Jedd Rawson seemed, she was timid about prying through his belongings in search of needle and thread to tackle the pile of mending. She well remembered how it felt to be caught going through a stranger's possessions.

The man called Gabriel had accused her of—

Snorting inelegantly, she began scouring a none-too-clean trencher. Forget him, she bade herself, it's not likely you'll ever see him again. "More's the blessing," she muttered under her breath.

She had more important things to consider than a yellow-eyed oaf who had treated her as if she were no better than the dirt under his boots. For the sake of her mother, she'd put up with years of that sort of treatment. But no more. She was a McNair. McNairs bowed down to no man. As young as she'd been, Maggie could remember hearing her father's proud claim.

"Except to you, sweetling," she crooned, leaning over the cradle to soothe the fretful Eli. Sara had mentioned weaning him now that there was someone with time to work at it, but having seen the thin blue dribble produced by Jedd's cow, Maggie didn't hold out much hope of success.

One day at a time, she repeated silently a while later, as she patted out the stiff cornmeal into flat cakes and slipped them into the potliquor. For once in her life, she was free to move on whenever the notion took her, and she rather liked the feel of freedom.

On the other hand, there was something to be said for having a fine roof over her head, plenty of food and a provider who was away more often than not. Dare she throw away such security for the sake of searching for a brother she hadn't seen in more than five years?

Three days later Maggie had still not given her word, although she was more content in Jedd Rawson's home than she had been in years. Not that there hadn't been problems.

There was Isaac, for one thing. So far, he had yet to speak a word to her, although his black eyes followed her constantly, as if accusing her of some dreadful crime.

"The boy's grieving," his father had told her at first. And later, "He's a mite stubborn, but that's no bad thing in a man."

Maggie dandled Eli on her knee just to hear him chortle. She had her own way of dealing with the silent Isaac and said as much to Jedd. "A body either trusts or he doesn't, and nothing you or I can do will change that. I'll see that he comes to no harm while he's at home, but I can't chase him over the island from sunup till dusk, not with Eli needing me here."

"The *Bridget* will be coming in most any day now. The boy'll have plenty to keep him out of mischief, for he fair worships Cabel. By the time she's ready to sail again, he'll come around."

The *Bridget*. It sounded familiar to Maggie's ears, but it was all she could do to sort out the new people in her life, much less keep up with who sailed what. There was the *Bridget* and the *Eliza Lea*. She knew those two now, and Sara had mentioned the name of the small sloop Jeremiah was presently working on at the boat yard, which she'd promptly forgotten. There was her father's lugger, the *Edenton Belle*, and the one Gideon had mentioned as being his uncle's favorite of all his wife's merchant ships, the *Morning Star*. If ever a ship called the *Morning Star* came her way, then that was most likely where she would find her brother. Knowing Gid, Maggie was increasingly certain he would follow their father and go to sea at the first opportunity.

"You'll take to Matthew," Jedd promised her after a day in which she had hauled four feather beds out for airing, boiled two pots of clothes, let out the hems of three pairs of trousers and sewn up so many split seams her eyes were fit to give out on her. Then, after settling Eli down for a sleep, she'd chased down the meanest old hen and wrung her neck and spent the next half hour scalding, plucking, singeing and drawing. "And Isaac, he'll come around."

"I'm sure he will," she said halfheartedly. At this point she didn't care if the little scamp never took to her, nor she to him. She had little doubt who had put the sand in her pallet the day before, and her so tired she'd been ready to drop. She'd spread her quilt on top of her pallet, sand and all, and been asleep before her eyes had closed.

"Matt's wild, but he's a good-hearted lad, full of pranks. As for Cabel, well, I'll not promise much, for he's never been one to ease up with strangers. Still and all, he's a fair man, and as good a sailor as you'll find anywhere. Set him down in the middle of the sea with naught but his own gumption to guide him and he'll find his way to port by dead reckoning. It's a gift not given to many a man, though I'm a fair hand, myself," he added modestly. "But Cabel was like that from the time he was a lad. Comes down to him from his mother's people, near as I can figure. His uncle, Anne's brother, was one of the last ones to walk the storm, they say. Strange folk, them Hatties. Not many left now, and them that is, keeps to themselves, even though most of 'em has all took white man's names."

Maggie was pleasantly surprised to find that the old man was such a talker, for she was used to silent meals with only the disgusting sounds of Nimrod's eating for company.

Isaac came in before the meal was finished, and without a word to either of them, slipped into his place and commenced eating.

"You've not made your manners to the lady, lad," Jedd reminded him.

Maggie shifted uncomfortably, unable to meet the boy's impenetrable stare. "It's all right, Jedd, I understand," she murmured.

"No, Maggie, I'll not have a son of mine acting like a heathen any longer. He's had three days of eating the food you set before him, wearing the clothes you washed and mended, and sleeping on the feather bed you beat up and spread fresh each day. It's time he learned his manners."

The child, his small face belligerent under a shock of unruly black hair, looked from one to the other, his dark eyes unreadable. When he finally spoke, it was to Jedd. "Some of the bigger boys said she was your whore, Pa. What's a whore?"

Chapter Five

Jedd reentered the room and stood silently, regarding the red-haired woman who sat at his table, her head bent and her thin shoulders hunched defensively. He had not made the boy come back and apologize, for he'd meant no harm with his question. Some of the lads had heard talk among the villagers and charged him with it, and Isaac, puzzled at their manner, had only repeated the question.

Jedd was not a man to turn away from duty. All the same, explaining such matters to his sons had always been an onerous task. Some men had little reverence for their womenfolk, which made it easier when time came to explain the he-ing and the she-ing that went on between a grown man and a woman. Most of his lads had learned it on their own, long before he worked up the courage to take them out to the landing for a talk.

But now he was faced with an even greater problem. The truth was, he didn't think he could abide many more weeks ashore. Houses were all right for womenfolk and youngers, but a man needed a solid deck rolling underfoot, needed the creak of timbers and the crack of canvas to set the blood to flowing through his body.

He'd not thought to marry again, for Anne had been woman enough to last him for a lifetime, but needs must be met, and the lass had a gentle way with her. Aye, and she was a worker, too, not like some who had walked through his door and started laying down the rules. If he'd been less than desperate, he would never have considered it, for she was young, yet. One day she would want babes of her own.

But damn all, he *was* desperate! Bailing out the leaky stern end of a squalling tyke was women's work, and as much as he loved his two youngest sons, he didn't think he could abide on dry land much longer.

"Lass, I've been giving it some thought, and I've decided the best way around this business is to get ourselves spliced," he blurted, striding into the room to clap a hand on her shoulder. He had meant it to sound cheerful, but seeing the way she flinched away from him, crying out in protest, he thought perhaps he should have dressed it up with a few flowery words.

Maggie was on her feet in an instant, backing away from him. Her shoulder throbbed painfully. Spliced? As in joined together?

As in *married*?

Surely she must have misunderstood. Not until her heel struck the wall did she halt. Arms crossed defensively before her, she stared warily at the tall, bearded stranger. A housekeeper was one thing, but a wife?

Jedd looked embarrassed, his weathered face even redder than usual. "I've not got much of a way with words, lass, else I would have fancied it up some. The truth is, I'm in sore need of a wife, and you're the likeliest one, I figure."

"No, thank you, Mr. Rawson, I don't care to wed any man," Maggie managed to reply.

"Now, Maggie, think on it some before you turn me down. You told me yourself that you've no home and no family save for a brother that run off years ago and an uncle you ain't never laid eyes on."

"But that doesn't mean—"

"Come back and set down, Maggie, and we'll talk it out."

She stood stiffly, her gaze on the large callused hand he extended toward her. "I don't mind standing."

"You've been standing since before sunup, woman, so set! And I'd be obliged if you'd stop looking like you was feared of me, for you know I'd not lay a hand on you in meanness."

Somewhat to her surprise, she believed him. He could have no way of knowing that a hand laid on her in kindness could be almost as painful. "I'm not afeared, it's just that I—that I don't like to be touched."

Jedd nodded slowly in understanding. "Aye, I'm an old man and you're a comely young thing. When I first set eyes on you I thought you'd be a runner, but you're a sticker, all right. A worker, too, and you've a way with the babe that beats all. He don't even cry in the night since you took him in with you." Jedd's bedroom had been curtained off, with Maggie and Eli sharing a space scarce big enough for pallet and cradle.

"It's not that I mind staying on, but I've no wish to be wed to any man."

"Then you'd do well to take my offer, lass, for being wed to me would be like being wed to no man, save for the protection of my name."

"You mean you'd be gone mostly." Maggie could still remember her father. He'd been gone mostly, too, but he'd come home often enough to keep his wife with child. And when he'd got himself killed, his widow had been left with two children to raise, and been forced to take the first offer that came her way or watch them starve.

Maggie shook her head, her chin set stubbornly. "No thank you. I don't believe I'm cut out for wiving. Some women aren't, you know. I vow I'll do as well serving as housekeeper, or perhaps teaching letters and numbers, for I was schooled by my mother, and she by Mr. Griffin near Nixonton."

Jedd shifted awkwardly. It had been almost thirty years since he had proposed marriage to a woman. The first time had been bad enough, with that yellow-eyed devil, Kinnahauk, glaring at him like he was buzzard droppin's. It was something that didn't come easier with practice, he was discovering, even when there was no one to stand between him and the woman, and her a plain little thing, except for her great shining eyes.

Damn all, a man shouldn't have to go through so much just to offer a homeless orphan the protection of his good name and a sound roof over her head! "If it's what Isaac said that worries you, why then, lass, you can put it from your mind. There's them that will talk, and nothing short of splitting their tongues'll stop it, but if we was to wed, why then, there'd be nothing to talk about. And if it's the other that bothers you—the bedding, I mean—why then, I . . ."

He shifted his considerable bulk once more, looking more and more embarrassed. Maggie moved away from the wall and without thinking, slipped into her chair again. Jedd began pacing the small confines of the room, running one hand over the back of his neck. When he spoke, it was without turning to face her. "I'd take it kindly if you was to keep what I say in confidence, for I'd not have it put about that Jedd Rawson was less than a man. But the truth is, lass, that since my wife died, I haven't been able to…well, what I mean is, twice when I was in Antigua, I visited one of them, you know, one of them houses. It didn't do no good. I thought if I was to take another woman, it would help me get over Anne."

He sighed, and Maggie found herself warming to the tough old sea captain. "Well, it don't work that way, more's the pity. The truth is, I don't want to get over my Annie. She was half redskin, and we had to go against her pa and mine both, but we never once regretted it." He shook his head, and this time Maggie was touched to see his eyes film over. "So you see, lass, even if we was to wed, you and me, Anne would still be the wife of my heart."

Maggie nodded, more touched than she cared to admit by the revelation. She knew instinctively that while Jedd was a fine one to spin a yarn, he was not a man to speak easily about such intimate matters.

"Do you understand what I'm saying to you, Maggie girl? I'd not be a bother to you in that way. I mean, you not liking to be touched and all…"

Maggie found herself wanting to reassure him, yet how could she agree to such a thing? In all fairness, she had to admit that it was tempting, there being gain on both sides. But *marriage*!

On the other hand, Jedd would be free to go, leaving Maggie to go on as she pleased, planting what she wished, rearranging her house—*her house*—to suit herself. And gently luring the boy Isaac out of his shell.

"I'll think on it," she said finally. She could tell he was disappointed, but it was the best she could do for now. He didn't press her, another point in his favor.

Swearing in disgust, Cabe sluiced his naked body down to get the musky stench of the bordello off his hide. Two of the overripe beauties had draped themselves all over him before he could even state his business, the smell of their soft, spoiled bodies putting him in mind of a pair of civet cats in heat. By the time he had routed half his crew out of the stalls, he'd been fit to be tied.

It was that redhead's fault. Maggie McNair, damn her soul. She'd got his men all stirred up, and the minute they'd hit port, they'd scattered like a school of mullet.

He'd lit into them the minute he'd got them back aboard ship, warning them of what they well knew. "An overdose of kill-devil rum'll turn your gut inside out and leave you with a splitting skull, but you'll damn well mend! One fandango with the wrong whore'll leave you with something you'll not get over so quickly. If you won't think of your womenfolk, then I damned well will! If it's wenching you want, then for God's sake, don't tumble into the first crib you come to. There's cleaner ones back off the waterfront, if you can keep your britches on long enough to find 'em!"

Shunning drawers, he stepped into his other pair of trousers and reached for a clean shirt from the chest. He'd meant to have that, and the hose the redhead had worn, laundered, but what with one thing and another, he'd never got around to it. They'd run into a line of storms three days out of Barbados and lost a jib. Then the deck cargo had come loose and damaged the winch. Women and washing had been the last thing on his mind.

Until he'd gone to round up his crew and finally tracked them down at the most infamous waterfront brothel of all. His own brother, still wet behind the ears, had sported a doxy on each knee when Cabe had located him. Grinning from ear to ear, Matthew had caught sight of Cabe, waved him inside, and generously invited him to share the wealth.

Wincing, Cabe recalled with painful clarity that Matt had changed his tune when he'd hustled him out of there—thank God he hadn't had to dress him first! None of the crew had been too happy about it, and they'd been drunk enough to let him know it. But then, Cabe had been called worse things in his life than a dried-up eunuch.

Combing back his wet hair, he anchored it at his nape with a strip of rawhide, his spirits somewhat restored now that he felt clean again. The bronzed planes of his stern face shifted subtly in amusement. Luckily, none of his men had any notion of how often this 'dried-up eunuch' had lain sweating in his bunk, dreaming about a homely little wench wearing naught but a pair of his own woolen hose and a shirt that left far too much of her shapely white limbs exposed.

For once he was glad to be on the homeward run. They were a few days late, but they carried a full cargo of muscavado sugar, cocoa and cotton, and a dozen baskets of limes and oranges to be shared out among the villagers for a treat. By this time, Gaffer would be back from across the sound with the *Eliza Lea*, all set for her outward run. Jedd's bos'n had his weaknesses, but he was a good man, and the crew worked well for him. Over the past few months Gaffer had taken on a few of the inland hauls while Jedd stayed at home with the youngers. It wasn't the best arrangement, but it was better than losing still more time.

The *Eliza Lea* lay at anchor some half mile off Jedd's landing. Among the first to recognize the distinctive rake of her mast when she'd come in sight, Isaac had been so excited that even Maggie had come in for a smile. Jedd had shoveled down his midday meal, thanked Maggie—something he never failed to do, to her amazement—and taken the boy out with him in the launch to check cargo against manifest. Gaffer, for all Jedd trusted his seamanship, was no businessman.

Sara came over shortly after they left, and together she and Maggie worked at getting Eli to accept milk from a rum bottle with a soft cloth tied over the opening for a wick. The infant was furious at being denied the breast, frustrated with the messy business of trying to suck his dinner from a wet rag, and not at all pleased with the thin, tasteless cow's milk.

"If he gets hungry enough, he'll settle down to drinking." Sara insisted.

"If he gets much hungrier, he'll march right up to the table and take stewed croaker and turnip greens with the rest of us," Maggie said, laughing at the tiny, flailing fists.

"Wouldn't do him no harm. He's got the teeth for it, I can vow to that." She shifted Charity Ann to her other breast while Maggie struggled on with Eli and the bottle. "Jeremiah's thinking we might leave out of here when the *Eliza Lea* sails next week. Two can get out the inlet and keep an eye out for trouble better than one. They do say Ned Teach is back at it again. Him and Governor Eden is thick as thieves.''

"Isn't he the one they call Blackbeard? I thought all the pirates had turned themselves in at Nassau and been pardoned.''

"Ha! You expect a thief to stand by his word? Sooner expect a weasel not to suck eggs.''

Maggie had no notion of whether or not weasels actually sucked eggs, but she conceded the point. "Then you're really going?''

Avoiding Maggie's eyes, Sara tucked a napkin under Charity Ann's wet bottom. "Would you mind so much? You took to Eli right off, and Isaac'll be no bother. Jedd won't leave before the *Bridget* comes home, and even if she goes right out again, he'll see that Matt stays home a spell if you ask him. You'll like Matt. He's sweet and full of mischief, and all the young girls are in love with him.''

Maggie went about her duties with a thoughtful look on her face after Sara left. She liked the Rawsons, leastwise all those she'd met. Even Isaac. In fact, she was coming to look on the solitary boy as more than just a challenge. There was so much about him that reminded her of Gid when he was younger—the rebelliousness, the stubborn set of his jaw. She'd known right off that he reminded her of someone the first time she'd seen him.

Just this morning she'd learned that it was Isaac who'd tended Anne's vegetable patch. There wasn't a ragweed anywhere, nor any of the hateful jimsonweed, yet he'd not touched a single one of the wildflowers that abounded in the sandy soil. That had gone a ways toward making up for the fact that just yesterday he had lined the tail of her shift with sandspurs while it was spread over the water bushes to dry.

She was almost of a mind to take Jedd up on his offer. What sort of future would a lone woman have? Even if she got herself to Charles Towne, how would she feel, showing up on her uncle Will's doorstep bareheaded, barefooted and empty handed? She'd heard tell that Charles Towne was a fine and fancy place. If the woman Uncle Will had married was truly as wealthy as Gid had said in his letters, then she might send Maggie packing right off, rather than be shamed by another of Will Lewis's shirttail relatives.

Maggie prided herself on being capable and biddable enough to fit in most anywhere, but common sense told her it would be foolhardy to throw away a penny in hopes of finding a pound.

If only Jedd hadn't complicated matters by asking her to marry...

On the other hand, he had promised not to touch her, and she truly believed he was a man of his word. A woman needed a man's protection, same's a man needed a woman to make a home for his children.

Ah, well, she would think on it a few more days, and then, when Jedd came back from wherever his next journey took him, she would give him an answer.

But as it turned out, Maggie gave her answer that very night.

"I've a mind to sail within the week, lassy, and I'd not go off and leave you here unprotected. The bloody freebooters gets bolder every day, for all they was supposed to have been cleaned out. Some says half the ships in and out of Ocracoke Inlet is pirates. A body don't know who's anchoring off his doorstep these days."

Maggie kept one eye on Eli, who lay on a quilt in a patch of sun, while she picked over beans for soaking. She'd been only half listening up to this point.

"What worries me, lass, is what would happen to you if trouble came while both ships was out and Jeremiah was up to Boston. Matt's a good boy, but he's a mite reckless. He'd be more apt to go looking for a fight rather than stay home and take care of his own."

"I don't see what that has to do with marrying," Maggie said, dumping the beans in a pot.

"If you was to bear my name, why any man on the banks would consider it his bounden duty to look after you if trouble come while you was here alone. I'd do the same for any of their womenfolk, and so would my lads."

Even so, she might have hesitated but for one thing. Jedd had actually trapped an Anglican aboard the *Eliza Lea*. Maggie knew as well as anyone that there were times when a man and woman had to wait for years to be joined in marriage, for the law was that no one save an Anglican or a justice could perform a marriage. And in North Carolina, one was as rare as the other, especially here on the banks.

"You mean . . . right now?" She tipped the lid and checked on the greens that were simmering on the hob, forking over the slab of ham that was floating in the potliquor. "Before supper?"

"Best get on with it. I'm not much of a one for ceremony, so if you don't mind, while Sara and Jeremiah tends to Isaac, we'll just take Eli and row out to the *Eliza Lea* and get the deed done. Unless you want all the fancy doings that goes with it?" he added uncertainly.

It was surely the strangest wedding Maggie had ever witnessed, but then, she had only witnessed one—that of her mother and Zion Johnston. At the last minute she had picked herself a bouquet of flowers, the yellow prickly ones that grew all along the sound. Jedd, who had worn a coat for the occasion despite the heat, looked uncommonly nervous as he hurried her into the longboat.

"If I'd knowed you wanted flowers, I'd 've picked some of Anne's red ones there by the cow shed. Them yeller things ain't no account."

Was there a man born who could tolerate something as useless as a flower, Maggie thought sadly as Jedd bent to the task of rowing them out to the sloop. The only one Zion had allowed on the farm was the dandelion, and that only because not a scrap of it went to waste. She'd roasted and ground the roots for coffee, boiled the tender green leaves for salad and made wine from the blossoms.

Maybe the good Lord had meant her to be a dandelion instead of a woman. She was tolerated only because she was useful, and like the seeds of a dandelion, she was blown from one place to another, putting down roots wherever she happened to end up.

Eli howled the whole time. Maggie thought he was often hungry, but Sara had told her earlier to pay him no mind, he would settle soon enough. She jiggled him in her arms, shushing him as she stood trembling on the deck of Jedd's work-worn old sloop until Jedd took him from her. Eli quieted instantly.

As for the minister, he was surely the strangest-looking creature she had ever seen, his beaver hat too large for his head, his nose too big for his face, and his fine broadcloth suit too short in the legs and too long in the sleeves.

Nevertheless, he stumbled bravely through the lengthy passage, pronouncing them man and wife almost before Maggie realized he was done. Jedd handed the baby over, presented her with a shiny new iron skillet, and mumbled something about the lack of a ring. "Had it fetched over from the main. Good iron wears as well as any gold ring."

The deed was done. They rowed ashore in silence.

Maggie went to bed Eli down, and Jedd waited for her to come out again. "Once my boys is home, I'd take it right kindly if you was to share my bed, Maggie."

Maggie went pale. "But you promised—"

"Aye, and I'm a man of my word, lass. Still and all, a man has his pride. I'd not have my sons thinking their pa is less than a man. But that don't mean I'd ever lay a hand on you. The bolster'll stay between us. There's room enough and more, and in time, you might even find comfort in having someone to talk to if you wake in the night."

Maggie was not at all convinced. Eyes narrowed, she watched him from across the supper table. They had announced their marriage to Sara when she'd brought Isaac home, and although she professed to be delighted, Maggie thought she'd looked rather startled.

"Where'd you find a marryin' man?" Sara asked.

Jedd mumbled something about the Anglican who had come across from the main, and Sara pounced on the news. "There's at least three couples I know of who's been waiting for months. I'd better go tell—"

"He's gone a'ready," Jedd put in. "Caught a ride with John Willis. He'll be halfway to Albermarle by now."

After Sara left and Isaac had gone to bed, Maggie lit a Betty lamp, wrinkling her nose at the smell of smoking oil. The first thing she would do as Jedd's wife was to make candles, for she couldn't abide the smell of burning grease. There was scarce enough tallow for both candles and soap, but there were plenty of wax myrtle bushes around. The boiling and skimming took forever, but the candles would be fragrant, and well worth the time spent in their making.

"You coming to bed, woman?"

"I, uh, thought I might sleep in my own bed tonight. There's no one here but us, and I doubt Isaac would know or care where I sleep."

"The *Bridget* was sighted off the inlet just before dark. Late as she is, it wouldn't surprise me none to see her anchored out back at first light. Not many men'll run the inlet after dark, but I know my sons. Cabel don't take kindly to delay. Come sunup, both him and Matt'll have their boots under the table by the time you get the coffee boiled."

Chapter Six

It was the smell of coffee that drew Maggie out of hiding the next morning. She couldn't remember falling asleep, but she must have. Surely she couldn't have lain awake all night, staring into the darkness while she listened to the sound of her husband's soft snores. All she knew was that every muscle in her body was sore from holding herself so rigidly, trying not to move or make a sound that would arouse him.

"My husband." She tested the words and found them strange, with no more substance than a moon shadow. Yet they were real enough. She was no longer Maggie McNair, but Maggie Rawson—Margaret Elizabeth Rawson, wife to Jedd Williams Rawson. Wife to a man three times her age, stepmother to a babe she had already come to love, to a child who wanted none of her and to a man nearly ten years older than she. Not to mention the two she had yet to meet.

She'd been so tense the night before, watching Jedd pull down the curtains that portioned off the small bedroom, that if he'd touched her she would have shattered like an egg shell. After hanging up her gown, she'd washed hastily while Jedd walked down to the landing for a last smoke. Then, wearing her shift in lieu of a night rail, she'd removed the bolster from the head of the bed and placed it in the middle, lengthwise, only to find that it was not nearly long enough. She'd had to decide between exposing her sleeping face to a strange man, or running the risk of having one of his feet accidently touch one of hers.

Her very first chore the next morning, she told herself, would be to make another length of bolster. Meanwhile all she could do was to turn her back and draw her knees up to her chest to avoid the possibility of any contact.

She needn't have worried. Jedd slept like the dead. Not even Eli's fretful crying had awakened him. Twice Maggie had slipped out of bed, changed the baby's sopping napkin and cuddled him until he stopped fussing, and Jedd hadn't stirred at all.

What a strange wedding night, she marveled as she eased herself out of bed the next morning and hurriedly began to dress, keeping a nervous eye on the sleeping man beside her. Never had she thought to marry, much less wondered what it would be like to sleep with a man.

So now she knew. It was no great thing. Her husband slept on his back without moving. He snored, but not too loudly. The snoring didn't bother her, nor did the faint aroma of tobacco that clung to his skin and hair, but she didn't see how she could ever relax enough to sleep with a stranger in her bed.

So this was marriage, she thought, flexing her shoulders before the small open window. Truly, it was no great thing. She would soon learn—

And then she heard the door open and shut, and the sound of low voices in her kitchen. That would be the other two, the sons she had not yet met. How was she going to face them? Did they know about the wedding? If they saw her coming out of Jedd's bedroom at this hour of day, they'd as good as know she'd slept in his bed. And though there was nothing shameful about it, she'd just as lief meet them later, when she'd had more time to get used to her new condition.

However, it was hardly practical to stay hidden for the next few years. Nor did she care to be still dawdling in the bedroom when Jedd awoke. No matter how fine his feather bed, she felt far more at ease in his kitchen.

In the thin gray light, Maggie peered into Jedd's looking glass and smoothed her hair, sorely missing her comb. Tied back, her hair wasn't so bad, but if she didn't find some way to get the tangles out soon, she'd have to cut it all off and start afresh.

Having done all she could to appear neat and orderly, she braced herself to go forth and greet her new family. Her sons. Leastwise, the only sons she'd ever be likely to have, married to a man who had promised to leave her be.

Never one to quail before an onerous task, she opened the door and stepped boldly into the kitchen. Her hand was still holding the latchstring when she felt her jaw go slack. There, seated at her table and calmly sopping a chunk of her cold pan bread in a cup of steaming coffee, was the last man on earth she ever expected to see.

Gabriel! "What are you—" she began, even while he was shoving back his chair and rising to his considerable height.

"What the devil? I thought I told you this was no place to ply your trade."

There were two of them, but Maggie had eyes only for the one. Now—why—what was the iron-faced Captain Gabriel doing seated at her table, breaking the bread she'd baked only yesterday?

"Where's Pa? What were you doing in his bedroom? Woman, if you know what's good for you, you'll be out of here before I can get around this table to lay hands on you."

"Hey, come on, Cabe, ease off a few points. That ain't very charitable," said the younger of the two.

"Charitable, hell! Do you have any idea who this light-fingered doxy is? The same one who stowed aboard the *Bridget* when we left Bath. The same thieving little baggage who tried to steal my best pair of hose and the shirt right off my back."

Outraged at the unfounded charges, Maggie found her tongue. "I didn't hurt your lumpy old hose, and as for your shirt, I only borrowed it! Besides, it wasn't on your back, it was in your chest. And any man with three shirts who's too stingy to lend one to someone in need deserves to have them all stolen!"

She could feel a wave of scalding heat creep up over her face as she struggled to deal with the unpleasant discovery that Jedd's Cabel and the man she had thought of as Gabriel were one and the same.

Falling back on a strength that had been born in adversity, she turned to the youth with the burnished gold hair and the beautiful blue-gray eyes. "And you must be Matthew. I'm right pleased to meet you." Flicking an accusing glance at the dark-visaged man towering head and shoulders above her, she marched to the fireplace and reached for the coffeepot, which sat steaming on the hob.

"Here, I'll get you a cup—or you can have mine, I ain't hardly touched it. Sit here. Do you want some bread and molasses? The bread's good. Can't say much for the coffee, but there's plenty of it, such as it is. Cabe makes it strong enough to melt the tusks right off'n a boar."

Before Maggie could prevent it, the eager young man had fairly tripped over his own chair getting her a cup and pulling out a chair for her to sit down.

"Thank you, Matthew. I believe I will take a bit of bread and molasses before I start the hominy and bacon." With a sweep of her faded gray skirts worthy of a grand duchess, Maggie took the seat her new stepson held. "And a bit of sugar for my coffee if it's as powerful as you say."

The coffee was abominable, but it was hot and strengthening. With Cabel Rawson glowering at her from his brass-colored eyes, she needed the courage it lent her. Her hands were trembling, but ignoring it, she took the quarter of a round of pan bread Matthew handed her and broke it neatly into three pieces. It was dark and crusty, and might even have been good, but it felt like a wad of raw cotton in her mouth, and tasted little better.

"What's your name?" Matthew asked. He had propped one elbow on the table and leaned his head on his fist, and now he watched every bite she took as if it were the most fascinating thing he had ever laid eyes on. "Are you going to let Isaac run you off like he done all the rest?"

"Her name is Maggie McNair, and she's not staying," Cabel said flatly.

Maggie ignored him. "My name is Margaret Rawson, and—"

This time it was Cabe who practically overturned his chair in an effort to get to his feet. "What the hell do you mean, your name is Margaret Rawson? Unless you've got a twin sister with red hair and a lumpy nose—" He paused, frowning as if there was something about her that puzzled him, and then he shook his head and continued. "Then you're the same woman who opened the hatch cover and damn near ruined half my cargo last month! The same woman who was going through my cabin, helping herself to—"

"The same woman who married your father." At his thunderstruck expression, Maggie smiled, unable to hide her pleasure at that small victory.

Cabel walked slowly around the table, his taut midsection at Maggie's eye level. There was no way she could tear her gaze away from the subtle flexing of sinew and flesh, as his trousers fitted shamefully close. There was something distinctly menacing in the way he moved. Nor was the set of his square jaw or the grim slash of his mouth reassuring. If she'd ever imagined she saw a glimmer of kindness in those golden eyes of his, she must have been blind.

Their eyes locked, and Maggie felt the shock all the way to the soles of her bare feet. He looked her over carefully, missing nothing. It was a knowledgeable inventory, and it was obvious from his expression that he was no more pleased with his findings than she was with her own.

She could have explained herself. She chose not to. Let him think what he would—he'd called her a thief and a whore. If there was one lesson she'd learned early in this life, it was that no woman's word would make an unreasonable man see reason. She might as well save her breath.

It was Matthew who broke the tension. Leaning back in his chair, his head thrown back and his long legs stretched out before him, he let out a chuckle that quickly escalated into a gale of laughter. "Married! Bless my soul, I didn't think the old man had it in him! Then that makes you—"

"Nothing."

Both of them turned to Cabel, who stared grimly back, his powerful arms crossed over his broad chest so that the seams of his shirt were sorely tried. "That makes her precisely what she was before I dragged her out of my cargo hold and dumped her off at the docks. Nothing!" His glaring gaze had not left her face since she'd entered the room. "Just as soon as you collect your *things*—" his emphasis served to remind her of their last meeting "—I'll see you aboard a ship that's leaving on the tide for Portsmouth Island. That's more your sort of place, taverns, seamen from every part of the world, hungry for just what you're selling. I don't care if you lighten every purse and pox every—''

Matthew leaped to his feet, toppling his chair against the wall. ''Damn all, Cabe, you got no cause to say things like that!'' he shouted. ''Just because you got no use for women ever since Lettie crossed her legs against you, that's no cause to treat Miz, uh, Rawson like she was dirt.''

It was Maggie who first noticed Isaac standing round-eyed in the door that led out to the back bedroom. She must have made some small sound, for both men turned. But it was Cabel who quickly knelt and held out his arms to the small boy in the outgrown nightshirt.

As Isaac flew into his big brother's embrace, Matthew dropped his chin to his chest, swearing under his breath. Maggie didn't hesitate to make her escape. Another time she would have to come to terms with the man's unreasonable attitude, but now just now. Not when she was red-eyed and shaky from her sleepless night, when Eli was beginning to fuss and when her brand-new husband was stomping around the bedroom in his stocking feet hunting for the boots she'd placed neatly under the bed after tripping over them on her way out.

As the sun climbed to its blistering height, Maggie found some of the tension draining from her. All three men, taking Isaac with them, had been gone all morning. The talk at the breakfast table had included everything from the price of corn and cocoa, to sugar and silk, to a tale currently making the rounds. It was Matt who told it, with a youthful eagerness that Maggie found completely disarming.

''This fellow Stede Bonnet—the one that took that Spaniard galleon last month off the Leewards—seems he was an officer in the army when he met Ned Teach, and old Blackbeard, he convinced Bonnet that he was a-wasting his life in the army. So Bonnet, he ditched the army, dumped his wife, and went out and *bought* himself a sloop! And then, damn me if the old fart didn't hire himself a crew to go a-pirating!'' He chuckled in disbelief. ''First time I ever heard of any pirate buying a ship and payin' a crew just so's they could steal another one, but you know what makes it even funnier!'' He broke off laughing, but managed to recover himself long enough to gasp out the rest of his tale. "He gets—the old crock gets—*sick as a dog* ever' time he sets foot on board anything bigger'n a longboat! If that don't beat anything I ever heard tell . . ."

Jedd cut through his son's laughter with a short retort. "Don't reckon you'll be laughing quite so hard when you're hull down and running, with one o' them damned bastards a-riding your wake."

Not a single word had been spoken about her marriage, but Maggie, servicing the menfolk with one hand and feeding Eli with the other, could tell at a glance that Cabe was far from reconciled. Just as she could tell that young Matthew was fair bursting with curiosity.

Matthew she could handle. He was enough like her own Gideon so that she had taken to him right off, but the other one . . .

How on earth could a body be expected to make her peace with a man who had despised her from the first time he'd ever laid eyes on her?

A man like Cabel Rawson would try the patience of a saint. Thank goodness he'd left as soon as he'd finished eating. She would hate for Jedd to learn through her that one of his sons had the sweet disposition of a bee-stung bullock.

With Eli snug in his hammock under the cedars, Maggie tackled the garden. Isaac had done well for a lad of only eight, but much still needed to be done. The herb patch had gone to ruin, with straggly patches of borage covering up new sprouts of mint, and weeds overtaking all.

Skirt tucked around her hips and tied in a knot, she crawled slowly along the barely visible rows, yanking out the largest weeds so she could see what was worth saving. A stone's throw away, the waters of the Pamlico lapped gently at the sandy shore. Gulls circled overhead, their raucous cries blending harmoniously with the soughing of the wind in the pines and the chattering of the tiny yellow finches that flitted from branch to branch in the live oaks.

It was a peaceable place. Now and then Maggie sat back on her heels to wipe the sweat from her brow. At such times she marveled that there was no longer a threat hanging over her, no Nimrod lurking in the bushes, hoping to catch her with her skirts hiked up, no Zion brooding in the shadows, waiting to catch her dallying so that he could descend on her with his cane.

The sun felt good on her back. It hardly bothered her at all now, only when someone touched her directly on one of the fresher bruises. She had no way of knowing what it looked like. All yellow and brown by now, probably, but at least the black and blue would have faded. It was almost as if the nightmare of the past ten years was fading along with her bruises.

She weeded on as the sun bore down on her unprotected nape, musing on the events of the past few days. Far too often for comfort, her thoughts strayed back to Cabel Rawson.

At least she would not be forced to see much of him. He'd be off again in a day or so, no doubt, gone for the better part of a month at least. Perhaps he would decide to sail round the world. Now that would be a pleasant happenstance, she mused, sitting back on her heels to smile dreamily at a patch of wild pinks. On impulse she picked a small bunch to take inside, for the kitchen, as pleasant as it was, could use a bit of color. Smoke had long since darkened the walls and ceiling, so that even on the brightest day there were dark corners.

When Eli began to grow fretful, Maggie got to her feet, dusted off her hands and lifted him from his hammock. He was hungry again, poor mite. And soon it would be time to ready a meal for the menfolk. Jedd liked to eat while the sun was overhead, and then work in the shade of the net shed on whatever needed mending until the cool of the day.

How quickly she had settled into the patterns of her new household. Marriage, Maggie concluded as she lingered long enough to poke up the fire in the outdoor oven, was not the frightening thing she had imagined it to be.

Jedd and Matthew brought Isaac home for the midday meal, and Maggie found herself looking past them for a glimpse of a taller man with a blue-black crop of hair that glistened like the wings of a blackbird.

"Cabe stopped off to Sara's for stewed drum. He'll be home directly. I'd appreciate it if you'd see to his bed, Maggie."

Maggie, struggling to lift the iron stewpan off the hob, could only nod. Grinning cheerfully, Matt removed her hands from the bail and lifted the heavy vessel easily to a place near the front where she could ladle out its fragrant contents without fear of burning her arm, and she smiled her appreciation.

Two days passed during which Maggie saw little or nothing of Cabel. To her relief, he continued to spend most of his time aboard one or the other of the two ships, taking his meals with Sara and Jeremiah. Then on the night before both Jedd and Jeremiah were to sail, Jedd called his whole family together after supper. Maggie, wishing she'd had time to change into her clean gown and smooth her hair, fixed Eli's milk and turned toward the bedroom.

Jedd ordered her back. "Feed the boy in here, Maggie. You're a part of this family now."

Her eyes flew to Cabel's face in time to see the thunderclouds form. "What about Sara?" she asked timidly. She could have done with Sara's cheerful chatter to bolster her courage.

"Sara's got her own youngers to see to, and trunks to finish packing. This don't concern Sara."

With a sinking heart, Maggie looked from one face to the other. Jedd was the same as always, his weathered features mostly hidden behind his bushy beard and mustache. Jeremiah, with his open, freckled countenance, seemed completely unaware of any tension. If Matthew was aware, he hid it well. He sent her a reassuring smile.

Against her will, Maggie's gaze was drawn to the other side of the table. There she encountered two unsmiling faces. Two sets of accusing eyes. Two pairs of arms crossed forbiddingly over two chests, one small and vulnerable, the other broad, hard—and surprisingly warm, as she recalled to her everlasting shame.

She could have laughed at Isaac's mimicking of Cabel if it weren't so discouraging. With a lift of the chin that was sheer bravado, she left to fetch the baby, taking time to change his napkin and smooth a bit of sweet oil on his pink bottom. If they wanted her, they could just wait for her. She might not be a blood Rawson, but Eli was, and none of the others seemed eager to take over his care and feeding.

"All right, we're ready," she announced defiantly as she reentered the room, the babe on her arm, and lowered herself to the hearth. Matt quickly jumped up and offered her his chair, but she shook her head. She would not push herself off on them that didn't want her, but she refused to bow down to them, either.

Jedd didn't waste time in preliminaries. "Maggie is my wife now, and I want her treated with the respect she's owed. She's a good lass, a hard worker, and I'll not have her shunned by my own flesh and blood."

Maggie felt her face burning as she concentrated on tipping just the right amount of milk to the nipple so that Eli could suck without strangling. She'd sooner they all ignored her than have her new husband force his sons to accept her. Damn all, she could fight her own battles!

"I'm not wanting to go off and leave her alone just yet, for with Jeremiah gone, she'd not know where to turn in time of trouble. One of you lads will have to stay back."

Dead silence greeted Jedd's pronouncement. Jeremiah looked at Cabel. Matthew looked at Jeremiah, and Isaac continued to stare holes through her with his dark, accusing eyes.

Jeremiah was first to speak. "Pa, I don't rightly see how I can put off this trip to Boston. Sara's all het up about going, and I've promised to meet with Mr. Cavendish about those oak timbers he's wanting to buy, and—"

Cabel interrupted to say, "There's time enough for at least one more sugar run before the season ends. We've lost enough time already."

"You've done two journeys back-to-back while I've stayed in with the youngers, son, but—"

"Oh, now hold on, Pa, that just leaves me," Matthew protested.

Maggie felt like a joint of beef being shunned by a whole pack of dogs. "Jedd, if you don't mind, I'd just as lief stay by myself."

"This don't concern you, lass," Jedd said firmly.

"It does so concern me! You said yourself I'm a part of the Rawson family now, and—" Seeing all five sets of eyes bearing down on her, she swallowed hard and forced herself to go on. "What I mean is, no one has to look after me. I'm eighteen years old, and I'm more than capable of looking after myself."

"It's not you Pa's concerned about, *Mistress* Rawson," Cabel replied, his tone of voice telling her clearly what he thought of her new title. "He'll be leaving behind two youngers, not to mention considerable property, and it's getting on toward storm season. How would you like to wake up in the middle of the night to find the whole island awash, the trees twisted backwards, and the waves breaking right up against the door?"

"Now, lad, don't be a-trying to scare—" Jedd began, but Maggie waved him to silence. She could fight her own battles.

"I've seen storms before!"

"Aye, but at least on the main you know you're well anchored. On the banks, with scarce a mile between sea and sound, it's a different matter."

"I'm not afraid of storms." Her head tilted defiantly, as if to say she wasn't afraid of him, either.

"Oh, no? I seem to recall finding a half-dead—"

Both completely disregarded Jedd's sharp, "Both of you, hush it! Cabel, I'll not have you speaking disrespectfully to your—"

"That's not true! And I was *not* afraid!"

"What about pirates? Are you afraid of those? Half the scum of New Providence is prowling the Carolinas these days. They've laid claim to half of Ocracoke already. If they decide to move their base to this side of the inlet, I'd not care to have my brothers depending on your tender care."

Maggie glared at Cabel, who glared back at her. Jedd uttered a sound of disgust, and the others stared at first one contender and then the other, as if wondering what had sparked the fierce animosity between them.

Maggie herself couldn't have told them, for it was a mystery to her as well. She only knew that from the first moment she had confronted this man, he had triggered a reaction in her that no other man had ever aroused.

Never—at least not since she'd first met Zion when she was eight years old—had Maggie hated a man on sight.

Cabel Rawson just might prove to be the exception.

Chapter Seven

With Cabel gone, Maggie's ragged nerves gradually commenced to mend. The following weeks were happier than any she remembered since her childhood with Gideon and her mother, awaiting her father's infrequent visits. Matthew, though his hair was a warmer shade of gold and his eyes a cooler shade of blue, reminded her more of Gid each day, for they were both of a mischievous nature. Eli had taken well to his bottle and Maggie had even tried him with a bit of pap, which he seemed inclined to take.

The only blemish on her growing happiness was Isaac, for the boy refused to warm to her.

"He'll come around," Matt promised, watching the small, proud back as the boy stalked silently to his bed after supper one evening.

"That's what Jedd and Sara said, but I'm beginning to wonder." Idly Maggie pinched a faded blossom from the bouquet of wildflowers she had placed on the table. "My own mother died this past May, and sometimes the hurt sneaks up on me and fair sucks the breath right out of my body. I reckon Isaac's hurt is just too big for him right now. He wants to kick something, and he doesn't much care what it is."

"He'll be mending soon, chattering away like a jackdaw."

"Hmmm," Maggie murmured doubtfully. "Your pa still grieves." She thought the words might be a comfort to him.

Matt nodded solemnly. "He still goes out to tell Ma goodbye before he sails. I don't reckon none of us is likely to forget her."

"He didn't marry me so's I could take Anne's place, Matt." Which was as close as she could come to telling him the way of her marriage without betraying Jedd's confidence.

"You didn't have to tell me that, Maggie—and he cares for you, we all do. Leastwise, most of us does."

Maggie made an effort to tease Matt back into his usual cheerfulness. "Looks like half the Rawsons want me and half don't. Eli's too young to have a say."

"'Pears to me he has right much of a say, 'specially if he don't get fed fast enough to suit him. Ma would thank you for taking on the mess of us Rawsons, Maggie, especially Isaac and Cabe. They ain't easy ones to get close to. Sometimes I wonder if the good Lord even knows what goes on under Cabe's scalp. He sure ain't like Jere and me, or Pa, either."

Maggie began collecting the heavy crockery plates. Matt had brought home a fish, and she had baked it with salt pork, onions and potatoes. He'd cleaned off his plate twice and gone back to the hob for more, and there wasn't a crumb of her clabber corn bread left.

"Funny, the way you 'n' Cabe got off on the wrong foot the first time you laid eyes on one another, ain't it?"

Maggie shrugged. "I left home sort of sudden like, and I didn't have time to book my passage in the proper way. I came up for air after a fierce storm had battered me fair to death, and your brother found me like that. He seemed to think I was . . . well, to tell the truth, I don't rightly know what he thought." She could laugh about it now, but at the time she hadn't felt much like laughing.

Matt grinned ruefully. "Oh, I can figure what he was thinking, right enough. Cabe don't like women on board his ship, claims they cause trouble."

"You mean bad luck? I heard sailors were a superstitious lot."

"I mean trouble, like fighting amongst the crew about who gets to—well, you know what I mean. He just don't care for women."

"You said that before. That doesn't sound very encouraging for the future."

Matt looked slightly flustered. "I don't mean he don't *like* 'em, Maggie, leastwise, he don't exactly *dislike* 'em. Cabe, he used to be a great hand with women, running up the banks or down to Ocracoke ever' chance he got, all done up in his best shirt. I used to pester him to take me across the inlet with him, and sometimes Ma made him do it just to get me out from underfoot, but he always dropped me off at the docks and picked me up when he was ready to come home."

Maggie could remember pestering her own father to take her to the docks and show her his ship. He used to tell her such wonderful tales about where he had been and all the wonders he had seen, how he had outrun the fastest pirates and the fiercest storms in his beautiful lugger, the *Edenton Belle*.

Matt plucked a honeysuckle blossom off her arrangement and sucked the nectar from the stem. "You know, there's times when old Cabe's more red man than white. Thinks a powerful lot, don't say much. Grandpa was the same way. Him and Cabe always got along real good. They could sit all day and never say more'n a dozen words between 'em, and walk away grinning like a pair o' possums. Clean, too. Scrubs down reg'lar, winter and summer. I've seen Grandpa crack the ice on a pond and wade in just to scrub himself down, but he heats water for Grandma to scrub down inside their lodge, come winter."

"Jedd said they'd left the island a while back, and he hadn't heard from them since." Maggie was curious about the Rawsons' mixed heritage. Perhaps if she understood it better, it might give her a clue as to how to deal with Isaac. She told herself righteously that it was only the boy who concerned her, not Cabe.

"Grandpa goes to visit his people over on the main—some that split off a while back. He says it's because he don't like all these cows and sheep a-running all over the island, but I reckon it's mainly on account of he misses Ma. She'd have been some kind of chief or something if she'd lived—it comes down through the womenfolk, and Ma was Grandpa's only daughter. Now I guess it'll pass on to Uncle John. His real name is Stormwalker, but when he left home, he took the name John Walker. Hell, he might even be dead, too, by now. Been years since he's been back. Funny if ol' Jeremiah turned out to be chief whatchamacallit of the Hatorask people, wouldn't it? With Becky Mary next in line."

Maggie poured the last of the water from the kettle over the dishes and then got out her bread bowl to mix the breakfast bread. It was strange to think of these men as being part redskin. The only one she'd even known to speak to was old Monty One Foot, a tame Matchapungo who peddled roots and herbs in town. Monty was never sober, and he had the saddest eyes she'd ever seen on any mortal, but he was certainly no threat to anyone.

Cabel Rawson was definitely a threat. And while he was not precisely what she'd call a handsome man, there was something about him, something that had lodged in her mind and refused to come unstuck.

"As I was saying, Cabe, he'll come around," Matthew went on. "He was right took with a widow woman some years back. She died on him, and he ain't never got over it, I reckon. Makes him a mite peculiar 'round women. Now me, I've had me a girl of my own picked out these past few years, only I ain't ready to settle yet."

"Oh, ah, have you told her yet?" Maggie was still caught up with the notion of Cabe as a heartbroken lover. The tight feeling inside her chest was probably no more than sympathy, she told herself.

"I reckon she knows it, all right, only she ain't about to let on. Like I said, though, I can wait. I got a while before I'm ready to settle down for the long haul."

Maggie had to laugh. She hadn't lived on Hatteras Banks a week before she'd learned of Matthew's reputation with the ladies. Sara had warned her, but seeing him in action was another thing. "It wouldn't by any chance be that pretty girl who lives down beside the boat yard, would it?" she teased, knowing from the way his face flamed that she'd scored a direct hit.

"Don't you tell nobody! It's between me and Lina, and I ain't at all sure I won't change my mind."

"After all these years?" Maggie scoffed gently.

"Well, I sure ain't going to let on I like her less'n she lets on first. Since she fattened up and filled out, she's so stuck up she has to pinch her nose to keep from drownin' in a hard rain."

"That's stuck up, all right," she agreed, trying hard to keep a sober face. Lord, he was Gideon all over again—a Gideon all grown up.

* * *

As if it were an ordinary occurrence, the villagers seemed to take as a matter of course Maggie's sudden appearance in their midst and her hasty marriage to a man who had left a few days later. Maggie met a woman who claimed to cure the best tea, another who claimed to grow the biggest figs by feeding her trees live oysters, and the miller who ground corn for most of the villagers.

She finally got to meet the widow Gaskins, who introduced herself by saying, "I'm Emma Gaskins, live down the road a piece on the sound side. When your time comes, send word. You're small, but you've a stout look to you. Shouldn't have no trouble. Jedd's babes was all long and narrow and come easy. Reckon you already heard his first wife was part redskin."

A bit shaken at the woman's outspokenness, Maggie could only stammer something about early days yet, and not being sure Jedd wanted any more children.

"He's a man, ain't he?" Emma planted her large, capable hands on her hips. Her apron was spotless, her gown as faded as Maggie's. On her head she wore a man's beaver hat, although her splayed feet were bare. "Besides birthing, I'm a fair hand with laying out and all manner of festering wounds, but I don't do fevers. Can't afford to. Might come down with one meself and give it to a newborn. I don't meddle with nothing that gets passed around, but I've got herbs and possets I can send if you're too bad off to do for yourself."

The days passed pleasantly enough, save for Isaac, who ate the food she prepared, wore the clothes she washed and mended, and continued to ignore her as if she were not even there. Eli thrived on solid food. Maggie knew little of babes, having been the youngest, but she seemed to remember hearing that they weren't supposed to eat real food until they were at least a year old.

Which was well enough as long as they had a mother's milk to nourish them, but Jedd's old cow gave little more than a few pints of watery blue stuff, and that unwillingly. Maggie had milked many a cow in her life, and her butter and cheese were as fine as any, but there would be no butter and cheese from Brownie. There was scarce enough milk for Eli, and that so poor you could see through it.

"We need a fresh cow and more grass to feed her," she told Matt a few days before Cabe was expected in. Jedd would be at least a week longer, according to Matt, who knew the routes well, having sailed them all with both his brother and father.

"Make a list. Pa'll see Thelbert Farrow about trading for one of his milkers before he leaves. Ain't much he can do about grass, though. Can't fence the whole island, and can't grow enough grass on what you can fence to do much good. What else do you need?"

"Well, Isaac needs some new clothes. His pants are all but splitting, and I've let out his shirts all they'll go."

"Isaac ain't the only one," Matt replied, and Maggie looked up quickly. Had he noticed that she had only the two gowns to her name, and not a single petticoat to keep them from hanging limp as a wet rag? Not to mention shoes. Going barefoot was no problem in the summer, but once it turned cold, she didn't know how she'd fare. Jedd hadn't offered to buy her anything, and she'd hated to ask, having suffered too many beatings in the past for the duel offence of greed and pride.

"Sara was laying off to sew Cabe and me some new shirts and a new pair of trousers, but she ain't had time to say scat since the babies come. A while back Cabe had him this woman over across the sound who was as fine a hand at sewing as ever you did see, only she liked to surprise him, so she never bothered to measure. Stuff she made was fine, all right, only it never did fit right. Maybe that was why he got rid of her."

Another of Cabe's women! No wonder the man was such a thunderpuss—he was likely worn to a frazzle. "I don't suppose your ma had a wheel or a loom hid away somewhere?"

"I never saw her at one. Some around here keeps sheep, but Pa never did. We traded for all our cloth. Pa says a sheep'll eat the grass right down to the grit, and then the whole island'll blow away. You keep sheep where you come from?"

"A few, just for spinning." It was as close as any of them had ever come to asking about her past, and Maggie was tempted to tell him all about her family—and about Zion and Nimrod and the farm, and why she'd run off, but Eli let out a wail that signaled either a wet napkin or an empty belly, and the moment passed.

* * *

Two days later the *Bridget* anchored off the island, having sold her cargo of sugar, cocoa and molasses on the main and taken on more grain and naval stores for another run to the Indies. There would be several days of repairing and reprovisioning, allowing the crew time with their families.

Jere and Sara were still not back from Boston, having been gone longer than expected. Which meant that Cabe would likely be taking his meals at home.

The thought brought a strange weakness to Maggie's belly, as if she had eaten bad meat or drunk foul water. After Matt and Isaac had taken off from Jedd's landing in the large rowboat, Maggie flew about the house straightening furniture, dusting and sweeping, and beating the beds up to billowing heights. She had scrubbed the floors and the outhouse just yesterday, leaving both as soft and white as any velvet, and now she wished she had taken time to sand all the iron pots until they were gleaming, even if it only meant she had to season them again.

After retrieving the eggs, still warm from the nest, she stoked the outside oven for bread and perhaps a molasses cake, and hurried back inside to see to Eli. As he was still sleeping peacefully, she took time to study her face in the small looking glass Jedd used for shaving.

The mark of the devil. If anything, it was even more evident. Her hair was as red as always, and twice as wild. After weeks of going without a bonnet, her skin had taken on a warm coloration that kept her freckles from standing out quite so much. Unfortunately, against the peach color of her cheeks, her eyes seemed greener and paler than ever. Sighing with displeasure, she wrinkled her nose at the image. At least she could do that without suffering, for the swelling she had arrived with had gradually gone down.

With no notion of whether or not the menfolk would come home to eat, Maggie had boiled ham and greens, baked a round of corn bread and a molasses cake, using the last of her clabber and most of her eggs. If they didn't show up until dark, why then they could eat it cold, for she would not sweat over a hot fire in midsummer twice in one day for them that didn't appreciate it.

She was coming from the outhouse when she saw the men returning. With deep water nearly a mile offshore, it was necessary to use lighters to unload both crew and cargo. All the islanders had a few small boats, whether or not they owned larger vessels.

She stood in the back door, shading her eyes against the sun, until she could make out the three men—or rather two men and a boy. "For pity sake," she muttered in disgust. "A body might think you were looking forward to seeing that iron-faced, hatchet-tongued man!"

Impatient at her own shilly-shallying, she turned and marched inside, slamming pots and pans against the hearth until Eli woke from his morning nap and demanded her attention.

It was steamy hot inside. Once she had mopped him off and changed his napkin, Maggie took the babe outside to give him his bottle. Matt had mended an old milking stool and placed it under the cedar grove for her several days before. Now she sat in the shade, her hair bundled up on top of her head and her skirt hiked up well past her ankles for coolness. There was a growing patch of dampness on her gown where her sweat mingled with that of Eli's hot little body, but it made it even cooler when a breeze stirred over them.

She had deliberately turned to face away from the landing, not wanting to appear anxious. And then she chided herself for such foolishness. She was a married woman. It was time she learned to think and act like one.

"Still here, I see."

She hadn't heard his footsteps, for he could walk as silent as a morning mist when he cared to. Matt and Isaac were still down at the landing, chattering away like blackbirds. Maggie looked up, and her gaze tangled with Cabe's until she could feel the heat rising up her throat. "Did you think I wouldn't be?" she asked in a voice meant to sound firm. Either he didn't hear, or he didn't like what he heard, for without a word, he turned and stalked away to disappear inside the house.

Taking Isaac with them, the men returned to the *Bridget* after eating. Matt complimented her on her cooking, praising everything until Maggie, embarrassed, hushed him. She knew he liked her cooking—he put away enough to fill three grown men. She also knew he would have taken it for granted as he always had if either Isaac or Cabe had spoken a single word at the table. Both of them had eaten in stony silence. Then Cabe had risen, signaled the boy and turned to go, still without so much as casting a glance in her direction.

Dear Matthew. For all his teasing ways, he was a kind boy, Maggie thought as she stood in the back door and watched them all go down to the landing, walking single file on the narrow path through the marsh.

But it was not Matt her eyes lingered on, but the broad shoulders and the narrow hips of his older brother. What a maddening man! What right had he to eat her food without so much as a nod of thanks? It would serve him right if she flattened his feather bed and poured sand in it!

It was the same that evening. They trooped in silently, Cabe and Isaac, the two dark ones, the two unsmiling ones. Matt came in later, having gone by the boat yard for a few minutes.

While Maggie served up the beans with a generous serving of wild onions chopped over the top, Cabe and Isaac sat out under the cedars. From time to time she peered out at them. They seemed to be talking earnestly, but she couldn't hear a word they were saying.

Finally everything was on the table but the corn bread, which was still in the outdoor oven. Taking two folded squares of canvas to protect her hands against the hot pan, she marched outside, ignoring the two who didn't bother to look up when she passed by.

"England lies to the nor'east, boy, not the south. There's a Plymouth up coast in the Massachusetts colony, same as there is in England. You'll have to know such things. Now spell out Plymouth and England for me. I'll not ask you to spell out Massachusetts, for I'm not sure I can, either. Then we'll get on with your numbers. By the time you're old enough to stand at my desk, I want you able to tote up a manifest for me. Pa's eyes won't last forever, Matt don't have the patience for numbers, and I'm too busy. We're counting on you, boy."

"What about Eli? He can't do nothing but cry and wet and eat."

"By the time he's twelve, he'll ripen some. He'll sail as cabin boy same's we all did. Same as you will when you're twelve."

"Supper's on the table," said Maggie, not ten feet from where they were sitting. Lessons? Cabe was hearing the boy's *lessons*? Somehow, that possibility had never occurred to her. If she had thought at all, she would have thought he might be asking the boy all sorts of questions about what she had been up to while he'd been gone.

Supper was eaten in silence, but for Matt's gossip. Finally Cabe had sent him a quelling look, and he, too, had subsided. Maggie watched as the three of them waded into her beans, bread and fried salt pork. There was molasses cake left over, and she served it with a dollop of clabber. They accepted in silence, ate in silence and left the table in silence. Only Matt turned back with a look of apology. "Thankee, Maggie. Reckon I'll be going down to the boat yard to see that everything's secured for the night," he said with a wink.

"Jere will appreciate the way you've looked after his interests while he's been gone," she replied solemnly. "Good thing it doesn't look like rain tonight. You might be obliged to pinch a nose."

The other two went outside in the fading light, and after a while, Maggie caught a drift of pipe tobacco through the back door. The dishes done and the food put out in the cool room, she fed Eli one last time and readied him for the night. He was a good baby. Now that he was getting enough to eat, he wasn't fretting near as much, even though she was almost certain he had another tooth working its way through his swollen little gum.

"Bye-o-my baby, bye-o-my baby," she sang in a tuneless monotone as she walked the floor with the infant over her shoulder. From outside she could hear the low rumble of Cabe's deep voice as he talked to his little brother. Who would have thought the man would have such a tender streak in him? Surely not Maggie.

With Eli bedded down, there was no reason to linger. Isaac always took himself off to bed, and Matt would be home when it suited him.

Still she lingered, a vague sense of incompleteness bothering her. The dishes were done, the baby sleeping, her house was in order. Morning would come before she was ready, with another huge pile of washing to be done, the cow to be milked, the meals to be cooked, and in her spare time, there was a pair of Matt's outgrown trousers she was trying to cut down for Isaac.

Remembering what Matt had said about Cabe's ill-fitting shirts, she wished the boy would allow her to measure him. But he wouldn't even speak to her, much less allow her to touch him. She had to content herself with trying to gauge by his old trousers that were too short, too tight in the seat, but still just right in the waist.

With an exclamation of impatience, she blew out the Betty lamp. She could do without the stinking oil, much less the added heat. One of these days she was going to have to find time to make more candles. And more soap, for with all the bedding and the baby's napkins to wash, that was nearly gone, too.

"I thought you'd be asleep by now."

At Cabe's words, she spun around, and to her horror, felt the heat rise to her face. God, he had only to speak to her to make her feel guilty! "You shouldn't sneak around like that! You'll scare a body out of her wits," she accused.

"I don't sneak in my own home, Maggie. I leave that for the likes of you."

"I didn't—I don't—" she sputtered, growing all the more angry as she saw the cool amusement sparkling in his yellow eyes. He was leaning up against the doorjamb as if he owned the place, as indeed, she supposed he did.

"I expect you do, every chance you get. Just keep this in mind, though—you'll not get the chance while I'm around." With that he turned and disappeared into the room he shared with Matt and Isaac, leaving her with no outlet for her impotent rage except for the dishtowel she held in her hands. That she threw across the room, striking the still smoking Betty lamp and spilling sooty oil across the floor.

Maggie cried herself to sleep that night. She told herself she was crying over having her freshly scrubbed floor ruined, but it wasn't the thought of having to spend hours on her knees with sand and lye soap that followed her into her troubled dreams.

It was a pair of yellow eyes set in a scornful face. Damn the man! Of all the ships that put into Bath Towne, why had she chosen his to hide aboard in her flight to safety?

Chapter Eight

Cabel watched his father's new bride like a hawk. He had always respected the old man. Resented him occasionally, and fought with him more times than he cared to recall, but always respected him.

Until now. Yet he was convinced it was not entirely his father's fault. Jedd had been anchored to the house too long. Dry rot had a way of setting in when a man was beached against his will. Some men were meant to abide on shore, some weren't. Jedd Rawson's place was a windswept, rolling deck, not sweating over a boiler full of baby napkins or a pot of beans and sow belly. If that old biddy from up Chic'macomico way hadn't got the wind up and walked out on him . . .

But the girl he'd hired after that had been even worse. She'd been so busy making eyes at Matt she hadn't even known Isaac was alive. And as for Eli, the poor little mite could have floated right out of his cradle for all the attention she paid him.

Jedd had been ripe for a woman like Maggie McNair. All she'd had to do was twitch her skinny little behind and roll those great green eyes of hers. He'd probably been so bamboozled by that time he'd tied himself a noose and invited her to slip it over his head.

Maggie Rawson! Cabe's profanity revealed a remarkable streak of originality. She was no more fit to take his mother's place than he was fit to fly! And what galled the fire of hell out of him was that there wasn't a bloody damned thing he could do about it! The old man had upped and *married* her!

Well, wife or no wife, she wasn't going to get away with a thing. He could see to that much at least. The first time he caught her prying into something that didn't concern her, she'd be out of there so fast she wouldn't have time to grab her hat.

If she even had a hat. She sure didn't look to have much, still wearing that same old rag he'd found her in. If she wore anything under it, it sure as shootin' didn't show!

It wasn't the fact that she was poor that bothered him. God knows, it was no sin to be dirt poor. Most bankers were poor when it came to gold and fancy geegaws, but those with the gumption to reap the woods and waters managed to live as fit as any lord.

No, it wasn't her poverty that bothered Cabel. He didn't know quite what it was, but—well, dammit, a woman ought to have more pride than to marry herself off to a man old enough to be her grandfather just because she happened to run into a streak of bad luck! Just like Lettie. Give a woman a shot at respectability, and she was hell-bent on hitching herself to the first set of trousers that come along.

Dammit, it weren't as if Maggie was outright ugly, either. Leastwise, she wasn't as ugly as he remembered her. In fact, brushed up and polished, she'd likely cut a right fine figure.

Against his will, a vision of his new stepmother began to take shape before his eyes. That hair... God, what a snarl! It fair made his hands itch to get into it.

And those eyes. He'd seen more than one set of green eyes on a woman, but hers were no ordinary shade of green. They were the color of a fox grape before it began to turn, and so clear a body could fall into them and drown before he knew it.

There was something different about her, but for the life of him he couldn't remember what it was. Not her hair. Not her eyes. God knows her chin was just as stubborn as ever, and her mouth clamped as tight as a bale on a barrel. And her nose...

Her nose?

That was what was wrong with her! She'd started out with a lumpy wad of a nose that was much too big for such a small face, only somehow it had shrunk up until it was no bigger than the tip of his thumb. Truth was, it was a right fine nose, as noses went. Which meant that when he'd first seen her, she must have...

Or someone else must have...

And then Cabe remembered the thing he had deliberately put out of his mind. The sight of her thin, rib-patterned back, all black and purple and red, with the yellowish stains of older bruises in between the fresh ones. Unconsciously he clenched his fists at his sides. His eyes narrowed until they were mere slits of fire at the thought of some bastard treating a woman— treating any creature so small and helpless—with such brutality.

And not just once, but again and again, from the looks of what he'd seen in that one sickening glance. Why hadn't she run away? Or perhaps she had, and the devil had caught her and dragged her back, and beat her for trying to escape.

But she had escaped. She'd hid out in his cargo hold and gotten clean away, though it couldn't have been easy on her. She'd won, and Cabe felt a small surge of pride in her that would have stunned him had he recognized it as such. He didn't hold with girls her age selling themselves. There had to be some other way to put food in their mouths.

But whether or not he approved, he was forced to admit that she was as spunky a bit of skirt as ever he'd seen. No bigger than a gnat, she had nonetheless turned Jedd's house upside down, scrubbing and polishing until the whole place shone bright as a new gold guinea. And on top of that, damned if she hadn't brought in every blooming weed for miles around and stuffed them in every empty pot and jug she could lay hands on!

Shaking his head as the irony of his own thoughts overcame him, Cabe swore again. With a feeling of restlessness he neither understood nor welcomed, he tapped the ashes from his pipe and stuck it into his pocket, only to have it fall through to the ground.

"Damned seams don't hold for nothing anymore," he grumbled, scooping it up and tucking it under his belt. He was going to have to find him another woman before he ran out of clothes. He'd tried Charlie the sail maker, but the canvas britches Charlie had made for him had flapped about his limbs like a luffing mainsail.

Come to think of it, he'd noticed that Isaac's limbs didn't hang so far out of his pant legs, and there was considerably more slack to the beam of his trousers these days. Evidently the woman could sew a bit. Maybe if he asked her nicely...

Sweat beaded his forehead at the thought of Maggie on her knees with her measuring string, one end held to his ankle, the other snaking slowly up to his crotch. Godamighty, he'd sooner go stark naked for the rest of his life than subject himself to *that*! He was hard as an oar handle just thinking about it—if she ever actually touched him, he'd likely set fire to them both!

Pride goeth before a fall. Pride was the devil's own sin. Pride led many a good man to his downfall. How many times had Maggie let such strictures flow over her head? Evidently none of Zion's preachments had sunk in, even though, as often as not, he'd hammered the lesson home with his cane.

Gazing around at the floor she had scrubbed just that morning, at the table scrubbed just as white and the newly cleaned hearth that took up one whole end of the room, she freely admitted her pride. It was hardly Sara's fault that she hadn't been able to keep up with everything. Doing for four grown men, two youngers, and two nursing babes was enough to run any woman ragged without having two houses to turn out. Maggie only hoped that Jeremiah was giving his wife the rest she deserved, letting her lie abed till all hours while a maid looked after Becky Mary and Charity Ann.

Meanwhile Maggie had made Jedd's house gleam, if she did say so herself. Every day the sun shone, she dragged the beds across the floor and hung them out the window to air, then dragged them back again. Her floors were white as cotton bolls—except for the place she'd spilled lamp oil, which would take a spell to fade. There wasn't a cobweb in any corner, and fresh flowers filled every spare container on every available surface. Even Matt had remarked on how pretty they looked.

"Looks like you're dead set on bringing the outside in, Maggie."

"I do like flowers, that's the truth." She hadn't bothered to add that for the past nine years, she'd lived with a man who couldn't abide anything he considered frivolous. If a flower didn't bear fruit, then he rooted it out. He'd once set off a fire that had burned half the woodlot and threatened the house, just trying to get rid of a single honeysuckle thicket. He was the only man she'd ever known who could look at a small, innocent wildflower and see naught but a vicious weed to be rooted out.

Thank heavens she no longer had to fear Zion's wrath. If only she could have taken her mother away in time . . .

But Maggie was not one to weep over what couldn't be mended. One day soon she would find a way to let Gideon know where she was, and then he could visit her in her new home. Gid and Matt would rub well together. It would be hard to find a more winsome pair than those two. Gid must be nearly twenty-one by now. He'd been tall for a lad. As a man he would've filled out all the hollows until he towered over every man in sight.

Except perhaps for Cabel.

With Eli on her hip and a blanket over her shoulder, Maggie set off, after putting away the food from the noonday meal. She had yet to explore her surroundings beyond what she could see from the house, for wherever she looked, there was something that needed doing.

The garden was coming along fine, although Isaac had deserted it since she'd taken to working there. Just that morning she'd noticed a narrow footpath that led from the garden into the woods, and now she was determined to follow it.

Within shouting distance of the house, on top of a small rise under a gnarled live oak that would have taken five grown men to reach around, was a single grave. Maggie knew instinctively that she had come upon Anne Rawson's resting place, for she'd seen Jedd walk up this very hill before he'd left.

Carefully placing the baby on his stomach in the center of the blanket, she seated herself beside him. "Anne Rawson," she read from the beautifully carved cypress slab. Somehow, it seemed quite natural to speak to the departed woman, for hadn't she continued to talk to her mother after poor Jane had slipped away in her sleep? Hadn't she talked to her with no response at all those last two months while the poor woman lay dying from the wasting disease?

"I'm Maggie. I was born Maggie McNair of Nixonton, lately from near Bath Towne, but last month I happened to journey out to the banks, and Sara took me to meet your Jedd. You see, they needed someone to help mind the youngers. Isaac still misses you something fierce, and it was getting too much for

Sara. Lord, she was plumb wore out, suckling the two babes, but Eli took to the bottle right off. He's starting to eat, too, now that he's got five teeth and another one busting through most any day. Chews on anything he gets his little hands on.''

She chuckled, and from the shore nearby, a chorus of laughing gulls set up a response. After a while she said, "I'd have been just as content to keep house, but when it came time for Jedd to set out again, he thought it would be best if we married. I reckon he was afeared I'd light out like the others did, but he needn't have worried. Truth is, I needed him more than he needed me."

Maggie wrapped her arms about her knees, enjoying the touch of the light breeze on her hair. She didn't feel the least bit self-conscious talking to a headboard and a border of conch shells. "'Course, I'm not a real wife to him. He still holds you to be his real wife, and truth to tell, I'm mightily relieved, for I don't think I'd care for all that . . . well, you know."

Maggie spent the better part of an hour with Anne, sometimes talking, sometimes just sitting in companionable silence while Eli kicked and dribbled and batted at every passing shadow. It was surprisingly comforting to be able to talk so freely, for not even to Sara, whom she counted as her friend, had she confided the details of her past.

Gazing at the meticulously worked pattern of shells that marked the small space, Maggie couldn't help but contrast it in her mind with the raw, unmarked plot where Jane McNair Johnston had been laid to rest. Someone—Isaac, she suspected—had made an attempt to transplant flowers at each corner. They were all shriveled up, some of them already blackened, as if the child had simply plucked the prettiest blossoms and stuck them in the ground, hoping they would take root and thrive.

Gazing down at the tiny bouquet of small blue and white flowers she had picked on her way up the hill, Maggie made up her mind to root some cuttings for Anne's grave. Perhaps if Isaac saw that she meant his mother no disrespect, he would soften toward her.

After a while, feeling greatly refreshed, she scooped up the drowsy baby, tossed the blanket over her shoulder and collected her wildflowers, which had already begun to wilt. She should have waited to pick them on her way back, but then, she was used to making the most of her opportunities. Who could tell when they would come again?

With Eli dry and sleeping in his cradle, Maggie retrieved her bouquet from the bed where she'd tossed it and tiptoed from the room.

"Star-of-Bethlehem."

At the sound of Cabe's voice, she whirled around, scattering flowers across the floor. "Who?"

"Star-of-Bethlehem. The flowers. What the hell are you doing, trying to bring the whole outdoors inside?"

"That's what Matt said." Maggie barely restrained herself from pressing a hand to her chest. Her heart had commenced to beating as if it were trying to escape her body. "I like flowers."

"Well, so do I, but not in the house. Place smells like a..." He grimaced, leaving Maggie to wonder what was wrong with any place that smelled like flowers.

"They smell better than your stinky old pipe," she defended. On her knees, she began gathering up the fragile, star-shaped blossoms and the few stems of blue-eyed grass she had found to set them off, burningly conscious of his gaze on her backside as she crawled across the floor.

"Your feet are dirty," Cabe observed from his vantage point above her.

"I've been outside," she snapped. "Your boots aren't any too clean, either."

"Tide's out. There's mud along the landing."

"Between your stinky pipe and your muddy boots, I don't see how you have the nerve to fuss with me over a mess of flowers," she grumbled. The truth was, she was far too aware of the big boots planted firmly in front of her, of the long, powerfully muscled limbs they covered, of the thighs that rose from their flaring tops, and...

Her face was already burning when she felt his hands on her shoulders. Crushing the pale stems in her damp hands, she let herself be lifted to stand before him, not having the strength to resist.

"Aye, and what do you smell of, Maggie McNair? All the men you've lain with? All the ones you've cozened out of a few coins? You owe me something for the two coppers I gave you, remember? And for the passage you stole aboard my ship."

Maggie's mouth fell open, and she struggled to think of some response to such an unfair accusation. But she was far too conscious of the feel of his hands on her arms, the scent of his body that hinted of salt, lye soap, leather and something essentially masculine.

Her mouth snapped shut and she swallowed hard, still unable to drag her gaze away from his face. "I don't owe—why do you—"

"Why do I what, Maggie? Why do I lie awake nights thinking of ways to get rid of you without shaming Pa? Thinking of who I could hire to take you so far away from this island that you'd never find your way back here?"

The pain was worse than anything she had ever experienced, and he hadn't even struck her. He'd only used words. Stricken, Maggie continued to stare at him until she felt her nose prickle and stop up. Next her eyes began to smart so that he appeared to waver before her like a reflection in troubled water.

It took every bit of strength she possessed, but she willed the tears back. Stretching her spine to its meager limit, she said coolly, "If you don't mind, I'd like to put my flowers in water before they wilt."

Cabe watched her walk away, and his conscience smote him. Dammit, why should *he* feel guilty because he happened to know her for what she truly was? Pa would never have countenanced a whore in his house, looking after his children. God knows what she'd told him to get him to marry her, but whatever it was, Cabe knew different. He'd seen her on the docks, approaching one man after another. She'd even approached him!

He felt his loins stir as he stared at the doorway where she'd disappeared. He could have followed her. He could have laid her out on that bed and stripped the pitiful rag she wore from her body and gazed to his heart's content at the riches it hid.

Red. She would be red-haired there, too, and even curlier. Her small white breasts would rise sweetly to fill his palms. He would suckle her first, until her nipples hardened under his tongue, and then he would cover her with kisses, lured on by the sweet musky smell of her womanhood, until they were both too aroused to prolong the delicious agony a moment more. Only then would he part her delicate thighs and ease himself into that sweetest harbor of all.

Ease himself! God, he would plunge! He would be on her like a rutting stallion, unable to control himself! And Cabel Rawson had yet to meet the woman who could make him lose control.

His father's wife. He swore softly, feelingly. Jesus, he had to get away from here before he shamed them all!

Maggie had never thought she'd be praying for the day when her husband would return, but as the week crept past and the tension between Cabel and herself grew even more unbearable, she found herself longing for Jedd's calming ways. Not even Cabel would have the nerve to look at her that way in his father's presence, as if he would like to wrap his hands around her throat and squeeze the very breath from her body.

Matt was no help at all. The boat yard took up all his time—or so he said. Maggie rather thought Lina had something to do with his diligence, for there was little but minor repair work going on at the boat yard with Jeremiah still away. One of the carpenters was doing something to the *Bridget*'s steering lines to keep them from fouling on a hard starboard turn.

At least she felt some encouragement when she noticed Isaac watching her transplant grape seedlings to a spot near the house that was sheltered from the fiercest winds. Without looking up, she said, "There now, with a bit of watering and some nice woods mold, they should grow just fine. No call to go traipsing all over creation hunting grapes when we can grow them right here by the door."

Isaac continued to watch her, his dark eyes solemn, but perhaps not quite so accusing as before. Bending over to gully the sandy soil around the stem, she murmured just loud enough to be heard, "If only I had another pair of hands, I might even set out some wild huckleberry plants over near those pines. I do like a good huckleberry pie, but it takes so long to hunt up enough bushes."

Sighing, she stood up, a hand on her aching back, and watched him disappear down the path that led to the landing. Oh, well, it was a start, anyway. At least he hadn't stuck his tongue out at her before he'd gone. Or belched. That was his latest way of showing his disdain. After polishing off whatever she served him, he would wait until Matt had thanked her and then he let out a long, loud belch before he left the room. With some folks, a belch might have been taken as a compliment for the cook, but Maggie was fairly certain that Isaac meant no such thing.

For all she was content, nothing had really changed. Some wanted her and some didn't.

Jedd came home the next day. Maggie, busy making conserve with the earliest figs from Sara's trees, didn't even know the *Eliza Lea* was back until she saw the four Rawsons walking up the landing path together. Only then did she look farther out to see Jedd's sloop, her sails neatly furled as she lay at anchor in the channel in the lee of the island.

Slipping the kettle off the hob, she stoked up the fire and set the water to boil. There was cold bread, and she could drop a few slices of ham in a hot skillet. She had pickled some beans before they could go bad, and with a few onions on top, it should do well enough. If she'd had more warning, she would have done more.

"If I'd had more warning," she said the minute Jedd walked through the door, "I'd have killed that old rooster that's got so mean."

Jedd grinned. "There now, lads, don't that sound just like a woman? Always finding something to fret about. Come here, lass, and see what I brought you."

Maggie ducked her head, suddenly shy as she became conscious of four sets of male eyes on her. Matt's and Jedd's were warm and teasing, but the others—the two who would as soon see the back of her as not—were harder to read. "I didn't want you to bring me anything," she mumbled. "You've given me so much as it is."

Cabe stood in the doorway, his gaze moving over her worn and faded gown. If the old man had given her more than the roof over her head and enough food to round her out a bit, it didn't show. And God knows, she'd worked for that much, he'd have to admit.

"Measured them by the length of my hand," Jedd was saying as he dug a pair of spanking new boots from his duffel bag and plopped them down onto the table. "If'n they don't fit, the boy'll grow into 'em soon enough, and I'll bring you another pair next time I go and come."

Disgusted, Cabe looked from Maggie's face to her feet and then back to the ugly pair of boy's boots sitting stiffly beside the mug of dainty blue and white flowers. Why the devil couldn't the old man have brought her something a bit more... feminine? Hell, you couldn't even bend a boot like that, much less wear it in any comfort! Maybe he'd ride up the banks to King's Point and get old Sits There to make her a pair of moccasins like his.

This time Maggie was unable to hold back the tears. As ever, her nose announced their imminence by turning red and stuffing up so that she could hardly breathe. "That's right kind of you, Jedd. They're lovely boots. They look like they'll fit just fine."

"Well go ahead, woman, stop sniffling and try 'em on," said the old man, as pleased as if he had brought her a pair of fine red kidskin boots with tiny heels and pewter buckles instead of a pair of plain black boy's boots of thick, dull cowhide. They were exactly like the ones she'd lost, and Maggie told herself that was the reason she couldn't keep the tears from streaming down her face.

"I won't wear her boots," Isaac declared truculently.

"Ain't they kind of big?" Matt chimed in.

Maggie, hopping on one foot as she tried to wedge her other one into the stiff leather, sprang another freshet of tears as she looked up to see Cabe glowering at her as if he begrudged her even a pair of new boots.

"Jesus, women!" Jedd grumbled, and strode across the room to pour himself a tankard of cider.

The days were long. Although the house quickly grew dark, and the Betty lamps were hardly worth the bother, there was enough light after the evening meal so that Maggie could see to sew if she took her work outside. Besides, it was pleasant. The air was cool and fragrant in spite of the pervasive smell of salt mud that heralded low tide on the sound side. There was just enough breeze to keep the mosquitoes away.

The men had gone down to the landing for their smoke, with Isaac tagging after them, as it was Jedd's first day home. Maggie leaned back against the trunk of a cedar and gazed out at her husband's distinctive silhouette as he sat on a piling, cradling his pipe in his hand. There was no mistaking that beard, nor the full crop of gray-blond hair. He was a handsome man for his age, even when one couldn't see the twinkle in his faded eyes.

Matt was easily recognizable by his gestures. He seldom talked without the use of both hands. There was no sign of the other two, but Maggie suspected that Cabe would be sitting on the sun-warmed planks, his back braced against a weathered piling, with the boy on his lap. Only with Cabe did Isaac forget his sturdy independence.

As the light faded, she finished hemming the trousers she'd been letting out for Isaac, measuring them against a pair of old ones. They looked about right, but it was hard to tell—there was more to a body than length and breadth, as well she knew from having sewn for Nimrod and Zion since her mother had grown too feeble to hold needle and thread. A string around the waist, one from waist to ankle, and another from ankle to seat would have given her all she needed, but she knew better than to ask. So far, she had yet to lay a hand on the boy. It was Matt who saw that he washed before he went to bed, Matt who tucked him in at night and saw that he was more or less dressed before he set out to do his chores of a morning.

She folded the trousers and tucked the needle away in its case. She'd found it in Anne's sewing basket, along with the scissors and coarse-spun thread. The men were just now coming up to the house, and she lingered, unconsciously wanting to be a part of their closeness. Jedd came first, then Matt, then Cabe, bearing Isaac on his shoulders. Cabe was laughing about something, and it struck her that she had never before heard the sound of his laughter. It set off a peculiar feeling under her bodice, as if her gown were too tight to allow her lungs to fill with air.

Matt took Isaac off to bed, and Jedd turned to Maggie. "Another tot of rum, Pa?" Cabe asked, coming up behind him. "I've got some ideas as to how we can get out the inlet without having every pirate on the coast on our tails."

"It'll keep till morning, son. I've a wife to see to." He drew Maggie to his side, hugging her so that her feet left the floor as he laughed down into her reddening face and winked. "Missed you something fierce, woman!"

Despite her momentary misgivings, Maggie knew she had nothing to fear from Jedd. She trusted him. It was Cabe who bothered her, and for reasons she couldn't begin to understand, it pained her to let him think she'd stolen even the smallest bit of his father's affection from him.

Turning back from the bedroom doorway to suggest that perhaps the two men would like to linger a while before Jedd came to bed, her gaze clashed head-on with a pair of glittering eyes.

Lord, he looked as if he *hated* her, and truly, she'd done nothing to him. He had no reason . . .

Suddenly Maggie wanted to run out into the night, to run and keep on running, to feel the wind on her naked skin. She hungered to hear Cabe's footsteps behind her, to know that he would catch her, and that when he did . . .

Dear Lord, how was it possible for a woman to think such things about any man, much less one who openly despised her? What would he think of her if he knew she had but to look at him—had but to *think* about him—to have her mind fill with all sorts of wicked thoughts?

Breathlessly she hurried into the room she shared with Jedd. Thank goodness they would all be leaving in a few days. She would simply have to control herself before her wicked imagination made her forget all about the vows that bound her to Cabe's father.

Chapter Nine

Sara, Jeremiah and the children came home the following day. Maggie was rather startled to realize how glad she was to see the woman she had known for such a short time.

"Did you sleep until all hours of a morning?" she asked. Sara was nursing Charity Ann while Maggie poked thin gruel between Eli's rosebud lips and then scraped it off his chin.

"Jere found me a maid, but not a wet nurse. Maggie, you'll never believe all the wonders I've seen. Roads full of carriages, fancy clothes—why the men outdressed the women! I vow we're twenty years behind the fashions here on the banks." She went on at length, and Maggie, thinking of her own limited wardrobe, could only count her blessings that she'd ended up on the banks instead of in a more fashionable part of the colonies.

"How're you getting on with Isaac?" Sara inquired.

"Did you ever try asking an oyster to open his shell for you?"

"When they get hungry enough, even oysters ease up. Which reminds me, you and Cabe getting along all right?"

Maggie shrugged. Lifting the baby to her shoulder, she patted his back until he let go his wind. "He's not much like Matthew, is he?"

"Bless me, no!" Sara laughed delightedly. "Gave you whatfor, did he? Cabe's got his soft side, but he'd sooner be keelhauled than show it. He'll come around, him and Isaac, both."

Maggie had heard that promise before. She didn't put much stock in it. All the same, the thought of discovering Cabel

Rawson's 'soft side' teased at her imagination long after Sara had taken her leave.

The nights were the worst. The men sat at the table with their rum long after the evening meal was finished, while Maggie went about clearing away, washing the trenchers, bowls and tankards and making up the breakfast bread to rise. When they left to stroll down to the landing, trailing a soft cloud of tobacco smoke behind, she hurriedly washed and changed into her shift. By the time they had considered the sky, remarked on the tide, and discussed the likelihood of an overnight shift of wind, she would be in bed, the bolster securely in place beside her. She always left a single candle burning to light her husband's way.

Her husband. How strange it still seemed—yet not at all unpleasant. Surprisingly, she had found comfort almost from the first in knowing that only an arm's reach away lay a strong and kindly man who had offered her his home and the protection of his name, asking nothing more in return than that she look after his children in his absence. There was something reassuring about Jedd Rawson, something she'd instinctively trusted from the very first.

It was hard not to contrast her present position with the one she'd escaped. Zion Johnston hadn't a kind bone in his body. As for his son, Nimrod had taken great pleasure in tormenting her from the first day she had met him. Nor had complaining to his father ever done her a mite of good, for invariably, she ended up being punished for lying while Nimrod looked on, a sly smile on his doughy face.

The wicked sluggard could have been caught with his hands around her gullet and still convinced his father he was only trying to save her from strangling by preventing a lump of bread from slipping down her windpipe.

That night Jedd came in before she was asleep. Maggie knew by the way he moved about that he was already growing restless. He'd told her in the beginning that he never slept soundly on shore. Maggie suspected that part of his impatience stemmed from the fact that there was too little for him to do while he waited to take the *Eliza Lea* across the sound for another cargo. The house was snug and in good repair, and any work needed on the sloop was done by Jeremiah's men or the ship's carpenter. Maggie tended the garden, and there were plenty to provide fish, turtle meat, crabs and other shellfish. Even the firewood had been cut and stacked by Matthew.

Maggie's days were full, and by nightfall she was tired. Still, she tried to stay awake for Jedd's sake. "It was kind of you to bring me boots, Jedd," she told him for the fifth time in as many days. "They'll come in handy when it turns cold."

"Wear 'em anytime you go into the woods, girl. There's snakes big around as a man's arm. Mostly they won't bother you, but now'n again you run across a testy one."

Maggie shuddered. There was little in this world she truly feared, but snakes made her flesh crawl. Nimrod had known of her abiding aversion to the evil creatures, using it against her on more than one occasion. "Snakes on an island? How did they get here?"

"Lord put 'em here, I reckon, same's He did most everything else. The food was good tonight, Maggie. You're a fine hand with bread, better than Anne was, though she done turtle and venison to a turn."

The unexpected praise took her mind off snakes, and Maggie wriggled herself a cozy nest in the bedding. They continued to talk about the two youngers, about the likelihood of an early storm and when to set out the last of the greens for winter.

They talked far into the night. The next day, Jedd patted her on the back more than once, a decided twinkle in his deep-set eyes. Amused, Maggie noted that he was far more demonstrative when one of his elder sons was around. She rather thought it had something to do with his manly pride, and would have been pleased to go along with the innocent deception but for one thing. The more attentive Jedd became, the more sullen Cabe grew. After the first few days, he was barely speaking to her.

The message that blazed forth from his eyes, however, was unmistakable. If Maggie had been the least bit timid she would have gathered her new boots, her spare gown and her quilt and lit out on the next boat to anywhere.

Which made it all the more necessary for her to disappear each evening as soon as her day's work was finished. Not that she felt much like lingering, for the summer days were long, and morning came early. Jedd usually followed her to bed soon afterward, leaving Cabel and Matt talking in low but still audible murmurs about who was to sail aboard which ship, and how best to deal with the increasing menace of Ocracoke's growing pirate community.

But no matter how tired she was, sleep didn't come easily. Just knowing that Cabe was only a few feet away, his long, powerful legs stretched halfway across her kitchen floor, one muscular arm hooked over the back of his chair as he nursed his last noggin of rum, was enough to bring on that strange, tightening feeling she'd first noticed when he'd caught her wearing his shirt aboard the *Bridget*.

As if the wall were not even there, she could picture him wearing the moccasins he often wore at home instead of the heavy jackboots that hugged his thighs. Midsummer heat and the dying cook fire would have left a sheen of sweat on his dark, angular features, and his hair—that darker than midnight crop that looked softer than the down on a blackbird's rump—would have begun to escape from the neat binding that held it at his nape.

How could she help but welcome her husband to her bed? At least Jedd's voice drowned out the sound of the voices from the next room. His stories could even distract her momentarily from dwelling on the enigmatic man who had yet to forgive her for hiding away aboard his precious schooner.

Jedd had a wealth of tales about the places he had been and the people he'd met. He was a fine storyteller, reminding Maggie of her own father in that respect. In many respects, come to think of it.

Sometimes they talked about Isaac, or about Eli's progress in learning to sit without toppling over. Once, after Jedd had been home for just on a week, he told her about Anne, and how he'd almost killed himself trying to prove his worth to her parents before he'd even been allowed to pay his court.

"Give the devil his due—if Kinnahauk hadn't come down so hard on me, I'd likely still be sailing under old Bartholemew Williams. Damned old redskin made me risk my neck proving I was worthy of his baby girl, and I've been at it ever since. Never ease off once you set your course, child, or you're bound to founder." He smiled, stroking his gray-blond beard. "Worth it, though, my Annie was. Worth ever' sweatin', cussin' minute of it, Lord keep her.''

Surely, Maggie thought in sleepy amusement, no wife ever had a stranger marriage than her own. Scarce broken in, and her bridegroom spent his nights telling her what a rare woman his first wife had been. Yet she found it oddly touching.

If it weren't for Isaac's stubborn refusal to accept her, and for Cabel's equally stubborn insistance on despising her, she could have been quite happy. Even so, she was more content than she'd been in years. She had all any woman could ask, and nothing at all to fear. If one discounted the constant strain of having Cabe's watchful eyes follow her every move.

He would appear at odd times during the day, when she was feeding the baby, or outside boiling the wash, with sweat dripping from every part of her body. She would feel his eyes on her with that trembling sureness, and look up just as he turned away. At times she would look up from her sewing to find that he'd come home for something in the mid of day and lingered to watch her, his eyes a bright flare of color in his dark, hard face.

"Did you want something?" she'd asked that first time.

"Yes, I—No!"

He'd turned and strode away then, and she'd been left with a feeling of guilt that had quickly given way to anger. Anger because there'd been no cause for her to feel guilty.

At first she'd considered confiding in Jedd, but quickly decided against it. There was an increasing strain between father and son that not even she could ignore.

It was all so unreasonable! Her only comfort was knowing that in all likelihood, Cabe would have resented any woman his father brought into their home so soon after his mother had died.

The days were in turn satisfying, frustrating, puzzling and exhausting. Only at night could she let down her guard. Of all unlikely places, Maggie found her greatest feeling of security in the small bedroom, with Eli on one side of her in his cradle and Jedd on the other side of the bolster. Her unexpected friendship with a man three times her age had grown surprisingly strong in the short while they'd been together. There was something about lying together in a dark room night after night, with the scent of honeysuckle drifting in through the open window and chuck-will's-widow calling from the pine woods, that seemed to invite confidences.

A little hesitantly at first, Maggie began to talk about her own past. "It's funny the way things turn out. I never thought I would marry. After Mama married Zion and took us to live on his farm, I swore I would never speak to another man if I ever got away from there."

"You were hurting when you come to me, girl. I've seen enough men flogged to know how they move, how they hold themselves, favoring the soreness."

Surprised at the observation, Maggie murmured, "You never said anything. You never even asked where I'd come from, or why."

"Figured when you was ready to trust me, you'd speak out. I ain't a man to lay a hand on child nor woman, Maggie. Now a man, he's different. Some deserves it. Some ain't fit to see the light o' day. If ever I lay hands on one o' them godda—them bloody bast— Beggin' yer pardon, them *pirates*, I'll do worse'n lay a cat across their yeller backsides."

Maggie shuddered at the bitterness in his rough voice. She knew from what Matt had told her that two local ships had been taken only this past spring, their officers killed and their crews set off in small boats that had capsized trying to make the inlet in a storm.

Jedd turned to her in the darkness, his voice losing its edge of tension. "But they'll not bother you here, girl, never fear. They've laid claim to parts of Ocracoke so that an honest seaman can't run the inlet without fear of seeing the skull and bones a-bearin' down on him. Charlie Vane, Ned Teach, ol' Calico Rackham—even that seagoing whore, Anne Bonny—they're a-swarming all over these banks, and any one of 'em would sink his own mother afore he'd bail her out. Gov'nor Eden sets up there in his fine house on Archbell Point a-sippin' Crown tea with the likes of Ned Teach. Hell, Teach even built himself a palace on Plum Point, right across the creek from the gov'nor, the bloody bold devil! Some favors sailing up to Virginie and asking Spottswood for help, but I dunno...I'm feared all politickers is tarred with the same brush."

Maggie knew that Ned Teach was the fearsome wretch they called Blackbeard, but her mind had set off on a different tack. "Ocracoke. Isn't that the island just across the inlet?"

"Aye, you can spit to it in a hard nor'easter. Some says they've put in to Hatteras more'n once, looking for quiet places to hide, but I've not seen 'em. Leastways, not yet. They say Rackham's a bloody fop, and I know for a fact that Teach is uglier'n a oyster toad. Once in Antigua I seen him run two fellows through with his sword 'cause he wanted their women, and him a-laughing all the time."

Maggie shuddered and pulled the coarse cotton spread up over her shoulders in spite of the steamy night. "I don't think I care to hear any more, if it's all the same to you. There's times when a body can't help but live with ugliness, but I'd just as leave not dwell on it before I have to."

"That was one of the reasons I wanted you wearing my name when I left from here, Maggie. Come trouble, the bankers takes care of their own. You're a banker now."

But Maggie had more on her mind than her own well-being. Somewhere out there, her own brother might be sailing into a nest of pirates right this very minute. Gideon had always had a reckless streak in him. He'd stood up to Zion more than once, knowing well that he'd get a thorough hiding for his prideful defiance. Unless he'd changed in the past half dozen years, he might take on a pirate ship and lose his life before she even had chance to find him.

She *had* to get word to him! Someone had to look after him, and she didn't know Uncle Will from Tom's turkey. For all she knew, he could be mean or weak or as conniving as any pirate.

For all she knew, he could *be* a pirate.

A thought struck her then. "But weren't all the pirates pardoned? Sara said . . ."

"Aye, and give their word not to sin again, for all the good it done. A man's word is only as trustworthy as a man is honorable, and there ain't enough honor in that whole bunch to piss on a fly."

"Lord, now you've got me scared to shut my eyes for fear a whole nest of pirates'll come swarming in through the windows," she said, only half joking.

Jedd chuckled. "If it'll comfort you, lass, I'll fetch you a belayin' pin to tuck under your pillow. I've laid out many a man with no more'n that."

"A skillet's more my style, and every bit as effective," she replied with a low chuckle.

In the next room, Cabe heard the soft sound of Maggie's laughter, and ground his teeth until the tendons stood out on his neck. Abruptly he stood, raking back his chair, and strode from the room. There were far better places to be on a hot night like this than sitting by his father's hearth, listening for a sound from his father's new bride.

And then hearing it.

After all the talk of pirates, Maggie started at the noise from the other side of the thin partition. Then, knowing that both Cabe and Matt were probably still up, she relaxed and let her eyelids drift shut. She was tired, but it was a good tired, a satisfied tired. "G'night, Jedd," she murmured.

"'Night, lass."

Truly, being married was a comfort, she thought drowsily. Graybeard or not, Jedd would guard her from pirates and storms and whatever troubles lay ahead.

But it was not Jedd's comforting presence that followed her into her dreams. Instead Maggie found herself back on the farm near Bath Towne. It was early May, and she was angry, frightened and aching with the loss of her mother. For too long she had suppressed the memory of her painful past, preferring to live in the present.

But some nightmares were not so easily laid to rest.

The heavy sweetness of night-blooming flowers that drifted in through the open bedroom window melded imperceptibly with the sun-warmed fragrance of the single thicket of honeysuckle that had escaped Zion's hoe and torch. A bee, drunk on warm nectar, wove its lazy way past, its wingtip brushing her cheek.

She ignored it. From the edge of the cornfield, she stared after Zion's retreating back as he strode back toward the barn. Damn him, she *would* get away from this vile place, for there was no longer anything to hold her there.

How many times had she sworn to escape this wretched place?

Her aching shoulders slumped as she answered her own silent question with another. How many petals did a dandelion have? How many feathers on a blackbird?

The noonday sun baked down on her unprotected nape, for she'd lost her bonnet while the old man was caning her. By now her nape would have more freckles than a blue jay's egg.

Defiantly she bent over to pick up the broken stem of honeysuckle she'd been weaving into a wreath when her stepfather had surprised her. The moment she'd seen him roaring down on her like a bull, waving his cane in the air, she'd known she was in for it.

"What did I tell you about dawdling away the Lord's good daylight while the weeds grow taller than the corn!"

"I've been chopping weeds since sunup, and well you know it."

Thwa-aack! "I'll teach you to sass me back, you devil's spawn!"

Squinching up her face, she'd borne the licks across her back in silence, knowing full well that her silence only angered him more. You wicked old heathen you, with your prating and parsifying, I'll be rid of you before these bruises fade, she vowed silently.

Thwa-a-ack!

Two wives he had driven into the grave, and not so much as a single marker to show for their having lived. If the people of Bath Towne knew how cruelly Zion Johnston used his womenfolk, his beasts—even his own son—they might not think so highly of him, she'd told herself bitterly. But the Johnston farm lay a full hour's walk from town, and few had time to visit. The old man kept to himself, sending Maggie to market. All too often, Nimrod was sent along with her to see that she didn't linger.

Thwa-aak! "No female—" he lifted the cane over his head again, holding her with one iron-clawed hand "—no female living under my roof, beholden to me for every bite she puts in her mouth, ever talked back to me." Down had come the cane on her thin, unprotected shoulders. "Spawn of the devil, you and that wicked brother of yours, both!"

Now Maggie whimpered in her sleep, but instead of another cruel blow, she was aroused by the touch of a hard, horny hand on her shoulder.

"You were cryin' out in your sleep, lass. Would a sup of rum help?"

"Mmm? No, I'm awrigh'," Maggie slurred without coming fully awake. She turned over onto her side, and Jedd's hand fell away, but the comfort of his touch followed her into another dream, less troubled than the last one.

Chapter Ten

The sun had already streaked the eastern sky with pearly color when Maggie opened her eyes the second time. For just a moment she thought she was still back on the farm, sleeping behind the blanket on her narrow corn shuck pallet. Then, in a flash, it all came back—Jedd and the strangely rushed wedding aboard the schooner. Isaac and Eli, Matt, Sara and Jeremiah. Last night's troubled dreams . . .

Cabel.

A short while later she was feeding fat slivers of pine into the oven out behind the kitchen, and fidgeting as Eli's fussing grew more and more insistent. She'd been late rising. She should have had breakfast cooked and on the table by now, she should be feeding the baby while the men ate their fill, and then she would have her own breakfast while Eli played in a corner of the kitchen.

She caught a glimpse of a small figure slipping out the door and whirled about. "Isaac, don't you dare leave this house yet. Go fetch the baby. His milk's warming on the hob."

"Won't."

"Oh, yes you will. If that baby wakes your pa, you'll think twice before you defy me again." It wasn't much of a threat, but then they both knew her threats were largely meaningless. She wouldn't know how to enforce them even if she could lay hands on him, and now that Jeremiah and Sara were back, she held herself lucky to see the defiant little scamp at all.

Or unlucky. For all his lack of size, Isaac was even more stubborn than Cabel. She didn't know which of the pair bothered her the most.

Oh yes she did, Maggie amended silently—and it had nothing to do with sassing her back, ignoring her commands and running away from her. Muttering something under her breath about women who spent too many hours working under a hot sun, she ran a testing hand inside the oven and felt the heat tug at her fingernails. She'd banked the fire the night before so it was already near hot enough for bread.

"Must have baked my foolish brain," she grumbled, slamming shut the heavy iron door. "No woman in her right mind would waste good time fancifying about a man she can't abide!"

Before the words were even out, Cabe appeared around the corner of the house with Eli tucked under one arm, and Isaac dashed off down the footpath toward Sara's house. Halfway around the bend, he turned to poke out his tongue at her, as if daring her to give chase.

Bless her soul, if she thought she had a hope of catching the little devil, she'd give chase, all right, and he'd not soon forget it!

Sighing, she turned to confront the man who strode across the backyard toward her, the squirming child doing nothing at all to diminish his natural born arrogance.

"I'm sorry he woke you," Maggie said grudgingly. And then she looked away, feeling the hot color rise to her face. Dear Lord, had the man no decency at all? He hadn't even taken the time to dress before coming outside. That first glimpse had told her more than enough—Maggie knew she would be a long time in forgetting the sight of a touseled Cabel Rawson in the early morning light, barefooted, bare-chested, his trousers riding low on his flat belly. Narrowing down from his chest, a dark wedge of hair curled against his bronzed skin as far as his waist and then began to flare out again.

Maggie forgot to breathe. Her hands were shaking as she held them out to take the baby from Cabe's arms, and she wasn't at all certain she could hold him without dropping him, but Eli had seen her. He lunged from Cabe's arms directly into hers, and there was nothing she could do but catch him.

"He's about to float out of his britches," Cabe said, his face a study in dubious dismay.

"You didn't change him?"

"I'll allow you the privilege—if you've got the strength. Judging from the way you were snoring this morning, I'd say last night about wore you out."

Stricken with embarrassment, Maggie lifted her head to stare at him. How could sleep wear a body out? Unless he knew she'd had nightmares. But how could he have known—unless she'd moaned in her sleep, or cried out? Surely he hadn't opened the door and seen her thrashing around in her sleep, trying to escape from dreams of Zion and Nimrod and their meanness?

The thought of his looking down on her while she lay sleeping brought a tightness to her chest that made it hard for her to breathe, much less speak. Nevertheless, Maggie managed to find a measure of composure. "I'd better dry him and fetch his milk. I think the cow's going dry. I couldn't even get half a pail last evening." She felt an awful compulsion to babble about anything and everything, as if words alone could erect a barrier between them.

Cabe watched her stalk into the house holding the baby away from her so as not to drench her gown. Not that another dousing could hurt it. It was the same drab rag she'd been wearing the first time he'd ever seen her. Evidently she was even worse off than he was in the way of clothing. If Jedd hadn't given all his mother's things to Old Sits There up at King's Point, she could've worn those.

Maybe he'd give her one of his own shirts. In fact, he just might dump the lot in her lap and let her try her hand at mending before they fell apart. One way or another, he was going to have to accept the fact that she was a Rawson now, a part of his life whether he wanted her or not.

Wanted her! God, when he'd come back after midnight from swimming until every muscle in his body was screaming in protest, only to hear her thrashing around behind the bedroom door, to hear all that moaning and groaning and whimpering, and Pa's deep rumbling voice. And her sated response! He hadn't been able to hear the actual words, but the murmur of her softened tone had been more than enough to keep him taut as a bowstring for the rest of the night.

Cabe's hands slowly curled into fists at his sides. He had only one more night ashore before he sailed. If he had any sense, he'd spend it aboard ship—where he should've been spending all his nights, instead of punishing himself with the thoughts of what was going on behind that closed door.

Night after night he'd heard them in there laughing, heard his father carrying on like a man half his years. It twisted his gut into a hard knot just thinking about it, yet still he couldn't stay away. Dammit, it wasn't that he begrudged the old man his pleasure! If he was man enough to take a woman to wife, he was surely entitled to bed her. Only why did it have to be someone like Maggie? Why not a woman of his own age, a decent woman who would do her wifely duty in silence and let the rest of the household get some sleep?

Cabe prowled about the small, snug house, his scowl deepening as he took in the blue and white wildflowers she'd placed on the table, and the yellow and red ones on the shelf. She'd used some of Sara's buttermilk paint to paint the chairs blue and the shelf yellow, and even though it pained him to admit it, the room was much brighter than he remembered.

Matt had probably done all the work. Cabe hadn't missed the byplay between those two. Before he'd sailed, he'd practically threatened the boy's life if he laid a finger on her, no matter how much she tried to beguile him. The old man had been dead set on making one of them stay behind, and Matt was the logical choice, but Cabe worried that he was too young to be wary of a woman like Maggie.

On the other hand, if it had been himself who'd stayed behind, he couldn't answer for what might have happened. He'd have probably wrung her neck the first time she came sashaying around him, teasing him with those big, innocent-looking eyes of hers.

Oh, she had the eyes of a saint, all right, clear as the water in the Indies Islands. But her lips were the lips of a sinner, made for teasing a man and luring him onto the shoals of destruction.

A mockingbird came scouting the fig tree for early fruit. Cabe ignored his melodious complaint. Morning sunlight slanted through the window to sparkle on the neat row of pewter spoons on a rack below the shelf. Through the soles of his bare feet, he could feel the grit of sand on the freshly scrubbed floor.

Maggie's soap was sweeter than that he was accustomed to using. It smelled of herbs and wildflowers, as did her hair. And he had to admit that the floors and the outhouse had never been so clean.

All right, so she had her uses, he allowed grudgingly, scowling at the open bedroom door where she'd disappeared with the babe. He heard his father's voice, and Maggie's soft response, and with a short oath, he whirled and stormed outside. His belly was hollow from hunger, but he would damned well wait. He would have taken all his meals at Sara's table except that he refused to allow any woman to drive him away from his own home.

Cabe prowled around the net shed, restlessly examining a neglected net for signs of dry rot. The sounds of Matt and Isaac's good-natured grumbling drifted out from the back room, along with the dull clink of the iron skillet striking the spider. After a while, the aroma of frying mullet lured him toward the kitchen, his stomach rumbling, but his mood no lighter than before.

He told himself he would probably have resented any woman who tried to take his mother's place, but he knew it was more than that. Far more. From the very first time he'd laid eyes on Maggie McNair, soaked to the skin, every freckle standing out in bold relief, her eyes wide with fright and her nose all swollen out of shape, he'd felt something...

He'd felt something. Aye, there was the snag. Cabe didn't like to feel something for a woman. Something besides a good, healthy lust, that was. As long as a man could control his own feelings, he could control his life. Look at Jeremiah. He'd been happy as a mud fiddler, making the Indies runs with Pa until Sara had come along. Now he was anchored to the shore, building ships for other men to sail, and dying inside with every new keel he laid.

Steeling himself not to look at the woman who stood ladling stew-fried corn into a trencher, Cabe stalked inside and took his place at the table. He was a Rawson, dammit! This was his home, and no conniving female was going to drive him away.

Gideon leaned over the rail and watched a flying fish lift from the surface of the sea and skim along beside them as if it were truly a bird of the air. Of all the wondrous things he'd seen since he'd first sailed with his uncle as cabin boy, the flying fish were his favorite. Not even the fire that sometimes danced in the rigging until a body expected the whole ship to go up in flames was as beautiful to see.

But some of the wonders were not nice to see at all, he thought soberly. And some were getting worse.

Gid's first run had nearly been his last. He'd been desperately ill the whole way to the Indies Islands, but on the way back, he'd managed to get his sea legs. And to some extent, his sea gut. After that, he'd learned quickly, seldom having to be taught a lesson twice.

He'd got on well with the crew right from first, for all they were a rough lot. He'd been big and strong for his age, even then, and once the men had discovered that he was no shirker for all he was the captain's blood kin, they'd accepted him.

Not that he hadn't been forced to undergo the same initiation as any other green hand. They'd sent him scrambling up the shrouds in a full gale, with the *Star* heeling over so sharply he'd come close to scooping up fish in the seat of his britches. They'd cheered him on when he'd climbed down into the forward hold to secure a hogshead of grain that had broken loose in a storm, knowing full well that he could've been crushed at any moment.

A slow grin breaking across his tanned and handsome face, Gid thought of the first time they'd taken him with them on shore leave, going him drink for drink before they'd all staggered off to the nearest sporting house. Thank goodness he'd been a good hand at telling tales—something he'd inherited from his own pa, no doubt. At any rate, the next day he'd spun a glorious yarn about all the women he'd pleasured before he'd grown tired of the game, and they'd never found out that he'd passed out early on and woken up on a pallet in the scullery the next afternoon. Alone.

Gid had known from the first that the *Morning Star* was engaged in the business of open trade. Smuggling, some called it. That hadn't bothered him at all, for what honest merchant would willingly pay half their earnings over to the Crown? All the taxes went for naught. The King's men couldn't even keep the damned cutthroats off their necks.

Two years after he had first taken command of his wife's ship, the *Morning Star*, Will Lewis had secured letters of marque, and they'd turned privateer, enabling them to prey on Spanish shipping. It had been a legal and honorable calling, although Gideon had to admit he'd liked it better when their only worry had been eluding the customs men. Which had been easy enough to do, as the government had only a few, scattered thin as ticks on a dead dog.

But along with the letters of marque, they had taken on a new quartermaster. From the very first, Gid had mistrusted the massive man who went by the single name of Turk. It had nothing to do with his wickedly scarred face, for Gideon knew better than most what it was to be cursed with a marked face.

It was far more than that. The man was totally without conscience. Vicious as a cottonmouth and greedy to boot, he had a look about his eyes that made Gid's blood run cold. Even more disquieting, there were those among the crew who were weak enough to follow any man who spoke with enough forcefulness. And Will Lewis was no longer a forceful man. Of late, his swamp fever had been recurring more and more often. Each time he appeared on the quarterdeck all yellowed and sweating, his eyes still glazed and his hands trembling so that he could scarce lift his glass from its rack, his hold on his men dwindled.

As Will had grown weaker, Turk had grown more powerful. It was as if the vicious quartermaster fed on the strength of his captain, leaving him little more than a hollow shell of a man.

Gid had managed to hold his tongue the first time Turk had taken command to plunder the *Plymouth Swallow*. He'd rationalized that even though she'd not been an enemy ship, but a chartered privateer like the *Star*, the *Swallow* was rumored to have preyed upon others of her own kind, leaving no survivors who might have gone bearing tales to the Crown's men.

With Will sick in his cabin, Turk had led the raid. They had swooped down on the unfortunate brigantine under cover of a rainstorm, crippling her with a broadside and boarding her before she could recover.

The fighting had been fierce and bloody, no quarter asked and none given. It was over within the first few minutes, and Gid, to his shame, had seen practically none of the action, having been too busy heaving his guts out over the rail. No stranger to senseless cruelty, he had nonetheless witnessed enough in those first few moments to tell him that he wanted no more of it.

But unless Will Lewis regained his strength enough to take back command of his own ship, he feared he'd only seen the beginning.

It was Gid himself who had protested against attacking the merchant ship bound upcoast a few weeks later. "She's from our own home port, for God's sake, Turk. They'll all turn on us! We'll never be able to go back to Charles Towne!"

All of which had earned him a merciless scourging from the crew, now blooded and growing greedier by the day. Turk would have surely prevailed, but just then, Will Lewis, weak, but still up to making his voice heard, had emerged on deck. Gid had stepped quickly up beside him, and after a brief hesitation, another of the crew had come forward. And then a few of the older hands had turned back to their work, and the moment had passed.

But Gid knew his days aboard the *Star* were numbered. One dark night he would find himself going over the side, his gullet sliced neatly open. As big as he was, he was no match for the evil quartermaster, and well he knew it. Sooner or later, it would come to open mutiny, and he had little doubt as to which side would prevail.

God, he should have known his luck couldn't hold. Just when he'd thought he had a fine career ahead of him, just when he'd been almost ready to send for Maggie and his mother...

There was still time to save his own skin. All he had to do was disappear the next time they were in port. He could find work on another ship, maybe up north somewhere. The *Star* line kept strictly to the Indies trade, using the southerly ports.

But how could he desert his uncle at a time like this? Will Lewis would never abandon his ship, not even to save his own life. And Gideon could never desert his uncle, for he owed the old man his loyalty, even if he'd never learned to care for him overmuch.

At least he'd have a spell of relief. They were going in soon for some structural work to the hull. For all his personal reluctance to come within range of his wife, Will had argued for having the work done in Charles Towne, knowing that his fearsome bride would be more than a match for Turk. But the wily quartermaster had known that his own power would diminish once the *Star* returned to her home port, where the old tartar held the reins of the shipping company in an iron grip.

Even though he was concerned, Gideon found it amusing that neither man was anxious to return to Charles Towne for fear of running afoul of the woman who had inherited a small shipping line from her first husband and doubled its size in less than five years.

Besides, Gideon had another reason for wanting to stay on at Ocracoke. His spirits lifted, even as his virile young body began to stir at the thought of the woman he'd recently met. Barbara was some years older, but there was a strength and a sweetness about her that drew him in spite of the fact that so far she had ignored all his attempts to get to know her better.

He was working on it. She'd not seemed to be put off by the mark on his cheek, and that was something in his favor. In hers, too, for he'd known other women to turn away in revulsion.

Maybe he could get a shore job on Ocracoke, Gid thought rather wistfully. He didn't know much about fishing, but there was always building to be done. The trouble was, he was a dead loss when it came to building anything more complicated than a slingshot.

Briefly he considered seeking work aboard one of the fleet of pilot boats that guided ships in and out of the inlet. The trouble with that notion was, he'd heard tell a man had to be born on the banks to be able to read those treacherous, ever-changing waters.

Besides, for all he was improving, he still had a tendency to turn green in a hard blow.

So maybe he'd take up farming. God knows he'd had that beaten into his bones before he'd ever left the main. Were there any farms on the banks, or was it all sandhills, swamps and hammocks, like Ocracoke, Portsmouth and all the other barrier islands he'd seen between here and Charles Towne?

Gideon sighed as he saw the quartermaster bearing down on him. No time for dreaming now, not if he wanted to survive long enough to set foot on solid earth again.

* * *

Maggie had spent the entire day preparing for the morrow's departure of Jedd, Cabel and Matthew. The last shirt was dried and folded into the duffel bags lined up against the kitchen wall, and she stood back with a look of satisfaction. There hadn't been time to mend all Cabe's things, for he'd only brought them to her that very day. All week she'd been patching Jedd's trousers where his boot tops chafed, and Matthew's shirts where his growing shoulders had split the seams. If Cabe wanted his mending done, he should've brought his clothes to her sooner. He could hardly expect her to ruin her eyes trying to sew by the light of a miserable dish of burning oil.

Drat! She still hadn't found time to make candles yet. Perhaps once the men were gone she could get Isaac to help her collect bayberries. There was hardly enough tallow on beef nor mutton around here to make soap, much less candles. At least with only the two youngers to see to, there wouldn't be so much to do. Matthew, bless him, had been helpful, but he'd eaten more than the rest of them put together. She could get by with a lot less cooking without his great strapping body to try and keep filled.

Hearing Matt's voice now as he greeted Cabe in the backyard, she called and asked if he would bring in the kettle of water as soon as it was hot. Not waiting for his reply, she hurried into the bedroom and began undressing. If she moved quickly enough, she could have herself a good wash and change into her clean gown before the men came trooping inside.

Knowing her limitations, Maggie was not a woman to suffer from vanity. All the same, it would be nice if they—if Jedd, that was—were to remember her looking neat and clean instead of damp, drooping and frazzled.

"Damn all, Cabe, if I don't go now, I won't get to see Lina before we sail!" Matt was saying outside the window. "She promised I could come to say goodbye to her, and I was planning on asking her—that is, I was thinking on telling her—" Red-faced and earnest, he stared at the older brother he had worshiped all his life. "The thing is, I thought I'd make my claim before some other fellow got in ahead of me. She ain't the type to wait on the shelf forever."

"If it'll keep you from sampling the wares of every whorehouse in Antigua, then for goodness sake, go throw a line aboard 'er and snub 'er down tight.'' Cabe managed a grudging smile. May as well send the boy off happy. God knows he'd grow up soon enough. "Go on, before I change my mind! But don't be out tomcatting all night. We'll be heading out by three in the morning.''

"Lina's not that kind of a woman,'' Matt said as they moved away from the window. A light southwesterly breeze picked up their words and carried them away from the house.

"They all are when they want something from a man. Remember that, little brother. Now get out of here before I send you back out to fetch Pa and Isaac. It's past the boy's bedtime.''

"Maggie's water...''

"I'll see that she gets it.'' Cabe watched his brother disappear around a bend in the winding sand path that led 'down below,' as the lower end of the island was called. Then, using the folded scrap of canvas Maggie had left outside for such purpose, he lifted the iron kettle from the fire and carried it toward the house.

It was no strain on his powerful muscles, but he couldn't help but wonder how a woman no bigger than a sand flea managed to tote and carry all the things that needed toting and carrying in a day's time.

With his booted foot, he kicked against the bottom of the bedroom door to let her know her water was ready, but the latch had not dropped into the slot, and the door swung open.

Cabe stood rooted in place, the hot iron kettle pressing against his tall leather jackboot. "Sweet Jesus,'' he breathed reverently. She was startlingly beautiful, even more than he'd remembered. Her long hair, a riot of fiery curls, fell over one shoulder, parting over her pale breast so that a rose-colored nipple no bigger than his thumbnail was perfectly framed by its tendrils.

Chapter Eleven

Maggie trembled as the fierce heat of Cabe's eyes raked over her body. Neither of them moved for what seemed an eternity, and then Cabe lowered the kettle to the floor and moved slowly toward her, like a blind man sensing his way on a hazardous path.

Her lips shaped a protest, but no sound emerged.

Cabe was beyond heeding his own common sense, much less the shock he saw in her eyes. Driven by a strange compulsion he neither sought nor understood, he entered the room, each step bringing an increase to the throbbing pressure of his loins. This was but another dream, he told himself, a dream that had grown all too familiar. How many times had he pictured her like this, her hair unbound, spilling over her milk-white breasts, the sweet curve of her waist an irresistible invitation to his sweating palms?

Her gown had settled low on her hips, the bodice dangling from the lacings that held it together. Beneath it, she wore...*nothing at all*! Dear God, if he'd known she went about all day wearing naught but the single garment, he would have gone quietly out of his mind long before now.

She's Pa's wife, a small voice whispered, and he tossed his head impatiently, past heeding the warning of his own conscience.

Hadn't she been flaunting herself before him since the first time he'd seen her on the docks of Bath Towne? He'd rejected her then, but he was only a mortal man, with the strengths and weaknesses common to all men.

You bloody bastard, she's your father's woman, his conscience shouted, but he shook it off impatiently. He wouldn't take her. He only wanted to touch her and prove to himself that she was neither more nor less than she seemed to be.

So near he could feel the heat of her body, inhale the wildflower scent of her hair mingling with the subtle musk of her womanliness, he lifted his hands. As if in touching her, he might exorcize the houri who had haunted his dreams for so long.

"No, Cabe—please, no," Maggie whispered.

Halting an arm's length away, he allowed his eyes to gaze their fill. The red-gold wisps of her brows lowered, then lifted, and he watched in fascination. Her lashes, incredibly fine though they were, were more black than brown, making an enticing contrast with her pale, clear eyes. Even as he watched, a tide of color rose up her throat to stain her face, making them seem greener than ever.

One part of him observed with wonder that her breasts remained unflushed. He had never known before that a woman's color came from the base of the throat, and no lower. But then, he'd known few women above the age of twelve who flushed.

Were her breasts as cool to touch as they appeared?

He saw her eyes widen as she read his intent, but the only sound in the quiet room was the thunder of his own heartbeats and the hiss of her pent-up breath as it bathed him in a warm, sweet current.

Cabe fought for control, knowing in his heart that what he was doing was sinful—hating the desire that had hardened him until he could barely stand upright—yet unable to resist. The woman had no right to tempt him this way, he told himself, yet he knew that she had done nothing to lure him into breaking every law of decency he'd been taught as a youth.

Living with her, there was the torment! Hearing the clear ringing sound of her laughter as Matt teased her over some bit of nonsense, or her husky off key lulling as she gentled the babe to sleep...

His breath came fast and shallow as he lighted her with the glow of his heated eyes. He would hold her for a moment, he promised himself, only that. No more. He would know the feel of her body pressed to his just once before he sailed, if only to prove to himself that it was no more than the flesh and bones of any mortal woman.

Pray God it would be enough to end this intolerable ache!

"No, Cabel—please, you mustn't," she whispered.

"Yes, Maggie, I must," he said harshly. "I'll not take what belongs to another man, but I will know the feel of holding you before I leave."

Even before he had drawn her to him, Cabe knew that holding her would never be enough. Yet she resisted even that at first, with a strength that was surprising in one so small. It was only when his lips brushed aside her hair to claim the tender place beneath her ear that he felt her begin to yield. As his teeth brushed gently over her skin, she shuddered, expelling her breath in a soft whisper.

He tasted her throat. One day he would taste her breasts. One day, he promised himself recklessly, she would know his touch, his kisses, on every part of her body. It could never be, and yet all his instincts told him that she belonged to him, that she had been his from the first moment he had set eyes on her one hot night in May.

She was still too stiff in his arms, as if she had never before known a man's touch. Impatient, he ground his hips against hers, telling her without words what she must have known. "See what happens everytime I even think about you?" He groaned as he felt the soft, receptive curves of her against the eager thrust of his manhood. His hands moved over her back, marveling at the texture of her skin. She was warm and incredibly silken, like touching the inside of his own cheek with the tip of his tongue.

He could hear the rasp of his callused hands on her shoulders, her back. Ruthlessly he tugged at her gown, wanting nothing between them, but it was of stronger stuff than it looked. "Maggie, Maggie, how is it that you of all the women I've ever known can witch me so? I wanted to despise you. God knows, I despise what you are, yet I can't leave you alone," he whispered.

It was breathlessly hot in the tiny bedroom. The feather bed where Maggie slept with Jedd took up most of the space, with Eli's cradle and the chest filling the rest. The mingled scent of salt marsh and some spicy herb drifted in through the open window, and in the rose-colored gloom that presaged darkness, chuck-will's-widow rehearsed her monotonous serenade.

Driven by a need that overpowered all reason, Cabe stroked the woman in his arms until she trembled against him. He fought the urge to throw her on the bed and plumb the depths of her sweet body, steeling himself to take only her mouth and then leave. He would sleep aboard ship tonight. There was no way he could sleep in this house, knowing that under the same roof, his own father was spreading those slender, silken thighs, suckling the sweetest berries of all—those that topped her creamy breasts—claiming by rights that very thing which Cabe wanted more than he'd ever wanted anything in his life.

"Kiss me, Maggie. Just once, and I'll go," he promised, his low voice tormented. She wanted him, too—the signs were unmistakable. The way she breathed, in tight, shallow gasps. The way her breasts peaked against his palm, hardening until he could barely control himself for the hunger that raged through his body.

And then he felt the timid pressure of her lips against his chest. With one hand, he ripped open his shirt, his chest swelling to meet her touch. "Kiss me, Maggie. Touch me there—yes!" he groaned as her cheek brushed across his nipple. "Use your lips, your teeth!"

"Oh, please—Cabe, this is wicked." Her mind told her it was so, but her heart told her that it was as natural as a blossom lifting its face to the sun.

Cabe tightened his arms around her until she could feel every contour of his hard body pressed against hers—the deep swell of his chest, the crushing pressure of his narrow hipbones, that terrible, wonderful thing that kept poking into her belly, making her feel all wet and wild and trembly. Uncertainly she peered up at him, seeing the film of sweat that highlighted the harsh angles of his dark face.

He began to shake. "Don't taunt me, Maggie. I'm not asking for much." Grasping her chin in his hand, he tilted her head, forcing her to meet his eyes.

What was happening to her? Why did she have this powerful urge to pull away her clothes, to rip the shirt from his body and unlace his trousers, and . . .

Maggie groaned and buried her face in his chest, and Cabe lowered his head, pressing his chin against the soft, warm curls. This wasn't the way it was supposed to be. He was supposed to hold her wicked little body in his arms, to look on her conniving face and know her for what she was, thus ridding himself once and for all of this terrible craving that fomented in his blood. Only it wasn't working that way.

The sunset's afterglow poured through the two unusually large windows, bathing her in an unearthly beauty. Unconsciously storing away the sight of her in his mind, Cabe knew he had never been so grateful to his father for giving in to Anne's need to see the night sky while she lay abed. "Dammit, Maggie, you'll have to kiss me, or I'll go crazy wondering what your mouth would be like! You've witched me until I daren't even fall asleep nights for fear of following you so deep into a dream I'll never find my way out again."

He kissed her temple, the top of one ear, and his lips grazed a cheekbone. Maggie moaned softly and burrowed her face deeper into the crisp hair on his chest. Her arms were wrapped tightly about his waist so that he could feel her from the knees up—from the rounded point of her small, stubborn chin to her soft breasts, from the delicate hipbones that framed the sweet hammock of her belly to her knees, one of which was jabbing into his shin.

If he'd wanted her before, he was possessed by her now that he knew the feel of her in his arms, the scent of her in his nostrils, the salt-sweet taste of her skin. Prying her face around, he traced the delicate curve of her lips with his forefinger, marveling at their softness. Then, with a groan of surrender, he covered them with his own.

She didn't resist. But neither did she respond.

Frustrated by what he considered to be her stubbornness, Cabe deepened the kiss, thrusting his tongue ruthlessly through the barrier of her lips, past her teeth, and into the warm dark cavern beyond. He felt her stiffen in his arms. Without lifting his mouth from hers, he opened his eyes in time to see hers widen.

In pleasure?

In fear!

God, how could she be afraid of him, when she'd practically unmanned him with her allure? Surely she didn't expect him to beat her? Had she been so badly used that she could no longer bear the touch of any man?

As shocking as that discovery was, it was no match for the hunger that raged through his body. Heedlessly he sought out her breasts, caressing them, teasing the peaks until they were like tightly furled rosebuds—hard, yet incredibly soft. Holding her tightly against him, he stroked her back, down over the gentle swell of her hips, lured on by the thought of the hidden warmth between her thighs.

Then using the last remnant of self-control he possessed, Cabe forced himself to ease his hold on her until she lay panting against his arm. His mouth hovering over her gleaming, swollen lips, he studied her face, noting with compunction that she was now so pale that each small freckle stood out in stark contrast, her hair the rich shade of Honduras mahogany.

"Ah, Maggie, Maggie, who *are* you?" The words were forced from him, nor did he wait for an answer. The sight of her dazed eyes, her parted lips, was too much for him. Just as he claimed her mouth for the second time, Maggie clamped it shut.

It was if she had no will of her own! The thought slipped through her mind, and she struggled to hang onto it before it, too, was lost. Cabe had robbed her of her will, her senses, and of every wildly mistaken notion she had ever had about a man and a woman and . . . love.

"Open your mouth for me, Maggie," he commanded urgently, his voice vibrating against her lips.

She was no match for him. As the tip of his tongue caressed her inner lip, she felt a languid heat steal over her body, saw the last of her reason melt away under the compelling flame that destroyed her brief moment of sanity.

As his hands cupped her hips to hold her tightly against him, she was blisteringly aware that the enticing bulge had changed until it was an iron-hard ridge that stood erect to grind against her belly. Unconsciously her hips began to weave in an instinctive pattern, her fingernails digging into the resilient flesh of his shoulders.

Cabe thrust against her, following her rhythm, increasing the pace. "Sweet glory," he moaned, "don't do this to me, Maggie." With a sound like the tearing of canvas, his breath left his body, and his head fell back. His arms still held her tightly so that their hips were pressed together, their chests barely brushing.

Maggie stared at the pulse that hammered in his throat. Through the fog that clouded her mind, she grasped at a single thought. She had to end this—this whatever it was that was happening to her.

Now!

Never in all her born days had she wanted anything so much as she wanted to follow this sweet madness until it had run its course, but she knew in her bones that it was wicked. A woman was born knowing certain things, and Maggie knew to her sorrow that what she wanted more than anything in the world, could never be.

Tears flowed down her cheeks unheeded as she struggled with a passion unlike anything she had ever known. "Cabel, I'm sorry," she whispered, unsure just why she should be the one to apologize, yet dimly recognizing that he was suffering even more than she was.

With a sigh drawn from the depths of his soul, Cabe lowered his head until it rested on the top of hers. His arms held her loosely as the passion that had driven them nearly beyond recall slowly diminished.

"No, Maggie. If anyone has the call to feel sorry, it's me. I should never have—"

"What in hell is going on in here?"

As Jedd's voice cracked over them, Maggie sagged against Cabe in horror. She barely heard the soft oath that escaped him, was only vaguely aware that he had quickly turned so as to shield her bare body with his own.

"Get out, Pa. And shut the door behind you," Cabe said in a voice that was unnaturally calm.

Trembling, Maggie waited for his wrath to fall on her unprotected back. It was only fitting. Zion had been right about her all along. Women like her were born to be used as the devil's tools, to lure decent men to their destruction.

"Maggie, are you all right?" Cabe said, his voice still rough with unappeased desire.

She lifted enormous, unseeing eyes to him, blind to the concern he'd expressed, knowing only that she had come between father and son. That she would have to leave this place. Just when she'd found contentment.

Cabe shook her gently, frowning down into her shattered face. He couldn't bear it that she was hurting for something that had been his own doing. All right, so she'd been tempting him. He'd made himself believe it was deliberate, but he was beginning to wonder. Unlike the whores at the One Eyed Cat, she had never touched him. If anything, she'd gone out of her way to avoid him. He had been the one to make the first move. The truth was, he'd been lusting after her ever since he'd first laid eyes on her.

No, not the first time. The first time had been there on the docks in Bath Towne. With her poor nose all swollen out of shape, she'd aroused more pity than lust. There'd been a look of desperation about her when she'd approached him, as though she'd not had an easy time finding custom for her wares. He'd suspected even then that she was fairly new to the trade, for she'd lacked a certain boldness.

He'd never told his father about that first meeting, about what she'd been before. By the time he'd come home again and found her here, it had been too late.

"Don't, Maggie," he said awkwardly, fumbling to brush away her tears with an unsteady hand. "It wasn't your fault. Whatever you've been in the past, you've been a good wife to Jedd and a good mother to Eli."

But Maggie was beyond hearing his words, much less understanding their meaning. "I'll have to leave. I was so happy here—and he brought me new boots, and he told me I baked better bread than—"

She swallowed hard, some shred of common sense preventing her from blundering even more than she already had. "I'll explain to Jedd that it was my fault, and he'll understand. He's a wonderfully understanding man, your father is. I'll even tell him—"

"You'll tell him nothing, Maggie!" Cabe whispered roughly, his hands tightening on her arms. "Listen to me, it wasn't your fault! I'm a grown man, I should've had more control. It's not the first time I've wanted a woman, dammit!'' Although it was the first time he'd ever been obsessed with one to the point where he'd lost all claim to reason. To his eternal shame, he wanted her still. God, was ever a man so doomed by his own foolish weakness! "Go to bed, Maggie. I'll talk to Pa. I'll make him understand somehow.''

In numb acceptance, Maggie nodded. Perhaps Cabe would eventually succeed in making Jedd understand. And then perhaps someone would make Maggie understand, for her whole world had turned upside down, and she didn't see how it could ever right itself again.

Jedd stood as tall and stiff as the sentinel cedar that had fallen victim to a storm years before yet refused to yield. His pipe was clamped tightly between his teeth, but it was cold. Cabe wished to hell he'd light it, say something, curse him, or do anything other than stare out at the bare poles of the two ships that lay anchored offshore.

"It was my fault, Pa. Maggie had nothing to do with it," he said for the third time. "I don't know what come over me. I knew what I was doing was wrong, but I . . .''

He swore long and fluently, striking a weathered piling with his fist. *Dammit, say something, you stubborn old bastard! Tell me to get out. Tell me to go to hell! Tell me anything, but don't make me stand here bleeding to death!* "Pa, I know I can't undo what's done. All I ask is that you don't send her away. She's a good woman, no matter what—"

" 'Pears to me you're right soft on the girl.''

"You know me better than that," Cabe protested quickly. Too quickly. "She's your wife, Pa. I respect her for that. If it'll make things easier—and I reckon it will—I'll see about having Jere build me a place up near King's Point before I get back. Ma was always partial to that first ridge past the Persimmon Swamp.''

To his great relief, Jedd turned. Seating himself on a piling, he went through the tedious process of lighting his clay pipe. "It just come to me that this might be a good time to tell you about Maggie and me," he said thoughtfully.

Cabe stiffened. "There's no call for that, Pa. Like I said, I'll move out tonight. What's yours is yours, and it's past time I was looking around for a woman of my own."

The old man drew deeply on the strong tobacco, spat, and began stroking his beard. Cabe recognized the gesture as a prelude to a rambling tale. One he didn't want to hear.

"Y'see, when it come time to sail, there weren't an Anglican nowheres south of Virginia. Now you know that me and your mother done things the old-fashioned way, with her pa saying the words and young Stormwalker scattering the corn for his sister, but times have changed. These days the Crown likes things done up all shipshape and Bristol fashion, with one of them frocked Anglicans a-crowing and a-praying over a man and his woman."

"What about the one that come through here on his way to Albermarle? Sara said he was in an all fired hurry, but you managed to get a line on him long enough to splice the two of you."

There was a considerable pause while Jedd examined the crust on his pipe, spat once or twice over the side of the wharf, and cleared his throat. "Mmmm, well-l-ll. What Sara told you ain't exactly the gospel truth, but near enough. Y'see, son, there weren't no way I could ask a decent woman like Maggie to sleep under the same roof with a passel of menfolk, and her not married to one of 'em. The folks hereabouts wouldn't stand for it. And that sugar crop to Antigua wouldn't wait forever, so I—well, you might say I sort of, uh, made me a Anglican preacher."

Cabe was in over his head, and the tide was running strong. "Pa, I don't have a notion what you're trying to say."

"You recall that poor feller that washed up near the inlet?"

"Oh, hell, Pa, don't tell me you got a corpse to marry you. There weren't enough left to—"

"Gaffer planted him out behind his pa's place, but he didn't see no cause to bury a fine black suit, especially when it come near on to fitting him."

Cabe exploded. "You didn't!"

Jedd shrugged his massive shoulders apologetically. "Well, I didn't see no real harm to it. She was willing, and we talked it out first. I—uh . . ." The old man muttered something in his beard, and then Cabe was towering over him, leaning down until their noses were only inches apart.

"You conniving old bastard, you tricked her into marrying you!"

"But that's it, son, we ain't really married. Gaffer done his part just fine, and Maggie and all the rest of the folk around here thinks she's my lawful wife, so I can't see what you're getting so riled about."

A vein was throbbing on the side of Cabe's brow. His eyes were narrowed to mere slits as he fought to control his temper. "Riled! Pa, don't you see what you've gone and *done*? You're living in sin with a woman who thinks she's your lawful wife!"

"Hell, son, there ain't no sinning taking place. You know how I felt about your ma. I explained that to Maggie before I rowed her out to meet Gaffer. She's like a daughter to me. So where's the harm?"

Cabe nearly strangled on his anger and frustration. "Where's the harm?" he asked in a voice that was dangerously calm. "The harm is that I want your woman, and she wants me, and there's no way on God's sweet earth that we can *do anything about it*!"

The men were gone when Maggie woke up the following morning. She had lain awake for hours, but Jedd had not come to bed. She didn't know how she could ever face him again, nor Cabe, either. By now, probably Jeremiah and Matt knew of her shame—Sara, as well—for in a small community like this, news of her disgrace would spread like a fever.

She was too miserable to cry. Tears would do no good. Seeing the remains of their breakfast on the table, she dragged herself out of the chair and set to work. There were two other Rawsons to consider, two innocents who should not be made to suffer for her sins. With Eli screaming for his milk, and Isaac goodness knows where, she could ill afford to waste time moping over something that was done.

The days passed with a sameness that gradually dulled the ache inside her. Maggie welcomed the drudgery of scrubbing and gardening, of drying fruit and beans for the winter, gathering bayberries for candles, of mending and washing the endless piles of napkins.

Time enough to worry about the future when the men began to return. Evidently they hadn't spread the word before they'd sailed.

Who would come back first, the *Eliza Lea* or the *Bridget*? She wasn't even sure which one Matt had sailed on, for it depended on whether or not someone named Douglas had decided to go in search of a preacher so that he and his Polly could finally marry, all of this according to Sara, who was pregnant again and suffering from morning sickness so that Maggie saw little of her these days.

It was a pity the preacher Jedd had found to bless their union hadn't been able to linger long enough to marry Douglas and Polly. He'd been in an almighty rush to sail, but at least Jedd had managed to keep him here long enough for their own needs. And by now, he was undoubtedly sorry he'd bothered.

Isaac, as if sensing Maggie's distraction, chose to be even more contrary than usual in the days after all the menfolk had sailed. He'd hidden a small green snake at the foot of her bed, and she'd let out a shriek that could've been heard all the way out to the reef.

No matter what small chore she asked him to do, he managed to slip away without doing it. Not five minutes ago she'd asked him to carry in a load of wood for the fireplace, and there he was out in the sound, wading about aimlessly with a stick and a pail, the firewood still in a heap by the cow shed where Matt had left it.

Maggie watched from the kitchen window. Now and then the boy would lunge at something just under the surface. Wishing it were her, no doubt. She didn't fool herself that she was any closer to winning his friendship, for all he'd mumbled an apology when he'd seen how deeply shaken she'd been over the snake.

While Eli was napping in the bedroom, Maggie wandered down to the landing. Friendship or no, Isaac was her responsibility. As long as he came to no harm, she could put up with his childish pranks. At least for as long as she stayed on.

If it happened that Jedd forgave her, she was going to do something about the boy, for they couldn't go on this way. Tie him down and give him a good talking to, most likely. One way or another, they were going to have to come to some sort of understanding. It wasn't good for a lad to grow up to be so willful. He wasn't lacking in intelligence, for she'd heard Cabe and Matt teaching him reading and numbers. He had a quick mind, and he talked freely enough. To all but her.

In the backyard, Maggie began to gather the makings for soap, meaning to start early the following morning. She'd lugged the crock of tallow out earlier, sitting it in the sun to commence softening. It was a hot task, not one she particularly enjoyed, but with the daily washings required because of Eli's napkins and her own limited wardrobe, she was running dangerously low again.

There was a blessedly cool breeze off the water. Maggie lifted her hair from her neck, allowing the air to play over her damp skin. As usual, her gown was soaked and none too clean. She'd meant to ask Jedd if he would bring back a bolt of Calcutta cloth this time, but she hadn't seen him before he sailed.

The thought of her husband stirred the old feelings of guilt and worry and uncertainty, and her voice sounded more impatient than usual when she called to warn Isaac not to go too far.

He ignored her, of course. Perhaps the breeze had carried her voice away before it'd reached him, for he was some distance away, wading in the shallows beyond a jutting point of marsh. Cupping her mouth, she was preparing to call again when she saw him drop from sight.

She waited for him to reappear, and when he didn't a frown formed on her face. Gathering her skirt, she leaped lightly off the end of the weathered plank dock and began wading through the knee-high marsh grass, for once oblivious to the possibility of snakes. The saw grass cut her feet, but she ignored it. Her new boots were every bit as miserable as her old ones had been without hose, and as she had none, she went barefoot altogether.

"Isaac!" she yelled, "You answer me, boy! I promise you, I'll—"

He was lying on his side in shallow water, doubled up awkwardly with his arms around his legs. Even at that distance, Maggie could see the agonized look on his face, and she set out at a run, splashing through the warm, ankle deep water near the shore. "Isaac, what's wrong? Tell me, please. I'm coming, don't worry, I'll help you!"

He twisted around, his face gray with pain. "No! I don't need you! Go back, there's jellyfish!"

Maggie had seen the strange, transparent blobs floating on the water and been mildly curious about them, but this was no time to satisfy her curiosity. Isaac was in trouble, and he needed her. Wet skirts hampered her progress but, panting, she finally reached his side and dropped down onto her knees. "What is it, boy? Tell me so I'll know what to do," she pleaded, almost in tears by now.

His mouth was a grimace of pain, his eyes shut tight against the tears that squeezed past. He was trying so hard to be brave, but she had to know what had happened before she could help him. Had he stepped in a hole and broken his leg? Had he cut his foot on an oyster shell? She couldn't see any sign of blood, but—

Something stung her foot and she rubbed it impatiently with the other one. The abrasiveness of the sand eased the pain almost instantly. "Isaac, you've got to tell me! Here, let me lift you up and—"

"They'll get you, too! I want Mama! I want Cabe!"

Oh, darling, so do I, Maggie agonized silently. Despite his lack of cooperation, she managed to get one arm around his stiffened shoulders and the other under his knees. It was only when she tried to lift him from the water that she saw the angry red marks on his legs.

"Is that it? Is that what hurts? How'd you do it?" She staggered under his slight weight, thrown off balance by the soft sandy bottom.

"*They* did it, dumb girl!" he growled, scrubbing his eyes with his fists. "Them poison jellyfish. Big ones, bigger'n a house!" But his belligerence was no match for his misery, and before Maggie had reached the shore with him, he was openly crying. "It hurts, Mama, it hurts bad," he sobbed, and Maggie's heart contracted with a pain of another sort.

Her right foot still burned. When she stepped onto the hard sand bank, she glanced down and saw that it, too, bore a distinctive red mark. Unconsciously she rubbed it with the sandy sole of her other foot, and again the friction seemed to ease the pain.

Acting purely on impulse, for she knew nothing of jellyfish, their poison or the remedy, she lowered Isaac to the ground and slapped a handful of wet sand on his leg, scrubbing it gently at first, then harder when he didn't protest.

"The other one—do the other one, Maggie," he pleaded, and she complied. She was Maggie again and not Mama. Even so, it was a beginning. But oh, what a cruel one. She would have waited forever for his acceptance rather than have it come at such a cost.

"What would your Mama do now, Isaac?"

His bottom lip quivered. "She'd hold me and m-make it stop hurting."

"But how?" she pressed. For all she knew, the poison could be working its way through his system even now. "Was there something she dosed you with, something she rubbed on it?"

"Leaves," he whispered.

"What kind of leaves?"

"Don't know. I want to go home. I want Mama!"

A little desperately Maggie lifted him into her arms and began hurrying toward the house. Leaves. What kind of leaves? Some were poison of themselves. She hadn't the slightest notion of what to do, but as she passed the crocks of tallow, she nudged his small arms around her neck and said, "Hold on a minute, sweet, Maggie will get something that'll make it feel better."

Tallow, lard and turpentine. She'd been dosed with all three for any number of ailments. Lard and sugar for burns, tallow and spider webs for cuts, and turpentine for sprains.

If Maggie had hoped that day would make a difference in their relationship, she was in for a disappointment. As if to prove his independence, Isaac defied her at every turn. He refused to lie abed until the redness went away, he refused to eat the molasses bread she'd baked specially for him, claiming that Sara's was better.

Leaving him playing with the toy boats Jeremiah had made for him, she took Eli the next morning and cut through the back path to Sara's house. She needed advice. She needed consolation. Most of all, she needed to talk to another woman.

"This is Lina Stowe, come to borrow a rooster," Sara said when Maggie had let herself into the kitchen. "Lina, this is Jedd's wife."

"Sakes alive, why, you're young! You mean you married the old man with them other two to pick from?"

Maggie was taken aback by the young girl's outspokenness, but she soon understood when Sara told her that Lina was a cousin. There was even a certain resemblance, although Lina didn't look to be more than fifteen.

"I, um, I've heard Matthew speak of you," Maggie said faintly, lowering Eli to the blanket where Sara's baby played.

"Fancies me, he does. He ain't too hard to take, but it's the other one I'm setting my cap for. Fair curls my toes, that Cabel does. If he was to kiss me, I vow I'd fall over in a dead swoon." She giggled, and Sara met Maggie's eyes with a look of amused resignation.

"Take my word for it," Sara said dryly, "the dark stormy ones is hard to live with. Just ask Maggie. If you want a Rawson man for a husband, best take one of the fair ones—they're as good for laughing as they are for loving, and there's many a time after the younguns start coming when a body wished she'd laughed more and loved less. Not that I didn't welcome every precious one of my babies, but Lord, I do get tired of spending so much time on my knees over a chamber pot!"

"Speaking of the dark, stormy ones," said Maggie, only too glad to shift the subject to one more comfortable, "Isaac had a run-in yesterday with what he said was a jellyfish. Big ugly round thing with strings hanging down from its belly—and you could *see* through it, clear as water!"

"They're bad some this year. Becky Mary got walloped last time Jere took her out clamming with him. I told him she was too little, but the sorry truth is, I was glad to be shed of her for a spell. Lordy!" She shook her head.

"Yes, but what do you poultice it with? Isaac said leaves, but he didn't know what kind. I rubbed it with sand and it seemed to help, but what happens now? Will it fester?"

Sara shrugged. She was stringing green beans for drying, and there were garlands of the things draped around the cozy, cluttered room. "Not likely. I'd smear on a tad of fat—it helps some. Anne was a wizard with herbs. Most of them redskins still swears by all manner of nasty remedies. Me, I'd sooner suffer than swallow some of the stuff I've heard tell of."

"He sure does look like Cabe, don't he?" With cheerful perseverance, Lina steered the conversation back to her own area of interest. "It's that old redskin's blood showing up. Some claims they're a sorry lot, won't have nothing to do with 'em, but they do say the men are—"

"Lina," Sara interrupted shortly, "tell Aunt Mercy she can borrow my rooster, but she'd better send Uncle Junius to fetch him. He's meaner'n two tomcats in a tote sack."

After the younger girl had skipped out the door with an assortment of messages for Matthew and a promise to bring Becky Mary a baby chick, Sara laughed ruefully. "Was I ever that bad? Lor', I reckon I was. Worse, probably. I was plumb gone on Jere by the time I was eleven year old, and he couldn't see me for sawdust."

Maggie murmured an absent reply, her mind filled with her own problems. She was longing to confide in someone, but how could she tell Sara of the shameful way she had behaved? Sara had trusted her. She had introduced her into the Rawson household in good faith, and Maggie had used the opportunity to come between a father and his son.

"Pretty, isn't she?"

"Who? Oh, you mean Lina? Yes, she's awfully pretty. Matt likes her a lot."

"I know, but like every other female between Currituck Banks and Ocracoke, she's set her cap for Cabe. There'd be fireworks for sure if anything ever come of it, with poor Matt so besotted he can't tell his east end from his elbow." She shook her head, knotted her thread and reached for another handful of beans from the large basket at her feet. "If there's one thing worse'n two tomcats in a tote sack, I reckon it's two brothers a-pantin' after the same woman. I hope she'll settle for Matt. Cabe's been heartbroke once already so that he'll not likely ever let a woman close enough to hurt him again, but Matt, he's still tender."

Maggie's response must've been at least marginally appropriate, for Sara's nimble fingers didn't pause. Soon after that she retrieved Eli from the blanket where he'd been gurgling and kicking alongside Charity Ann and left.

What would Sara have said if Maggie had confided in her? Thank goodness Lina had been there, or she might've spilled it all out before she'd had time to think. It was bad enough knowing that she'd lost Jedd's respect. As for Cabel's, she'd never had it. But to lose Sara's friendship would be too much.

Shifting her wriggling burden to her other hip, Maggie told herself that it was hardly the first mistake she'd ever made, nor would it be the last.

All the same, she had a feeling that it would be the one with the most lasting effect on her life.

Chapter Twelve

Knowing that Ruben Quidley would be in from fishing his gill net before the sun was a handbreadth above the horizon, Maggie took her basket on her arm and Eli on her hip and set off to fetch a small croaker to stew for the midday meal. Isaac tagged along, making it seem as if he weren't with her, but he soon spotted a group of young friends fishing the shallows for minnows and ran to join them.

Maggie sidled carefully through a thicket of Spanish bayonet, their pale, waxen flowers nodding silently in the salt-tanged breeze, and joined several other women who were also waiting to fill their baskets. She greeted those she knew, smiled at those she had not yet met, and then turned to watch the swooping, screaming gulls that marked the return of the fisherman.

She'd felt thickheaded ever since she'd woken up that morning. Eli had been fretful all night; he seemed to be cutting another tooth. She prayed he wasn't sickening, for she knew little enough about the ailments of children. She'd run to Sara so many times for advice she was ashamed to bother her again.

All around her the women made use of their time to visit and exchange news about who was expected home when, who was rumored to be in the family way, and whose man had said what about the increasing problems that beset them all—taxes, storms and pirates.

"My Henry says they lay up alongside you in port like you was two birds from the same nest, but just let 'em meet you offshore, riding low in the water, and they drop a sail over their nameplates, uncover their guns and run up the skull and bones and it's devil take the hindmost."

"And then swear on their mother's graves that they're naught but honest sea traders while they auction off your cargo before your very eyes," chimed in another one.

"If they ain't already shut your eyes with six fathom of water. I heard tell Ned Teach was bragging how he strung up every man jack aboard that old tub he took off the Virginie Capes last month—leastwise them that wouldn't throw in with him. Towed their dead bodies all the way up the Pamlico and dumped 'em off Archbell Point, and told Eden he'd brung 'im a present."

"The way *I* heard it," confided another woman, "he was showing off down to Ocracoke—"

"Showing off! I heard he poured gunpowder into his rum, lit it, and then poured the whole flaming mass down his gullet, a-laughing like a banshee!"

"Yes, but have you heard about the one they call the Turk aboard the *Morning Star*?" Lina Stowe asked, her piquant features avid with excitement. "Bald as a darning gourd, they say, and *mean*? Lawdy, they say he set a live rat on a man's belly and turned a pot down over it, and then set hot coals on top of the pot. The rat didn't have no way to go but down!"

There was a chorus of groans, and a few gagging sounds, but Maggie's ears had perked up at the mention of her uncle's ship. If the locals knew of her, she must be using Ocracoke inlet and the customs agent at Bath Towne instead of her own home port of Charles Towne. Which meant that the chances of finding Gideon might be far better than she'd ever dreamed.

"I ain't heard nothing about no man called turkey, but they do say the *Star*, for all her spit 'n' polish, stinks like New Providence when you get downwind of her."

"Not a turkey, Hester—the *Star*'s quartermaster is called Turk. Leamon Burrus told me he was down to Ocracoke just last week, and..."

But Maggie was no longer listening. She'd heard enough talk from the men at her own table to know that New Providence on Nassau was the foulest den of pirates anywhere. The scum of the seas had named it their own, gathering there between raids as far north as the Carolinas. As a joke, the pirates had even elected their own governor—an old drunk named Sawney.

If the *Star* dared sail within range of New Providence, it would have to be with the consent of its unsavory population, and that could only mean one thing.

Maggie was still distracted by the time Ruben came alongside the landing with his silvery cargo. The women swarmed closer, and eventually Maggie was able to select two small croakers—just enough for Isaac and herself—but her mind was not on fish.

She would have to ask Jedd, that was all there was to it. She had to know, and it was hardly a matter she could discuss with any of the women who obviously already considered the *Star* an outlaw ship.

Besides, she would need the advice of an experienced man, for if Gid were actually involved with any such unsavory characters, then the sooner she found him and got him away from there, the better off they would all be. He'd grown increasingly rebellious before he'd run away, but he would never willingly have thrown in his lot with a bunch of vicious, seagoing thieves—not the Gideon she remembered.

For days Maggie worried over her newest problem. Her eyes grew shadowed, her collarbone stood out in fragile relief above the rounded neck of her faded gown. Right this very minute, while I'm scalding cornmeal for a pan of bread, she would tell herself, Gideon could be fighting for his life. Picturing him lying bleeding and helpless on a deck somewhere at sea, a victim of some cutthroat's blade, she would be overcome by feelings of helplessness and anxiety.

But then anxiety would turn to exasperation. "Gid, if you've gone and gotten yourself in trouble, I don't care if you've grown big as an oak tree, I'm going to wallop the daylights out of you!" she would mutter as she beat the heavy mixture with a cherrywood spoon.

In her deepening concern for her brother, Maggie's own problems were largely forgotten. It never once occurred to her that Jedd might not listen to her troubles, might no longer be willing to help her at all. She *needed* him! She had no one else to turn to, and if that meant that she had to try and explain about what had happened between her and Cabel...well then, she would do it. No matter how mortifying it might be.

And then a dreamy expression would steal over her face, replacing the look of strain. For a moment she might stand there, the wooden batter bowl cradled in her arms, as she recalled the rare sweetness of his touch, the feel of his arms around her.

It had been so long since anyone had held her. Being held by a man—by Cabel—was vastly different from being held by her mother. Could she explain all that to Jedd?

She would have to try. Surely if she could make him understand, he would forgive her. How could she have known that she would be overtaken by a sort of momentary madness? At least it'd had no lasting effect—she was the same old Maggie, married to Jedd, responsible for his children and his household, and doing her very best to live up to those responsibilities.

As for that brief wild sweetness she had known when Cabe had kissed her, it was about as lasting as a patch of moonlight. Come morning, there was no silver sprinkled across the bay, no moonbeams scattered across the garden—just plain old dirt and water.

Maggie had quickly discovered that living in a small banker village was vastly different from living on an isolated farm. Here, rumors swarmed thicker than mosquitoes. Newcomers were held at a distance for a time, but having married a banker and been accepted by Sara, who had wasted no time in spreading the tale about how Maggie had jumped in the ditch to save Becky Mary, Maggie was considered one of them. She was now included in their network of gossip concerning everything from cosmetics—it was said that a certain notorious redhead from Portsmouth Island had got that way from the judicious use of gunpowder and potash—to whose ship had been sighted where, and which was expected home when. Even the cargos were open to speculation.

Actually it was from Isaac that Maggie learned that both the *Bridget* and the *Eliza Lea* were expected to make landfall before dark.

"Jimmy's pa come in today, and he said they cleared customs and loaded a new cargo right behind him. I'm gonna ask Pa to let me go with him next time out. I'll be ten years old in a little while, and I'm big."

He was barely eight and small. Maggie smiled indulgently at the thin, dark child. He burned up energy with his very intensity, and couldn't sit still long enough to clean off his platter. "I reckon you are at that, but I'd miss you. Who would stay behind and take care of me and Eli?"

His look of disgust told her that a single jellyfish episode was not enough to change the course of their relationship. Maggie sighed and vowed to be patient. At least he was speaking to her now, sometimes almost a dozen words a day.

With a feeling of breathlessness that was not altogether due to the weather, she put on greens and beans to cook, using the outside fireplace so as not to heat up the house. Then she set her wash to boiling and dragged the feather beds out for airing. By midday, she would have her heavy work done, and then she intended to steal an hour for her own use.

Isaac sat at the table for all of five minutes before bolting, taking a cold corn dodger with him. Maggie watched him go with a look of mingled fondness and irritation. For once, she was just as glad to be finished early. She'd bathed and fed the baby and now he was lying peacefully in his cradle, gnawing on the clean bone of a chicken leg to ease his swollen gums.

Meanwhile she had saved the last tub of rinse water for her own use. When she faced her menfolk for the first time in almost a month, she meant to be clean and neatly dressed. She would even wear her new boots, although they still chafed her feet. When she'd washed her best gown a few days before, she had mixed a little flour water with the last rinse and shaped the skirt over a rounded yaupon bush. Now it belled out almost as nicely as if were lifted by a ruffled petticoat.

Having learned her lesson, Maggie made sure the bolt fell into its slot and the latchstring was in before she dared strip down to bathe. Knowing that Isaac had gone to the boat yard to wait for a sight of the menfolk, she had one less worry on her mind.

Which was just as well. Now that the time had come, she was beginning to feel a nervous sickness in her belly at the thought of seeing Cabe again. What must he think of her for allowing him to look on her naked body, to kiss her and fondle her as if she were no better than one of those poor women who haunted the docks, selling the use of their bodies?

Quickly she splashed her burning cheeks, her breath coming in shallow little gasps. Dwelling on it wouldn't help; she'd done it, and that was that. However, just in case Cabe thought she was a loose woman, she would twist up her hair until no curl could possibly survive and then cover it with a clean white cloth, for good measure. And while she was at it, she would tuck a dish towel in the neck of her gown so that no part of her showed but her face and her hands.

Pity she could think of no reason to wear a veil. It might make those first few minutes when Cabe and Jedd walked through the door easier to get through.

She bathed quickly, enjoying the faint scent of her new soap. Zion had never permitted any hint of fragrance to leaven the smell of potash and tallow, but Jedd had even gone so far as to show her some of the shrubs that Anne had used to sweeten her soap and candles.

Now, freshly bathed and wearing one of Jedd's soft, worn old shirts, Maggie took a sliver of soap she had softened in water and carried it out to the backyard. She wore her new boots, for she'd scrubbed until her toes were all shrively and pink, but she daren't put on her clean gown just yet.

There was no one to see her there, with only the cow shed, the net shed, and the fowl run. Beyond those, Jedd's landing nestled in the salt marsh that bordered the sound. Like all the other islanders, he'd built his house in a sheltering grove of yaupon, cedar, bay, pine and live oak, and those covered over by curtains of grapevines and the yellow flowering vine that had smelled so sweet when she'd first come to the island. The backyard was her private bower, open to the breeze off the water, but hidden from view of any passerby.

Humming tunelessly, Maggie dunked her head in the wash boiler. She slathered on the softened soap and scrubbed with her fingertips, bending over at the waist so as not to get soap in her eyes. Then, using the gourd, she poured water over her head until it ran clear, and repeated the process once more. Sara had brought her a comb from Boston, and she had laid that, along with a towel, on the stool beside the cool house.

What a wonderful feeling! If only she had the time and patience, she would wash her hair every single day. Nothing was quite as effective for clearing a troubled mind.

From nearby came the contented murmuring of her laying
hens. Farther out, screeching sea gulls dived on a school of
finger mullet, while underlying it all was the ceaseless beat of
the ocean. The sound was as comforting as her own heartbeat.
How quickly one could adjust to contentment after years of
misery.

Blinking as a trickle of water found her eyes, Maggie blun-
dered her way toward the cool house bench and reached out for
the clean cloth she'd left there.

Cabel had felt no particle of guilt as he'd watched her rins-
ing and twisting the water from her hair, her steps hesitant as
she turned blindly toward the fowl run. He'd been stunned
when he'd come around the corner and seen her, and while he'd
been gawking at the sight of her small, damp body encased in
nothing more than one of his father's old shirts and those confounded boots, the time for announcing his presence had come
and gone. Now it was too late. If he spoke out, she would be
embarrassed. If he left her stumbling all over the backyard with
her eyes squinched up tight, she'd end up hip-deep in marsh
without ever coming close to her drying cloth. And so he stood
and stared.

Under the circumstances, there was only one course he could
set. Taking a last look at the glorious sight of her pale, shapely
limbs and the pink flush of her bare skin shining through the
thin weave of his father's worn shirt, he snatched up the coarse
cotton square and strode forward.

God, why did women insist on covering up such loveliness
with all those skirts and petticoats and long drawers and what
all? Not even Lettie had ever let him see her completely uncov-
ered. Oh, it was all right to see her topside—like every whore
from Bath Towne to Bristol, she'd displayed that proudly
enough with her low cut gowns—but a well-turned calf, a delicate ankle, that was another thing altogether. Shameful, they
deemed it! As if the Lord hadn't fashioned all the different
parts of their bodies, top and bottom.

"Here," he said gruffly, shoving the cloth into her groping
hand.

Of course, she dropped it. She blinked her eyes open, the
green irises suddenly surrounded by red, as tears swelled to fill
them. Covering her face, she turned her back, thus providing

him with another thorough look at her delectable stern quarter.

Those damned boots! He'd meant to get up to see old Sits There before he'd left, but with one thing and another, it'd slipped his mind. He'd simply have to buy her some decent shoes the first chance he had. No foot as dainty as Maggie's should be shod in such a clumsy fashion.

"Go away," Maggie agonized. "I don't want to see you. If you have one shred of decency in your body, you'll go back where you came from and forget you saw me. Like this, I mean. Oh-h-hh, *piety*!" she wailed.

"It's not the first time I've seen you like this," he reminded her. Bending over, he picked up the cloth, shook out the sand and placed it in her hand, closing her fingers around it.

"You aren't supposed to be here until this evening!" Her voice was muffled as she struggled to cover her whole body with one small square of cloth.

A rare smile rearranged his stern features. "Why, Maggie, a body would think you're not glad to see me."

"I hate you!"

"Do you? I wonder. Maybe you hate me same as I hate you. Maybe—"

"Worse!" she cried, scrubbing her stinging eyes and then trying to cover herself with the towel. "I wish you'd—I wish..."

Cabe stepped closer, his hand closing gently over her fragile shoulder. An image streaked through his mind of the first time he had ever seen that shoulder, with its bruises, both old and new, and he forceably restrained himself from gathering her in his arms.

She was too damned vulnerable. What had they done to her, the pair of them? What Jedd had done was bad enough, but what Cabe was doing was little better.

"What do you wish, Maggie?" he asked quietly.

No response. Was she crying? Was she hiding? Was she that frightened of him? "I wanted to talk to you before you see Pa," he said without the slightest notion of how to begin. How could he tell her that the man she looked on as her husband was no more than a stranger who had taken advantage of her for his own ends, even as she'd tried to take advantage of him? Trusting him, she had slept in his bed, called herself by his name—and worse, she was looked on by all the villagers as Jedd's wife. It was hardly a matter that could be explained away as a slight miscalculation.

The cloth Maggie had knotted about her hips came loose and slid, and she caught it before it touched the ground. Blotting her eyes once more, she absently wrapped it around her dripping head. "I don't see that there's anything to talk about," she said. "What's done is done. If it can't be undone, then it'd best be forgotten." Reaching up, she began squeezing moisture from her hair. Then, as if suddenly remembering her scant attire, she whipped it off and wrapped it around her hips again, never once meeting his eyes.

Cabe bit back an oath of sheer frustration. Dammit, he wasn't the world's greatest hand with women, but she wasn't helping matters with her stubbornness! "Maggie, would you just *look* at me? How the hell can I talk to you when you keep hiding?"

"What woman wants to talk to a man who can't pass the time of day without swearing?"

Bracing his feet as if he were riding out a storm on his own deck, Cabe hooked his thumbs under his belt to keep from grabbing her and shaking some sense into her stubborn, mule-headed, reckless little body. "Dammit, woman!"

"There, you see? Go back to your taverns and your—your own kind of women! Decent women don't want the likes of you around!"

"*Decent* women! Are we talking about Mistress Maggie McNair, late of the Bath Towne docks? The woman who's sleeping in the bed of—"

"Never you mind who I'm sleeping in the bed of, you foul-mouthed—you foulmouthed *toadfish*!"

In her fury, Maggie had whirled around to confront him, her eyes swollen and red-rimmed, her small chin jutting threateningly. Cabe began to smile. All his anger and frustration heaped together were no match for the sight of the tiny redhead, mad as a wet hen—*wet* as a *mad* hen—wearing only an enormous shirt, a square of cotton and a pair of ungainly black boots. His smile broadened, and soon he was chuckling. And the more he laughed, the more her chin quivered, the more her eyes sparkled.

Cabe saw it coming, but he did nothing at all to evade her wild punch. It fell short, and with a string of inept profanity, she turned and ran into the house, boots flopping and buttocks bouncing with every step.

His laughter quickly faded, and he sighed. Things were not going the way he'd planned. And he *had* planned—at least he'd thought of little else for the past month. God, what a mess that old man had got them all into, and all because he'd been too damned impatient to wait until a suitable woman had come along. Instead he'd snapped up the first one who'd come his way, anchoring her down with a false wedding that would be the ruination of all of them.

At this point, Cabe usually reserved a few choice words for his meddlesome sister-in-law. It had been Sara who had introduced Maggie to Jedd. The rest had followed as naturally as day follows night. Jedd had been desperate, and Maggie had obviously been running away from something or someone. She'd needed a place to roost, and he'd needed a broody hen.

How the bloody hell were they going to get out of this mess, after living together as man and wife in the eyes of the whole community? The Rawson name would be dragged through the mud, and if a man's name was naught, then he might as well move on and try to start afresh in some new place. As for Maggie . . .

Aye, as for Maggie. Cabe was no longer quite so certain she'd been one of the dockside whores. Now that he'd had time to think on it, it seemed to him that at least one of the sailors she'd stopped would have tumbled her, for most of them had been too drunk to see clearly in the dim light. Besides, even then, she hadn't been all *that* bad.

And then he remembered her bruises, and the awful feeling that had gone through him when he'd caught a glimpse of her tortured flesh. It had been all he could do not to spill his guts on the cabin floor. When she'd looked him square in the face with the clearest, steadiest eyes he'd ever seen, something had happened to him. Only he hadn't realized it at the time.

Then, later, when he'd returned and seen her again, her face all healed, when he'd thought about some bastard actually striking her with his filthy fist, he'd felt like killing the man for the sheer joy of seeing him die!

God, what was he going to do? He'd never felt so helpless in all his life! He was reefed in with no way out. Legally or not, she was Pa's wife, living under Pa's roof. Which meant that one way or another, he would be seeing her far too often unless he cut himself off from his family.

She was a good wife, too, he'd give her that. The house shone, Eli no longer smelled like sour milk and worse. She set a fine table, and except for Isaac, she'd won them all over. Matt was half in love with her himself.

It had been Matt she'd asked to bring in her bathwater. Had she been expecting him to open her door? To see her like that?

No! Cabe couldn't allow himself to believe that. She was a decent woman, not the whore he'd once thought her to be. He had to believe that, or he would lose his mind.

Jedd greeted Maggie as if nothing untoward had happened before he'd sailed. He gave her a quick squeeze, a wink, which left her more confounded than ever. Did that mean that she was forgiven? Surely he hadn't forgotten already—goodness knows, she'd not been able to put it from her mind, no matter how hard she'd tried.

"I need to talk to you, Jedd," she said uneasily.

He patted her shoulder and then sat down and yelled for Isaac to help him with his boots. "Later, lass. We'll talk after the household settles for the night. Is that greens I smelled cooking when I come past the fire? I vow, I'm hungry for a mess of greens. All Cookie knows how to make is beans, hard tack, salt pork and more beans."

"It's mustard and dandelion. Eli had two new teeth since you left. I think his hair's beginning to curl, too."

"I got stung by a jellyfish, Pa," put in Isaac, grunting as he strained to pull off the thigh-high jackboots.

"Lucky it weren't a stingeree, boy. Hurt much?"

Isaac cast a sidelong look at Maggie. "Naaa...I didn't hardly notice it. Jimmy got the night sweats and his ma makes him wear a stinkbag round his neck. Phoo-ee! Can't hardly get downwind of him no more!"

As the evening wore on, with gifts given—a bolt of calico and one of muslin for her, and a real knife for Isaac—Maggie thought she must have imagined the tension that shimmered just under the surface. Matt arrived and caught her up in his arms to swing her around until she was clinging to him and laughing helplessly.

"Miss me?" he demanded, refusing to lower her to the floor.

"Matthew, put me down! It's unseemly."

"Not until you tell me how much you missed me," he teased.

"All right, I missed you, you big buffoon!" He lowered her until her toes bumped the freshly scrubbed floor.

"How much?"

"A smidge, maybe even a smidge and a half, but not near so much as someone else missed you."

Setting her down gently, Matt braced his hands on his thighs and bent over until his eyes were on a level with her own. "Would that someone happen to have dark brown hair and hazel eyes?"

"Hmmmm . . . I disremember."

"Mag-gie," Matt said, his brows lowering into a comical grimace.

"Can't seem to remember much of anything. Only her initials—I believe they were L.S."

Jedd and Cabe watched this teasing byplay with varying expressions. Cabe's was speculative, Jedd's indulgent . . . and more than a little troubled. Maggie, flustered from all the attention and the excitement of having her menfolk back again, turned to the fireplace, where she'd kept a low bed of coals under the yaupon tea. The men would drink rum, and Isaac was of a mind to join them. Maggie knew that most women allowed their babes to drink rum, but her own mother had always claimed it was too harsh for young bellies, and Maggie was not about to take the chance of having her charges fall ill in her care. She'd insisted on cider or yaupon tea for Isaac, and lately he'd come to prefer the tea, well sweetened and laced with Brownie's thin milk.

"Food'll be on as soon as I can bring it in," she said, pouring the tea and lifting the rum jug down from the shelf.

"I'll help," said Matt, but it was Cabe who got to his feet, waving his brother aside.

Jedd's face grew even more troubled as he watched the two of them disappear into the backyard. By tar, he'd really done it this time. If he'd only had the patience to wait a few days, she could've been his daughter instead of his wife, and he wouldn't be wrestling a guilty conscience. It was plain to see that she and Cabe were stuck on one another, and it was his fault they couldn't do anything about it.

Oh, his intent had been good. She'd needed a home, and he'd needed a mother for his youngers. It weren't his fault that Anglicans was scarcer'n balls in a henhouse.

Once he'd gotten over the shock of seeing the two of them together, he'd cooled down right enough. Should've expected it all along, should've seen it from the way they'd huffed up every time they come together. Only by then he'd heard all the talk in the village about how he was looking right peaked after taking on a fresh young wife, about his hair turning yellow overnight instead of gray, and he'd let himself do a little bragging. Not so much in what he'd said as the way he'd said it.

Oh, he'd strutted around, liking the way his crew looked at him, but the truth was, he was a damned useless old relic who didn't deserve to have a decent woman, not even an old and ugly one. And what was worse, he knew himself to be too much a coward to confess that he'd been lying all along, that he hadn't bedded his pretty little bride at all, much less had her fair begging for him night and day.

He ought to be keelhauled!

Jedd downed his noggin of rum just as Cabe and Maggie came through the back door. She was carrying a pan of bread while Cabe toted in the heavy pot of greens. Maggie's face was red, like she'd taken too long to pull the bread out of the oven, and Cabe, well, he looked all closed up. Kinda like old Kinnahauk had looked when Jedd had first told him he wanted to marry his daughter.

"Pa, we need to talk," Cabe said.

"Directly, son. First let's set and eat what Maggie'n the good Lord seen fit to provide." And then he bent his head in a moment of silent prayer. *Annie, you got to help me get out of this mess I made. You took real good care of this old fool while you was here—for God's sake, don't quit on me now!*

Chapter Thirteen

By the time the dishes were washed and Cabe had put Isaac to bed, Maggie's nerves were strained past bearing. Matt had changed into a clean shirt and gone out after the evening meal without mentioning where he was going—as if everyone didn't know. Cabe had followed Jedd outside, and through the window, Maggie had heard them quarreling before they even reached the landing.

"Dammit, Pa, it's not right! You can't just go on . . ." He'd turned his head, and part of it was lost.

"Well, I don't rightly see how I can set about telling her now."

"Hang a blanket across—!"

Hang a blanket? She must have misheard. Hang the bastards, more likely. She'd thought they were having words over her, but they must be going on about the pirates again. That was all anyone ever talked of lately.

Dropping into a chair, she stared unseeingly at the oil stain that still shadowed a streak across her kitchen floor. So far Jedd hadn't said a word about what had happened the day before he'd sailed. If he didn't speak out soon, she was going to bust wide open! She was still fretting when he returned. Alone. "Cabe'll sleep on board tonight. Jeremiah's meeting him at first light to talk about some fool notion the boy's taken about mountin' a slew of four-pounders on deck."

Maggie dragged her attention back to the present. Evidently she'd been right. They'd been discussing the pirate menace, not her own misdeeds. "Is . . . everything all right, Jedd?"

"Shipshape 'n' Bristol fashion, lass. You look frayed around the edges. The boy been giving you a rough haul?"

"Isaac?" She ventured a tired smile. "I think he's coming to trust me. Don't let on I told you, but he was so scared after he tangled with that jellyfish, he even let me carry him ashore. For a few days after that, he almost forgot he didn't like me, and I'd hoped . . ."

Her smile wavered. She was so weary. Sometimes it felt as if she were swimming against the current, with the shore growing ever more distant.

Chiding herself for being fanciful, Maggie paid a last visit to the outhouse while Jedd got ready for bed. By the time she returned to blow out the candle and change into her shift, he had already arranged the bolster. She'd tarried, hoping he would be asleep, but she could tell by his breathing that he was still awake. Here it came, she thought. He was bracing himself to ask her exactly what had happened, and why, and although she certainly knew *what*, she still hadn't a notion as to *why*.

"Thought you looked a mite peckish tonight," he said after several moments had passed in silence. "It's too hot to be working all hours, Maggie. Take some time off. You and the youngers walk down to the beach of a morning. There ain't a boy alive that don't like combing the shore to see what's washed up. Did it myself when I was a lad. If my pa had caught me playing by myself in the surf and it a-pounding fit to beat the devil, he would've whomped me good, but I never come to no harm. Why there was days when the beach was so thick with bounty, I'd not even get my feet wet for gathering."

Maggie murmured a suitable response, but it was not her own weariness that filled her thoughts, nor the sea's largesse. Even if Jedd had forgiven her for her unseemly behavior, she couldn't forgive herself. She needed to talk with someone who could help her understand what had come over her, but confiding in Jedd, or even Sara, would take more courage than she could lay claim to.

Perhaps this was part of her punishment—suffering her guilt in silence. Jedd's kindness was certainly heaping coals on her head!

"Tomfool notion, if you ask me. Come the day an honest seaman can't clear Ocracoke Inlet 'thout a passel of four-pounders a-clutterin' up his deck, then it's time he quit the sea and went to farmin'!''

"Four-pounders? You mean guns?"

"Said guns, didn't I? Thought Cabe might've mentioned it when the two of you was out fetching in the food."

"No, he didn't mention guns." The truth was, she'd refused to hear anything he'd had to say, busying herself with the fire and ignoring him until he'd sworn a blue streak and snatched up the big pot without using any padding, and then she'd been busy smearing grease on the angry red marks across his hands. It was a good thing his palms were like leather, or he'd be suffering even more than he was.

Jedd stroked his beard. He liked it to lay neatly on top of the coverlet while he slept. "Just thought maybe he'd said something to set you off. When the two of you come inside, you was still throwing off sparks like you'd had a real set-to."

"Well we hadn't!" Maggie snapped. "I may not be perfect, but at least I know how to keep a civil tongue in my head! I know my place, and I'm not about to let any mule-headed—to let that—Jedd, the truth is, there's times when that blessed son of yours comes near to making me raise my voice!"

Crossing her arms over her chest, she waited until her breathing evened out. Just *thinking* about Cabe Rawson made her raise her voice. Lord only knew what she'd have done if she hadn't long since had the temper beat out of her by that wicked old man.

"I expect it's only the weather," she murmured when there was no reaction from Jedd. "A body can't move without getting wringing wet." It wasn't the weather. It was her own guilty conscience. More than that, it was Cabe himself, and the way he made her lose sight of all that was decent and reasonable. And on top of that, there was her worry over Gideon, wondering how she was going to get word to him that their mother was dead, and that she herself was married and living a stone's throw away. At least she was if the *Morning Star* she'd heard so much talk about was the same one Gid had sailed on.

And if it *was*, then she had far more to worry about than she'd first thought. So much, in fact, that she didn't know where to begin. It seemed that they'd both made a mess of their lives, and since Gid didn't seem inclined to look after himself *or* his family, then it was up to Maggie to yank him back to salvation.

On impulse, she turned to her husband. "Jedd, you recall I told you I had a brother?"

"Mmmmm."

"Now I don't know this for a sure certain fact, but what would you think if I was to tell you that he was sailing aboard a, um, a..." She swallowed hard. There was no way to prettify it, not if she wanted his advice, much less his help. "Aboard a ship they say might've hoisted the skull and bones a time or two," she finished in a small breathless rush. "I can't swear to it. You know how gossip is. Let any strange ship come too close to another one, and there's all manner of clacking tongues. But all the same, what if it happened to be true? What if Gid has gotten himself mixed up with such trash through no fault of his own, being a poor, fatherless lad with no one to guide him into the ways of righteousness? Could a body—I mean, would there be any way—"

From the other side of the bolster came the low sound of Jedd's breathing. He was asleep!

With a sigh that came from the very roots of her soul, Maggie let her tense muscles go slack. She'd been braced to pour out the whole wretched business onto Jedd's broad shoulders—Gid's possible involvement with pirates and her own wicked doings with Cabe. She could have taken his anger, knowing that with Jedd it would blow over like a summer storm, and then he would set about advising her as to the best way to go on. She needed the wisdom that came with age, and nothing in all her life, most of which had been spent on an isolated farm, had provided her with the experience she needed now.

The days seemed to flow together as the men sweated to get the guns mounted and Maggie fretted over whether or not Eli was getting enough to eat. She would swear he'd put on pounds just since she'd been there, but she knew so little about babes—was it enough?

Matt was racing in and out to bolt his food each evening before changing from his work clothes into his courting clothes, which were the same, only cleaner. It turned out that Cabe had not only ordered guns for the schooner, but for Jedd's sloop as well, and that was all any of them could talk about in the rare times when they came home to eat.

If she'd been worried about having come between father and son, Maggie told herself she could forget that problem, at least. The fact that Cabe took most of his meals with Sara and Jeremiah and slept aboard the *Bridget* was dismissed as being no more than practical. As he was the one who'd insisted on having protection, he was most concerned to see that the work was done properly, and Jeremiah had never installed deck guns before.

Maggie found more than enough work to occupy her hands, but there was too little to occupy her mind, nothing to prevent her thoughts from straying back to those few magical moments when Cabe had held her in his arms and kissed her and...touched her.

Wherever she went the talk was of pirates. The village seethed with gossip about the daring raids that were taking place practically within sight of land. Though some of the outlaws had taken advantage of the pardons the year before to escape the hangman's noose, others had disdained them. Still others had accepted the Crown's pardons and continued in their lawless ways, daring the feeble authorities to give chase.

Talk was that Ned Teach had captured a French Guineaman mounting some forty guns, and was now openly calling Ocracoke his second home, having somehow cozened Governor Eden into ignoring his outrageous deeds. The women pirates, Mary Read and Anne Bonny, were seen more than once in the area, and one of the Hatteras men claimed to have been stopped by Mistress Bonny for provisions while he was fishing in the bight of the Cape. She'd gotten away with no more than a few fish, a keg of fresh water, a pot of beans and three pans of bread, for the catch had been small that day.

A right fair woman, she'd been deemed by the local crew. At least they'd lived to tell the tale, although some had not been so fortunate. Two sloops out of Ocracoke had been taken by Calico Jack Rackham, the officers killed and the crews allowed to row ashore. One of the murdered officers had been Lina Stowe's kin.

Maggie decided that this was definitely not the proper time to bring up the subject of Gideon and his possible link with such notorious outlaws. Not when the whole banks was up in arms, vowing to oust the pirates themselves if the governor's men would not.

On a morning when the men had been home almost a week, she sat quietly under the cedars, letting out the seams of a pair of Matt's trousers while she listened to the deep voices drifting up from the landing. Ruben Quidley, Jeremiah, Cabe and several others had come by after the evening meal, migrating toward the weathered dock where Jedd's longboat, an oyster flat and two battered skiffs were tied up. Along with the pungent smell of cow manure, pipe tobacco and salt marsh, the soft breeze blew their words directly to where Maggie sat working.

"Stede Bonnet's been taken. Him and his whole crew's waiting down in Charles Towne for trial. If'n ye ask me, they'll not escape the noose this time."

"Waitin' in Charles Towne! I heard tell they was the ones that fair wiped out the town."

Charles Towne gone? But what of Uncle Will and his wife? Could Gid have been there at the time? Better alive aboard the Star than dead at home.

"Aye, they was in on it, but I hear Teach led the raid."

"Reckon they finally caught that black-bearded devil?"

"You know ol' Ned. They say he tricked Bonnet out of the loot and left him and his men aground on a sandbar. Come high tide, Bonnet's sloop lifted off and they was all set to give chase, but her rudder was fouled. She headed out, but then damned if she didn't come about again and ram her bowsprit right up the gullet o' some South C'lina militiaman. It was all over but the shoutin' after that."

"And the hangin'," Matt added gleefully. "Lordy, what a sight that must've been!"

Cabe remained silent. He was working a monkey's fist onto the end of a heaving line, and not for the first time, Maggie marveled at the varied talents displayed by these island men. Builders, fishers, planters and seamen, any one of them could splice two lines together with naught but a wooden fid, while she, who'd been spinning and weaving practically since she'd hatched out, made a botch of splicing no matter how many times Matt tried to show her.

She heard no mention of the *Morning Star*. Perhaps the talk had been wrong. A cat could take up in a henhouse, but that didn't mean it would ever lay eggs. Like as not the *Star* had only been doing a bit of smuggling. Many an honest merchant seaman had been forced to take up smuggling to avoid the heavy Crown duties, and were thought no less of for it. She'd heard of some who weren't so honorable, who purchased their cargoes at pirates' auctions and then smuggled the goods into the northern ports, selling them at a great profit, but even so . . .

There was black and white, and then there were shades of gray, Maggie concluded, nipping off her thread. Who was she to say which men were law abiding citizens and which were not? Jedd was as honorable as ever a body could be, yet even now he was having guns mounted on his deck—guns that were never meant to bring down fowl for the table nor venison to be larded and smoked.

Holding up the pair of trousers, she shook her head. With the meals he stuffed under his belt, that boy got up from the table a size larger every day. If Jedd's youngest three continued to grow up the way they were doing, she would likely end up using the last scrap of her precious hoard of calico and muslin on their backs instead of her own.

"I'll be headed out tomorrow, Maggie." Cabel spoke from so close behind her she jumped. Wearing those moccasins of his, he could slip around silent as a shadow.

"Tomorrow? Then I reckon the guns are all finished." She formed a cool little smile and tried to ignore the fact that her heart was flopping around in her breast like a beached bluefish.

"I reckon. At any rate, we've wasted enough time in port. Sailing the southern seas can be chancy this time of year."

She could almost feel the heat of the tropics as his golden eyes moved over her. Restlessly she snatched up her sewing and stood.

"Maggie? Has Pa talked to you?"

"Of course he's talked to me. Jedd's not like you and Isaac."

"You know what I mean. Has he *said* anything?" And then it was Cabe who seemed restless. He flexed his shoulders, threatening the seams she'd recently restitched, and Maggie tried not to stare. For a man who was far from perfect of feature, he was strangely compelling, and she couldn't say why. His nose? It was only a nose, if haughtier than some. His cheeks were lean and weathered, grooved with two deeply carved lines. It was his mouth, she thought with a sudden fluttering in her middle. How could a mouth look so stern and set when she knew to her sorrow that it was warm and sweet and yielding?

Then she tangled with his eyes. Closing her own in defeat, she shook her head. "Go away. Leave me be, Cabe. I don't know what you're trying to—"

"Maggie," Cabe interrupted. "Things aren't always the way they seem."

It was then that Matt joined them, shattering the tension between them like ice on a winter pond. "Hey, Maggie, I'm obliged to you for your help! Them britches was getting so tight I was feared of bending over." He looked pointedly at Cabe's closely fitting trousers, and Maggie, against her will, followed his gaze. "Maybe you ought to see to Cabe's next, before he comes a-busting out all over—"

"Matthew," Cabe said with barely leashed fury, "If you've nothing better to discuss than the fit of my britches, you can damned well start hauling your gear aboard. We'll be leaving before calm of day."

Maggie, watching the byplay between the brothers, knew that he was referring to the brief, breathless period just before the sun broke over the horizon. And she was missing him already.

"Well, as it so happens, I *do* have something else to say," Matt retorted. "Pa's taking Isaac along tomorrow, and he wants me on board special to keep him from getting underfoot. And since Doug's gone off preacher huntin', I reckon you'll have to pick up another man tonight or go short."

"I'd sooner sail shorthanded than have a couple of moonstruck layabouts tripping over their own feet."

"Moonstruck! 'Pears to me that Doug and me ain't the only ones who's gone soft-pated. Leastwise, the women we're a-courtin' don't belong—"

Face burning, Maggie stepped between them. "Just hold on! You're worse than two fighting cocks! I don't have all your things ready, so you can't sail yet. I've not had time to seal all your boots yet, and what's more, Isaac's too young to go sailing off to God knows where!''

"I'll grease my own boots," Cabe snarled, glaring at her as if she'd threatened to burn them instead of offering to dope them with beeswax and tallow.

"We ain't really going nowhere yet," Matt explained. "Just headed out overnight to see how she goes. Pa don't like to set out any distance after he's had his deck altered without trying her out first, and Jere, he don't know no more about mountin' guns than a fiddler crab knows about flying. Pa told me himself he'd have taken her down to Ocracoke, only the *Star*'s got every carpenter on the island tied up working on some mysterious contraption or other."

Maggie grew still at the mention of the infamous ship. Her heart felt as if it were about to burst from her bodice, but neither of them seemed to notice anything amiss.

"Show some respect for your brother," Cabe ordered.

Matt tilted his head in challenge. "Huh! When it comes to showing respect, I'd say you had a few lessons long in coming. It 'pears to me like you and M—"

Cabe didn't shout, but the effect was much the same. "I'd suggest you keep your notions about something that's none of your business to yourself. If I was you, I'd head on out and look for Lina. Last time I saw her she was fixing to go off riding with Joe Willis on that moon-eyed roan of his."

Matt's sun-bleached brows lowered in a scowl. "I'll fry him in his own lard first," he muttered, setting off at a lope.

Cabe turned to Maggie, and she braced herself instinctively. The look he gave her left her completely baffled as, without a word, he turned and strode off as silently as he had come.

Maggie had too much on her mind to mope, even if moping had been her nature. Except for Eli, she would be alone for the next two days, and the *Morning Star* lay only an inlet away from where she stood that very minute. Never one to waste an opportunity, she made up her mind even before she'd watched the men disappear in the morning mist that drifted just over the surface of the water.

There was always the risk that she would be discovered. She'd have the devil's own time explaining what she was doing rowing around in the middle of the sound without so much as a net or a pole.

And there was Eli. Unless Sara would agree to look after him, she would have to forget the whole thing. Still, Sara had been feeling better lately. And Maggie had taken Becky Mary and Charity Ann under her wing more than once while Sara had suffered the worst of her sickness. Could she ask her to look after Eli without explaining why?

There was but one way to find out.

"I've a mind to get off to myself for a bit, Sara. So much has happened, and me without a minute to catch my breath..." She had brought along the bottle, a handful of napkins, and the spare blackberry tart she'd baked special for breakfast.

"I've been admiring Isaac's new calico shirt. Don't let on I said so, but I think he's right proud of it. When're you going to make yourself a pretty frock?"

"Lor', before I sew myself a new frock, I'd best see about making myself a pair of drawers. I hate to say it, but I've not had time nor cloth since I gave Ma my last pair to be buried in." She leaned forward and whispered. "Could you tell? You know I don't own a single petticoat, either, save the one I sleep in."

"Land sakes, Maggie, half the women I know leave off wearing all them trappings in the summertime. A body could faint from the heat buried under so many layers. Come winter, though, you'll need every stitch you can lay hands on to keep warm. That wind off'n the water cuts right through to the bone."

"Then I reckon I'd best get sewing."

"And I reckon you'd do better to take advantage of having all your menfolk out from under to lie abed and put your feet up. Jere said they were headed down past Portsmouth, likely be out till tomorrow evening. If I was you, I'd sleep all day, sleep till I couldn't sleep no more. It'll ward off the megrims better than any potion I know. Go on now, leave that baby here with me. I hate to say it, but I been missing him since you took up with Jedd." She patted her plump belly. "This time I swear I'm going to give Jere his boy, though I don't know where we'll put him."

Sleep was the last thing on Maggie's mind when she left Sara's small neat house. She'd likely not get another chance, for once Isaac was home, such a venture would be out of the question. The boy might not talk much, but there was little that went on without his knowing it.

Within the hour she was headed out into the channel, praying she wouldn't overtake either the *Bridget* or the *Eliza Lea*. And then she laughed at her own foolish optimism. A rowboat overtaking a sloop and a schooner, and them with a three hour head start? Not likely.

Someone—probably Jedd—had told her that Ocracoke was near enough to spit on in a hard nor'easter. She only prayed he hadn't exaggerated, for already her shoulders were aching and her hands were growing tender. She should've taken the smaller skiff, but the rowboat had looked faster.

Ever practical, she'd borrowed a pair of Matt's old trousers and one of Jedd's spare shirts. She'd planned on borrowing a hat to keep the sun from blistering her neck, but the only one she could find came down to her nose, blocking her vision, and she'd had to content herself with turning up her collar and praying her hair would shade her well enough.

The sun was fierce. And she hadn't counted on the weight of the oars. Resting them for a moment, she wiped the sweat from her face and felt it sting the palms of her hands where a blister had broken.

She was beginning to think that before the day was over, she'd have blisters in more places than her hands. How could a plank seat be so hard? It must be the trousers. Lacking the fullness of a skirt, there was little between her tender flesh and the hard rowing seat.

A new respect for the suffering of seamen was slowly kindled as she shifted her weight first one way and then another to ease the pressure.

Somewhat to her surprise, she seemed to be drifting rapidly toward the southwest, the direction in which she was bound. It seemed that even the current was working in her favor.

Now that she thought on it, there were any number of things working in her favor. First she'd heard that the *Star* was being worked on at Ocracoke, and then her menfolk had decided to leave her alone, taking Isaac with them. And Sara had been glad to keep Eli for a day without pressing her for a reason.

Oh, yes, things were going her way, all right. And while Maggie had never set much store by omens, she couldn't help but be heartened at the way everything had fallen into place. With a bit more luck, she would find the *Star* quite easily, and Gideon would be there to greet her, and they could have a grand visit, and he would agree to return with her and give up his dangerous companions, and...

Licking a drop of sweat from her upper lip, she commenced to pull hard on the oars again.

Cabe knew before the village had dropped from sight that the bow mount was not going to work. The forward rise of the *Bridget*'s deck was steeper than most, to allow for more headroom below deck.

Jeremiah had insisted on the forward placement. Against his better judgement, Cabe had given in. Now, dammit, he was going back and get that fifth gun remounted astern. He'd been hearing too many tales lately about the way some of those bloodthirsty bastards came a-swooping in close under cover of darkness, clapping on to a ship's stern before she was able to bring a one of her guns to bear. After lobbing a single shot amidship to scatter the crew, they would heave on a line and swarm aboard without risking so much as a single scratch to their own vessel.

Pa could make up his own mind where he wanted the *Eliza*'s fifth gun mounted, but Cabe was heading back in. He'd lost enough time on this business, as it was. Another month and they would be left with nothing but coastal runs, which meant higher duties and half the profit, and with the added cost of ten four-pounders they could ill afford, there was no more time to waste.

Cabe had no sooner ordered his crew to come about than he spotted the single small craft being swept dangerously close to the inlet. From the crow's nest, where he'd been watching for shoals, Amos sang out, "Cockleshell there to the starboard, Cap'n!"

"Aye, I've already got a glass on her. Ease off on the main, lads, and prepare to heave a line! We'll take her in tow."

But the closer they came to the hapless skiff, the deeper Cabe's scowl grew. He'd seen carrot tops aplenty, but he knew of only one head of hair so bright it almost hurt a man's eyes. Trousers or no, that was no lad.

What the bloody devil was Maggie doing here? His first thought was that something had happened to Eli and she'd come after him, but even Maggie would've known to send a man for a man's job.

"Stand by for towline!" someone sang out. To a man, his crew lined the starboard rail, ready to bear a hand.

Cabe was at the helm, for he never trusted another helmsman near inlet waters. From his vantage point he could see the small figure quite clearly now. His hands gripped the spokes until his nails whitened as he thought of how close she'd come to being lost forever.

And then came anger. The little witch! Stealing a boat was bad enough, but to dress herself up in that shameless getup—

Never had he been more aware of the physical differences between a man and a woman, and that angered him most of all. He'd ordered her to leave—advised her that first day to go in search of richer hunting grounds, but damn her wicked hide, she'd had to wait until Jedd had come to depend on her! Wasn't there a speck of gratitude in her wicked little heart for the man who had taken her in and given her his name? Or at least, lent it to her. No doubt she'd grown tired of playing the part of a decent woman—too much hard labor involved when she could just as easily earn her keep flat on her back.

Cabe made an effort to control his wrath, telling himself she wasn't worth it. He was half tempted to set her adrift again, he vowed, knowing in his heart that he was deceiving no one but himself. No matter what she was, she was still in his blood. God knows what it was going to take to rid him of her wicked spell. If Pa hadn't messed things up so that none of them could do anything without shaming the whole family, he might have taken her for a mistress—at least until he tired of her.

Now, dammit, he couldn't even do that. "Bring her aboard," he ordered tersely, glowering at the twelve men in case any one of them should suggest that it was tolerably peculiar to come on Jedd Rawson's new bride out in the middle of the sound, and her dressed in trousers, no less. As if any woman with a sense of decency would allow herself to be seen in public with her limbs hanging out for all the world to gawk at!

It quite escaped Cabe that only a short while before he'd been wondering why women felt they had need to cover such an attractive portion of their anatomy.

By the time Maggie, looking frightened and utterly miserable, was led before him, he was so furious he could barely speak. "My cabin," he said through clenched teeth. By God, he'd let her wait. He'd be anchored off the village in another hour, the crew dismissed until Jere's men could remount the forward gun. Let her stew until then! Let's see how she enjoyed pondering her sins while she wondered what was going to become of her.

And Maggie had ample time to stew. The door of Cabe's cabin had no sooner slammed shut behind her than a hoard of memories rushed in on her. It had been here that she'd had her first good look at him. When he'd found her half in and half out of his cargo hold, she'd been too far spent to register anything but cool rain, fresh air, and relief that she was still alive, but by the time he'd brought her below to his cabin, she'd accepted the fact that she was not about to die. She had taken account of her surroundings, and of the man who had rescued her—or captured her. She was never quite certain which.

This time she had no compunction about curling up on his bunk, wet and salty though she was. Her hands were in raw agony, and she feared her face would soon look like an undercooked joint of fresh pork.

"Would you care to tell me where you were going?"

She jumped at the sound of his voice, trying not to appear as guilty and as miserable as she felt.

"Well, really, I'm sure it's none of—"

"Maggie." The way he drew her name out left her in no doubt as to the state of his patience. "For half a copper, I'd have let you go."

"And if I had a guinea, I'd give it willingly to see the last of you!" But her small defiance had cost her in other than gold, for she was discovering all over again that she had no liking for ships that rolled under her like a ox plodding over a rutted field.

"Where were you bound?"

"Fishing."

"Where's your pole?"

"I lost it."

"You're lying."

She exploded. Disappointment was bad enough, and sunburn and queasiness did nothing to improve her disposition. "Then what if I am?" she cried recklessly. "What do you expect me to say, that I was off to meet with a bloody pirate?" She took great pleasure in hinting at the truth, knowing he would likely disbelieve whatever she told him.

"I could break your foolish little neck! Do you have the slightest notion of what could've happened to you?" His brows lowered over his eyes in a ferocious scowl as he towered over her.

"Don't shout at me!" she yelled, jutting her chin for emphasis.

"I'll damn well shout whenever I feel like shouting!"

"Then get it over with! Do your shouting and hopping about, and then take me home before I empty my belly all over your nice, clean floor!"

"You do and I'll take you across my knee and beat the daylights out of you!"

"My, your kindness fair melts my heart," she jeered. She wouldn't give him a mouse if he were up to his neck in bobcats.

Cabe swore at length, and she closed her eyes and let it wash over her, her brief rebellion threatening to fade away like fog in the morning sun. "Maggie—dammit, woman, I'm about two ticks away from feeding you to the sharks, so if you ever hope to set foot on dry land again, you'd better give me some straight answers. *Now!*"

How easy it would be tell him everything—about how she worried about Gid, and how fearful she was that he would be injured or worse before she could find him and persuade him to come away with her. But she couldn't. For Gid's sake, she didn't dare take the risk. "I don't feel like talking. Cabel, I'm not trying to rile you," she added hurriedly when he leaned down as if he might drag her bodily up from the bunk. "Um, it's the sun. Too much sun always did rob me of my wits."

For a moment she thought he was going to argue with her, but instead he turned and poured out a measure of rum, handing it to her. "Drink it down."

"I'd rather have cider, if you please." She could have drunk the rain barrel dry, but cider would do well enough.

"Maggie." Once more he threatened her with his tone of voice, and she snatched the glass from his hand.

"All right, all right," she grumbled, and sipped the fiery liquid, shuddering as it burned its way down her throat. In truth, it was some strengthening. And she feared she was going to need all the strength she could summon.

Cabel raked his hand through his hair and began pacing. "So you were going to meet a man, were you?"

Startled, Maggie bid for time to think by sipping her drink. She hadn't expected him to believe her, else she'd never have skirted so close to the truth. If it'd been Jedd, she would have poured out the whole miserable mess on his broad, comforting shoulders, knowing that he would hear her out without interruption, and would not have blamed her for her brother's indiscretions.

But Cabel? He'd been seeking a chance to discredit her from the moment he'd laid eyes on her. She'd have to be a bigger fool than she was to hand him this opportunity to send her packing.

"Well, the truth is," she ventured cautiously, "I was going in search—that is, I wanted to see if I could find—" Her courage wavered. If he'd looked the least bit understanding, she might have surrendered, but the more she hesitated, the angrier he grew. And the angrier he grew, the more she hesitated. He was like a towering thunderhead feeding on its own fury to grow taller and blacker by the moment.

"I-I only wanted—" she whispered, when he cut her off.

"What? To go ply your wares in a bigger market? To see if you couldn't do better for yourself than thick black boots and calico? I've heard tell the pirates bring back all sorts of trinkets for their whores—silk shawls, pretty red shoes with silver buckles, beads and bracelets and sweet-smelling perfumes. Is that what you want, Maggie? Is that what you were hoping for when you hid out aboard my ship?"

He turned to her then, his scornful gaze increasing her misery a hundredfold. In two strides he was beside her, grasping her wrist. "Was it gold you were wanting to get your greedy little hands on—or was it a younger lover? Is that it, Maggie?"

No longer merely miserable, Maggie was suddenly frightened. Of all the Rawsons, Cabel was the one with the most unpredictable temper. He was the one who remained an enigma to her, the one she spent the most time thinking about, yet understood the least.

"*Why*, Maggie? Pa made mistakes—God knows, he's not perfect, but was he ever unkind to you? Did he ever strike you?"

She shook her head slowly, unable to look away from his terrible, beautiful eyes.

"Then why couldn't you tell him you weren't happy? Why did you wait until his back was turned and run away?"

"I wasn't running away," she managed to whisper.

"No? I'd like to know what the devil you call it. Did you tell anyone where you were going?"

Her gaze fell to her lap. She was still seated on the bunk, her shoulders propped against the bulkhead and her feet tucked close to her hips. One hand lay curled on her lap, the other still in Cabe's possession. "Sara—that is, I told her—I mean, she's keeping Eli for me. And I was only going for the day, just over to Ocracoke to see if I could find my—"

"Just over to Ocracoke!" he exploded.

"Stop yelling at me, blast you! It's not all that far! Jedd told me himself that he could practically spit across the inlet in a hard wind."

"Pa says a lot of things. There's also a lot he doesn't say and should! Dammit, don't you have any notion of what would have happened to you if we hadn't come along when we did?"

Maggie tugged at her hand. She could scarce breathe with him towering over her. "I'd have got where I was going. I've rowed boats before. I'd have met—" No, she simply *couldn't* tell him about Gid, no matter how much she wanted to ease the burden from her own shoulders. Cabe would be sure to hold it against her, and he already held her in such low regard. She owed Jedd the truth, and she must find some way to tell him quickly, before Cabe dragged it out of her and told him first. Jedd needed to know, but she must be the one to tell him so that she could make him understand . . .

"You'd have met . . ." he prompted, his voice dangerously soft.

"The man I was looking for. And then I'd have gone back home." And then, unable to help herself, she blurted, "Honestly, Cabe, I only wanted to see him, just to be sure he was all right."

Her eyes pleaded more eloquently than she knew, and with a muffled oath, Cabe stood, dropping her hand. Before she knew what he was about, he'd lifted her feet aside and sat down on the bunk, crowding her against the bulkhead. "You stubborn, hardheaded female, you'd have been swept out to sea and drowned before you ever got near the other side. Only a fool would go near that inlet in a small boat with the tide flowing out. There's currents stronger than any man can fight, much less a scrap of a woman."

With a sigh that had the unlikely effect of making her ache to comfort him—sore, sunsick and angry though she was—Cabe took her hand, holding her prisoner when she would have eased away. "And in case you'd forgotten, Maggie Rawson, you're no longer free to go and come as you please. One of these days, you'll have to understand—that is, there's things you don't know—" He broke off, swore under his breath and gave her a look that squeezed the wind right out of her lungs. "Oh, hell, Maggie—just trust me, will you?"

It was then that he slipped his fingers between hers, palm to palm, and pressed her hand tightly.

It was then that Maggie groaned and bent over with the agony of a dozen raw blisters against his hard, salty hand.

Chapter Fourteen

As the pain of her tortured hands subsided, Maggie became aware of a look of concern on Cabe's face. It was gone in an instant, replaced with something more enigmatic, but even that was better than his anger.

Now, if only she could get him to leave her alone before she inadvertently set him off again. "The oars were heavier than I'd expected. I might've gripped them a bit too hard."

A corner of his mobile mouth twitched a bit and then was still. "I thought you claimed to have rowed a boat before."

"Well, of course I've rowed a boat. That is, I've paddled about a bit." She brushed her hair back from her face, careful to use the back of her fingers and not her palm, and then concealed both hands behind her.

"And that wouldn't be a mess of fresh blisters you're hiding behind your back, now would it?" he taunted.

"I might have worn a small blister," she allowed. Small! She'd fair ruined herself! By now she couldn't even unbend her fingers without crying out at the pain.

"Ah, one small blister. I recollect once when Matt was about knee high, that he borrowed Pa's fowling piece and set off after a mess of black ducks. He ended up with a blister, too—one that damn near covered his whole backside. Youngers who don't have no better sense than to take up a man's gear and try to do a man's job sometimes has to be taught a lesson for their own good."

Maggie squirmed uncomfortably. When Cabe moved suddenly, she scuttled back as far as the shallow enclosure would allow, but he'd only stood to fetch something off his shaving table.

"Sit still, woman, and give me your hands—this stuff don't smell so sweet, but it'll take the fire out of your blisters." He reached for her right arm, and as she didn't care to engage in an undignified set-to, she gave in and held out her hand, palm up.

Her fingers were curled, and she was unable to restrain a small whimper when he carefully unfolded them. Silently he frowned at the raw, oozing flesh. Dipping his forefinger into the small pot, he smeared one palm with a thick, greenish balm, instantly easing her pain.

Hesitantly she extended her other hand, which was treated in kind. About to set the pot aside, he subjected her face and neck to a frowning scrutiny. "Bless me if you haven't gone and par-boiled yourself. And God knows when you'll be able to use those hands again. Even if you was to stay home, you'd be worthless until you mended."

"Worthless! I can work circles around any woman you can name on my worst day, and this—"

"Still, I reckon there's no point in offending Pa with the sight of your homely face, all scaly and peeling like a half-shed snake," he said, ignoring her outburst as he dipped his finger into the pot again and reached out to pull her toward him.

Rearing back, Maggie gave him her most quelling glare. "If the sight of my face offends you, you can bloody well—"

"Mind your temper, madam—and dammit, hold still! 'Pears to me you don't have a whole lot to complain about."

"And it appears to me that you've got entirely too much to say about something that's none of your concern! If the day ever comes when I can't earn my keep, it'll be up to Jedd to tell me to go, not some—some—! And what's more, I don't have a temper!"

"No, and a blackberry don't have thorns, either." He reached around behind her, grasping a handful of hair, and jerked her closer, frowning as he smeared a streak of the pungent-smelling ointment down her nose and across each cheek. "This stuff'll make you feel some better, but it won't do much for your looks."

"I don't *care* about looks," she protested, unreasonably hurt by his words. "Uggh! It smells like a wet henhouse!" She tried to twist away, but he held her fast, his short-lived patience obviously at an end.

"Dammit, didn't I tell you to sit still?" Placing one hand flat on her chest, he shoved her back onto the bed. "Where else are you burnt? Your neck? Your chest?"

"Leave my chest alone!"

"Your feet! For God's sake, woman, you have shoes, why not wear them? Don't you know what sun can do when it shines down through the water?"

She knew well enough...*now*. The few inches of water in the bottom of the rowboat had felt deliciously cool, but it had only increased the sun's power to burn, and her feet felt as if they'd been baking in an oven for days.

She gave herself over to the pleasure of his cooling touch as he smoothed the ointment down the tops of each foot, to the tip of each small toe. His touch was bothering her far more than the sunburn, and in an effort to distract herself, she mentioned the fact that she'd left Eli with Sara. "I'd better hurry back before she starts wondering if I've forgot all about him."

"The boy'll keep for a spell longer. Sara served well enough before you come along, she'll serve as well after—"

After I've gone, Maggie finished for him. Closing her eyes, she allowed herself to sink momentarily into sheer physical misery. She ached, she burned, she throbbed—and what's more, she sadly feared she stank.

However, she still had a responsibility, and Maggie had never been one to shirk her duties. Unlike *some* she could name, who went traipsing off to sea with never a thought as to who stayed behind.

Thinking of the Rawson men, she'd been pleasuring herself with a bit of righteous resentment even though she knew the charge to be unfair. And then the uncomfortable notion struck her that the description came far closer to fitting her own brother.

Poor Gid. He'd always been quick to leap into the fray. Ma had hauled him away from trouble more than once before they'd ever met up with Zion, and after Ma had fallen ill, it had been Maggie who had kept him from flying off the handle and doing something that would have likely ended in his being jailed or worse.

She could only hope that with age had come a degree of moderation, but from all she'd heard, that hardly sounded likely.

Pirates! Good Lord, why couldn't he have settled for something less likely to end in disaster? As for her uncle Will, she'd never even met the man, and felt no responsibility for his well-being. He was old enough to account for his own misdeeds. It was Gid who needed her, and she'd let him down. She'd simply have to try again the first chance she got.

"Feeling better?" Cabe asked silkily.

"Much better, thank you," she said with grudging honesty.

"Then you might stop glaring at me that way. If I was a pan of milk, I'd have clabbered by now."

"I'm not glaring, I—it's that foul-smelling mess you put on me. How do I know you're not trying to poison me?"

He stared at her mouth so long she licked her lips nervously. "Because if I was wanting to poison you, I'd scarce have wasted my precious poison on your feet."

"There's poisons that soak through the skin. I've heard tell of redskins who used all manner of evil plants on their victims without having to pry open their..." Her voice dwindled off. She could have bitten her tongue for saying what she had about redskins. To Cabe, of all people! His own mother had been half redskin, and it pained her to think she could have said something so hurtful, for truly, she'd never have willingly hurt him. "I didn't mean—I only meant some potions were, um..."

Ignoring her embarrassment, Cabe resealed the small pot and replaced it on the table. "My mother swore by this stuff," he said. "Never would say what was in it, but I seem to remember her drying the leaves of the white-flowered sumac and grinding them in a mash of pokeberries."

Both of which Maggie knew well were ruinous. With a glint in her eye, she inquired innocently, "Then why is it green and not purple?"

"The gall of all them blow toads, I reckon. Probably what gives it that rich odor."

As unlikely as it seemed, Maggie knew he was teasing her. Sara had once told her that although Anne's father had been chief of the Hatorask people, her mother had been an English-woman, an herbalist who'd been highly respected by the red-skins as a healer. In fact, Sara had intimated that they'd even called her a "white witch."

"I do believe you're right," she said thoughtfully. "Still, it's passing strange. I recollect hearing that blow toad gall is a specific against swollen heads. Is that why you have such a store of it?"

"I wouldn't be knowing about swollen heads, madam, but I've found it right handy for silencing witchety women who don't know enough to keep a civil tongue when they talk to their betters."

Maggie's aching shoulders sagged deeper into the mattress. She was hardly up to a battle of wits, yet she hated to allow him to get off the last shot, after having caught her at such a disadvantage,. Truly, he had a talent for it!

Her mind scrambling for some handy barb with which to prick him, she was forced to admit that he was more than a match for her. He could put her off balance with a single look. From the very first time she'd laid eyes on him, there'd been a subtle untamed quality about him that had both drawn her and repelled her. Seeing him now in this rare teasing mood, she didn't know what to make of him. Was he trying to catch her unaware? To trap her into revealing where she'd been bound and who she'd been searching for?

It was as if he'd read her thoughts. His smile held more than a note of mockery as he reached out and stroked her hair away from her face. It had long since unraveled from the single braid she affected to swirl about her head in a tangled red cloud.

Edging away, Maggie felt the familiar weakness invade her limbs. He ran a callused fingertip around her hairline, from brow to temple to nape, as his smile grew positively diabolical "Don't worry, paleface, we Hatorask warriors gave up scalping some years back. Ma said it was no longer considered polite."

"I wasn't thinking that!"

"What were you thinking? Shall I read your thoughts in those wicked green eyes of yours?" Cabe grinned. "Let me set your mind at rest, paleface squaw. If you're thinking I'm abou to attack you again, I'll fetch you a looking glass. That should set your mind at rest.''

She managed a scathing glance and that was all, for he'd come altogether too close to the mark. ''If you don't mind, I'd like to go home now,'' she said stiffly.

Still smiling, Cabe replied softly, ''You'll go when I say you can go, and not before.'' He eased down onto the bunk beside her and before she could protest, he'd gathered her onto his lap. Maggie began pounding the iron-hard arm that held her, even though the blows were far more painful for her than for him.

''Hand healed to fighting fit already? My foul redskin potion must be even more effective than I'd thought.''

''Your foul—'' she struggled for her release against his overwhelming strength, and lost ''—your foul redskin potion stinks to high heaven!''

''I'm touched by your gratitude, but then you were ever a meek and grateful creature, weren't you? No wonder Jedd was so anxious to take you in and give you a home. He knew—ow! You shark-toothed little trollop! Bite my shoulder one more time and I'll drag you home with the anchor cable!''

''Dammit all to hell and back, Cabel, if you don't let me go I'm going to tell your Pa on you!''

''Tsk tsk, I should've known sooner or later you'd trip over your tongue. It don't become a lady to swear, Maggie.'' He clamped her tightly against him so that she couldn't even move her head.

''Damnation and hellfire!'' she yelled deliberately. She'd not learned to plow behind a team of oxen without learning the use of a few persuasive phrases. ''You're squashing my bones, you lummox!''

Cabe's hold on her eased just enough so that she no longer felt as if she were about to be crushed like a hollow gourd. She tried to slip off his knees, but she might as well have pitted her strength against a bear trap.

Too weary to fight such an unequal match, she sighed and let her head loll for a moment against his shoulder. Water. What she wouldn't give for a long, cold draft of water. Although, if someone handed her a gourdful at this very moment, she'd be hard pressed not to toss it in his sneering face.

A familiar warm, melting sensation began to creep into her limbs, tingling alarmingly, especially where her bottom came into contact with Cabe's muscular thighs. His hand stroked her shoulder, and the tingling increased. Maggie stiffened, feeling a strange stirring underneath her hips.

Oh, no, not again! Never again, she swore fervently. Cabel Rawson might've inherited some wild magic from his witching grandma, but the McNairs had ever stood fast against tyranny, and no McNair would ever be softheaded enough to fall under the spell of a savage, seagoing despot!

Drawing in a deep breath, she prepared to eject herself forcibly from his lap. But the breath that filled her lungs was no longer redolent with the pale green potion, which seemed to have seeped into her skin, affecting its cure without leaving a trace. Instead it whispered of healthy male sweat, leather and some exotic essence that was his alone.

And dammit, she resented it! It wasn't fair to use such weapons against a woman who had no knowledge of how to fight back. How could a body fight against something so unreasonable as a man's particular *scent*?

She felt him harden and stir beneath her, and she stiffened in alarm. "Open the window—please, Cabe," she gasped. "I can't breathe in here!"

He whispered something under his breath, something shockingly profane, but he eased her off his lap and onto the cool linens. She huddled there, eyeing him warily. She was frightened, but not so much of him as of her own feelings. How could she stand fast when her own body threatened to betray her with these unsettling...urges?

"I expect you're thirsty," he said, after studying her silently for a long, uncomfortable moment.

She pounced on it. "Truly parched!"

"Promise me you won't try to shin out the porthole the minute my back is turned, and I'll fetch you a cup of cider."

"I'd hardly be likely to try something so unseemly with your whole crew looking on. Besides, I can't swim all that well."

Cabe allowed his gaze to wander down her body, from the place where Jedd's shirt billowed about her slender waist to the gentle swell of her hips, the tapering of her thighs, and the length of ankle revealed below the button tab that struck Matt just below the knee and her just below mid calf.

"Unseemly? Of course you wouldn't," he drawled, and coals were heaped on the fire as her face flamed anew.

Nor did he bother to tell her they were already anchored off the island, and all but the watch crew had already gone ashore. "I'll have your word, all the same," he said.

"I said I'd stay!" she snapped, already regretting having asked even that small favor of him.

He left, but before she could think of a way to take advantage of his absence, he was back again, bearing a sweat-beaded tankard. "Just a few sips, mind you. Too much sun can cause the belly to turn, and I don't want you ruining my clean bed."

Muttering something between a grunt and a snort, Maggie reached for the tankard. Before she could down more than a third of its contents, he removed it from her hand. "Slowly, I said! You're bound and determined to defy me at every turn, aren't you?"

"If you've had enough of me, you may take me home."

"With the whole village looking on? The crew's already gone ashore. By now, the whole village knows we plucked you out of Pa's rowboat, and you fried to a frizzle, a-flauntin' yourself in a pair of trousers so that any man who weren't blind could see the shape of your limbs all the way up to your—"

"Hush! I didn't. It's not—"

"Crotch," he shouted, pushing his face within inches of hers until she was reeling from the force of his blazing eyes. "What were you doing out there, Maggie? Who were you going to meet? Do you feel up to explaining all that to the busybodies waiting for you on shore?"

She might have known he hadn't forgotten. Nor would he rest until he'd dragged it all out of her.

Turning away, Maggie reached for her drink, and before he could stop her, she'd finished it. Cabel snatched the empty tankard away, and she tossed her head triumphantly. Out of the entire war, she'd at least won this small battle.

"Go ahead, then, make yourself sick! You deserve all the misery you're going to suffer!"

"It's my belly, and I know what's good for it!"

"Bullheaded female. I should've heaved you over the rail the first time I ever laid eyes on you!"

"I should have known better than to take passage with a selfish, mean-hearted devil who begrudges his own father a wife to look after his home and family!"

"A wife! You're no more a wife—"

"Oh, and it galls you to have to call me Mistress Rawson, doesn't it? But let me tell you something, Cabel Rawson, I *am* your pa's wife, and there's nothing you can do about it! And what's more, all the rest of the family likes me just fine!" She was wound up good and proper now, blistered palms, sunburnt face and feet forgotten.

"And Isaac, does he like you just fine, Mistress Rawson?"

She took a deep, steadying breath and began to shape the truth to suit her needs. "He's coming to. He's just shy of showing it, that's all."

Cabe hooted. "Oh, aye, the lad's shy, all right. Shy like all those seamen on the docks at Bath were shy. I saw them walk right past you, don't think I didn't. Not a one of them would give you the time of day, would they? You're a great success, you are, Maggie McNair. Why you're almost as great a success as a wife as you were a whore."

She sat down suddenly, her mouth gaping and her eyes wide with disbelief. "Cabel Rawson, you take that back."

"Why should I?" he taunted.

"Because it's not true, and you know it's not!" She could have wept. Was that what he truly thought of her? Was that why he'd done those things to her that day when he'd come upon her bathing? Because he'd thought that she— "Oh, no. You're only trying to make me leave," she said in a voice that was soft, but quite firm, nonetheless. "You've never wanted me there, though I've done my best to take your mother's place."

It had been the wrong thing to say. He was suddenly livid. "The day will never come when you could take my mother's place. You're there because Pa was desperate for someone to—"

"I know why I'm there!" she shouted. Suddenly she'd had enough. All the stress of a day ill-spent bore down on her until she could hardly hold up her head. "So if you don't mind," she said with the last bit of pride she could muster, "I'll be about my job. There's Eli to fetch and feed, and a wash to do, and with Jedd and the others on the way home, I'd best see about setting a pan of pone bread to working.''

"You'll do all that with the skin wore plumb off your hands, I reckon," he jeered. Some of the fire had gone from his eyes now, but all the same, she didn't trust herself in his presence another moment. They'd likely end up killing one another. "Let me see your hands, Maggie," he demanded, and she hid them behind her. Ruthlessly he dragged her arms around in front and pried open her fingers.

She clamped her teeth tightly against making a sound. They still hurt, though not nearly so bad as they had earlier.

"Tell me something, Mistress Rawson, if you've spent all your time in a cornfield instead of a dockside crib, where are all your calluses from hoeing and chopping!" His smile was anything but solicitous. "How come they didn't protect your hands better?''

She snatched back her fists and hid them behind her again. "You try soaking your calluses in hot water and lye soap every livelong day and see if it doesn't soften your horny hands up some! Don't waste your time worrying over *my* hands, Cabel Rawson. I'm no wilting violet to be crushed under your boot heel.''

"Oh, no, you're a tough little weed, aren't you? A real survivor." With a single short expletive, he let her know just precisely what he thought of her. As if she hadn't already known. As if he hadn't spelled it out for her. "What are you going to do," he sneered, "Beg Sara to take on your care as well as Eli's?''

But Maggie had had all the bearbaiting she could take. Planting her fists on her hips, she ignored the twinge and thrust her chin at his. "Listen to me, you bloated croaker, I don't *need* Sara. I don't need *you*! I don't need *anyone*, and what's more, I never will!''

Truly, she told herself, she must be delirious. For a moment there, she had almost been convinced she saw a trace of respect on Cabe's stern features.

But when she looked again, it was gone. "Come on," he said tiredly. "I reckon I may as well take you ashore. Pa seems to set some store by you—God knows why.''

A day later, just before dark, the *Eliza Lea* dropped anchor off the back of the island. A crowd had gathered on shore for word had just reached the village that the sloop had been attacked at first light that morning by an unknown three-master flying a red skull and bones on a black field.

Cabe's longboat was the first to reach her, and from the shore, Maggie watched him board. She held Eli in her arms, for sore hands or not, she'd had too much pride to ask Sara to take over her responsibilities.

"They say one ball went clean through the aft'deck and come out right beside the rudder," someone marveled.

"From the way that boom's hanging, I'd say she come damned close to losing her pole. They say it was that quartermaster o' Will Lewis's."

Maggie grew numb, her thoughts working feverishly until Eli's squirming got her attention. "There, there, dumpling, Papa's going to be all right." He *had* to be all right, she told herself, somewhat surprised at how much the old man had come to mean to her. "Was anyone hurt?" she asked of Lina Stowe, who had edged through the crowd to stand beside her.

"I don't know yet. That looks like Gaffer furling the jib, and—is that Matt helping him? Oh, God, please let it be Matt!"

"He left home wearing his blue shirt. He didn't take his other one." Both men at the bow were wearing sleeveless jerkins.

"How'd she get away?" asked a wizened old man, but before anyone could supply the answer, there was a murmur and then a hush fell over the crowd as a small group of men appeared on deck and began climbing down into Cabe's longboat.

Eli gurgled noisily, and Maggie bounced him in her arms, her eyes straining against the glare of sunlight on water for a sight of a familiar gray beard, a head of golden curls, and a small dark figure.

Isaac! If anything had happened to Isaac!

Suddenly Lina grabbed her arm and began dancing up and down. "There he is. Matt! Matt!"

"Oh, Lord, there's my John—he's all right," moaned another woman, who promptly covered her face with her apron.

As soon as it became evident that one small boy and all nine men were back safely, although one carried his arm strapped to his side, the crowd on the shore pushed forward, each wanting to be first to welcome their own.

Maggie stood back, her joy dimmed by the knowledge that her own brother could very well have been involved in the attack. This time someone had actually mentioned Will Lewis by name. There could no longer be any doubt about it. Unless Gid and Uncle Will had parted ways, her brother was definitely a pirate.

It was a sober group that turned away from the waterfront and scattered to go home to the evening meal. Even the younger ones were quieter than usual. Doug, who'd returned that morning without a preacher, walked hand in hand with his patient Polly. He'd been one of the first to arrive at the landing. Matt carried a subdued Isaac on his shoulder, his other arm being wrapped around Lina's plump waist. None of them would have much to say until later, after the initial shock had worn off.

"They come upon us blind," Jedd said after he'd fortified himself with a double potion of rum and lit his pipe. They all sat around the kitchen, Cabe and Jeremiah, Matt and Isaac, while Sara helped Maggie put the food on the table. She'd brought over beans and corn bread from her own house, and Maggie had fried butterfish and new greens.

More aware than ever before of the powerful bond that held this banker family close in the face of adversity, Maggie felt herself drawn, like a cold and hungry child, to the warm hearth of their mutual love.

While the small children played underfoot, Jedd accepted another tot of rum from his eldest son and began relating the tale of how the morning fog had burned away to reveal an unfamiliar schooner bearing down on his stern. Not until she was practically on top of them did she hoist her infamous colors.

"Not a blessed one of them fine new guns could I bring to bear on 'er, neither," he swore. "It was like she knowed we had 'em, and knowed just where they was a-mounted. I never seen nothing to beat it."

"You didn't recognize her?"

"She flew the skull and bones—red on black—but her jib was swagged down over her bowsprit."

"To cover her nameplate," put in Jeremiah.

"So they could get a clear shot at us, more likely," said Matt.

"I hear Rackham's a bad one for clapping on astern where a man's least able to defend himself, and jamming a rudder with his bowsprit so a man can't even sheer off," Cabel remarked, but Jedd shook his head.

"This weren't Calico Jack, boys. Soon's I seen the sun a-shining off that dome, I knowed who we was up against. Lewis's man, the one they call the Turk. Stands head and shoulder over any normal man, with a skull as nekkid as a pun'kin. They say he saw Teach jam a bunch of lucifers in his beard and light 'em one time, and Turk, he set himself on fire a-trying to outdo the old black-bearded bastard."

"So it was Lewis's gang." Jeremiah frowned thoughtfully. "I'd heard they'd done a lot of work on the *Star*, but I didn't know she was off the ways again."

"It weren't the *Star*, boys. I'd know that ship of Will Lewis's anywhere. No, this was a three-master, built some'ers up in the Massachussets colony from the look of her. But they'll hang, ever' last one of 'em. Don't matter what they're a-sailin', they can't outrun the hangman much longer." And without a pause, he said, "Set that trencher of butterfish right here, Maggie. Boys, let's set to. I ain't had a decent meal since I left home. Bless the food, Lord, amen."

There was more talk during the meal, and Maggie listened with a growing feeling of helplessness. She knew in her heart that Gid was no pirate. He might be caught up in a situation he didn't know how to get out of, but with her help...

That was just it. How could she help him when she couldn't even get word to him without arousing suspicion? She could hardly ask one of the Rawsons to take her across the inlet to see a member of the crew that had attacked Jedd and would've murdered them all had it not been for a bit of luck.

"Grounded 'em, did you, Pa?" Jeremiah repeated admiringly. "I always said there weren't a shoal in the Pamlico you didn't know like the warts on your nose."

"Pa ain't got warts on his nose," Isaac defended, and Cabe, laughing, scooped the boy up and sat him on his knee. "Warts is what happens when a lad disobeys his elders. You going to eat that food Maggie set before you? You heard Pa, little brother—set to!''

But the younger men were still too excited to concentrate on food. ''You shoulda seen Pa, Cabe,'' said Matt, as soon as he'd washed down a mouthful of Sara's white beans with a long draft of hard cider. ''He was cursing something fierce. It took both of us to get the wheel over, and when we come about, it was so fast we damned near went beamside over, smack dab in the middle of the inlet!'' He bit off an enormous chunk of corn bread, chewed hastily and washed it down with more cider, his eyes sparkling as he relived the near disaster.

Cabe smiled at his brother's bloodthirsty enthusiasm, but the smile never reached his eyes.

''That old Turk, he was bearing down on us like he was a-gonna ram his bowsprit right up our arse—uh, aft cabin hatch,'' he amended hastily, catching his father's stern look. ''But we was riding high in the water, and Turk, he had enough guns aboard to sink the King's navy. God knows what all he had in his hold, but he sure didn't have no freeboard to spare. So Pa, he led the old bastard right onto that big shoal that's made up over southwest of the channel. Boy, you shoulda seen us fly! Half our canvas was shot full o' holes, but Gaffer run up everything but Amos's drawers, and we come a-flying across the edge of that shoal so fast we damned near piled up on the far side of the channel before we could come about.''

Maggie stood at the hearth, her own plate in her hand as she nibbled a crisp-fried tail of fish. Her mind seethed with questions she dare not ask. Had Jedd fired back? Had the schooner broken up, or was she still grounded fast, at the mercy of seas that could batter a ship into kindling in the space of a few hours?

''Was anyone hurt? Anyone at all?'' she asked when she couldn't bear it any longer.

''Junius busted a pinion when the boom knocked him into the shrouds, is all. We was lucky.''

Yes, Maggie thought despairingly, but were those aboard Gid's ship so fortunate? Had she discovered her brother's whereabouts only to lose him again?

"I'll send Ruben on down to Ocracoke come morning to see if we can get a spare set of sails," said Jeremiah. "If there's news, he'll hear about it. I heard this morning they've sent word up to Spottswood to see if he can send down some of his men to clean up this mess. Maybe now we'll see some action."

"Past time, if you ask me," Jedd grumbled. He was beginning to look pale and drawn now, the shock having settled in on him. Quietly Cabe arose and poured his father another tot of rum, allowing his hand to rest on the old man's shoulder for a moment before taking his seat again. "Hang the whole bloody bunch of 'em and be done with it. Pardoning the bastards off don't do no good—just gives 'em something to laugh about while they make plans to take over the whole damned Atlantic coast. Run 'em all back to New Providence and then set a torch to the stinking hole! If Eden can't, and Spottswood won't, then we'll just have to do it ourselves."

Maggie was no longer listening. If Jedd was sending someone across to Ocracoke in search of a new set of sails, likely they'd be back the same day. Ruben, he'd said. She knew his boat, having watched it come in from his pound nets many a morning. A small shallop, neat and tidy, with enough room for one small body to hide. All she had to do was slip aboard before he set out.

But what excuse could she give for wanting to go to Ocracoke? What excuse for leaving the children unattended, for leaving her menfolk to fend for themselves?

None. It was too late to waste time on such niceties now. She would simply do what had to be done and worry about excuses later.

Chapter Fifteen

The shallop was cramped. Having surveyed the small space before, Maggie had expected that. What she hadn't expected was that she'd have to share it with a bale of musty canvas, a stinking net and a pair of worn-out boots. Huddled under the low forepeak, she told herself the journey couldn't take much longer, for they'd been rolling along for an eternity. If there'd been any other way...

But there wasn't. She couldn't afford to reveal herself, nor could she afford to wait for more comfortable accommodations, not with the talk of Spottswood sending men down to clean out the infamous mess on Ocracoke. After all these years of wondering and worrying, what if she were too late? What if Gid had truly thrown in his lot with the other scum and refused to come away with her?

Gradually she became aware of a sharp pain in her injured hands and realized that she was digging her fingernails into the tender flesh of her palms. Not even to herself would she admit that she was afraid of what she might find—or worse, that she would find nothing at all, that Gid had been—that he was—

The hull bumped against something solid, jarring her against the sharp edge of an exposed rib, and she heard a male voice raised in greeting. Thank providence! She'd been afraid every moment of the journey that Ruben would discover her. After the first hour, she'd almost prayed he would, for she was dying of thirst and every bone in her body ached.

Now that she'd arrived, she was almost sick with anxiety. How would she find Gid? Ocracoke was even smaller than

Hatteras, but where to start? Who to ask? What if word got back to Jedd?

Outside, Ruben and the unknown stranger went about securing the shallop. Go, Maggie willed silently, hurry up and be on your way before I jump up screaming!

On and on they nattered. To think that men accused women of rattling their tongues! By the time the garrulous pair finally set off for the sail maker's loft, she had learned who on Ocracoke was smuggling what and how they managed to elude the customs men; which old man suffered from dropsy, and which local woman had been bedding down with the pirates. And more.

Crawling out of her miserable prison, Maggie brushed down her gown and stretched to get the kinks out of her limbs and neck. Resolutely she tried to take comfort from the fact the Ocracoker had made no mention of a man named Gideon who bore a blaze mark on his right cheek—although he'd had plenty to say about Ned Teach, someone called Meathook, and the *Star*'s quartermaster, Turk, who was reputed to be ugly enough to scare a billy goat right out from under his horns.

It was small comfort. It might even mean that Gideon was no longer on the island, which brought on a whole new line of worry. What if he'd had the good sense to leave when the *Star* had turned to piracy? How would she ever find him? What if he'd been injured and was even now lying sick and abandoned in some rat-infested hole in New Providence? What if—

Feeling chilled in spite of the relentless heat, Maggie stiffened her resolve. She'd come this far; she refused to lose heart before she'd even begun to search.

There were some dozen or so men and as many children along the waterfront, all either busy with their own affairs or gathered in small groups talking quietly among themselves. The children played about the shallows, and Maggie was able to slip away without being seen.

This time she'd been wise enough to wear her own gown, for the last thing she wanted was to be noticed and questioned. From a distance, one woman looked much like another, she told herself, so that her presence should not arouse much interest.

Pausing in the deep shade of a spreading live oak, she took stock of her surroundings. The few houses she saw were much like those on Hatteras. Smoke rose from the chimneys, as well as from backyard ovens, reminding her that it had been hours since she'd eaten, and even then, she'd been too tense to get down more than a bite or two.

Where to start? She could hardly go from house to house, inquiring for a fair-haired man with a mark on his right cheek. Nor did she care to ask the local fishermen. If they knew Gid for a pirate, it was hardly likely they'd help her.

She was on her own. And it was entirely possible that Gid might have changed over the years. Would he have grown thick about the middle? Perhaps he'd grown a beard to cover his mark. Would she be able to recognize him after all? Would he know her? She'd been little more than a child when he'd last seen her.

"Was ye a-looking fer ol' Meathook, lassie? Well now, ain't that cozy?"

Maggie started at the sound of the voice behind her, but before she could turn, an arm was thrown around her neck and she was pulled back against a solid wall of hot, stinking flesh.

She screamed, and immediately, a hand was slapped over her mouth. "Ain't had me a redhead since Quick Mary down to Portsmouth died o' the pox. Right partial to reds, I be. The more fire on top, I allus say, the more fire betwixt the—"

Maggie kicked back and caught his bare shin with the heel of her hard leather boot. He roared a frightful curse, and his arm loosened just enough for her to duck out from under. She spun away, but the deep sand was a trap. He was on her before she'd even reached the rutted road, knocking her down and landing hard on her back.

She spat out a mouthful of the stuff as he roughly turned her beneath him. "Get off me, you filthy beast!" She aimed her fingers at his small eyes, but he was fast, for all his unwieldy bulk.

Grabbing both her hands in one of his ham-sized fists, Meathook jerked them over her head, almost pulling her arms from their sockets. Maggie tried to scream again, but she was paralyzed with fear. Her throat refused to utter more than a dribble of sound. He was lying on top of her, crushing the air from her body. Burning sand ground into the skin at the back of her neck, into her scalp. Her skirt was yanked up, and she felt her legs burning.

"No, oh, no, please no," she mumbled over and over.

He shifted his weight and began rooting around her bodice. She heard it tear, and it was as if the small sound charged her with new strength. He would *not* destroy her gown! She had little enough as it was, and if this great stinking boar thought he was going to rip her clothes off her, he was sadly mistaken! Straddling her hips, he raised himself on one elbow, pressing her down with his loathsome belly. Maggie managed to work one knee free of her tangled skirts, and then, using every bit of her strength, she brought it up as hard as she could, and was rewarded by a piglike squeal of pain.

Meathook rolled over onto his side, rocking and clutching himself in agony. "I'll kill you for that, you bleedin' little whore!" he threatened when he'd run out of curses.

But Maggie wasn't listening. Scrambling quickly to her feet, she took off at a run, tears of shock, fear and horror blinding her eyes. Lifting her skirt, she fairly flew along the rutted path, uncaring where she went as long as it was away from the animal who was every bit as frightening as Nimrod had been. Head down and arms pumping, she didn't even see the tall figure step out of the cedar grove to block her way. Instead she slammed into him at full force, and would have fallen if he hadn't caught her about the waist.

"Whoa, there, dearlin', you'll never get there this way."

Heart pumping, Maggie sucked breath into burning lungs. If this was another of those rutting bastards who thought he could—

The words sunk in, and she grew still. Afraid to wipe her eyes and look up, she stood stiffly in the unlikely shelter of a stranger's arms. Something about his words had . . .

No. It hadn't been his words. It had been his *voice*.

She gave herself another moment to recover before she blinked away her tears and drew back. It wasn't, of course. It couldn't be. But it had sounded almost like . . .

"Gideon?" she whispered wonderingly as she lifted disbelieving eyes to a familiar face.

"Do I know you? Aren't you the—"

His arms fell away and he stepped back to stare at her. He shook his head, blinked once, and then stared again. "No. Oh, no. I ain't that far gone. I've not had more'n a dram all morning, and that's the blessed truth."

He might not recognize her, but there was no way on earth Maggie could have forgotten that sweet, teasing grin. He was older, his face stamped with a new maturity, but some things would never change. "Gideon, it's me, Maggie. Don't you even know me?"

He winced as if a painful cramp had caught him unaware. "Maggie? Is it truly? Sweet Jesus, little sister, what the bloody hell are you doing out here on the banks?"

It took all the strength she possessed not to throw herself at him and cry until there were no more tears left inside her. But she'd wasted too much time as it was. "I see your manners haven't improved over the years," she observed calmly. "Do all seafaring men spew forth curses every time they open their mouth, or do I simply bring out the worst in them?"

Gid let out a whoop of sheer joy, and then she was back in his arms and he was swinging her around, laughing as if he couldn't quite believe what his senses were telling him.

"Oh, Gid, I was that worried when I heard—"

"Maggie, Maggie, what the devil are you doing on Ocracoke, of all bloody places?"

"—and they're saying that Uncle Will's man was the one who—"

"God, is Mama here, too?"

That stole the wind right out of her sails. He didn't know. Of course, he couldn't have known, and now she would have to break his heart by telling him that he was too late.

"Gid, Mama's dead. She took the sickness sometime back, and it never let up on her, and she . . ."

"When?" Like a cloud covering the sun, the laughter was gone from his eyes.

"Back in May. She just slept and slept for a long time, and then one day she didn't wake up. It was an easy passing, Gid." Her throat constricted, and she dug her fingers into the back of his hand as he led her up a slight rise to the shade of the cedar grove. Some distance beyond, she could see men swarming around a ship and hear the double beat of their hammers echoing in the still air.

She sat, and he dropped down beside her. "Too late. I was too late," he said slowly. "I kept thinking, planning, honest I did, Maggie. Only I could never put together enough to buy a fine house where you and Mama could live together in comfort. I wanted it to be just right—a patch of land with a garden, big windows with real glass. A sleeping room with a door instead of a rug hung over a pole. I kept thinking, one more trip, just one more trip."

"I know, Giddy, I know." She stroked his arm, wanting to take away the pain from his eyes, in spite of all the times she'd condemned him for not coming for them. "Mama couldn't have left her bed, even if you'd come for them. She was too weak. And I'd never have left her, so you see, it's just as well. It eased her mind, just knowing that you'd got away free."

"Away, at least, if not free," he muttered darkly. "Still and all, you're here now, and—" He broke off, and Maggie watched his hands slowly curl into fists. A light breeze swept up the hill from the waterfront, stirring her hair against her brow, cooling her body under the sweat-damp gown.

He was still beautiful. The rough life he'd been leading had not marred his handsome face. Smiling sadly, she recalled how she used to think God must have made him on one of His good days, and then added the blemish to his right cheek in case the angels grew jealous.

Lord, she'd worshiped her brother. He'd been her friend, her only friend. He'd been protector, confident, and coconspirator. She'd been lost when he'd left, even though she'd known he had to go before Zion drove him too far.

"How'd it go after I left, Magpie?" The pet name he'd given her when she'd been a tot, stumbling after him and babbling incessantly, brought the sting of fresh tears. Laughing unsteadily, she mopped them away with a sweaty forearm.

"I survived," she said airily, and then wished she'd put it another way. Their mother had not survived, and Gid would be long in forgiving himself for that, though even if he'd stayed he could have done nothing to save her from the fever.

"You've grown," she remarked.

"You ain't, but you've filled out some. You look a lot like Ma."

"I've never looked like Ma. You're more like her than me. I've got Papa's hair and Papa's temper, but you're the one who got his wandering ways."

Which left them both silent for a while. There was so much to catch up on, Maggie hardly knew where to begin. But there'd be time for that later. First she had to find a way to get him to leave with her.

A thought struck her then. How on earth were both of them going to fit under Ruben's forepeak? There'd been hardly enough room for one, let alone the great towering hulk Gid had grown into.

Gid's voice roused her out of a muddle of half-formed plans, none of them workable. "So you've finally grown up, little Magpie. 'Strewth, you don't look much different from when you used to beg me to let you bait the turtle hooks on the trot-line down at the creek."

She smiled, giving in to the joy and relief of simply being with her brother after so many years. She'd find a way to get him to Hatteras with her. There was always a way, one only had to search for it.

"You've changed some. The sun's turned your hair nearly white, and I swear, you've grown twice as tall as you were when you left." There was a hardness about him now, she admitted silently. It hadn't been there before, but then, he was a man grown, a member of a pirate crew, whether or not he'd thrown in his lot with them.

Maggie took heart. Some things, at least, had not changed—his rich blue eyes, and the sweet teasing curve of his smile were still much the same as she remembered. He loved her still; she was sure of it, and that gave her comfort, too. Everyone needed one person in the world to love and be loved by, and she had no one left but Gid.

Did he have anyone else? By now he could even have a wife. Perhaps she was an aunt. She was on the verge of asking when he spoke again.

"Why were you running just now, Maggie? You were crying, too. Had someone said something to frighten you?"

She toyed with a twig of white cedar berries, twirling it in her fingers. If she told him what had happened, he would likely do something foolish, and she didn't want him getting embroiled in any more trouble, not now that everything was turning out so well.

"I was afraid—that is, I didn't know where to find you, and—"

"Magpie," he interrupted gently. "You were never even a fair liar. It was Meathook, wasn't it? I saw him sitting back there beside that big oak, looking like he'd sat down on a red ant hill. Did he—that is, he didn't—"

His dark brows were settling lower and lower over his eyes. Maggie knew what was coming, and knew she had to deflect his anger. "He tried to—to kiss me, that's all. And I didn't care to be kissed."

She thought he was going to strangle before he got control of himself again. "That lowdown son of a bleedin'—" She clamped her hands over her ears, and Gid managed to moderate his description.

"Let it be, Gid. He'll not try it again, at least not unless he's wearing a suit of armor."

Reluctantly he agreed to let the man live, but only after Maggie had vowed to walk off and leave him if he engaged in a brawl on her account. "We've more important things to think of now, such as how we're going to get away from here."

"Back to the main, you mean? How did you get here?"

Which meant another rather involved explanation, one that took them well into the afternoon and drew forth some rather painful recollections along the way.

"Never a day went by that I didn't think about you and Ma and wonder how you was faring. A hundred times I started to go back, even though I'd nothing to offer you. If I had, I'd likely have ended up killing them both—the old bastard and that snake of a son of his."

"I know, dearling. You were wise to stay away."

"Don't say that Maggie. God, I feel so guilty for leaving you and Ma alone with that pair. I just kept hoping, I kept on thinking that in a little while I'd have enough put by to make place for you. But by the time I had a bit saved up, Uncle Wi was in bad trouble and there was only me, and I couldn't turn my back on him—not after he'd taken me in."

"I know. Sometimes it's hard to see where a body's real duty lies. Did I tell you they were going to marry me?"

"They?"

"Nimrod." She ignored Gid's profane outburst. "Zion told him he could have me on his seventeenth birthday. I'd been planning to leave, anyway. I only stayed to be sure he put a marker on Mama's grave. But when I heard that, I had to get away." She shuddered. "Nimrod! Lord, I'd sooner marry Monty One Foot! They'd have worked me like old Belem and Jonah until I dropped in the field, and then plowed me under and found themselves another poor fool."

Gideon pounded a fist against his thigh, his eyes closed against the pain his womenfolk had endured in his absence. "I swear to you I'll kill the pair of 'em, Maggie. For Ma's sake and yours."

"And hang for your pleasure," she snapped.

Throwing an arm across her shoulder, he drew her into a tight embrace. "It'd be worth it. God, it'd be worth it, Maggie! I've got more accounts to settle than you'll ever know, but I swear to you—"

"Yes, and I wish you'd stop it. I've been sworn at quite enough lately, thank you." She'd been only half teasing, but she had no intention of going into all that. It was growing late in the day, and she'd yet to broach the matter uppermost on her mind. It wasn't going to be easy, for where she was determined, Gid was downright stubborn. A roundabout approach would likely work best. The trouble was, she'd never had the patience to cultivate guile. Clearing her throat, she said, "Speaking of hanging, Gid—"

"How come you look like a scaly-bark hickory?"

Thrown off stride, she blinked. "How come I *what*?"

"Your face, it's peeling something awful. Didn't you know it?"

"Oh-hh . . ." Tentatively she touched her cheek. "Do I look that bad?"

"Not less'n you get up close. Leastwise, it's no worse'n you always looked when we used to sneak down to the creek and go swimming the first hot day of summer."

She wrinkled her nose at him and felt her tender skin protest the abuse. "Well, let's just say I've done it again, but that's not what's important. Gid, I've come to take you away."

His eyebrows—brows that were several shades darker than his sun-bleached hair—lifted comically. "To take me a *where*?"

"Away. From here." She sent him a look of exasperation. "From this dreadful mess you've gotten yourself involved in. Gid, don't you know what they *do* to pirates? Do you realize that the bankers are so mad they'd as soon fry the lot of you in your own lard as not? Eden's naught but a weak-willy, so now they're sending up to Virginia for help. And if Spottswood won't drive all the pirates out of these coves and bays around here, then the bankers are planning on going after the lo themselves. Gid, you've got to get away! Save yourself whil there's still time. As for Uncle Will, he can go or stay as h chooses, but I'll not allow my brother to ruin his whole life ou of sheer recklessness."

"Yammer, yammer, yammer, little Magpie," Gid taunted though his eyes were no longer laughing. "Them folks yo work for sure do like to gossip."

"It's not just gossip," she exclaimed, angry that he refuse to take her seriously. "And they're not just folks I work for they're my family!" She'd told him only that she was stayin over on Hatteras with a family that needed her. "That is, m husband and his sons. What's more, it's not just the men bu the womenfolk, so you can see they're serious."

"Husband! You're *married*?"

"That's the only way I know to get a husband. What's more I have five stepsons, and they were all spittin' mad after you friend Turk nearly blew my husband's ship out of the wate yesterday. Jedd said—"

"That was your *husband*? That battered old sloop that cos Turk the spanking new three-master he'd captured less than week ago?"

"I don't know about that, but Jedd recognized your frien Turk, and—"

"Now hold there a minute, little sister, Turk's not my friend. A shark don't have friends, though there's always a few that'll suck up to the meanest son of a bitch around. And right now, the crew's about evenly divided—half wanting Uncle Will to run him through and feed him to the buzzards, and half wanting Turk to take command and go after every prize ship that passes offshore. Trouble is, Uncle Will's half is mostly old men. I'm the only one with any hair, teeth or gizzard left."

Maggie took a moment to digest this news. Then she asked, "Well, why doesn't Uncle Will just get rid of this Turk, if he's the one causing all the trouble? Then those who want to can follow him, and the rest of you can go back to whatever it was you were doing before."

"Ah, Magpie, you ain't playing with your corn shuck dolls no more. In the first place, it does something to a man to see a coffin full of gold and know that there's more for the taking, and he can have his share. Some of Uncle Will's oldest friends can't help but be sore tempted. And gold ain't all. There's richer cargoes than a man could ever dream, and beyond that, there's the ships, themselves."

He paused to stare out at the harbor, where some half a dozen vessels of various types and sizes were moored, and Maggie wondered if she'd come too late. Had Gid, too, become infected with a fever even more deadly than the one that had taken so many lives last winter?

"It's too easy, Maggie. It sucks a man in before he knows what's got a-holt of him. The men see all them ships Teach brings in and think they might just as well get their share. That schooner Turk lost yesterday in the inlet? She was a prize he took last week without firing a single shot. Enough silk and spices and China Tea to fill a warehouse. He was just waiting for things in Charles Towne to cool off some after the raid to set up an auction, but then he spied that sloop headed in, and she looked to be an easy mark. He damned near took her, too."

"Yes, and he damned near got his head blown off for his troubles," Maggie retorted. "My husband's the best seaman on the banks, and what's more, he's got a slew of great big guns mounted on his deck. And so has Cabel."

Ignoring her outburst, Gid continued. "Besides, there's plenty more sea scum where Turk and the others like him come from. There's been murdering thieves as long as there's been men. Put a deck under their feet and you can call 'em pirates, but you sure as hell can't rid the world of the lot of 'em just by sending a handful to their maker.''

"Maybe not, but at least you and Uncle Will don't have to turn the *Morning Star* over to men like that Turk and get yourselves hanged from the same gallows.''

"It ain't that simple, Maggie. If it was, I'd be working somewhere on dry land, where my feet don't threaten to slide out from under me and my belly don't act like a butter churn every time we hit open water.''

Maggie's brows lifted. "You, too?"

Gid grinned in commiseration. "Yep. You, too?"

"Every time. Does it ever get better?"

"Some. Depends on the weather, the course, and the build of the hull. And how much work you got to keep your mind off your belly.''

"Then it's simple," Maggie announced with satisfaction. "You can just quit and get a job with my oldest stepson. He has a boat yard over on Hatteras.''

"No, it ain't simple, either, dammit! Uncle Will's sick. He's got swamp fever that comes on him unexpected like, and when it does, he's so weak he can't even sweat without help. So far, the crew don't know how bad off he is. I've sort of let 'em think he's drinking heavy—they'll respect that in a man. But it's getting worse, and I just can't go off and leave him, not after he took me in when I was fifteen and taught me my trade. He's a fair man, Maggie. Oh, he's too weak to stand up to Aunt Cindy—hell, no man can do that—but he's not a man to let his weakness turn in on him and make him mean, like some does.''

Heartsick, she stared at him for a long moment. "Just tell me one thing, Gideon. Is it the gold? Would you walk away from all those riches if you had the choice?"

"Ahh, Maggie," he groaned. "It ain't the gold. I can make my own fortune without having to steal it from another man, and some day I will. But first I have to pay back Uncle Will for taking me in and teaching me a trade.''

"Ha! Some trade!"

"I ain't no blasted pirate, and I won't be! I hate the whole stinking mess.''

"Then walk away!"

"If I go, Turk and his kind will take over, and anyone who don't like it will be strung up. Uncle Will don't deserve to end up as crow bait on the end of a rope. It ain't his fault he weren't born with a whole lot of gumption. Him and Ma were brother and sister, just like you and me, Mag. For Ma's sake, I've got to stay."

"Oh, Gid—then what are we going to do?" Maggie whispered.

"What I'm going to do is borrow a boat and get you back to Hatteras to this husband of yours. Is he a good man, Maggie? Does he treat you kindly?"

"He's a fine man. He's some older than me, but he's kind and generous—he brought me these boots, and two bolts of cloth."

"I'm glad you're happy. I hope Ma knows. She worried so about you, and about Will, too."

"Did she, Gid? I never knew that."

"She didn't want you to. You were her baby, but sometimes I'd come on her crying, and when I asked her why, she'd say she missed her family. And I don't think she meant Papa."

Maggie sighed. She was coming to realize every day how little she knew of what went on in the heads and hearts of those around her. She was a woman's age, with a woman's responsibilities, but sometimes it seemed as if she were still waiting to grow up—still waiting for something, at least.

"Don't fret, Magpie. You've got that longing look in your eyes again."

"I don't have any look at all," she scoffed. "I'd best be getting back, Gid, and I want you to think about what I said. Ma might have missed her brother, but she'd be heartbroke if she'd known the trouble you're about to bring down on your head."

Gid stood and dusted the sand from the seat of his britches, and Maggie thought she'd never seen such a handsome man. Except for Cabel, of course, but they were so different, that hardly counted.

"You stay right here. Don't stray out of this grove, and I'll be back before you know it."

As if she would have risked being set upon by Meathook or one of his kind. Lord, what must the women of this island have to put up with. Like as not they went about armed with rolling pins and butcher knives.

Lying back in the shade of the cedars, Maggie breathed in their spicy fragrance and felt some of the tension drain from her body. It had been gathering for so long that now she felt almost let down. Of course her job was not done yet. She still had to convince her brother to turn his back on what he considered his obligation, but she'd given him something to think on.

Poor Gid. All his life he'd been bound by a duty to others. First Mama, and then Uncle Will. At least he wouldn't have to burden himself with her now. When would he ever have a chance to live his own life? What would he choose if he could?

What would she have chosen if through some magic she'd been offered anything in the world she wanted?

The picture that formed in her mind's eye was familiar—a snug house on the water, protected from the fiercest storm winds but open to the summer breezes. Children, food cooking in a fine oven, flowers everywhere and a garden flourishing under her care.

Only the man in the picture did not have gray-blond hair and a flowing beard. Instead his hair was black, drawn back from his dark, angular features and caught at his nape with a scrap of rawhide. His eyes were the color of pale honey, and his body was tall and strong and lean—a body that offered comfort, shelter and a wondrous excitement that made her grow warm just thinking about it.

To the west the sun bled out its life color as it slipped into its watery grave. The small boat reflected the color as it turned into the cul-de-sac of Hatteras harbor. Maggie had considered having Gid take her to Jedd's landing, but dismissed it as too risky. She could only hope the local men were anchored fast at their own supper tables so that she could slip in unnoticed.

A short distance offshore, several of the larger vessels, including the *Bridget*, rode at anchor. They appeared to be deserted. Pray that was true, for the last thing she needed now was to have one of the Rawsons present himself and demand to know where she'd been all day—and why.

Gid eased off the sheet and allowed the sail to flap uselessly as he came alongside the main wharf. Maggie had been silent during most of the voyage, dreading the coming confrontation. This time there would be Jedd to face as well as Cabe. What excuse could she possibly make for having walked out without a word to anyone? Jedd might be made to understand, but it would only give Cabe another weapon to use against her, and his arsenal was formidable enough as it was.

"Home safe and sound. Have you far to walk, Mag?"

"Not far. I'll be home before you're halfway out the channel," Maggie reassured him. Her belly was tightening up into a hard knot, just when she'd been priding herself on coming all this way without a single twinge of seasickness.

"A right handy little craft, ain't she? I might see if Barbara'll sell 'er to me when I get ready to leave the *Star*. She'd be good for fishing, oystering, or even smuggling. Knowing Barbara, she'd probably want to go along, though."

Barbara? Who was Barbara? He could have mentioned her on the way across the inlet, for the wind had snatched his words more than once.

But Maggie was far too distracted to waste time worrying over Gid's entanglement with some woman. She was sorely tempted to drag him home with her and introduce him to her family and be done with it. May as well get the thunder over with the lightning.

He lifted her onto the wharf and she turned to him impulsively. "Gid, come home with me—now. Don't go back at all. Jeremiah would take you on if I told him you were my brother, and we wouldn't have to tell anyone where you'd been or who—"

"Maggie, love, we've been through all that." He took her by the shoulders, challenging her to meet his eyes. "I've obligations to meet before I can go my own way."

The image of his beautiful, stubborn face shimmered through a window of tears as Maggie glared at him. "What about me? Aren't I an obligation? You promised—"

"I know I did, and it's fair killing me. I failed Ma. I can't fail Uncle Will, not when I'm the only one he can trust to—"

"But what about *me*?" she fairly shouted.

"You've your own man to look after you now. You don't need me anymore."

"I do *so* need you, Gid!" Sobbing openly now, she threw her arms around his waist and pressed her face against his chest. "I need you most of all. I worry about you. I've always worried about you, but now that I know you're mixed up with those—those awful p-pirates..." She broke off, unwilling to accept the threat of losing him again so soon after she'd found him.

"I'll be safe enough, love—leastwise, as safe as a body ever is in this world. Now quit ruining my new shirt and let me get on back before Barbara thinks I've run off with her boat."

With red-rimmed eyes and a trembling chin, Maggie stepped back and lifted her head. "If you get yourself killed, Gideon McNair, I'll never forgive you!"

"Then I'd best set about staying alive. Lord help me, I wouldn't want to get crosswise of your temper. You ain't improved all that much since you sawed the ears off ma's kitchen chairs for catching in your apron every time you walked past."

The memory of her childish rebellion brought a watery smile to her face, and Gid leaned over and kissed her wet cheeks, first one, then the other. "There now, that's better. I wouldn't care to have your husband coming after me for making you weep."

With reluctant acceptance, Maggie said, "He'll likely come after you, all right, but it won't be on my account. Gid, *do* be careful! I love you so, and if anything ever happened to you, I'd want to die."

Pressing his cheek against the top of her head, Gid held her, stroking her back and murmuring clumsy words of comfort. She was all he had. God knows he loved her more than anyone on the face of the earth, but he couldn't go with her now. She didn't need him, she only worried. She'd always been one to worry—quick to anger, but even quicker to forgive. "Don't waste your tears on me, little Magpie, I ain't worth it. Give me one last kiss to be going on with. I've a mind to sleep in a soft bed tonight instead of wandering up and down those infernal, 'skeeter infested banks, trying to find the mouth to Barbara's creek."

Slowly Cabel lowered the glass from his eye, his fingers gripping the brass tube with nearly enough force to dent it. He had followed the entire scene on the wharf once he'd recognized that crop of wild red hair in the bow of the sail skiff.

So that was the one. She'd followed him out from the main and waited her chance to join him. Yesterday he'd caught her at it, but today she'd succeeded. How many other times had she slipped away to meet her lover? Why had she settled on Hatteras instead of joining him on Ocracoke?

He'd have his answers, by God, if he had to flay them out of her one by one!

A cold, hard anger settled down over him as he thought of how she'd gulled them all—even him! After seeing her work the docks, knowing her for what she was, he'd let himself be taken in by her gentle ways and those lying green eyes of hers.

Carefully Cabe replaced the spyglass in its rack, every muscle in his body rigid with disgust. He felt all the savage blood of his forefathers rise up in him, stripping away generations of civilization. Reason argued that she was his father's woman, and nothing to do with him.

To hell with reason!

Instinct told him he could conceivably be misjudging her, and he damned himself for a weakling. His eyes could tell goose from gander before it even came within range of his fowling piece. Those same eyes had watched her on the docks of Bath, slipping in and out of the shadows to accost every drunken sailor who staggered by. And only yesterday, those eyes had seen her dressed in an outfit no decent woman would wear, headed hell-bent for leather to meet her lover.

Had she thought that just because her husband wouldn't bed her, she was free to take a lover? Not as long as she called herself a Rawson. He'd see her in hell first, and as for the scar-faced bastard she'd slipped away to meet, one day soon, Cabe promised himself, he would have the joy of slicing that mark off his cheek and handing it to her all done up in pretty ribbons.

No, he wouldn't soon forget that face. Nor the fact that the pair of them had conspired to deceive an honest and trusting man.

Dropping silently down the few steps into his cabin, Cabe grimly poured himself another tot of rum. He'd had more than enough already, for he'd been restless and moody all day. The fact that Maggie McNair was directly responsible for his restlessness only made it worse.

In his cups, he could no longer deny the truth. She had witched him good and proper. Even knowing her for what she was, seeing her as she'd looked that first night—filthy, pale, her nose all swole out of shape—she'd managed to work her spell on him. He hadn't been able to get her out of his mind, and then to come home and find her installed in his own house!

And the worst of it was, that even knowing all that, he still wanted her. She'd worked some wicked magic on him all right, and now his very survival depended on breaking it.

Moving none too steadily, he poured himself another shot, tilted his head and downed it in one fiery gulp. Where were the old sweat houses? Where were the potions and notions the old medicine chiefs used to use to drive out evil spirits? He'd heard the tales from his grandfather's people back when he'd scarce been big enough to understand the words, but the meaning had lingered in his mind.

Swearing softly, Cabe made his way topside once more. He stood swaying on his feet as he watched the tip of a gleaming sail disappear in the salt haze to the southwest.

Narrowed eyes reflecting the golden color of the sky, he made a promise to himself. One day he would seek out that curly-haired lover of hers and ruin his other cheek. And then he would murder the son of a bitch for the sheer pleasure of seeing Maggie's face when he told her what he'd done.

Chapter Sixteen

Not trusting himself to confront Maggie in his present frame of mind, Cabe remained aboard the *Bridget* that night. He drank too much, which was highly unusual, for knowing that he was responsible for the lives of some twenty men, he had long since learned the value of moderation. When his head grew thick with rum, he shed his clothes and dived over the side, swimming until his mind cleared.

And then he repeated the procedure. Drinking. Brooding. Swimming. In the old days, he would've whistled up his own horse and raced with his devils along the shore. Like the rest of the shaggy herd that roamed the island, the half-wild stallion, Cinnabar, had been trained to respond to one distinctive summons.

But Cabe had been too long away. By now, some other youth would have claimed his mount. Besides, which, he'd long since learned that a man can never outrun his troubles.

Had Pa thrown her out yet? Or had she lied her way out of it? What pretty little tale had she spun for him? Hoodwinked him with some cock-and-bull story of visiting a sick friend? One look from those big, sea-green eyes of hers, and a man might well believe the sun rose in the west and set in the east.

Sleep eluded him. His eyes grew sunken and red-rimmed, his thoughts ever darker. Pa had likely accepted whatever tale she'd told him by now, just as Matt or Jere would have accepted. Why couldn't he be as trusting?

Sometimes he wondered why he alone of all the Rawsons had been cursed with such a mistrustful mind. Isaac showed signs of it, but neither Pa, Matt nor Jere ever wasted much time searching for the truth beneath the truth. His grandfather had once told him that all men lived in three worlds at once—the world of What-Had-Gone-Before, the word of What-Was, and the world of What-Was-To-Be. Some men, he'd said, were unable to deal with so many realities, choosing to live only in one world at a time. Some of those men were called crazy, and were to be pitied. Others acted with reckless disregard of the consequences, bringing sorrow to themselves as well as to those who loved them.

Cabe had watched as his grandfather and the handful of his people who still remained on the island had been forced to accept yet another world—the world of the white man, in which they could never thrive.

It had been too long since he'd seen his grandparents. Instead of drowning himself in rum, which solved nothing and left him with a sore head, Cabe longed for his grandfather's quiet wisdom. Perhaps only a man like Kinnahauk, who had despised the English, yet married an Englishwoman, would understand the devils that tormented him now.

How was it possible to despise a woman and be drawn to her at the same time? Maggie McNair had set herself in his pathway, and nothing he'd been able to do could dislodge her. If she'd deliberately set out to ruin his life, she couldn't have done a better job of it.

She was not a part of his past world, Cabe told himself firmly, nor would she be a part of his future! Absently rubbing his belly, which was burning from an absence of food and too much kill-devil rum, Cabe told himself that she would not be a part of his present much longer, either. Pa was too soft for his own good. He tended to take the world as he found it, but Cabe was cut from a different bolt. As long as that woman was under his roof, flaunting her lovers under all their noses while she pretended to be all she was not, he would never rest.

Maggie fully intended to tell Jedd where she'd been and why, for she was full to bursting with trying to keep it inside her. She'd come to trust in his fairness, and she desperately needed his help, for nowadays, the very whisper of piracy was enough to get a man hanged, guilty or not.

Isaac met her as she came up the path. Distracted by worries and weariness, she didn't see him until he jumped out in front of her, waving a stick and crying, "Boo! I'm Blackbeard, and you're a goner!"

Catching her breath, she clutched her heart and glared down at the wicked little imp. "That's a dreadful thing to say, and what's more, you shouldn't go about scaring a body that way."

"Pa's gonna skin you alive for running off," he confided, sounding quite pleased at the prospect.

As if she hadn't considered that possibility, Maggie sniffed at the notion. "Oh, and is that what he does when you run off?"

"Nah—he fans my britches, but he don't take his strop to me, 'cause he knows I'm big enough to take care of myself."

"Well, so am I, and it's past time you were in bed." Guilt made her add, "Have you had anything to eat?"

"Blackberries and clabber. Got it myself. Pa ate some, too."

She'd left greens and bread and part of a joint of salt beef in the cool house—surely they'd found it there? More guilt descended on her, like the swarm of mosquitoes that whined about her unprotected parts. "I'm going inside before these 'skeeters carry me off. You'd best wash your hands and feet for bed."

"I ain't dirty, and 'skeeters don't bite me—I chew wild onions."

"Does it help?" she asked wistfully, scratching her neck.

"It won't help *you* none. You have to b'long here 'fore wild onions'll help, and you don't b'long."

Maggie took the enlightenment with a grain of salt. She'd seen Sara slapping and swearing at the pesky things, and if Sara didn't belong by now, having lived there all her life, then Maggie could never hope to.

Sara had already brought Eli home, and now he lay kicking on a pallet in the corner of the kitchen while Jedd and Ruben Quidley sat at the table with their pipes.

Maggie eyed Ruben warily. Had he known all along that she was aboard his shallop? Had he come to tell Jedd on her? Oh, Lord, what if he'd followed her and seen her meet Gideon!

But if he'd followed her, then surely he would have helped her when that wretch, Meathook, had attacked her, she reasoned, struggling under a burden of guilt and relief, worry and weariness.

"Well, lass, did you have a good day?"

"Good day?" she repeated blankly. With both Ruben and Isaac looking on with every evidence of interest, it was impossible to tell him what a wonderful, dreadful day she'd had. Instead she busied herself with Eli, lifting him up and nuzzling his fat neck. If she had to give him up, if Jedd turned her out after learning about Gid, she didn't know what she'd do. She'd come to love her new family almost as much as she'd loved her old one.

Jedd leaned over and took him from her, tossing him over his shoulder easily. "Boy's getting to be a big tote, ain't he? He ate a bate of food, and I bailed him out and went to put him down, but he commenced to grizzling some, so I brought him out again."

"Another tooth? He seemed all right when I—what did he eat?"

"Some o' them greens and a piece of cold meat. Ruben held him and I poked it in his mouth. He's a right hearty eater—seems like it weren't no time ago he was only good for milk and a bit of pap."

Maggie shook her head impatiently. "Just because he has a few teeth, that's no reason to think he can eat whatever you poke in his mouth."

"Ah, he'll not come to any harm, lass. Rawson boys is tough, else not a one of mine would'a made it. They ate anything that didn't move out of the way fast enough, and it didn't kill 'em."

She wasn't about to argue. "Yes, well . . . I'd better see to bedding him down."

"Aye, you do that. You look a mite peaked, yourself, don't she, Rube?"

The fisherman nodded silently as he pulled on his pipe, and Jedd rose and followed Maggie from the kitchen, carrying his sleepy son in his arms.

Maggie scarcely waited until they were alone. "Jedd, about today—"

"I'll not ask after your comings and goings, Maggie. If you've a mind to tell me, then I'll hear you out when I get back home."

"Home? But you're already here." Maggie felt as if the wind had been knocked from her sails. She'd been all wound up to unburden herself, knowing she could trust Jedd not to fly off the handle and condemn Gid out of hand.

"Once the moon rises, I'm headed out. Henry Austin come in from Edenton this morning with a load of cypress shingles, and him so sick with the ague he hardly had the strength to lie down. Them shingles was promised to a man up in the northern colonies more'n a month ago. I offered to haul 'em up coast for him while I'm waiting for Jeremiah to get done with Cabe and get onto the *Eliza*."

"But Jedd, can't we—I mean, I need to speak to you about a matter that's been on my mind for some time."

"Then it'll hold for a mite longer, lass. The tide won't. She'll be turning in another few hours, and if I can slip out under cover of night, I'll not have to worry about them bloodsucking pirates coming down on me."

Her disappointment not unmixed with guilty relief, Maggie persisted. "But don't you even want to know where I've been?"

"A woman has her needs, and a wise man gives her enough slack for 'em. Anne used to go off by herself now and again when the youngers got too much for her. Times she'd set out under a tree and stare out over the water all day. I learned early on not to go after her, for she was downright mean less'n she got her listening time. That's what she called it," Jedd said softly, his faded eyes focusing on another time, another woman. "Claimed there was this voice inside her a-wantin' to speak to her, and she a-needin' to listen, but shut up in the house with a mess of youngers, she couldn't hear thunder if it lifted her plumb off the ground."

"But Jedd, that's not—"

"You're back, lass. That's good enough for me."

Knowing it was useless to protest, that now was not the time to add to his worries, she said a little forlornly, "Please be careful, Jedd. I'm already missing you."

"That's right kindly of you, lass. I'd be much obliged if you could pack my bag. Cabe and Matt'll be here should you need anything afore I get back."

Wordlessly she nodded. Offhand she could think of nothing short of a disaster befalling one of the children that would make her call on Cabe for help. Nor would he, if he followed his usual pattern, go out of his way to seek her company. No matter what she did, it was wrong in Cabe's eyes. She seemed to strike sparks off him without even trying.

The sun rose in a blaze of white heat that promised squalls before nightfall. All day, while Jeremiah's men swarmed over the deck of the *Bridget*, Cabe paced, heedlessly scattering the curious workmen before him as he brooded over the puzzle that was Maggie McNair. He'd first laid eyes on her under the most damning of circumstances. No decent woman would dare set foot on the docks at night. Especially not alone. Not only had she come alone to a place where only whores, thieves, and sailors abided—most of them in their cups—but he'd watched with his own eyes as she'd accosted every man who passed by. She'd even tried to lure him off his ship.

After stealing passage, she'd gulled his father into believing he had to protect her good name with his own. And Sara had taken to her right off, as had Matthew and Eli. Hell, he'd even begun to soften, himself. She was a tempting little morsel, and plucky, too. And he had to admit she was a worker. There was something about her that got under a man's skin before he knew it and set up a fever that twisted his reason until he couldn't think straight.

But now he'd caught her—not once, but twice—slipping away to meet her lover. No wonder she'd been content to marry an old man who refused to touch her, with that young bastard slipping up the creek to meet her every time their backs were turned!

Cabe swore, more in pain than in anger. He should've let her go that first time. She'd have been swept out through the inlet and capsized as soon as she caught a breaker broadside, and Jedd could have worn a long face for a few days and then set about finding himself some decent woman to take over his household.

And you, Cabel? Would you have mourned her? his own voice silently mocked.

He shook his head in resignation. Damn her beautiful green eyes to hell and back, even now, knowing full well she wasn't worth it, he couldn't put her from his mind.

Ignoring the noise all about him as the carpenters rolled the gun carriage across the deck on a series of peeled saplings, he leaned on the weathered railing and stared out at the hazy shoreline. From here he could easily make out the main harbor, but Rawson's small landing was lost in the flat, featureless streak of marshland that bordered the sound side of the island.

With cruel clarity, his mind taunted him with pictures of Maggie bending over the oven. Or sitting on that old mended stool under the cedars, picking over dried beans and reaching out now and then to give Eli's hammock a swing. As he recalled the day he'd come upon her while she was washing her hair, his manhood began to stir, and he leaned over the rail and scowled at his reflected image.

The face of a fool gazed back at him.

A wife who was no wife, a woman who couldn't be faithful to one man if her life depended on it, and *still* he couldn't put her from his mind. And even if he succeeded in putting her from his mind, his traitorous body could not forget the way she'd fit in his arms, her naked breasts crushed against him and her wide eyes staring up at him in wonder, as if she'd never been so close to any man before.

Turning away, he swore in cadence with the tapping of hammers and the muttered grunts of the men who struggled against heat and mosquitoes to secure the gun in its newly constructed cradle near the stern. God help him, no matter how much he tried to deny it, there was no escaping the truth; Jedd had her, and Cabe wanted her.

He had known women before. Once he'd even asked one to marry him. Pricilla King had been a young woman from Virginia, wife of a man Cabe had sailed with his first few years at sea. Rolph had been a likable sort, but once he hit port, he'd been unable to stay away from the brothels. Neither beatings nor robbings had prevented him from frequenting the roughest districts of every port city in Europe and the Indies.

Cabe had paid her a visit of condolence as soon as he'd learned that Rolph had been robbed and murdered outside a Liverpool brothel. If she'd been ignorant of the circumstances of her late husband's death, he'd been determined she would remain so, for she was far too fragile and gently bred to withstand such a blow.

She hadn't wanted to discuss Rolph, and he'd contented himself with seeing that her house was in good repair and that the woman who lived with her had money enough for her needs.

Not until some six months later had he asked her to marry him. There'd never been anything resembling passion between them, but they shared a mutual need. Prilly wasn't thriving since her husband's death. While she didn't seem to be grieving outwardly, she'd lost weight she could ill afford to lose, and her color had faded until she looked more like a ghost than the smiling, pleasant woman he'd first met when he was in his teens.

She needed a man. And he needed someone of his own, someone kind and understanding, who would welcome him home after his voyages and bear him sons. And perhaps a few daughters, for he'd had enough of living in a house full of men. Prilly would be a fine mother to daughters. They would be sweet and well behaved, smelling of soap and lavender instead of fish bait and tar.

It was on a Christmas day that he'd asked her to marry him. Smiling a bit sadly, she had thanked him and declined. He'd argued, but she'd been adamant.

"Ask me again come spring," she'd said, but when spring had come, Prilly was dead. According to the old woman who looked after her—a distant cousin—Rolph had brought her an unwelcome gift from one of the seaport cribs. By the time the old woman had recognized the pox, it had been too late for any attempt at a cure. In her weakened condition, Prilly would never have withstood it.

He had had his share of mistresses since that time, and enjoyed them every one, being faithful to each in turn. He could say in all honesty that they had fared as well, for he'd been both a good provider and a skilled lover.

Yet he'd always held a part of himself in reserve. If now and then he dreamed of a woman who could fill the barren places in his heart, he knew better than to take such things seriously. He'd long been aware that there were thoughts in his head he'd never dared give tongue to for fear of being thought daft.

Cabe told himself it was senseless to be thinking such things. A grown man didn't waste time looking for a woman to share his dreams. What would such a woman say if he told her he wanted her to be a part of his three worlds—the one past, the one that was, and the one that was yet to be?

She'd likely run screaming off into the night, and he'd be the laughing stock of his whole crew. They were enough of a handful without that.

No, he'd best set about finding another woman to share his bed. And this time, he'd marry her. It was time he built his own house and started a family of his own.

But the image of a green-eyed wraith drifted between Cabe and his plans for the future. Maggie. The wind whispered her name, and the tap of the hammers echoed it.

Cabe swore and swore again. Dammit, Maggie McNair was *not* the woman of his dreams! She was naught but a faithless will-o'-the-wisp, blowing in the wind like some wild seed, content to bed down wherever she happened to land.

His mind knew all that, why couldn't he convince his heart?

Cabe groaned the following morning to see Sara and the two children in the longboat with Jere and two seamen, rowing out to the *Bridget*. Jere had planned an inspection that morning to see how the work was progressing, and Sara had threatened to come along, as that was all her menfolk talked of anymore.

"My, they're not very big, are they?" she declared, brushing down her skirts after having been lifted aboard. "Stop that running about, Becky Mary, you'll trip and break your—come down from there this minute! Amos, would you catch her before she gets too far up that ladder?"

Shifting the baby on her hip, Sara strolled about the deck while Jere conferred with his carpenters. Finding herself alone with Cabe near the bow, she began questioning him about the dangers of having the guns aboard with a crew who had never handled anything larger than a fowling piece.

"They'll learn," he replied, more interested in learning the answers to his own questions. "Sara, what happened the other day—that is, what did Maggie have to say about where she'd been?"

"Maggie? Why, not much, as I recollect. Where do you suppose that little scamp has got to now?"

"Dammit, Sara, stop trying to shield her! Two days in a row she sneaks off, and you not only *help* her, you cover for her afterwards! I'd have thought you had better sense!"

"Help her! What did I do to help her?"

"You took Eli off her hands without even trying to stop her, for one thing. Why the devil didn't you tell Pa or me she was fixing to run off?"

Sara's dark eyes snapped fire as she glared up her brother-in-law. She was no more intimidated by Cabe than she was by Eli, and what's more, it was about time some woman jerked him down a few rungs. "Now you listen here to me, you—"

"No, *you* listen for a change! Pa nearly lost his lights and liver out there, and she goes traipsing off like she didn't have a care in the world! You think that's any way for a wife to show respect for her husband?"

"Well, saints alive, it ain't as if she didn't do what she bargained for. There's always food in the cool house and a change of clothes fresh every week, and she keeps that baby bettern'n most women would. Come the day you have to lift a hand to feed your own belly or boil your own clothes, then you can rant all you want to, but Maggie don't need you to tell her when to sneeze and when to say grace."

"Where'd she say she was going? Did she tell you who she was going to meet?"

Sara scowled at an osprey that had dived and then lifted above the water, shaking his plumage dry before carrying a flapping bluefish off to his nest. Her lips remained tightly clamped.

"In other words, you won't tell me," Cabe said flatly.

"In other words, you yaller-eyed hard crab, I don't *know* where she went, and if she was fixing to meet someone, I never heard about it!" Spots of color appeared on her plump cheeks as she stepped right up under his nose. "What's more, if I *did* know, you'd be the last man on God's sweet earth I'd tell!

You've had it in for that poor girl since the first day she ever set foot on this island, and don't try to tell me no different! And if you think I don't know why, then you're even dumber than I thought, Cabel Rawson. I can spot a prowling tomcat quick's the next person!''

Cabe stepped back, his thighs striking the rail, and nearly overbalanced. Sara grabbed his arm, and her face softened. She loved all the Rawson men, but she'd always had a special place in her heart for Cabel. He alone seemed to take the world and its problems so seriously. Would he ever find what he was searching for? Did he even know? Most men contented themselves with what the Lord put in their path, but not Cabe. He was forever looking for something no mortal was meant to find. She only hoped he'd recognize it if it ever came his way.

Maggie had slept fitfully. Eli had been restless, and finally she'd taken him into bed with her, patting and lulling him while she pondered whether or not to confide in Matt or Jere. She hated this feeling of dishonesty, yet if word got out about Gideon's connection with Uncle Will and the *Star*, he'd be tarred with the same brush, and even if he gave it up and came to Hatteras, he'd likely be shunned as a criminal.

She'd thrown off the light cover, sweating in the humid heat. How could a body think when she could hardly catch her breath?

Morning had finally come, and with a discipline learned over many years, she dragged out the wash boiler and began filling it from the rain barrel. Thank goodness there were clouds over to the southwest. If she hung every bush and fence with wet shirts, Isaac's trousers, and Eli's napkins, it would be sure to rain. Then, for a few hours, it would be cool again. Poor Eli was suffering from heat rash as well as from his Pa's feeding.

"Salad greens and cold meat," she muttered. No wonder the poor child had fretted all night long!

With both the *Bridget* and the *Eliza Lea* in port, Matthew was at liberty. Maggie was poking more pine under the wash boiler, conscious every moment of the thickening sky, when he came out to join her. "Reckon you can get along without me tonight?"

"Reckon I'll manage to survive."

"Lina wants to go down to Ocracoke—her grandma's ailing. I promised to take her across and bring her back tomorrow evening."

Maggie didn't even want to think about Ocracoke. She'd made up her mind to tell Jedd everything as soon as he got home, trusting his fairness to hear her out without flying into a rage, as at least one of his sons would have done. "Did Jedd get off all right?" she asked, whittling shavings of soap into the wash boiler.

"Caught the tide right on the turn. Henry's old tub ain't got too much draft to her, but then, she weren't loaded too heavy. They say Teach's been hanging out just inside the bight of the Cape, waiting for them rich Yankee merchant ships to come down the banks."

"Oh, Lord, why couldn't he've waited until Cabe could have gone with him?"

"Pa'll be all right. He probably doused his lanterns and skimmed by right under the old bastard's warty nose. By now, he's likely halfway up the Chesapeake."

With another glance at the clouds that were beginning to pile into a threatening tower, Maggie set the first load to boil and went about her outside chores. She threw a handful of corn over the fence for the hens, shucked back a few more ears for Brownie, and stoked the fire under the oven. There was bread to bake, whether or not Matt would be there to share it.

"What time are you leaving? It's fixing to storm."

"I'll outrun the squall easy—just give me time to change into a clean shirt."

"What, just to sail across the inlet?" she teased. "You'll just get all hot and sweaty again, even if you don't get rained on."

"Awww, c'mon now, you know you like to see me looking all slicked up and handsome."

"When you're all slicked up and handsome, about the only thing I'm like to see is your backside disappearing through the door."

"Can I help it if I have to spend so much time down at the boat yard?" A gleam of mischief danced in his eyes.

"You know, you're a good brother, Matthew. All the time you spend helping out Jeremiah, and now you're willing to waste even more time ferrying Sara's little cousin back and forth across the inlet, it must pain you to be so obliging."

"Not half as much as it would pain me to be left here with Cabe. In the mood he's been in lately, he'd as soon heave me head foremos' over the side as pass the time of day."

Her expression must've given her away, for Matt began to chuckle as he held the door for her and followed her inside. "Don't let him rile you, Maggie. Ol' Cabe ain't half as bad as he looks." Waiting only long enough for her snort of disbelief, he added, "He's *twice* as bad!"

By dusk the rain had still not come. Nor had Cabe. Did he know Matt had gone? Did he know she was there alone, for even Isaac had gone home with Sara for the night as a special treat for Becky Mary's birthday.

Maggie didn't know whether to be relieved or disappointed. It was like a storm hanging over her—like the clouds that had built up all day, darkening until the sun was blocked out and even the birds had fallen silent.

She would have welcomed even his anger, anything to clear the air between them. Waiting had always been a burden to her, and sometimes it seemed as if she'd spent her whole life doing just that. Waiting. First for her father, then for Gideon, and now for Cabe.

She didn't even know why she was waiting for him. Jedd had said he'd be here if she needed him; Cabe had never said anything. She hadn't even seen him since the night he'd brought her home after her first abortive trip to Ocracoke.

And so she paced. And she waited. Every nerve in her body told her that a storm was about to break over her head. She'd just as soon get it over with.

The storm struck while Cabe was making his unsteady way up the path. He relished the head wind that made even walking a perilous business. He'd not meant to come home at all, but the more he'd thought on it, the more it had eaten at him. Dammit, a woman was no man's property until her bride price was paid! Pa hadn't paid so much as a copper for Maggie. He'd paid a hell of a bride price for Ma—old Kinnahauk had seen to that. If the old ways had been good enough for his forebears, they were good enough for him!

In truth, if any man had paid Maggie's bride price, it had been Cabel, himself. He'd tossed two coppers at her feet the first time he'd ever seen her, which was enough for a woman like her, a woman who went from one man to another like a bee on a honeysuckle vine.

How many horses had her blaze-marked lover paid out? How many canoe loads of oysters, how many pelts? A gold ring? Hell, no! The truth was that she was no man's woman. Any man could take her and walk away with no dishonor, for she was no maiden, nor was she the property of another man.

That had been the way of the Hatorasks since before the first white man had set foot on these banks. And tonight the blood of his mother's people simmered hotly in Cabe's veins.

As the wind shrieked through the trees, twisting the powerful sinews of the live oaks until they writhed in agony, Cabe's teeth shone in a feral smile. Rain lashed his face, stung his body, plastering his clothes to his skin—and he gloried in it. Knowing he would likely be drenched before he ever reached shore, he'd left his boots aboard ship. Now he moved silently and swiftly, his bare feet familiar with every root, every tuft of grass on the hard-packed sand trail.

Tonight he would break the web she'd spun, rid himself of the spell she'd cast that made him want her, even knowing what she was. She'd witched him so that he couldn't sleep, couldn't eat, couldn't think of anything but her soft, pale body, her sea-green eyes, and the red hair that flamed and enflamed until he knew he must discover the source of her fire and quench it before it consumed him.

Maggie had put out three of her new bayberry candles, their scent enriching the smell of smoked juniper walls steeped in a generation of living. Eli was fed and settled for the night, and she felt oddly restless. Worry, she supposed. It was hardly surprising.

Were Matt and Lina safe? Where was Gideon tonight? At sea, trying to keep his feet from slipping from under him and his belly from turning inside out? Was he out in the rain, or lying snug and cozy ashore in the arms of his friend, Barbara?

Suddenly the door burst open, allowing a gust of wet wind to enter. Leaning across the table where she'd been trying to see to darn a pair of Jedd's hose, Maggie shielded the flickering candles with her hand. "For goodness sake, shut the door!"

"Is that any way to greet your stepson?" A cruel smile curled Cabe's lips, but he did as she'd asked, leaning against the door with his bare feet braced widely apart, as if her freshly scrubbed kitchen floor were the rolling deck of a ship. He smelled of rum and salt air and rain, and there was something distinctly unsettling in the way he was looking at her.

"Cabel? Are you all right?"

He made no reply, but as he moved away from the door she could tell he'd been drinking far more than usual. His gait was slightly uneven, and there was an unholy glint in his eyes that sent a shiver down her spine.

She got to her feet, nearly upsetting her chair in her nervousness. "If you're hungry, I could set out some cold meat. And I made bread this morning. Have you had anything—"

"Don't talk, I don't want to hear your charming lies."

His voice was deep, rough, though not noticeably slurred. Maggie found her limbs frozen as she watched him come around the table to where she stood. "Cabe—please, what's wrong?"

"Why, nothing at all, dearling." His hands touched her throat, then slipped down to her shoulders, biting into her tender flesh. "Nothing that you can't cure." He dragged her roughly against his chest, where she struggled against a rising surge of panic. "Don't fight me, dammit!"

"No! Cabel, for God's sake!" Eyes widening in terror, Maggie clawed at his hands, but she was no match for his sinuous strength. "Don't do this," she whispered, twisting her face away when he would've taken her lips forcefully.

His thumbs pressed against the vulnerable flesh under her chin, hurting, threatening, frightening. "Kiss me, damn you. Don't deny me what you give so freely to others!"

Dear God, did he not know? Did he think she cared more for Jedd, and Matthew and even Isaac than for him? "Oh, Cabe..." She trembled as he jerked her hard against him, holding her as though he would never let her go. "Not like this. Not again. It isn't right."

"Don't talk to me of right and wrong," he growled. Once more he captured her chin in his fist, lifting her face slowly upward.

Maggie's heart raced as she fought to stand against a force more powerful than any storm. It wasn't fear, she told herself, that made her tremble in his arms. It wasn't fear that made her rise on tiptoes until she could feel his sweet, rum-scented breath stir her hair against her cheeks. Nor was it fear that elicited the low moan when she saw the reflection of her own pain and uncertainty in his fire-bright eyes.

As the rain beat against the side of the house, and the wild wind screamed around the corners, seeking entrance to their small haven, there was only one certainty in all the world.

Cabe's arms. Cabe's lips. Cabe's body against hers, his scent in her nostrils. His touch warming her until she glowed with an incandescence that outshone the glowing coals banked in the far corner of the fireplace, the sweet-scented candles on the table.

She felt the coiled tension in his body as he slipped her gown down over her shoulders, baring her for his pleasure. Unable to endure the sensations that swept over her as she watched his searing examination of her small, pink-tipped breasts, unable to withstand the strange melting feeling that touched the most unlikely places in her body, she closed her eyes. There was something wild, almost savage, about him tonight—something that sent a shiver of unease through her mind.

But it was her own treacherous memory that finally betrayed her. As his hands grew gentle on her face, slipped down her throat, over her shoulders, to move slowly down her back, he groaned and shook his head, like a man waking from a nightmare.

Was he remembering that other time, as she was? The time he'd come upon her in her bath and . . .

She caught her breath as she felt his hands cupping her breasts, pressing their soft weight while his thumbs stroked the cool slopes, barely brushing the sensitive peaks. Her knees threatened to give way. Feeling her nipples begin to shrink into tight buds of exquisite pleasure, she opened her eyes and stared down at them curiously, struck by the contrast between Cabe's dark, work-hardened hands and her own pale flesh.

"God in heaven," he breathed raggedly. Bending his head so that his rain-spangled hair brushed her chin, he nipped at the vulnerable hollow just above her collarbone. "*Roosomme wisto*...my own *waurraupa* witch!"

Gooseflesh rose along her flank, and her eyes opened wide at the strange-sounding words. But before she could ask their meaning, she felt his mouth close over the tip of one breast.

Nothing on the face of the earth could have prepared her for the sensations that swept over her. It was wildfire and honey. It was sparkling May wine and chain lightning. Her knees buckled, and just before she collapsed, he lowered her to the bare floor.

Maggie felt the grit of sand beneath her back. She was past caring. She knew little about what was happening to her; she only knew there would be no turning back. Drowning in the tide of passion he'd created the first time he'd ever touched her, she lifted her arms, and with a harsh groan, he lowered himself beside her, half covering her body with his.

The flickering glow from the hearth bathed her skin as he fumbled at the lacings of her skirt and drew it down over her legs, and she was shamed to have neither petticoat nor drawers. What must he think of her?

But then she forgot false modesty as he ripped off his own wet shirt and flung it into a corner. In the faint, shadowy light, she could see something straining against the front of his trousers, and suddenly she stiffened. Never in all her life had she felt so vulnerable. Right or wrong, she loved him. No longer could she pretend, even to herself, that it was not so. Whatever happened here tonight, there would be no going back.

Cabe leaned over and buried his face in her soft belly, and lightning streaked through her body. Part pain, part pleasure, it was so exquisite she could see it in her mind as it coursed through her limbs, touching her in secret places, melting her, leaving her breathless, trembling. In shock.

"Please Cabe, I can't bear it. I'm frightened!"

"*Sehe!* Don't talk." She felt the heat of his body reach out and envelope her like a warm hand.

Why was he speaking in that heathen tongue? What was wrong with him tonight? She lay stiff as a board, trembling helplessly as she watched him strip off his trousers, and then her eyes widened and she moaned.

How could she—no, it simply wasn't possible, she told herself, her gaze riveted on the fearsome thing that stood rooted in the darkness at the base of his belly.

"I can't," she whispered. "I could *never*—"

He silenced her in the most effective manner possible, by grinding his mouth down on hers.

It was a ruthless kiss. In the first few moments, Maggie tasted her own blood. She could scarcely breathe with his weight on her, but not until she began to pound on his back with her fists did he ease off to one side. Before she could roll away, he'd flung a powerful, copper-hued thigh across her hips and was turning her face back toward his.

"God, I can't think of anything but feeling me inside your sweet body, racing the swiftest tide of all! Open your mouth for me, dammit—you even *taste* like wildflowers," he accused, as his lips slid away from hers to trace the line of her jaw. "Sweet grass and honeysuckle." He expelled his breath in a long, shuddering sigh, both his voice and his hands growing gentle. "And your hair, like wild red silk, begging for my touch. Jesus, Maggie, why'd you have to come here? You're killing me!"

But before she could think of a response, he was kissing her again, and this time it was his gentleness that was her undoing.

With the tip of his tongue, he bathed her bruised lips, licking them lightly until she could stand it no longer. With unsteady hands, she reached up to touch his thick, damp hair, caressing his nape, his velvety ears, and the oddly soft skin at his temples.

And then it was Cabe who trembled. His tongue darted, and then he twisted his head to seal their lips, and Maggie gave herself up to the dizzying experience of being thoroughly seduced by a kiss. Lightning streaked through her body once more, jabbing again and again at the hidden place between her thighs until she was all but senseless.

"My little wildflower, my little shaman. Put your hands on me, I want to feel your touch," he murmured huskily.

Timidly she slipped her hand down his neck, over his shoulder, until her fingertips brushed against the thicket of silky hair on his chest. She heard him catch his breath. "Yes—there! And there... Don't hold back, Maggie, we both know what we're about.''

Cabe might know what he was about; Maggie had never been so lost in all her life, but it was far too late to turn back now. All she could do was hang on and pray that he would see her safely through to the other side.

Taking command of her hand, he guided it to the places where he most wanted to feel her, and Maggie wondered at the way he stiffened when her fingers raked across his nipples. Feeling the hardened points, she feared she'd hurt him, and she wanted only to please him. Driven by a compulsion she didn't even try to understand, she sought the tiny nuggets with her lips. Finding one hiding in it's silken nest, she raked it gently with her teeth, and Cabe's whole body shuddered. He shifted so that she could feel him pressing against her thigh.

And then his hips began moving rhythmically.

She moaned. As if she'd been tippling beyond her meager limits, she was caught up in the compelling rhythm. Soon her own hips were writhing in response. Of its own accord, her hand moved down his side, between their two bodies, toward that mysterious masculine part that burned so hotly against her. As if somehow sensing that it alone could bring her relief from this aching, this seeking, this great *need* that was throbbing inside her.

How could anything be so soft and yet so hard? she thought wonderingly.

Oh—had she hurt him again? He'd gasped as her hand closed around him, and she snatched it away. ''I'm sorry—I'm so sorry, I never meant to hurt you.''

Without a word, he took her hand and replaced it, pressing her fingers around his thick shaft. He muttered something under his breath, something that might have been either prayer or curse.

Tentatively she began to explore the different shapes and textures of him. What a strange thing a man was... so full of contradictions. Hard and soft, rough yet gentle, so cruel and sweet, seeming to despise her yet seeking her out to bring her this wondrous gift.

And then she felt his hand on her belly, and she gasped, drawing herself in as if to escape his touch. When his fingertip circled her navel, she began to whimper. "Cabe, please—I can't stand it!"

"*Sehe*," he whispered. "Hush." Gently removing her hand from his shaft, he gathered both her arms and drew them above her head, holding them there with one hand. Then he lowered his head and began to suckle her breast.

Maggie died. There was no more breath left in her body, so how could she possibly be alive? Yet when his tongue ceased circling the straining tips of her breasts and his mouth moved down to nip at the soft flesh of her belly, she drew in great, shuddering gasps of air and died all over again.

But there was yet another dying in store for her, one which she could never in this world have imagined.

First his hands prepared the way, caressing her trembling thighs until they willingly parted. Searching the nest of fiery curls, he unfolded the tender petals hidden there.

And then he kissed her until she was writhing helplessly, certain her heart would burst under such a strain.

"Oh, no, oh no, oh no," she moaned.

"Oh yes," he answered hoarsely, moving over her. Placing himself between her thighs, he lifted them around his hips and lowered himself probing with the tip of his manhood until he found the channel he sought.

And then he plunged. Maggie screamed, but the sound was lost as he covered her lips with his, driving his tongue deep into the soft hollow of her mouth even as he drove himself again and again into another vulnerable hollow.

Tears rolled unheeded down her cheeks. Gone was the magic, the wonder of what had happened to her, stripped away in one single terrifying moment of pain.

Cabe rode her hard, but the ride was mercifully short, for his obsessive hunger had been building for too long. As wave after wave of indescribable pleasure swept over him, burning the soul right out of his body until he was no more than an empty shell, he collapsed on top of her, allowing her to feel his full weight for a moment.

Consciousness slowly replaced his oblivion. Now maybe I can get you out of my mind, he thought as he felt her fragile softness beneath him. God knows, if this hadn't done it, nothing ever would.

When he could find the strength, he rolled off to one side. He was still stunned by the force of what had happened. Never had it hit him like this. No woman had ever carried him so high, to a place where he could look down on all the splendors of the earth, soar above the eagles, ride beyond the moon.

"Maggie? Are you all right?" Unwelcome doubts began to creep in when she made no response. Usually the women he'd bedded had wanted to cuddle afterward, hoping to lure him into another round of loving. And more often than not succeeding.

Her silence bothered him, and that fact in itself irritated him. His head was still slightly befogged by the rum he'd been drinking all afternoon. It had come over him gradually, the knowledge of what he must do to exorcize her from his soul.

She was no man's woman. No man had paid her bride price. She had taken other lovers—why not one more?

Ah, his inner voice whispered, but even a woman who belongs to no man is free to choose her lovers. Did she choose you? Or did you force yourself on her, like the damned rutting savage you are?

Restlessly Cabe rolled onto his side, and then he heard her quiet sobs. He closed his eyes as an anger that felt oddly like shame washed over him. Dammit, why should he feel shamed? It weren't as if he'd stolen something she hadn't given to dozens of other men. Or even worse—sold!

He frowned in the darkness, slowly coming to remember certain things he would have given his soul to forget. Like the momentary resistance he'd felt—or thought he'd felt—when he'd entered her.

Like the sharp cry that had escaped her lips just before he'd kissed her. Could he have imagined all that?

Of course he'd imagined it! Who ever heard of a virgin whore?

Chapter Seventeen

Maggie scooped a spade full of ashes into the iron pot, poured in a gourd full of water, and set it aside. So far, she'd burned two pots almost beyond salvation, and the day was only half done. Leaning on the handle of the spade, she gazed unseeingly out across the marsh and told herself that she hated him. She loved him and hated him all at once. He had cursed her, used her, taken her to within sight of heaven's gates and left her there, without a word of regret. Or even a word of good-bye.

"Damn you, Cabel Rawson, I hope you rot in hell." Her voice was bitter, her eyes deeply shadowed, but quite dry. She refused to weep over any man who could treat her with such callous disregard.

Inside the house, Eli experimented with a few new sounds before letting her know that his bottom was wet and his belly was empty, and he'd had quite enough of being alone.

With a sigh dredged up from the depths of her soul, Maggie stirred the potash with a stick of kindling wood and left it to eat away at the mess she'd made of Jedd's good iron pots. No matter how she felt about Cabe, no matter how much she wanted to run away and keep on running, she was needed here. The children needed her. Even Matt needed her—and she'd promised Jedd to stay.

There was more than enough work to keep her hands busy, but her wayward mind was not so easily distracted. She might be rocking Eli's cradle, humming an off-key lullaby while she darned a pair of hose, or baking a batch of molasses cakes that

Isaac professed to disdain but managed to devour by the dozens, when with no warning at all, Cabe would appear.

As clearly as if he were actually standing before her, she could picture the way his worn leather jackboots creased at his ankle, then skimmed his long, muscular limbs, hugging his calves before flaring out just above his knees. In her mind's eye, she could see the way his trousers stretched across his lean hips. She could actually smell the clean masculine scent of his body, see the glint of sun off his warm-hued skin, the diamonds of sweat glistening in the dark hair that spread across his chest.

Even the washpot was a reminder. As she poked a boiler full of napkins just coming to a simmer, she remembered the time he'd come home while she'd been struggling to lift a coverlet from the boiling pot with the end of her wash stick. He'd taken the stick from her, removed the coverlet and wrung it out, then spread it over the topmost branches.

"You'll burn yourself," she'd warned.

"It's too heavy for you," he'd told her, and she'd replied that Eli was heavier than a wet coverlet, and she managed to tote him without any trouble.

"But he's not dripping hot water," he'd reminded her.

"Often as not, he is," she'd retorted. It had been one of the rare times when they'd shared a genuine smile. It had been fleeting, the way the sunlight seemed to dance in his eyes when he'd looked directly into hers. The way his lips had twitched once or twice before parting to reveal his gleaming white teeth. As if he didn't want to smile, but couldn't help himself.

She'd tried telling herself it was only his way. Matt was an endearing tease, Jedd was kind and uncomplicated, Jeremiah was quiet, but a wonderfully considerate man. Even Eli exhibited a cheerful set of mind when he wasn't wet or hungry or teething. Cabe and Isaac were simply of a more somber nature. Over and over she had told herself that it had nothing to do with her.

But of course, it did. The truth was that neither one of them liked her; neither one of them wanted her there. And now Cabe had made it near on impossible for her to remain.

Yet how could she uproot herself again? She was stuck here. At least until Jedd returned, or until Sara felt able to take on Isaac and Eli for more than a few hours at a time—or until she'd gotten in touch with Gid and forced him to see that he had a responsibility to her as well as to Uncle Will.

Matt came home the next day, changed into his work clothes and left again, this time to help Lina's pa fence his garden to keep the deer from devouring his greens as fast as they sprouted. Isaac had been in and out a dozen times, and Maggie noticed to her amusement that each time, more of the molasses cakes were missing.

Of Cabe she saw nothing. Rather to her surprise, she was more relieved than sorry. She couldn't have faced him so soon after what had happened between them. It had been hard enough to come to terms with the fact that she loved him. It was hopeless. It was wrong, and she was heartsore over the whole miserable business, but she no longer tried to deny it.

Maggie was no simpleton. She knew that just because Cabe had—had done what he'd done, that didn't mean that he loved her, too. With his arms around her, it had been all too easy to let herself be swept into believing, but she'd come down to earth quickly enough when he'd walked away without so much as a backward glance.

She sighed now, thinking of what an ignorant fool she'd been. Cabe had made her feel things she'd never even known existed, and for a few brief moments, she'd dared to dream. But then he'd hurt her. And even before the physical hurt had ended, he'd got up, pulled on his clothes and left her there, limp and aching and utterly shattered. And that had hurt more than anything.

"Bye-oh, my ba-by, bye-oh, my ba-a-by," she crooned. Eli lay hot and heavy in her arms, smelling faintly of soap and milk and sun-dried garments. Wisps of straight, dark hair clung damply to his pink scalp, and she gazed down at the silky fringe of black lashes that fanned across his plump cheeks, pretending for a moment that he was her son, not Anne's. And that Cabe, not Jedd, was his father.

Matt brought word that evening that the *Bridget* was finished and that Cabe had taken her out on a trial run, and Maggie felt the knot inside her grow just a bit harder, a bit colder. He had not even come home to tell her he was leaving. What plainer way to show his contempt?

"Did he say how long he'd be gone?" she asked quietly, trying hard to keep the hurt from showing in her voice.

"No more'n a day or two. Just long enough to be sure he can maneuver without fouling the running rigging or tripping over one o' them gun carriages. We ain't used to having the rail side cluttered."

"The whole idea is crazy," she grumbled. "If you ever have to use one of those awful things, you'll probably forget which end is which and end up shooting your own sails full of holes." Maggie hated conflict. She saw no reason for it, but that hadn't kept conflict from dogging her footsteps like a persistent shadow for practically all of her eighteen years. Even the fact that her own father had sailed safely around the Horn a dozen times and then come home only to run afoul of a stray arrow when the war was all but ended was proof of what an insane place the world was becoming.

Haunted by what he'd done, Cabe managed to focus his mind on the business at hand during the daylight hours, but on the endless night watches, when all slept save the few needed for the safety of his ship, he brooded. If he could have erased that entire event from both their lives, he would have done so. If he could have thought of words that would make up to Maggie for the grievous injury he'd inflicted on her, he would have knelt at her feet and sung them until he turned blue for want of air.

Lacking the words—indeed, lacking the courage—he stayed away for three days and four nights. Then, with a cargo bound for Barbados waiting in a warehouse across the sound and the storm season already upon them, he headed in to collect his full crew.

They met outside Sara's gate. Maggie had gone in search of Isaac, and Cabe was on his way home to say what had to be said before he sailed.

For a long moment he could only stare. The easterly wind had turned her bright copper hair to a riot of wayward curls. In her small, flushed face, her eyes were like the clear waters of the Indies with sunlight dancing in their pale green depths.

"Maggie, I—" His voice rough, he cleared his throat to try again. Yet, even as he watched, the color faded from her face, leaving each tiny freckle standing out in bold relief. Her mouth opened as if she would greet him, but then she clamped her full bottom lip between her small white teeth, and Cabe felt the sweat breaking out on his back.

God, she was so small! Standing there as boldly defiant as if the wind couldn't lift her off her feet and hurl her away, as if she hadn't been half dead the first time he'd ever seen her. Yet from some source he could only imagine, she had found the strength to defy the very fates.

"Maggie, I'll be headed out again directly." *Tell her you're sorry, you bastard! At least give her the words, for you can never give back what you took from her.*

"Will you be wanting to see the youngers before you sail?" Her voice was as calm as the creek on a midsummer morn.

"Aye, I'll have a word with Sara and then I'll be along home."

"There's food a-plenty." She seemed to be looking him directly in the eyes, but when he tried to read the thoughts behind her prosaic words, he realized that her gaze was unfocused.

"I'll not trouble you, Maggie. I only wanted to have a word with the boy before I set out."

Cabe's eyes narrowed as he saw her swallow hard and turn away. He would've given a fortune to know what she'd been thinking, but he hadn't the courage—nor the right—to ask.

Half an hour later, Maggie watched as Cabe and Isaac trailed up the path together. Instead of coming inside, they went around the house to where Eli napped in his hammock. From the kitchen, Maggie watched as Cabe lifted the infant and then sat on the white sand, dandling him on his knee. Isaac perched on the old milking stool, and the two of them seemed to be talking while Eli chortled and waved his fat fists about.

Gazing wistfully out the window, she wondered how any man could be so tender and understanding with a babe and a troubled child, and at the same time, so distant toward someone with whom he'd shared the most intimate act possible between a man and a woman. If she lived to be a hundred, she would never understand how he could have forgotten so quickly. Her own conscience had bedeviled her until she'd scarce been able to sleep or eat. She had sinned against her marriage vows, and Maggie was not a woman to take sin lightly.

And yet it hadn't seemed like a sin when it was happening.

Cabe strolled into the kitchen, where Maggie was bottling the blackberry conserve she'd made earlier. "You'd best take him, for he'll not stay in his hammock now that he's wide awake."

She dried her hand on her apron, avoiding Cabe's probing gaze, and took the heavy child from his arms. When she would have turned away, he stopped her with a hand on her shoulder that burned right through the worn stuff of her gown.

"Maggie, let me say this, and then I'll go."

There was no way she could have hid the way her heart leaped into her throat at the tenderness in his deep voice. She dared not meet his gaze for fear he would know, and if he knew, he would hold her in even lower esteem.

"I'm sorry. No matter what, you didn't deserve to be treated like a—" Swearing under his breath, he let his hand fall away from her shoulder.

Maggie was trembling so hard she was afraid she would drop her wriggling burden. "Yes, well, you'd best go now. Tell Isaac he's not to run off again before dark."

"Maggie, won't you—"

"You'd best hurry—the tide . . ." she said in a soft rush of words, and was both relieved and hurt when she heard him slam out the door.

Isaac had evidently been waiting nearby, for she heard his rare young laughter ring out quite clearly. Laying the sodden infant down on the chest to change his napkin, she told herself that the ache in the boy's heart was beginning to mend.

Perhaps in time her own would mend as well.

Three days later, word came that Henry Austin's sloop, which Jedd had sailed north, had been attacked off the Virginia capes on the homeward journey. This time, there'd been no mistaking the identity of the attacker, for the whole episode had been witnessed by two fishermen.

The *Morning Star* had been headed north when she'd come upon the sloop riding high in the water. According to the fishermen, who'd been terrified that they, too, would fall victim, Lewis must have known she was carrying little or no cargo, but with the cruel arrogance for which his quartermaster had become noted, he'd taken her simply because she was there for the taking. The schooner had been completely unprepared, for her owner had been one of the last to order guns. Ironically they were the only cargo carried on the return voyage, but crated against the weather and lashed securely to the deck, they'd been totally impotent.

The *Star* had been on a trial cruise, testing her newly raised and reinforced sides and her flush cabins, according to the information pieced together from witnesses and from several of the Ocracokers, who'd come forth as soon as word had spread along the banks. Fully ballasted, she'd easily outmaneuvered the smaller vessel, raking her again and again with a barrage of iron, nails, broken glass and explosive balls from her bank of twenty-pounders. Half the two-master's crew had been dead or maimed by the time the *Star*'s men had swarmed aboard.

"Lord bless us, he's gone." It was the first Maggie heard of the tragedy. She'd been in the backyard stirring a pot of fig conserve when a delegation from the village, led by Sara, had come to break the news.

"Them filthy murdering bastards sent ever' single of 'em to the bottom," someone hurried to explain.

"May Will Lewis and that Turk o' his rot in hell!"

Maggie looked from once face to another, seeking a denial. *Uncle Will—Gideon.* Oh, dear God, no! The earth suddenly tilted under her naked feet, and closing her eyes against pain and disbelief, she stood there, syrup dripping on the sand from the bowl of her wooden spoon. *Not Cabe. Please, God, don't take him from me. I'll never look at him again with sin in my heart, but don't let him be dead.*

"I'm sorry, Miz Rawson. Ain't none of 'em coming back. Them Virginians had a glass on 'em the whole time. Saw him go down right off."

"But there could've been a mistake—they can't be sure."

"Jedd was the onliest man aboard with a gray beard. At least they didn't—what I mean is, sometimes them bastards sets the officers aside and tor—"

"For God's sake, Thomas, stow it!" someone growled. "Ma'am, what he means is that Jedd didn't have time to suffer much, if that's a comfort to you."

Jedd! Oh, please—no. Not her friend, her anchor. Her beloved companion. Dear Lord, it couldn't be true. He'd only been doing a favor for his cousin. A man didn't die for helping out his kinfolk.

Maggie began to shake. Swaying on her feet, she struggled with crushing waves of grief, fear, relief and guilt—grief for Jedd, fear for Gid, relief that Cabe had not been taken from her. And guilt at feeling such an overwhelming sense of relief.

Suddenly it was all too much. With scarcely a whimper, she crumpled to the ground. Emma Gaskins was beside her in an instant, cradling her head. "Here, Douglas, tote her into the house for me," the midwife ordered gruffly, and a young man with drenched eyes and an unsteady chin stepped forward and lifted her carefully in his arms. "Where's Cabel?" Emma muttered. "Jeremiah, go after Isaac. He don't need to be alone with this burden, and him not even over losing his ma yet."

It was Matt, his face a sickly shade of gray, who followed Isaac down to the landing. Jeremiah and Sara took Eli home with them, and after a while the others left, promising to return. They went in small groups, the women weeping and supporting one another, the men stony-eyed and silent. It was too soon to be speaking of revenge, but it was in their eyes, in the set of their shoulders and the curl of their fists. Not a single household was untouched by the tragedy. Mothers would mourn their sons. Wives would weep and try to comfort their fatherless children. Brothers and sisters would draw closer, feeling the circle narrow about them.

Almost guiltily, the crew of the *Eliza Lea* avoided looking directly at one another, for all were thinking the same thought. If Jedd had taken his own crew instead of the men who regularly sailed Henry's schooner, not a one of them would be here today.

Emma stayed the night. Maggie had revived even before Douglas had lowered her onto the bed, but Emma didn't like her color, nor the strange, wild look in her eyes. God knows, grief was a fact of life, but there'd been something more than grief in Maggie's eyes the moment before she'd collapsed. Lord help the poor thing if Jedd had left her with a babe in her belly.

Maggie was up with the sun the next morning. When Emma opened her eyes, having napped on a pallet dragged in from the back bedroom, she was going out the door with the milk pail.

"Child, you don't have to do that. Eli's with Sara, she'll see he don't go hungry."

"Brownie expects me. She'll get swole if I don't milk her first thing."

"That wore out old bag o'bones don't give more'n a teacup full on 'er best day, and you know it. Good thing you started the boy in on food. Most don't start feeding until at least the first year's past, but I say if they can get it down and keep it down, it ain't likely to hurt 'em. Don't give him rum less'n he has trouble with his gums. There's some says I'm daft, but I'm right partial to water for drinking, and I ain't sickened from it yet."

Maggie went about her chores, moving as if she were asleep. Emma's words poured over her half-unheard. She wished the woman would leave and allow her to think. She needed to come to terms with what had happened.

Where was Matt? Where was Isaac? Where was Cabe?

Oh, God, where was Gid? Had there been many losses aboard the *Star*? Who could she ask? *How* could she ask?

That night there were four of them under Jedd's roof. Matt and Isaac in the back bedroom, Eli and Maggie in the front. All the next day neighbors came and went, leaving gifts of food and words of comfort. Like as not, the food would spoil before it was eaten, for Maggie knew she would choke if she tried to force down a single morsel. Matt had been crying again. His eyes were red and swollen, and ever since they'd learned that with the help of the Virginia fishermen, some of the bankers had recovered most of the bodies and were bringing them back home for burial, he'd stayed off to himself.

Isaac had disappeared again. Maggie noted the fact and then moved through the crowded room until she located Sara. "Would you listen out for Eli? Isaac's run off again, but I think I know where to find him." No matter how much he resented her, she couldn't leave him alone with his grief now. He was too small to bear such a burden alone.

If only Cabe were home. Dear Lord, how they needed his strength!

Her own eyes were burned dry by now, for she'd shed a lifetime of tears. For Jedd, who had been her good friend during the brief time they'd been together. For Cabe, who had yet to hear the news. And for Gideon, who had cut himself off from her forever with this barbarous attack.

Maggie made her way swiftly to the hilltop overlooking the sound. There, just as she'd suspected, she saw a small figure sitting forlornly beside the cypress headboard, tracing the carving with a grubby finger. His face was streaked with dirt and tears, one sleeve of his shirt was wet, and he'd torn the knee of his best trousers.

How in God's name had she managed to fall in love with two such difficult males? This child, who defied her at every turn, who rejected her every overture, and who despised her for no reason that she could divine, other than that she was not his mother!

And the other one, who despised her for reasons that were even more obscure. Was there something about her that brought out the worst in men? Perhaps even Zion and Nimrod would not have been so hateful had she been any other woman.

"Isaac, I know where there are some wild roses. It seems to me your mother would be right pleased if you were to set some out up here on her hill."

The boy ducked his face, ignoring her. She tried again, forcing her voice to a steadiness she was far from feeling. "I made circlets out of honeysuckle for my mother's grave. My ma didn't have a headboard. I was meaning to plant buttercups there, too. Do buttercups grow here? I haven't found any."

"I hate buttercups. I hate you, too."

"I know, but I reckon if your pa were here, he'd want us to try to be friends now. It troubles your brothers to see us fighting like this, and these next few days are going to be hard on them. Matt goes off by himself, and I don't know what to do or say to make him feel better. Maybe you do?"

"I hate Pa, too. He shouldn't have gone off and left."

Maggie sank down on the scraggly grass beside the forlorn little figure. He'd been down on the sound side. She could smell the mud mingled with the little boy smell of his skin. Funny how a body could come to know a person by their scent. "I expect he just missed your ma too much, Isaac. We used to talk into the night, and he told me so many times what a wonderful woman your ma was, and how he'd never have taken me to wife if he hadn't thought Anne wanted a woman in the house to look after her babies.''

"I ain't a baby!"

"No, you're growing like a weed. Like one of those wild rose bushes I was telling you about. One day it's a little bitty sprout, so small you'd scarce notice it, and the next it's climbing over everything to get to the sun, all full of pretty pink blossoms.''

"I don't like flowers, neither," he mumbled, twisting a stem of grass around his fingers. "First thing they do is go and die on you, just when you get to—" he swallowed hard, and it was all Maggie could do to keep from gathering him onto her lap "—to liking 'em!"

"You mean the petals fall? But that doesn't mean they've died, Isaac. It only means they've passed on to another stage. If flowers bloomed forever, they'd never bear fruit. Then there'd never be any more flowers. Fruit and nuts and seeds can't be born until the petals fall.''

"Why?"

Why? Dear Lord, how had she gotten into this subject? She didn't know how to talk to an eight-year-old about anything, much less about death and grief and such. She wasn't at all certain she understood it herself.

But one thing she did know about boys, about children of every age—they could never resist a secret. And Maggie had a secret that was burning a hole in her heart!

"Can you keep a secret, Isaac?"

He cut his dark eyes her way, and his small fingers grew still. "'Course I can keep a secret," he muttered. "Jimmy blabs ever'thing, but I know lots of secrets.''

"Well, if you'll promise not to tell Jimmy, not to tell anyone, I'll tell you my secret," Maggie confided, lowering herself until she was stretched out on her belly beside him. She propped her chin in her fists and whispered, "I've got a brother, too. I reckon you didn't know that, did you?"

Isaac plucked up a withered weed and flung it away in disgust. "That ain't no fitten secret!"

"It is so a fitten secret, because we're the only ones who know.''

"Who cares about your old brother? I bet he's mean and nasty and ugly. I bet don't nobody like him, and—and I bet he has to wear a stinkbag 'round his neck on account of night sweats.''

Maggie didn't know whether to laugh or cry. But one thing she would not do was give up. Gid might be lost to her, but she would see to it that someone, at least, remembered him with kindness and admiration. "He's the kindest brother ever a body had, and what's more, he's tall and handsome and the angels kissed his cheek when he was born and left a strawberry there, and—''

"A real one?''

Noting that suspicion had been supplanted by a reluctant interest, Maggie went on to tell Isaac about Gideon's boyhood triumphs, and even a few of his disasters, drawing a small chuckle from him on one occasion.

Heartened, she confessed that the reason his existence must be kept a secret was that his life might be in danger if anyone learned of his whereabouts. "For he's vowed to protect a kinsman," she confided. "And until he's freed from his vow, no one must know where he is.''

"But we do," Isaac boasted.

"That's right. And now, let's talk about the roses we're going to set out up here on the hill after your Pa's laid to rest tomorrow." She could actually see him withdrawing again. "Pink roses?" she pleaded.

"I hate pink.''

"Buttercups?''

"I hate buttercups.''

"Dandelions, then—you like them because they're all around the edge of the garden patch.''

"I blow their heads off," the boy said belligerently, as if regretting his earlier lapse.

"So do I. And that's all right, because that's what they're for. It just means there'll be more dandelions come another spring, because wherever the wind blows them, they flourish.''

"What's flursh?''

"Thrive. Take root and blossom. They're one of God's gifts to the earth, like tiny little suns scattered all over the ground.''

"Can we blow some seeds up here now?''

"Tomorrow, after your pa comes up here to join your ma, we'll cover the whole hill with dandelion seeds so that next summer it'll look just like a bright yellow blanket."

For a moment she thought he was going to shut her out again. His small face grew pinched, the tip of his nose suspiciously red, but then he stood up and held out his hand. "I reckon we'd best start c'lecting them seeds before Eli commences to hollering for his supper."

"Let's go fetch something to carry them in, else the wind'll blow them away fast as we pick them."

Hand in hand, they walked down the hill, following the narrow sandy path that was bordered by scrub oak and yaupon. Maggie's eyes were blurred with tears, and she kept them cast down, hidden from the child who jogged along beside her. Not until they were almost at the edge of the clearing did she glance up.

With a joyous cry, Isaac broke away from her, running to throw himself into the arms of the man who stood there, watching them through pain-dark golden eyes.

Chapter Eighteen

The house was never empty. From the time when they'd first gotten word of Jedd's death to the day of the burial service, the villagers gathered there to mourn and to comfort. The men migrated toward the landing, as was fitting. Maggie had wondered aloud why they congregated at the Rawson place and not at the homes of the others who had been lost.

It was Sara who supplied the answer. Jedd had been the captain.

The women were everywhere—cooking, washing, taking over Maggie's chores as if she'd suddenly ceased to exist, as if a body didn't need the endless demands of everyday living as an anchor when all else seemed in danger of being swept away.

Matt took to staying aboard ship, but Cabe remained stoically at home, as befitted the new head of the household. As for Isaac, most of his waking hours were spent on the shore, poking idly at the piles of dried eelgrass that had washed up there, flailing the saltwater grass with his stick, or simply sitting and staring out across the water. Now and them Maggie would find him standing silently beside her. He would run off again without speaking, but she would be warmed by the brief contact.

Maggie grew desperate. It showed in her long moments of utter stillness, moments in which she hardly seemed conscious of the chattering voices all around her. It showed in her eyes, which appeared larger than ever, surrounded as they were by dark shadows.

Cabe saw the look and wondered at it. There was something wild about those eyes, something bewildered, like an injured animal that was unable to comprehend the source of its pain.

His own pain caused him to strike out blindly. She had no goddamn *right* to mourn Jedd Rawson, he told himself. They'd been scarce more than strangers, even if they had shared a bed. Why should a woman like Maggie, who was young and beautiful enough to win the heart of the devil himself, why should she pretend to have loved an old graybeard like Jedd, who'd snored and belched and farted, who'd told the same old stories over and over, with the same gestures, always breaking up with laughter in the same places?

God, he was going to miss that old man! They'd had their share of troubles, what with Cabe rebelling at every turn, determined to test his own strength. From the time he'd been Isaac's age, he'd been bound to make his own mistakes. He'd sorely tried the old man's patience too many times to remember, but the bond between them had held fast.

Although now that he thought back, it had frayed a time or two. Like the time when he'd been about ten, and had accidentally stampeded a herd of wild ponies right through the middle of King's Point, flattening damn near every lodge in the village. And again when he'd almost lost the *Eliza Lea* by racing that French sloop through the inlet at low tide that time Pa had been down with a fever. Not to mention the time he'd got himself stranded aboard a floating whorehouse in Jamaica when he was fifteen and, thinking he was asleep in the fo'c'sle, they'd sailed without him.

It had been spark-to-tinder the night Pa had come home unexpectedly and walked in on him and Maggie. He'd been damned lucky the old man hadn't taken out after him with his fowling piece. Not that Pa's conscience had been setting any too easy on that score.

God, what a muddle! One of them wanting her, one of them claiming her, and her off lying with some blaze-marked bastard, making fools of them both!

Much as he'd wanted to at the time, Cabe could hardly blame his father. If the poor old man had gulled her into a false ceremony, it was only because he'd been chafing to get back to sea where he belonged. Some men were like fish out of water between voyages, restless without a deck under foot.

It should have been easier once he'd learned the truth. At least he hadn't been forced to spend every night wondering what was going on with the two of them closed up in that bedroom. Pa had confessed that he'd never laid a hand on her, and Cabe had to believe him.

But he hadn't stopped wanting her. If Pa could have brought himself to send her packing, they'd both have been better off. But he hadn't. Now Pa was gone, and it was far too late for Cabe to save himself. He would go after her lover and carve him into a hundred small pieces, he told himself. The thought brought a wintery smile to his face, the first since he'd heard the news of the attack and come rushing home, leaving half his cargo on the wharf at Edenton.

But even as the smile faded he knew he couldn't do it. She'd come to enough grief through the Rawsons—he could never bring her more.

The heat had already grown oppressive by the time they gathered at the grave site for Jedd's burial service. Around the deep sandy pit, wild blossoming vines tumbled over the nearby trees with irreverent exuberance, and the smell of spices lay heavy on the air.

Jedd's was the first. Afterward the villagers would lay to rest each of the other crew members in turn, moving in a group from one house of mourning to the next. Likely they'd not be done before sunset, but it couldn't be helped. The only ones missing were the two sail makers who had sewn the recovered bodies into canvas bags. Word had it they'd quietly drunk themselves into oblivion.

From the looks of the man who stepped forth to say the words over Jedd, he would much rather have joined the sail makers than face the task ahead of him. Maggie stood stiffly beside Cabe and Matt, with Sara and Jeremiah and their youngers on her other side. Cabe held Isaac's hand, but she drew comfort from Eli's warm body. Her best gown was freshly washed, thanks to someone from the village, and a sprig of some sort of evergreen had been tucked into the neck. Sara had given her a bonnet and a pair of new drawers, and Matt had blacked her boots along with his own and Isaac's.

Her dull gaze moved over the speaker and then returned. She frowned as something tugged at her memory. She'd seen him before, but where? Who was he? In his ill-fitting black suit, which had faded out to a rather unfortunate shade of purple, he looked startlingly like a plucked buzzard, with his beaky nose, his red, sweating face, and his long neck.

"Jedd Rawson were a good man," the speaker intoned. "He weren't a one to lie or cheat. Most times, he didn't even lock his crew up when he hit port. He knowed we'd be there come time to sail, if we had to drag one 'nother aboard." He swallowed, and Maggie stared, fascinated, at his prominent Adam's apple.

Where *had* she seen him before?

The words droned on, and Maggie, shouldering Eli and clutching a bunch of wilting beach daisies, swayed on her feet. She should have eaten something today—yesterday. How long had it been? She'd lost all track of time.

"—didn't need no astrolabe nor no compass. You could set him down on the darkest night in the middle of any sea, and he'd find his way home straighter'n a snow goose. Had the feel of it in his bones. Some men does—most don't. Jedd did. Wherever he's a-headed, I ain't got ary a doubt in my head he'll make it. Ol' Jedd could whistle up a wind in hell."

A deep, rusty voice lifted from the congregation. "Cracka mast, pecka meal, one aig."

A shiver ran down Maggie's spine as a ragged chorus of Amens rose around her. Almost as if in response, a light breeze stirred the leaves, tilting their pale undersides for a moment. She glanced in bafflement at Sara, who was weeping openly. "T'was Jedd's way of calling up the wind," she whispered, and Maggie tried unsuccessfully to swallow the painful lump in her own throat.

The momentary breeze had died, and Maggie told herself she'd only imagined it. She blinked away the spots that danced before her eyes and looked downward as someone tugged on her skirts. Isaac, his tear-stained face more solemn than ever, was holding up a bunch of short stems with a few straggling seed heads attached. Most had been blown in the plucking.

She glanced at her own withered bouquet, and something flickered in her mind. The homely red face of the man in the dark suit. Another bouquet, stiff yellow wildflowers hastily gathered on the shore just before she clambered into a long-boat to go...

Memories rushed in of a young woman clutching a prickly bouquet—hurting, terrified of the future and trying not to show it. And of a gray-bearded groom, grim and more than a little intimidating.

The service was over, and already the villagers were moving away. Leaning over, she whispered, "Isaac, wait for me right here. I'll tell Matthew we're staying behind, and then I'll bed Eli down."

But first she needed to speak to Sara, who would go on to a few more of the services before going home. Women with small children weren't expected to follow the procession all the way to the last grave site. Some of the babes were already grizzling, being lulled with sugar tits and kerchiefs sopped in rum.

Maggie waited for the others to pass, the men with an embarrassed nod and the women with a brief embrace or a word of comfort. Sara handed Charity Ann over to Jeremiah and slipped an arm about her shoulders. "You looked plumb beached, Maggie. Why don't you stay here? If you want me to set with you, I will. Jere can go on and stand in our stead, him and Cabe. No one expects you to go through it again today."

"I'm all right, Sara. I'll catch up, but first there's something I need to do with Isaac. I promised him."

"Stay with him, then. Lor' knows he needs you, and there ain't a thing you can do for the others. They understand."

"Sara, wait—who was the preacher? What was his name? I think I've seen him before."

"Gaffer Hooks? I reckon you have, he's Jedd's—that is, he *was* Jedd's bos'n. They go way back. Poor old Gaffer, I don't reckon he'll sober up again in many a day."

"But—but he's an Anglican, too, isn't he? Along with being Jedd's bos'n? I've heard of some that farms and preaches. This man Hooks *is* a real—I mean, he *does* have the power to..." Her voice trailed off uncertainly.

"Gaffer Hooks? Lor', girl, where'd you ever get that notion? The only thing Gaffer is, besides being Jedd's mate, is a rip roaring old sot. Many's the time I've heard Jedd say that drunk or sober, Gaffer can shinny up a mast faster'n a cat up a tree. Oh, I'll not deny that Jedd set a lot of store by him, but on dry land, that old croak's about as reliable as a crowing hen.''

Maggie was in no condition to deal with ambiguities. "Well, is he or isn't he?''

"A preacher? He ain't.''

"But Sara, Gaffer Hooks is the same man who married us," she said, desperation widening her eyes until the whites showed all around. "He couldn't do that unless he was Anglican, or at least a justice, so you must be wrong about him. Maybe when he was younger, before he took to sailing. I remember he had on that same suit—''

"Took it off'n a corpse. It don't mean nothing.''

"—and it was only May then, but I was thinking how hot the poor man must be in all that wool, and me feeling miserable because I didn't even have a petticoat to hold out my skirt.'' The sun beat down on her borrowed bonnet, and Maggie felt a trickle of sweat start just between her shoulder blades and work its way down to the waistband of her stiff new drawers. The air was so still and heavy that even the birds were silent.

"Maggie, are you sure?'' Sara demanded.

Miserably she nodded. "Jedd took me out to his sloop. He said we had to hurry because the preacher was sailing on the top of the tide, but I made him wait while I picked some of those prickly yellow flowers. He said there wasn't time to fetch you or anyone else, so we had to make do with a witness who was too drunk to stand up.''

Sara sighed. She shook her head, sympathy struggling with amusement, both shadowed by the events of the last few days. "That wily old goat,'' she said finally. "Jedd was never a one to bide his time once he'd set his course, and he'd had two women and a girl run off on him. Maggie, I'm sorry some. Do the boys know?''

Maggie shook her head sadly. "At least, I don't think they do. Cabe would have found some way to get rid of me by now if he'd known I didn't have any right to be here.''

"Don't you believe it! It ain't seemly to mention it with Jedd not even—well, you know—but from the way Cabe looks at you, I'd say getting shed of you's the last thing on his mind."

Maggie felt a rush of heat burn her cheeks. "You're wrong. He despises me."

"Mmm-hmm," Sara said thoughtfully, tapping her small foot in the soft sand. "About the same way you despise him, I'd say. Poor old Jedd set the cat among the pigeons, didn't he?"

Eli was beginning to fret, and Maggie shifted him in her arms. She'd had about all she could take for one day, but she couldn't afford to let down, not while a few neighbors still lingered behind to offer her comfort.

Comfort that wasn't even her due, she told herself after the last one had left.

Woodenly she went about settling Eli while Isaac waited for her to join him outside. Not until the babe was sleeping soundly did she dare slip away, and then only after she'd opened the window wide so that she would hear if he cried out.

Isaac reached for her hand, and she gripped his small fingers tightly, vowing not to take out her bitterness and her bewilderment on him, for it was no fault of his that every man she ever came to depend on had let her down. First her father, then Gideon, and now Jedd.

And Cabe? Was he any different? At least he'd never promised her anything, never offered her anything.

Largely in silence, they gathered dandelion seed heads and carried them carefully up the hill. Once the sowing was done, Isaac slipped his dusty hand in hers and they went back toward the house, still without speaking. From the brittle look on his small young face, Maggie knew the boy would've been shattered if he'd tried to talk. As for herself, she was too bewildered by what she had just learned.

A few at a time the womenfolk returned to see that she was all right. Jedd had been the captain. She was his widow. It was their duty.

Maggie prayed for them to go and leave her alone so that she could scream or curse or weep, and at last they did. But by that time, she was too weary for emotion. The funeral foods had been disposed of, mostly devoured by the same families who'd supplied them. Eli had been fretful, upset by the heat and the crowds, and Isaac had finally fallen asleep. The men had been out at the landing, so she'd been the one to see him to bed.

"What if the wind blows our seeds away, Maggie?" he'd asked from his low pallet.

"Then we'll plant more, and keep on planting until the whole hilltop turns gold."

Satisfied, he turned to the wall and closed his eyes, and when she touched him softly on one thin shoulder, he didn't flinch away.

For three days—ever since word had come—Maggie had been unable to sleep, unable to eat more than a morsel or two. She'd tried to keep busy, only to have her work taken right out of her hands by well-intentioned neighbors. The frustration of having nothing to do after a lifetime of hard work had been even more wearisome. She felt as if she might fly apart at a single word.

Cabe was scarcely in better shape. She couldn't bear to have him out of her sight, nor could she stand to be around him. The vital energy that was so much a part of him seemed to bounce off the walls until she could have screamed. That evening after the funeral, he'd paced the limited confines of her kitchen, finally coming to rest with his shoulders braced against the cold fireplace wall. From the set look of his jaw and the way his fists were clenching and unclenching at his sides, it would take only a word from her to set him off again.

Maggie stole a look at him, only to find his eyes boring into hers. "You looked peaked," he charged, as though she'd gone out of her way to look bedraggled just to irritate him.

"What did you expect?" she shot back. And then she could have bit her tongue. She knew better than to cross swords with him, for he always drew the first blood. It was just that she had too much on her mind to be cautious, what with burying a husband only to discover that he hadn't even *been* her husband—and the everlasting worry over what was to become of Gideon.

For the first time, it occurred to Maggie to wonder what would happen to her when the others found out that she had no real right to Jedd's home, much less his name. Sooner or later they had to know, for Sara couldn't keep a secret from Jere, and if Jere knew, they would all know.

The strain on her face, the pain in her eyes, reflected Cabe's feelings, causing him to speak more sharply than he would've if he hadn't been so distraught himself. "Don't think that just because Pa's gone you're free to go traipsing off again. You'll stay on and care for the youngers, same as always." It wasn't a request, it was a statement.

Maggie was too tired to bristle. She'd had no intention of running away, at least not until she had to go—not until they sent her away. She stole a look at him, wishing he weren't quite so intimidating. How could she ever have thought that his man might come to love her? It was impossible to believe they'd ever shared anything more intimate than a few grudging words.

She shifted uneasily in her chair, and then she stood, as if standing would lend her the dignity she sought. "I'll stay for as long as Eli and Isaac need me." From somewhere she summoned the courage to look him directly in the eyes, praying he would not be able to read the pain and confusion she felt. "That is if you're sure you want me to stay."

Nerves abraded by weeks, months, even years of strain, Maggie clasped her arms over her chest, dimly aware of a bone deep coldness that crept through her very soul. God, she was so tired! It seemed to her that a hundred years elapsed before he spoke, and when he did, his voice seemed to echo from a great distance.

"I want you to stay, Maggie."

"You'll be headed out soon? Matt said you left your cargo on the warehouse docks."

"I'll be headed out, but before I collect my cargo, there's something else I have to do. Something personal. Something that will give me great pleasure." There was a harsh gleam in his eyes, and Maggie stared hard at the Betty lamp that swung from its chain over his shoulder, schooling her features not to reveal the pain his words had brought.

Something personal. Something that would bring him great pleasure. It could only be a woman. He was going to claim a wife now that he had a home to bring her to.

Maggie summoned up an unreasoning anger to hold back the anguish. If it was a woman he spoke of, then she pitied her. The look in Cabe's eyes had been far from loving, and she knew to her sorrow that he was capable of taking what he wanted from a woman and crushing her under his boot heel.

"Maggie? Are you all right?"

She blinked, and lifted her chin a fraction. "All right? Well of course I'm all right."

Cabe's eyes narrowed. He'd seen the last bit of color drain from her face. She'd been pale enough before; now she looked almost transparent, as if she were disappearing before his very eyes.

"Maggie? Have you—" She swayed, and he reached out to catch her in time to keep her from falling, sweeping her up in his arms.

God, she weighed no more than a wisp of smoke! "You haven't eaten a morsel today, have you?" he accused.

"I think so. I'm certain I did." Maggie clutched his shoulders as the smoke-darkened ceiling tilted and then righted itself again.

Cabe was certain of no such thing. Suddenly he could recall seeing her at first light this morning, patiently poking gruel into Eli's mouth while her own breakfast went untouched. Someone had cleared away and washed the dishes, as if it were a mortal sin to leave a dish unwashed in a house of mourning. And then, later on, she'd been out under the cedars where she could keep an eye on Isaac while she gave Eli his milk. She hadn't gone near the kitchen. When the table had been spread again, she'd been...somewhere. She hadn't come into the house, at least not while he'd been there, and he'd been there most all day until time to go up the hill.

"Maggie, you have to keep up your strength." Cabe's voice held a grudging tenderness of which he was totally unconscious. Holding her in his arms, he tried to ignore the pleasure of feeling her slight weight pressed against him, feeling her unruly hair tickle the sensitive place just under his chin. As always, she smelled of wildflowers.

"Set me back on my feet, Cabe, I'm perfectly all right now." She wriggled until he lowered her to the floor, but he held her tightly against him.

"You don't look all right," he muttered to the top of her head.

"Don't let my lack of size confuse you, I'm strong as an ox." As if to prove her words, she pushed against his chest until he was forced to ease his grip. Still he refused to let her go entirely, keeping one arm about her waist.

Sighing, Maggie realized that she could no more free her body than she could free her heart. "I'd best see to milking Brownie. I forgot all about the poor old thing. If you've nothing more to say to me, I'll leave you."

"Will you, Maggie?" There was an undercurrent in his voice she didn't understand, one that made her distinctly uneasy. "Do you really think I'd let you go until I was ready for you to leave?"

Confused by his words as well as his manner, she hesitated. "I only meant—well, of course I'll stay as long as I'm needed, but now, right now, Brownie needs me more." Surely he didn't mean . . .

No, of course not. It was only her wild imagination that was reading all sorts of crazy things into a perfectly innocent statement. The silence drew out between them until she could have screamed just to end it.

It was Cabe who finally broke it. "I'll be leaving you now, for we'll sail at moonrise. Take care of yourself, Maggie, and keep a weather eye on Isaac. You might think he's finally come around, but don't be surprised if it wears off after a few days. He'll mend in time. We all will."

The talk was more than ever of the pirates, and Maggie was torn between wanting to hear every word and wanting to forget their very existence.

"Hanged Bonnet's men down at White Point, I heard tell," the toothless old man who had greeted Maggie the first day she'd come to the island told her. He was too stiff in the joints to do more than sit in the sun and talk. "Aye, the whole mess of 'em. George Rose and Billy Livers and Tom Price, all went a-dancin' at the end of a rope."

"I see Ruben got a nice mess of flounders this morning," Maggie mentioned in an effort to deflect him from his gory tale, but she was no match for the bloodthirsty old fisherman.

"Aye, an they planted that Amand feller in the marsh, they did. Come spring, his bones'll likely wash up on the point like that pore old feller Gaffer found. They say he was—"

"Why, I think I hear Eli! He'll climb out of his cradle if I don't fetch him this minute," Maggie said with a bright false smile.

She hurried away, all her fears brought to the surface again. Where was Gideon? Had he perished in the battle? If he was alive, surely he would have got word to her somehow! Where was Cabe?

"Lord, please take care of those I love, for not a one of 'em can look after himself," she muttered as she hurried into the house.

Familiar chores brought a measure of comfort over the next few days. As long as her hands were occupied and her mind too weary to do more than drift above a sea of troubles, like a sea gull hovering lightly on unseen currents of air, Maggie could avoid thinking of Gid and Cabe. Sometimes hours would go by when she wouldn't give either of them a single thought.

Working like a small whirlwind, she caught up on all that needed doing and dug out the bolts of calico and muslin Jedd had brought her. She would sew. She'd already made shirts for Isaac and Matt, and now she would make something for herself—another pair of drawers, a petticoat, and a new gown of the calico. Her two old ones would scarce make it through another winter.

The calico was pale blue, patterned in scarlet and black. She chuckled softly for the first time in ages as she considered Zion's reaction should she suddenly turn up at the farm again wearing such a frivolous creation. He would likely accuse her of selling her soul to the devil.

After bedding the children, she cut and basted until she could no longer see her own stitches, and then she washed and changed into her night shift. Just as she'd always done, she continued to place the bolster along the center of the bed. Somehow, it seemed more necessary than ever now that she knew she had not truly been married to the man whose bed she'd shared all summer.

A deep, shuddering sigh was drawn from the depths of her, and she turned over onto her stomach. Sinking down into the billowing feathers until she could feel the rope netting underneath, she burrowed one fist close to her chin to clear herself a breathing space and commenced to think of her future. Sooner or later she must make plans, but somehow, she couldn't seem to bring her mind to focus on what lay ahead.

One thing was increasingly clear. Before she could plan for the future, she was going to have to root any dreams of Cabel Rawson out of her heart as relentlessly as Zion had rooted out every wildflower that dared desecrate his precious farm.

It was just after daybreak two days later when she heard the first rumors. Emma Gaskins stopped by on her way up the road to a confinement. "They gone after them bloody devils, Maggie. Gonna get rid of the whole plague-taken mess of 'em without waiting no more for the Crown to send help."

Maggie must have uttered some suitable response, for Emma hurried on to her birthing with a satisfied nod. All morning, though, her mind was fevered with thoughts of Gid. She pictured him running from a fleet of angry bankers, all armed and bent on revenge.

Lord knows, she would have cheered them on under any other circumstances, but her own brother! For all she knew, he might already have perished, and no matter what he'd done, she couldn't wish that on him.

By midday, Maggie had almost succeeded in convincing herself that Gid would never have taken part in the killing. He might have been a mite reckless, he might be misguided in his unswerving loyalty to Uncle Will, but he was no murderer. She knew it as well as she knew her own heart.

Because she couldn't bear waiting helplessly, not knowing what might be happening or who might be suffering at this very moment, Maggie threw herself into another frenzy of cleaning. Taking time out only to feed and change Eli, she scrubbed the already spotless floors, washed down the clean walls, and sanded the crust off every pot until they gleamed like dark mirrors.

It was midafternoon when Isaac burst into the kitchen just as she finished scouring.

"They got 'im, Maggie, they got 'im!" the boy shouted.

Sitting back on her heels, Maggie felt a sliver of dread slip into her heart. She composed herself before the excited boy. "Mind where you walk, that floor's still wet."

Isaac, his bare feet grimy with the black dust that seemed to filter through even the palest sand, tiptoed across the freshly scrubbed floor to perch on the hearth. Maggie hadn't seen him so animated since before they'd got word about Jedd.

"Maynard chopped off his head and he swam 'round and 'round till somebody poked him under with an oar!"

With methodical thoroughness, she wrung out her scrub rag and draped it carefully over the rim of the pail. An unformed prayer hovered just beyond reach of her tongue. Folding her hands on her lap, she asked, "Maynard?"

"Not Maynard—Blackbeard," the boy corrected, as if any fool should've known that much. "I never heard of nobody swimming with their head chopped off, but chickens do it all the time. Leastways they—"

"Chickens *swim*?"

"Oh, Maggie," Isaac cried, obviously quite put out with her dimwittedness. "Chickens can't swim, silly. They only flop around after you chop off their head, getting everything all full of blood and sh—"

"Isaac!"

"Well, they do," he said plaintively. "Ma used to tie their feet together and hang 'em over a limb until they—"

"Yes, but we don't have to talk about it. Wash your hands and I'll set out some cider and molasses cakes before Eli wakes up. I vow I could do with a sup of cold cider, it's that hot."

Maybe it was someone else, some other ship, she thought frantically. What had Emma said? Only that *they* were going after *them*. She hadn't mentioned any names. The *Morning Star* was probably halfway to Charles Towne this very minute, knowing the bankers were hell-bent on revenge.

And guilty or not, Maggie could only pray they would make it.

Isaac wiped his grimy hands across the seat of his muddy trousers and held them up for inspection. "Don't need washing, see? Jere says Maynard's going to take his head to Bath Towne and serve it up on a platter to Gov'nor Eden."

Maggie hung on to her last shred of patience. He was only a child, and a grieving child at that. But enough was enough. "Fetch me the cider, will you? And before you commence talking such foolishness again, I don't want to hear it."

"Ain't you even glad ol' Blackbeard's dead, Maggie? He was a pirate, an' pirates killed Pa. Some says Blackbeard was the rottenest, meanest, ugliest man that ever lived, but I bet when Cabe catches up with old Lewis, he'll be even uglier. I bet he has long black fangs, and red eyes, and—"

"Hush!"

"—and knives sticking out of his—"

"Isaac, if you don't stop that this minute, I'm going to—"

"—ears," the boy yelled as he dashed out the doorway, obviously quite pleased at the effects of his colorful account.

Without finishing her threat, Maggie slumped over the table and buried her face in her hands. She didn't want to hear about it, she didn't want to *think* about it! How could she not want her husband's murderers caught and punished?

Yet how could she wish her brother dead?

What had he said about Cabe catching up with Uncle Will? But Cabe had gone to meet some woman . . . hadn't he?

Oh, how did she know? No one ever told her the straight of anything, she had to discover the truth for herself. And in every case, it was a truth she'd just as soon not have learned.

That evening, Isaac's energy seemed boundless. He ran and whooped with several other boys along the shore while Sara and Jeremiah sat at her table, avidly recounting the events of the day. Maggie felt it was hardly her place to tell the eldest Rawson that she didn't want to think of pirates and killing and such, so she heard it all again, in more accurate, if less colorful, detail.

Jeremiah confirmed that Governor Spottswood of Virginia had indeed sent his two sloops, manned by British crewmen and under the command of a young lieutenant named Robert Maynard, down from the James River. It had been late the previous day when they'd reached Ocracoke, only to find their two sloops greatly overmatched by Blackbeard's heavily armed *Adventure*.

The battle, clearly visible from shore, had been fierce and bloody. Blackbeard had found himself outnumbered and outmanned, but he'd had the advantage of having eight working guns. The attacking sloops had been badly underarmed. One of Maynard's sharpshooters had finally managed to shoot away the *Adventure*'s jib stay and fore hallyards, allowing the disabled sloop to drift hard onto a shoal, but even then Teach had refused to surrender. Using bottles filled with powder, shot and slugs of iron, with a quick match rammed into the opening, he'd proceeded to bombard both of Maynard's smaller vessels.

Fortunately Maynard, fearing just such an attack from the infamous *grenados*, had ordered his men below only moments before.

Maynard's damaged sloop had drifted out of control until she'd been captured by the swift current and carried directly broadside the stranded *Adventure*. Seizing his opportunity, Blackbeard and his crew had begun swarming aboard, armed to the teeth. The pistols of both law and outlaw had been primed and ready when the men met face to face on the deck of the HMS *Pearl*. Maynard had fired first, hitting his target, but he hadn't counted on Blackbeard's phenomenal strength. The pirate had grabbed his sword and lunged before Maynard could reload.

It had been one of Maynard's crew who had slashed down into the pirate's neck, thus saving the officer's life. And still Blackbeard had fought on, staggering over the bodies of dead and wounded of both sides. A lesser man would have been finished.

Growing paler by the moment, Maggie listened while Jeremiah described how, mortally wounded, the notorious pirate had hacked and slashed his way ruthlessly across the deck until he was almost upon his opponent. Maynard had barely managed to cock his pistol when the black-bearded giant had slowly toppled to the deck.

"The rest of the scum—leastwise, those who were still able—jumped over the side," he said in conclusion.

Maggie swallowed the nausea that rose in her throat. "What'll happen to them now?" she managed to whisper.

"Teach's men? They were hauled off across the sound. Like as not they'll be tried and hanged, if'n they make the trip, that is. Weren't nobody in a forgiving mood. I heard tell, and I be lieve it to be true, that Maynard jammed ol' Teach's head onto his bowsprit and swore he was going to present it to Eden on a silver salver."

And then, as if it were the greatest news possible, he added, "You'll be right pleased to hear that Cabe was sighted yesterday headed south, hard on the heels of the *Star*. Lorable Gaskins was out on the reef when he spied Lewis's ship hull down and running abreast Portsmouth Island, and then here come Cabe, sails bellied out like the devil himself was a-blowing into 'em."

Cabe. Then he had left home with revenge, and not romance in mind. Maggie felt the goosebumps rise on her arms. She had no doubt that if Cabe caught up with the *Star* in his present mood, there would be no mercy shown to the captain or any member of the crew. Maynard had been only doing his duty. How much more vicious would be a group of bankers bound on revenge for the killing of twelve of their own? And could she blame them?

Chuck-will's-widow called plaintively from the edge of the woods, adding to Maggie's feelings of restlessness a few nights later. An autumn moon had risen just as the sun was setting, and she leaned in the doorway, staring unseeingly at the spectacle.

"Maggie?"

Her imagination was finally getting the best of her. That had sounded almost like a human voice. Cabe's voice.

And then she heard it again, and this time there was no mistaking it. Nor was there any mistaking the lean, broadshouldered man who came walking slowly up the front path. She stood stock-still. Chuck-will's-widow, resenting the intrusion, fell silent.

Even with the moon at his back, she recognized him. The tremors inside her never lied when Cabe was nearby. "You're back."

By now he'd reached her side. He turned so that the moonlight shone down on his face, and she was shocked by the changes she saw there. Exhaustion had turned him into a stranger. There was a dark stubble on his usually clean-shaven face, and his eyes were sunk so deep in his head their color was no longer visible. Only their intensity.

His shoulders sagged, and for one long moment she dared hope that he had failed in his mission. "Are you . . . all right?"

"If by that you mean, am I injured, the answer is no. Not bodily. I find I've no taste for killing, Maggie. Funny, isn't it? God knows, I've had my share of fights, but sending a man to his death, hearing him cry out for mercy—" Breaking off, he swore, and Maggie caught at his arm when he would've pushed past her.

"What happened? Cabe, you've got to tell me what *happened*!"

"You'll be happy to hear that Pa and all the others have been avenged," he said tiredly. "The last of the bloody bastards are gone from Ocracoke. For now, at least. There's plenty more where they came from—God knows, half of New Providence could move in on us by morning."

"The—the *Morning Star*?" She could barely bring herself to ask, yet she would die, not knowing.

"Gone. Every last stinkin' one of 'em, gone to hell a-beggin'. We managed to get close enough before daylight to hole her good right at the waterline, and then the best hunters among us started cutting down her rigging with our muskets. She was taking on water, slewing around broadside. She'd have been beamside over if she hadn't sunk first, with every man jack aboard swarming over the sides like rats. Now, if you don't mind, would you please get out of my way?"

"But where are you going?"

"I'm going to the kitchen for a bar of your soap, and then I'm headed out into the sound. I don't think I'll ever wash the stench of killing off me, but I'm damned well going to try."

Maggie didn't even hear his last few words. She had finally succumbed to too many sleepless nights, too many days without eating, and too many frantic hours spent worrying over those she loved.

Quietly, just as chuck-will's widow resumed her dirge, she crumpled into a small heap at Cabe's feet.

Chapter Nineteen

Cabe lifted Maggie in his arms, resisting the urge to crush her tightly against him. For so long she'd loomed large on his horizon, filling his waking hours with frustration and his sleeping ones with dreams, that he tended to forget how very small she was.

"Maggie?" he murmured, not overly concerned. He'd yet to meet a woman who wasn't given over to vapors now and again. Likely 'twas nothing more than her monthly tide.

"Maggie?" A note of urgency crept into his voice when she failed to respond. "Come on, dearling, wake up before I drop you. I've not slept for three days and nights—I'll be landing us both on the deck in another moment."

He rocked her gently in his arms, frowning when her head lolled like an overblown blossom on a slender stalk. "Damn all, Maggie, stop playing possum! If you're feeling poorly, just tell me and I'll fetch Emma, but don't do this to me!"

What the devil had she done with all the lamps? Granted the things gave off more smoke than light, they were still better than nothing.

Maggie was already beginning to stir by the time he lowered her onto a chair. "Whoops—careful there," he cautioned as she threatened to topple sideways. With one hand he shored her up while he drew another chair from under the table and seated himself near enough to catch her if she fell. Cabe could no longer trust himself to hold her. To his great disgust, his exhausted body was reacting to her nearness in an all too familiar manner.

He located a nub of candle, and after several tries, managed to light it, placing it just out of reach of the draft from the open door. The light flickered on her pale face, making her eyes as luminous as sea fire on a dark night. The shadows under her cheekbones were more pronounced than ever, and in contrast to her pallor, her lips were berry red.

Eyes rimmed with sleeplessness, he stared at the woman beside him. She looked so small, so desolate. But her vulnerable looks were a lie, for she was a survivor if there ever was one. There would always be a man somewhere to take care of a woman like Maggie.

And God help him, he was one of those men.

Cabe tried telling himself that it was the lack of sleep that had scattered his wits, not the feel of her in his arms again. Not the warm wildflower scent that always seemed to hover around her. But it was no use. The warm smell of the candle reached his nostrils, and they flared. Bayberry. Did everything she touch smell of plants? They were all over the house, and as if that weren't enough, she'd dug up half the forest and set it out again nearer the house until a body could scarce find the door.

He edged closer. He might as well not even be there for all the mind she paid him, he told himself churlishly.

Even as he watched, she closed her eyes, still sitting upright in her chair. He couldn't tell if she was sleeping or praying.

Sleeping, most likely. And too bloody stubborn to fall over.

She was shutting him out, and suddenly he wanted in. "Maggie, say something. And dammit, open your eyes so I can see if anyone still lives there." His voice cracked on the poor attempt at a jest, and it occurred to him for the first time that her senses might have fled under the strain of losing the man she'd thought of as her husband. Or more likely from losing her lover.

For the hundredth time, Cabe pondered the identity of the man he'd seen embracing his Maggie on the docks. He wasn't from this island, nor Ocracoke either, for he knew every banker by sight, and most by name.

Still, she'd been headed across the inlet. Which must mean the young bastard was off one of the ships that had lately laid by in Ocracoke Harbor. There'd been several in port about that time, most notably Teach's *Adventure* and Will Lewis's *Morning Star*—both of which had since been taken with all hands killed or captured.

Suddenly Maggie's spell of fainting began to take on a horrible significance, coming as it had right after Cabe had an nounced that he'd sent the whole bloody crew of the *Star* to the bottom. He'd been doing a bit of bragging, but she couldn't have known that. Actually, only a few men had been killed in the fighting. A few more had died of wounds, one old man had come screaming up from below and run under a boom, breaking his neck, while two more had gone over the rail. Weighed down with sabers, handguns and bandoliers, they'd never come up again.

As for the rest, they'd been taken prisoner, trussed up and sent on their way to Williamsburg, where Teach's crew was awaiting trial. Like as not they'd all be hanged together, but at least he wouldn't have to witness it.

He'd been disgusted enough at his own weak belly for killing. Some aboard the *Bridget* had wanted to cut them all into bits and feed them to the sharks, but Cabe's only desire had been to rid the seas of the maggoty lot and go home.

Abruptly he got up and poured himself a generous measure of rum, downing it in one go. Not that it would help, at least not unless he drank himself senseless. Even then it would change nothing. The only reason he hadn't killed Maggie's lover was because he hadn't seen the son of a bitch.

"Godamighty, what a mess," he muttered.

"What?"

Slamming the tankard down on the table, Cabe began stripping off his shirt. He needed air. What he really needed was a long swim in cold water, if he had to wade halfway across the sound to find it. Summer had lasted well into October, and even now the water was warm along shore.

Throwing his shirt aside, he began unlacing his pants. And then, swearing, he remembered his boots. Sitting on the edge of the hearth, he struggled to peel the cumbersome things down his thighs. He tugged at the heels, twisting and pulling. By now he was swearing openly, with Maggie staring at him as if she expected at any moment to see the top of his head fly off.

"What the devil are you staring at? Don't tell me you've never seen a man undress before!"

Maggie blinked, her own heartache momentarily forgotten. He looked wretchedly tired. "Cabe, I'd be glad to help if you'll only tell me what to do."

"Go to bed!" One boot came off with a jerk and he threw it across the room. He tugged at the other one, cursed, and tugged again. "If it's watching you like, maybe you'd care to journey up to Williamsburg and watch while they hang the murdering scum that sent Jedd and his whole damned crew to their reward!''

He looked to see what effect his words had had on her and then wished he hadn't. Wished he'd never come home at all. One glance at that stricken face as she disappeared into the bedroom was enough to sicken him. God, why couldn't he keep his mouth shut?

Cabe closed his eyes against the pain of his own conscience. It had plagued him for too long now, always the loudest when he'd had a bit too much rum. After his deliberate brutality almost from the first moment they'd met, he would count himself lucky if she didn't cut and run the minute he turned his back.

He couldn't blame her if she walked ·out this minute. He'd done nothing but torment her—cursing her, accusing her of crimes his heart told him she was incapable of committing. Raping her.

Even now he cringed at the memory of that night. He could no longer delude himself that it had been anything more than the most brutal offence, for she'd been innocent and he'd taken her forcefully, in vengeance and in frustration.

In love, too, only he hadn't known it at the time.

Tonight's twist of the knife had been the most vicious of all, he told himself. For though she'd cared enough for Jedd to be a good wife to him, she had plainly loved the yellow-haired devil with the mark on his right cheek.

Cabe waded out under the light of the moon until the water reached his chest. Diving under the surface, he swam until his head cleared enough to think. Finally, wading ashore, he stumbled into the house as naked as the day he was born, and in that same state, he finished off the jug of rum. Only when the sun had turned the tiny bedroom into an oven the following morning did he awake, unable to remember falling into bed. Someone—probably Matt—had tossed his clothes in after him, for he was still clutching a boot in his arms.

Cabe's head was splitting. Maggie recognized the signs. He was tiptoeing instead of striding around as if he owned the hall and half of China. At the slightest sound, he winced. Beneath his perennial tan, his color was gray, and if she could have felt anything at all other than a merciful numbness, it would have been joy at the sight of his suffering.

Eli let out a wail, and she turned tiredly to go tend him. She would feed him first, and then force herself to eat something. For the sake of the youngers, she had to keep up her strength.

Isaac and Eli. No matter what the past or the future, they still needed her. They'd had no hand in any of this, and until Cabe deemed it otherwise, she would stay on for their sakes.

Sighing, she lifted the heavy child over her shoulders, tenderly untangling his chubby fingers from her hair. She loved her two charges more every day she spent with them. Leaving them would pain her, but she was no stranger to pain.

Nor was she a stranger to Cabe's dark moods. He'd been blaming her for one thing and another since she'd first set foot on his precious schooner, and nothing she could do was likely to please him now. Lord help her when he discovered she hadn't even been married to his father!

He'd obviously forgotten the night he'd come home the worst for drink and attacked her like some great rutting savage, leaving her bleeding and weeping on the kitchen floor. Would that she could forget so easily.

But to her shame and sorrow, Maggie knew that it was not the pain and humiliation she would remember to her dying day, but the glory of his caressing hands, his seeking lips.

By the time she'd finished feeding Eli, Maggie was giddy with hunger, herself. She should've eaten sooner. It had always been that way. Whenever she'd been worried or angry or upset, her belly had reacted by tightening into a hard knot, rejecting all thought of food. Which meant that she'd gone hungry to bed as often as not, she recalled with a rueful smile.

Ignoring Cabe, who sprawled morosely in a chair with his bare feet propped on the cold hearth, she ladled herself a bowl of turtle stew, poured a tankard of cider and laced it with rum—for once she felt need of something stronger than yaupon tea or coffee—and carried the lot to the table.

Neither of them had spoken a word since she'd come into the kitchen and seen him there. Maggie ate, feeling his presence like an oppressive storm cloud hovering over her, but not once did she turn her head his way.

Let him grieve. Like Isaac, he would feel his grief all the more deeply for not being able to express it, striking out at those who attempted to come close to him.

But damn all, she was grieving, too! She'd lost the last member of her family—she was completely alone in the world. And Cabel Rawson had no right to mope about as if the sun would never rise again, because the world would not stop turning for Jedd, nor for her mother, nor for Gideon.

It only seemed that way for a while.

Silence shrouded the room like smoke on a rainy day. Perhaps it was just as well. There'd been times when she'd wanted to kill him and times when she'd wanted to lose herself in his arms. To her everlasting shame, Maggie knew he had still not managed to trample her love to death. In time it would wither and die. Neither love nor anything else could survive for long in such a hostile climate. Meanwhile she would simply have to stand brave and wait it out.

She managed to get down three bites of Sara's cold turtle stew. Gid had always been partial to turtle stew, she recalled with a sudden dimming of her vision. Staring at the gray congealed mess in her bowl, she pictured him baiting his trotline in Adams Creek for snappers and then trying to make pets of the vicious creatures. More often than not, he managed to allow them to escape before Zion could scald them for cleaning.

And now Gid was gone. She'd heard the words from Cabe's own mouth, and still it wasn't real. They'd been apart so many years, with her waiting for his letters, waiting for him to sail into Bath Towne harbor. Why couldn't she simply go on waiting? Where was the harm?

Suddenly Maggie could feel her nose prickle. Her eyes burned and then they began to fill, and she gripped the edge of the table until her fingers cramped. *Damn you, Maggie McNair, you are not going to cry now!*

One of Cabe's feet struck the floor, and he uttered a foul oath. It was the last straw. Maggie whirled about, glaring at his shimmering image. "I'll thank you to keep a civil tongue in your head when you're in my house!" she snapped. Impatiently she swiped at her overflowing eyes, and her hand struck the edge of her bowl, tipping the contents onto the floor.

Cabe jumped to his feet and glared at her. "What the devil have you done *now*.?" he demanded in an aggrieved tone.

"Nothing you need worry about. I simply ruined my floor for the pleasure of spending the morning crawling about on my hands and knees with a rag and a pail!"

"Oh, so it's *your* floor, is it?"

Maggie had already fetched the scrub pail. She poured water from the kettle onto a sliver of soap, hiked up her skirt and got to her knees, glaring at the mess she'd made. "I'm the one who scrubs it."

"And I've got two lads holystoning my decks, but if one of them was to lay claim to my ship on account of his labors, I'd be forced to point out the error of his ways."

Maggie was in no mood to bicker. It had not taken her long to discover which one of them would come out the winner in any battle of wits. Unfortunately her tongue was not always subservient to her common sense. "I do beg your pardon. It's *your* floor, *your* house, *your* bucket and *your*—"

"All right, dammit, you don't need to talk a body to death. As it happens, I've a bit of a head this morning. If I offended you, then I'm right sorry."

If he'd offended her! Maggie seriously considered crowning his aching head with the scrub pail. Anger flooded through her, seeping into crevices left by too much grieving, too many uncertainties. It lent her the strength to rebel against everything she'd ever been taught about a woman's duties.

She stood and dried her hands on her apron. "I'm going out for a spell. I'm taking Eli—Isaac's out somewhere. If the mess on *your* floor bothers you, you can clean it up yourself, Captain Rawson!"

Cabe's head snapped back suddenly, and he winced. "Hold on there!" Moving with exaggerated caution, he sidled around the table toward where she stood. He was wearing his oldest trousers, so threadbare they only served to emphasize what they were meant to conceal. He was barefooted, bare-chested and, unfortunately for Maggie's peace of mind, he'd never looked more magnificent.

Not that she noticed at all. She'd had her fill of men. *All* men, and Rawsons in particular. Bent only on escape, she marched into the bedroom and snatched Eli from his cradle, where he'd been cheerfully chewing on an ivory geegaw. Mentally she exempted him from her wholesale condemnation of the Rawson clan—for the time being at least.

She didn't even make it as far as the door before Cabe called her back. Ignoring him, she stripped off her apron with one hand and flung it at a chair, her mind set on escaping before she lost her temper.

"Maggie! You come back here!"

Her hair was uncombed, her gown a disgrace, and she hadn't a notion of where she was going. Other than simply *out*.

"Maggie, I'm warning you, if you take one more step..."

Turning slowly, she confronted him, taking in his unhealthy color and his bloodshot eyes. His soot-colored hair was no tidier than hers, for he'd not taken time to comb it and fasten it at his nape with a band of leather as he usually did. It gave him a wild look, bringing to mind his savage redskin lineage.

"Well?" he prompted, not giving an inch.

"You, sir, may go to the devil for all I care, but don't you *dare* raise your voice to me. For the sake of the youngers, I've decided to stay on until you find someone to take my place. But hear this, Cabel Rawson—I'll not be mistreated by any man, especially you!"

Cabel, one hand pressed to his temple, attempted a grin that was more of a grimace. "What's so special about me?"

For a moment she couldn't harness her tongue to her wits in order to reply. What *was* so special about him, after all—except that she'd had the great misfortune to lose her heart and her soul to him, when all he'd wanted from her had been the use of her body. And that but once.

She tilted her chin, her cool eyes flashing. She'd made herself a promise once, and Maggie was a keeper of promises. For the sake of her mother she'd put up with years of cruelty, but never again.

With a calmness that did her proud, she said, "There's nothing the least bit special about you, other than the fact that you have a nastier disposition than most."

Never would she have believed he could move so fast. For her one step backward, he took three steps forward, until suddenly he was blocking the doorway. "Not so fast, little witch-eyes."

She stared pointedly down at his hand on her arm. Like the rest of him, it was browned by a lifetime of exposure, strong from years of hard physical labor. "If it's my bones you're after, then kindly use your knife. Prying them out with your fingers is not only painful, it's apt to be messy."

Lips tightening in annoyance, Cabe nevertheless eased his grip to something just short of a caress. Likely she would bear his fingermarks for many a day. "Maggie, we need to talk."

"We've said all that needs saying."

"About the future, dammit! I mean ... about the future."

She could tell he was trying hard not to give offense, and she hardened herself against her own weakness. "My future is none of your concern, and yours is of no interest to me."

He shook his head in exasperation, winced as the pain slammed through his skull, and then swore softly. "What about the youngers?" he demanded. "Would you go off and leave them to Matthew and me?"

"You'll find another woman to care for them. Likely you've only held off on account of—"

"Damn all, Maggie, you're their stepma! Don't that mean anything to you?"

"Did Gaffer include that in the marriage words? I'm afraid I wasn't paying attention."

"Jesus," Cabe whispered reverently. Turning away, he dropped onto a chair, propping his chin on his fist. "How long have you known?" he asked finally.

Maggie shifted Eli to the other shoulder and felt a warm wetness dribble down her back as he gave back a bit of his breakfast. "Since the burial. I recognized that suit, and Sara told me who he was."

"Then she knows, too?" Answering his own question, he stared morosely at the coarse weave of the tablecloth. "So that's why she was looking at me so funny. Likely she was wondering if I knew."

A rumble of thunder had them both turning toward the open door. In the past few minutes, the sun had clouded over.

"What about Matt? Have you told him?" Cabe asked.

Maggie shook her head and felt Eli grab a curl at her temple. She winced. "And I don't think Sara has, or he would've let slip something. He's not as closemouthed as some."

With a look she was at a loss to interpret, Cabe stood and poured himself a mug of coffee. "Go for your walk before it rains, Maggie. I'll straighten this mess out someway." Maggie didn't hesitate.

Black and strong, the coffee began to revive Cabe's wits. He had much to do, and in truth, he'd never felt less like moving. There was the business of Jedd's mock marriage to settle, and the sooner the better. If it had to come out, it would have been better while Jedd had been in a position to stand up for himself and take his licks, for the blame was rightfully his. Maggie had been a victim, in spite of what he'd once thought.

Gaffer would take the secret to his grave, for he'd loved that old man like a brother. As for the others, they would understand Pa's reasons, even if they couldn't condone what he'd done. Nothing would be served by letting the truth out now. As far as the world knew, Maggie was the widow Rawson, and she would remain so until she took herself another husband.

Which brought him to the next matter to be dealt with. Maggie's lover. One way or another, he would have to find the young bastard—that is, if he was still alive. He owed her that much. There were hundreds of places on the banks where a man could hide, but Cabe knew most of them. There was also a good chance that he'd been a member of the *Adventure*'s crew, in which case he would be in Williamsburg awaiting trial like the others, and there'd be little chance of getting him away.

On the other hand, if he'd been aboard the *Star*, Cabe would have remembered him. There weren't that many big, yellow-haired devils with a mark on their cheek and a face that would have drawn women to him like a dead mullet drew flies.

No wonder Maggie had loved him, Cabe thought miserably. And there wasn't a doubt in his mind that she did, for he'd seen the two of them together himself, and she'd been hell-bent on meeting him, even at the risk of her own life.

All right, he would damned well go out and find the young bastard for her! If she wanted him, then she would have him if it lay within his ability to grant her wish. Perhaps in that way he could make up for all the harm he'd done her. And if his own suffering would count for the rest, why then the score would be even!

Under the sloping ceiling of a small cottage some miles to the southwest, Gideon stretched and turned to the woman beside him. "God, I'm thirsty! Barb, what day is this?"

"Hush now and I'll fetch you a sup of cider, and then you'll go back to sleep."

"Is Will back yet?"

"You're not to worry about Will Lewis, and you with a crack in your noggin big enough to let in the wind."

"Ahrrgh, Christ, woman, stop yammering and give a man a drink, will you?"

"Stop swearing and lie back down there, or I'll give you something stronger than any drink!"

"I'll fetch it meself, then, you bullheaded female." Gid fumbled weakly with the coverlet and attempted to sling one leg off the low bed, but an unexpected shaft of pain brought a groan from his throat, and then Barbara was bending over him, her work-hardened hands gentle as she wiped his brow and straightened the woven spread again.

"There now, and I'd like to see you prancing out to the rain barrel in no more'n a few lengths of bandages, and them on your head, your foot, and your shoulder. Wouldn't that just set the town on its tail a-laughing!"

Gid grinned weakly, sweat beading his face and body as he came fully awake. "Woman, get your greedy little hands off my carcass. Just because you've happened to catch me at a slight disadvantage—"

"Slight! A cracked skull, a broke foot, and your arm fair sliced right off your chest?"

"My working parts is in good enough order. Leastwise, I got better sense than to lie here all day when there's things to be done."

"Your sister?"

Gid nodded, and then wished he hadn't. His head felt as if it were about to explode. "If she gets wind of trouble, she'll be taking on the whole island. I'll need to set her mind to rest, and then I might see about making plans for the future. I ain't likely to be sailing with Turk no more. I seem to recall . . ." His voice trailed off and he frowned at the elusive memory.

"As to the future, I've this house and the sail skiff. I've a pound net all staked up and an oyster bed Thomas put in. He left me well fixed. Now I know I'm some older than you, Gid, but I'd make you a good wife. You could go farther and do worse."

Gid closed his eyes against the wistfulness in her sweet face. He'd come to care deeply for this young widow, but a man could only be stretched so many ways without flying apart. And he had Uncle Will and Maggie to think of. "I'd not live off a woman, love, no matter how kind and generous she be." He made another attempt to sit up, and this time Barbara didn't interfere.

"Thunderation, I'm weak as a water worm! How long have I been here, a day? Two days?" He remembered the fight. That had been yesterday, hadn't it? And he could dimly remember Barbara sewing on him and dosing him with something that had tasted like wormwood and gall. It had knocked him clean off his pins.

"I ain't marked 'em off, but I'd say it was more like two weeks."

Gid came up from the pillows as if struck by lightning. "Weeks! *Two weeks!*"

"Don't take your nasty disposition out on me, you proud young devil, for you ain't the only man I could have! If it hadn't been for me you'd likely have sprawled out there on the dock where they threw you until the wharf rats finished you off, for there ain't many would lift a hand to help a pirate—not after all they've done!"

"I ain't a damned pirate, and you know that!"

"Lie down in a hog wallow and you'll get up muddy."

"I need a drink."

"You need to eat. I've dribbled broth down your throat till I like to drowned you, but it ain't hardly enough for a big strapping lad like yourself."

"Then give me something more, dammit. Why was I here so long? It ain't the first time I've had a crack on the skull, nor the last, most likely."

"I'll tell you anything you want to know, but first lie back down while I fix you a morsel to eat."

Gid didn't need a second urging, for his head was beginning to pound, and he'd just realized that his skin was hot as the breech of a twenty-pounder. He tried to recall precisely what had led up to the fight with Turk, but the more he tried to chase down the pieces, the more they eluded him.

He could remember Turk's crowning him with the haft of his broken sword and leaving him for dead, but why was his sword broken? Because—ah, now it was coming back. It had been only his own nimble-footedness that had saved him from being skewered on the business end. He'd jumped aside just as the enraged quartermaster had lunged, and the sword had sliced through his shoulder and plunged through one of the gun mounts, snapping when it struck iron.

That would account for his shoulder and his head. As for his foot, it had probably been injured when they'd thrown him onto the dock. Which still didn't tell him *why* they'd fought.

Not that they hadn't fought before, only this time something told him it had been in deadly earnest. One of them had been meant to die. The fact that he'd survived could be set down to Barbara's unflagging care and Turk's own impatience to be—

To be where?

It hurt, but he forced himself to remember as much as possible: the raid Turk had proposed, Uncle Will's sweating and trembling as he pleaded with Gid to stop him...

Barbara came back, bearing a trencher of stewed goose with yellow turnips, and Gid forced down a few bites for strength before he began to question her.

"Did I dream it, or was Turk threatening to take over the *Star* and go after Jedd Rawson's sloop to repay him for that business in the inlet a few weeks ago?"

"You didn't dream it," said Barbara, taking over the task of feeding him when Gid would have set the trencher aside. "Said he'd do it and he did, only it weren't Rawson's sloop. Jedd was sailing for Henry Austin."

Gid closed his eyes at the thought of what could have happened. But Jedd was an able man. Maggie had said he was the best seaman anywhere, and he'd certainly shown more than average skill and daring when he'd left Turk stranded on a shoal in his spanking new prize.

"Did, uh, did they...meet?"

Barbara cast him a bitter look. "They met all right. That devil of your uncle's weren't satisfied to take his prize and be done with it. He had to go and murder ever' one of Rawson's crew!"

She poked a bite of dark meat at him, and numbly, Gid chewed and swallowed, and then wished he hadn't, for the thought of what must have happened made his gut threaten to turn on him. "Killed 'em all, you say? Godamighty, woman, didn't they even put up a fight? It ain't like Turk to kill off good seamen that might sign on with him."

"A banker sign on with the likes of him?" Barbara scoffed. "They'd sooner pimp for the devil. But never you mind, he got what was coming to him! One of Rawson's sons caught up with the *Star* off Portsmouth Island, and they made 'em pay."

"Uncle Will?" Gid knew before hearing the answer. It had had to happen sooner or later. Nearly every one of the crew was now siding with Turk, and Gid couldn't have held them off much longer. Like as not, the both of them would have found themselves as shark bait one moonless night.

"After all he did for me, in the end, I wasn't able to save him. What about the rest of them?" To his great shame, the sadness he felt was laced with relief that it was finally over.

"Some was killed, some drowned, and the rest was hauled off to the gallows over across the sound. As for your uncle, word has it he run up on deck and broke his neck. Don't reckon he suffered much."

"I'll have to go to Maggie. Like as not she thinks I'm dead, too."

"You ain't going nowhere right soon, lad. I packed your wound with sugar and turpentine, and it's healed without a pucker, but you ain't got the strength to stand, much less to get yourself over to Hatteras. Stay on a while, and then you can take the boat again."

But Maggie had waited long enough for her brother to go to her. Five years too long. He must go to her now, if he died in trying.

Chapter Twenty

The days were growing shorter, the air perceptibly cooler. Matt had cut a large supply of firewood before he'd left, and Maggie, with Isaac helping her boil and skim, had made another batch of bayberry candies. Both children were growing, changing almost daily. Eli was scuttling about like a small crab, and had already begun pulling himself up. It was all Maggie could do to keep him from harm, but she welcomed the challenge. Unlike most of her other chores, that, at least, engaged her mind.

She prided herself that she could go whole days now without once thinking of Cabel. But then came the nights, and she would relive their every moment together.

Just before he'd sailed, Cabe had brought her a pair of moccasins made of incredibly soft hide, with a lovely design of green and yellow beads. Embarrassed, she'd put her hands behind her back, but he'd drawn them out and forced her to accept his gift, embarrassing her still more. From the look on his flushed face, he'd been every bit as discomfited, himself.

"Friend of Ma's made them," he said gruffly. "Says her eyes aren't what they used to be or she'd have done better with the beadwork."

"Oh, Cabe, they're lovely! I never had anything half so fine," Maggie had protested. In truth, she'd never had anything but heavy black boots, each pair cobbled for Gid, outgrown by him and passed on to her—that is until Jedd had brought her a pair of her very own. "Yellow flowers," she'd murmured, fingering the slightly uneven design that adorned the toe of each small slipper. "I'm right partial to yellow flowers."

"Yeah, well. Just see that you wear 'em. They'll ease your feet after a day's work."

He'd looked so magnificent standing there with his own booted feet braced on her freshly scrubbed kitchen floor, scowling until his eyes were slits of pale fire. Maggie had somehow known that it wasn't anger that lowered his black brows. Whatever emotion had burned behind those proud features, it had struck a note deep inside her that had left her trembling and weak.

For long moments they'd stared at one another. Maggie had wanted to beg him not to rush off again. There were so many things she'd wanted to tell him, words she'd lacked the courage to say. And if he left and later returned with a woman at his side, as well he might, they would never get said. If he brought back another woman to take her place, Maggie knew her own heart would wither and die, like those pitiful little blossoms Isaac had planted on Anne's grave.

She treasured her moccasins, not only because they felt far better than her stiff black boots, but because they'd been a gift from Cabe. His hands had held them. He'd wanted her to have them.

Far too often he crept into her dreams. Dreaming had no place in her life, she reminded herself repeatedly. For all the good it did. Just because she'd agreed to stay on until she was no longer needed, that was no cause to go weaving dreams about things that would likely never happen. How many women in this world married for love? None that she knew of, save perhaps Sara, but even then, it had probably been more a case of growing up together and being handy when it came time to settle down.

On one score, however, Maggie felt justified in taking pride. Isaac had come to accept her as the authority in the Rawson household when the *Bridget* was out. Which didn't mean he obeyed her without question; it only meant she had an even chance.

She'd come to love the tough little scamp for his own sake, and not just because he reminded her so much of Cabe. Now and again he made some reference to their secret, and Maggie could have wept all over again. She hadn't the heart to tell him that in all likelihood, she no longer had a brother. It wasn't just that she was ashamed to confess that Gid had probably played a part in the raid that had taken Jedd's life, but the child had seen enough of death. It was time he learned that loving didn't always mean losing, and if that meant she must hide her own grief, then so be it.

Sometime during the night, the wind shifted. After a long spell of cool drizzling weather, the day dawned still and sultry. Both Maggie and Isaac were weary of being housebound. While it rained every day for a week, she'd searched her memory for childish games, and then turned to story-telling until she'd run out of tales. She was dying to get outside, if she did nothing but sit in a clearing and watch the fish hawks circle overhead. Thank goodness Eli still napped after his midday feed. Sara's Charity Ann woke with the chickens and never closed her eyes again till long after dark.

Seeing Isaac headed out the door, she called after him. "Watch that sky, it still looks a mite uncertain over across the sound."

"Aw-ww, Maggie . . ."

"You'll do more'n 'aww, Maggie,' if you take one of your pa's boats out and a squall blows up."

"I ain't gonna take no boat. They're all swamped."

"Then bail them out."

"Then can I take the skiff?"

"Not while the weather's still uncertain."

"It ain't gonna come no bloody squall!"

"Mind your tongue, Isaac Rawson. No boats today, you hear me?"

"I hear you," he said with exaggerated wariness. "Kin I have a molasses cake?"

"Have two."

He was gone before the lid settled on the crock, and Maggie grinned after him. The little imp. He knew very well she had a soft spot for him. Why else would she work so hard to keep that crock filled with his favorite sweet? She couldn't abide the things, herself.

As the sun simmered down through a pale gray haze, Maggie thought longingly of yesterday's bath. Knowing that Isaac was playing at Sara's house, she'd done something incredibly daring. Taking a bar of soap, she'd peeled down to her shift and gone out in the rain, standing under the edge of the roof where the water cascaded over the eaves. There, she'd lathered herself from stem to stern, as Jedd would've said, glorying in the freedom of not having to dip every gourdful of water and carry it inside in a pail.

Of course, she'd been covered with goosebumps before she was half done, but it had been worth it. Later on today, when sweat began beading her back as she hilled up the winter greens, she would remember how she'd shivered then and savor the feeling.

Eli rubbed mashed venison and turnips into his hair and looked to her for approval. His eyelids were drooping, but he fought against surrender.

"Num-num ma?"

"Yes, dumplin', there's a smart boy. Here, let Maggie wash your face."

"Mmmm ma-a-aa."

Her heart swelled as she removed a shred of meat from the silky dark hair. He was calling her 'ma' now, she was certain of it. And while it thrilled her, she dreaded to think what Cabel would say when he heard it. He would swear she'd taught him the word deliberately.

If he ever heard it. From the looks of it, he'd deserted them for good. She'd not seen hide nor hair of him for weeks, not since the morning he'd given her the moccasins, stared into her eyes until her knees had fair crumpled beneath her, and then stalked off without so much as a word of farewell.

It hadn't been the first time he'd forced her to face up to her deepest feelings for him and then walked away without a word. Did it give him a sense of power? Was that why he did it? Lord knows, if he were any more powerful, he wouldn't even need a ship to carry him across the sea!

If only Matt and Lina were ready to wed, Maggie told herself she would get away, as far away as possible before Cabe returned. But Lina was far too young to take over her responsibilities, even if she could bring herself to relinquish them.

Besides, Matt still showed no signs of being ready to settle down. He and Gaffer were doing coastal runs with the *Eliza Lea*, with a contract for hauling lumber that promised to keep them busy well into the next year.

Maggie missed the young man's cheerful teasing. There were times when her spirits sagged so low that it was all she could do to get out of bed, stoke the fire and set the water to boil for another meal, another load of laundry. If there was a way to keep a leaky baby from wetting through a whole set of bedding in the wink of an eye, she'd yet to learn about it. Sara had been no help, declaring that only time and patience would ease the situation.

It had been Sara, however, who had told her of the decision to keep secret her dubious marital status. There was no cause to blacken Jedd's name, she'd explained, and him no longer able to speak out in his own defense. His motives had been selfish, but not unreasonably so. At least no one had been hurt by the deception.

No one, Maggie had thought bitterly, except for herself. She'd been both hurt and angry at first, but she'd eventually come to accept what couldn't be changed.

Now, settling Eli in his cradle and opening the window so that she would hear him from outside if he woke, Maggie quietly slipped off her gown. She'd put it on clean after her bath the day before, but already it was spattered with turnips and venison. Her oldest gray was practically falling apart, which left only her new calico.

If she'd ever hoped the bright blue color would dim the green of her eyes and the red of her hair to more circumspect shades, she'd been sorely disappointed. It only accentuated her bold coloring, as the plain cut of it accentuated the new roundness her body had developed since she'd taken to eating regular meals and not cringing every time a shadow fell over her.

In a strangely reckless mood, Maggie slipped on her moccasins. Though her first impulse had been to keep them forever as a memento of a rare tender gesture from a harsh and difficult man, she knew as well as anyone that leather unused soon stiffened and cracked. Besides, when she finally left this island, the last thing she'd be needing to carry with her was a bundle of foolish tokens.

For a long moment she studied the dainty slippers, admiring the stylized sunbursts of yellow flowers that decorated the tops. They were only shoes, she told herself, nothing more. Certainly not a declaration of any tender feelings on the part of the giver.

Shoes were shoes, and a woman alone must be frugal. Therefore, she would keep Cabe's gift, but from now on, she would use it instead of placing it on the pillow beside her where she could reach out and stroke it with her fingertips in the dark, lonely night.

With one last glance at Eli, who was sleeping in his favorite position, with his small rump lifting the light woolen spread, Maggie tiptoed from the bedroom. She took down a basket from the wall, one that was already stained from many years of service. She'd a mind to go wandering with no particular goal, but it was simply not in her to waste time when she could just as well gather grapes, or acorns to parch on the hearth on a cold winter night.

Cabe waited impatiently for the longboat to be lowered. He'd hoped to be home a week earlier, but they'd followed up one false lead after another, combing the whole damned coast, from Virginia almost to Georgia. At every possible port, he'd set forth seeking word of a tall pale-haired young man with a blaze-mark on his right cheek.

Cabe knew well the dangers of asking such questions in any seaport town. A man's affairs were his own private concern, and a wise man damned well heeded that fact if he wanted to keep lights and liver together.

Even so, he'd been compelled to take the risk, for his own sake as well as Maggie's. He needed to resolve this matter one way or another—either with word of her lover's death, or by bringing the young bastard home with him so that she could choose between them. Even knowing which one she would choose, he could do no less, for he had wounded and shamed her in an attempt to deny his own feelings.

But in spite of his efforts, all he'd been able to bring her was a bundle of rose slips he'd collected in Williamsburg. He was bone-tired, frustrated as hell and no nearer a solution than when he'd left nearly a month before.

The wind had kicked up out of the east about half an hour before they'd dropped anchor, and even though the *Bridget* had been built for the shallow waters of the Pamlico, they'd damned near ripped the keel off her hull dragging over oyster shoals. It was near dead calm in the lee of the wooded village, and Cabe could see similar shoals rising above the fast ebbing tide on either side of him. Already dozens of women and children with baskets and several small boats were taking advantage of the unusually low tide to gather shellfish.

As he set out in the longboat, gulls circled overhead in search of stranded clams. At any other time, he might have lingered to gather a few himself, for he was right partial to salty raw clams, but his mind was not on seafood, nor food of any kind.

Would she still be there? God, what if she'd left!

Of course she'd be there, he told himself. He knew his Maggie, and she was not one to walk out from under her responsibilities. Besides, she loved those two babes almost as if they were her own.

But what if he'd driven her away by his constant coldness, his cruelties? One pair of moccasins couldn't make up for all the pain he'd brought her.

Bending to his task, Cabe sent the longboat skimming over the wind-whipped waters, skillfully dodging the shallows as he kept his sights on the familiar cove that sheltered his home and his heart's desire.

Isaac shifted the heavy bundle to his other shoulder. His feet were numb with cold, but he refused to turn back until he'd filled the sack with oysters. Maggie would be so proud of him . . .

Pausing in his labors, he watched a small sail skiff nudge a shoal, heeling over so that the boom raked the water. There was no anchor line out, and her tiller was untended. Someone was going to lose a fine boat if he didn't—

"Hey! You aboard yonder skiff, are you ailin' or something?" he called out cautiously. What he'd taken for a rag dangling over the gunnels was an arm, the fingers trailing in the water.

Picking his way carefully through the clusters of razor-edged shellfish, Isaac edged closer. The skin on the back of his neck prickled, and he braced himself for what he might find.

Somehow Maggie found herself on the hill beside Anne and Jedd's graves. It was a peaceable place, close enough so that she could hear if Eli woke, but sheltered, too. With its vine-hung trees and its windowlike opening onto the water, it was the closest thing to a church she could think of. Maggie had some praying to do. And perhaps some weeping, too, for she'd been bottling things up inside her for too long now.

Half an hour later, she sat up and rubbed her swollen eyes. "Well, that's mostly what's been bothering me, Lord, but if he's in your hands now, then I reckon I'll have to face up to it. The thing is, I don't feel it in my bones, and I always thought I would, somehow, if anything ever happened to Gid. Shows how foolish a body can be. And while we're on that subject, Lord, I—oh, glory, that looks like the—it is! Lord, he's come back! There's the *Bridget*, and here I been sitting, a-weeping and a-wailing over my troubles while I should've been poking up the fire and setting out food! 'Scuse me, Lord, I'd better get on down the hill.''

She heard the voices even before she reached the door. Isaac was holding forth, his voice high-pitched with excitement. He was always that way when Cabe came home. There was a closeness between those two that none of the others shared.

''My Pa was a seaman, too, and he was the best and the smartest, and the—and the—only the pirates killed him, but Cabe, he went after them and chopped off their—''

''Isaac!''

At the sound of Maggie's voice, the boy jumped to his feet. ''I found Gid, Maggie. I knowed him by the mark on his face. He says the Lord put it there 'cause he liked strawberries so much, and I saved him. If'n it weren't for me, Maggie, he'd 'a' never made it to shore. Tell her, Gid, tell her!''

A man appeared beside Isaac in the doorway, his arm in a canvas sling, one foot booted, the other bare, and his head wrapped in a clumsy bandage. He grinned at her, and for a moment Maggie could only stare, too stunned to react at seeing the brother she'd believed dead.

''Gideon,'' she whispered. Finally some force other than her own set her feet into motion, and with a soft, broken cry she ran forward, ready to launch herself into his arms, and stopped short to gape at his injuries.

No one had noticed the sharp intake of Cabe's breath, nor heard the single terrible oath he'd uttered. They'd been too busy hanging onto the bastard he'd just spent three weeks looking for to pay him any mind.

Cabe had been full of noble intentions—that is, until he'd seen Maggie practically knock the young scoundrel down greeting him. He'd come up from their landing just as she'd hurried into the house, and he'd gone after her, his feet silent in the soft sand. He'd been just in time to hear Isaac tell her all about saving the bastard's life, and to see her response.

What a waste of time. One Rawson saves him, and another one was going to scalp him and throw him out for the buzzards to pick over!

Cabe stepped inside the door. "Get away from her, you son of a bitch." The quiet words seemed to shatter even the golden shafts of sunlight that slanted into the room.

"Cabe!" Maggie cried as she felt herself wrenched from her brother's one good arm. His eyes were glittering with a deadly determination. "Cabe, what is it? No—please!"

Cabe's fist smashed into Gid's face, and the younger man crumpled silently to the floor. Maggie followed him down, cradling his head on her lap. "Gideon, wake up. It's all right, love, he'll not hurt you again." Glaring up at Cabel, who had turned away to stare out the door, she said, "He was injured. If you've hurt him, I swear I'll kill you myself."

Visibly bracing himself, Cabe turned, his eyes going from Isaac, who was cowering in one corner, his black eyes round as acorns, to Maggie, kneeling on the floor with Gideon's bandaged blond head clutched to her, his neck bent at such an awkward angle that Cabe thought if the poor devil didn't die of his other wounds, he would likely die of a broken neck at Maggie's hands. "If you love him so much, then get him the hell out of here and don't let me see either of you again," he said, pain robbing his voice of expression.

"Well, I can't drag him out, he's too heavy—and I can't stop loving him! He's my brother, dammit! You're just going to have to put—"

"Your brother!" The word exploded from Cabe's throat. "Your *brother*?" he repeated, a stunned look on his face. "Christ, Maggie!"

"Would you stop swearing and lift him up?" Maggie cried, but Cabe was gone. Without another word, he swung out the doorway and strode off into the woods.

With Isaac's help, Maggie was able to get Gid upright and move him into the bedroom, where he collapsed on Matt's bed. "Maybe I'd better fetch Emma," said Isaac, worried lest his new hero should die on him before he'd heard the rest of his story.

"'M a'right," Gid muttered weakly. He grinned, and it too was a feeble effort. "Don't know's I can take any more Hatteras hospitality, though. Ocracoke's some better. Leastwise, they wait'll a man's steady on his pins to knock 'im down again."

"Oh, Gid, it's just—Cabe didn't mean it. He's just got back from—well, with losing his Pa and all, he's not been himself."

"See, Cabe don't know 'bout you fighting Turk and all that. Tell her about it, Gid. Tell Maggie like you told me. Maggie, he took on that ol' Turk all by hisself and whomped the daylights out of 'im, and—"

"Sorry to disappoint you, little feller, but it was Turk that laid me out and left me for crow bait."

"Yeah, but you took 'im on! You walloped 'im real good before he laid you out, didn't you?"

Maggie looked from one to the other, needing to hear all Gid had to say, but with a fiercer need to reassure Cabe. If he'd been angry because he thought Gid had had a hand in the raid that had killed Jedd, at least she could ease his mind on that matter. The rest would follow. They would sort it all out, one way or another.

"Gid, let me get your feet up on the bed and—"

"Ow! That foot's been broke, Maggie! A man ain't safe around you. Leave us. If I need anything, the boy'll fetch it for me. Go find that savage of yours and keep him away until I get my breath back."

Maggie didn't need a second prompting. If Cabe returned in his present mood, Gid wouldn't stand a chance. She had to find him, to make him understand that Gid hadn't been a part of the fatal raid.

Five minutes later, Cabe, his temper held in check, returned to the house. Her brother. After he'd hunted the poor blighter from one end of the coast to another, intending to do the honorable thing if it killed him, he'd laid him out at her feet. Damn near knocked his head off, and him no fair match for a day-old duckling.

Her brother! Why the hell hadn't she said something before now? She could have saved him all this agony.

And why should she have told him anything? When had he ever spared her?

"McNair—if that be your name—we've some talking to do. No, don't try to get up. Isaac, fetch Pa's jug. The man needs something to take away the taste of my fist."

The water swallowed up the sun in a blaze of fire, and even as Maggie watched, storm clouds swiftly eclipsed the color. What a changeable world they lived in! Cold one day, warm the next, calm one moment, stormy the next. Gideon missing, feared dead, then restored to her when she'd all but given up.

And Cabe.

Sighing, she shook her head and nibbled another grape. She'd searched all the places she knew, short of banging on every door and asking if he were hiding there. Finally she'd come to her favorite place on the shore to think. Either he would return or he wouldn't. Nothing she could do would make a difference.

Three night herons stalked the shallows, and she watched them unseeingly, licking the purple juice from her fingertips. They were stained with it, her lips were stained, too, and her hair had collected all manner of twigs and leaves. Soon she would have to go back. Gideon needed rest, but he would need food even more. He'd lost weight since the last time she'd seen him.

As though something had startled them, the herons unfurled their wings and stepped, hopped—and then they were aloft, skimming just over the water and out of sight around the point that shielded her from the house.

A rumble of distant thunder quickened her pulse. There was something wild in the air this evening, something that whispered of exciting changes to come. Never in all her years on the mainland had she been so aware of the forces of nature as she had since coming to the banks.

Throwing back her head, she filled her lungs with tangy salt air just as an unseasonably warm breeze moved the curling tendrils on her brow.

That was how he found her. Stopping dead in his tracks, Cabe feasted his eyes on the sight of Maggie staring out across the water, her arms wrapped about her knees, the moccasins he'd had Sits There make for her cupping her feet the way his hands ached to do. She was more beautiful than ever, with her eyes closed and her lips parted, as if waiting for a lover's kiss, and the strange half-light splintering into liquid fire as it struck her hair.

At the sight of her softly swelling breasts above her gown, he felt a familiar hunger begin to stir in his loins, the hunger that had made it impossible for him to remain in the same house with her without taking her again and again. In spite of the breeze that had picked up only moments before, he felt a film of sweat break out on his body.

Maggie, Maggie—could she forgive him? Was there a chance she could come to accept him as a lover? A husband?

How was it possible for any woman to look so innocent and so sensuous at the same time? He hadn't even touched her and his body was standing forth like a damned bowsprit!

There ought to be a law against Maggie McNair, he thought, swearing softly.

As if sensing his presence, she turned slowly and met his eyes. Thank God he was half-hidden behind a wax myrtle bush, or she'd have jumped up and run screaming into the house. Short of wearing an apron himself, there was no way he could hide his lamentable condition.

They stared at one another for an eternity. Neither of them spoke. After a while, Cabe began to wonder if he'd finally placed himself outside her forgiveness by this latest brutality. But how could he have known the man he'd thought was her lover was her brother?

"Cabel?"

He hadn't even greeted her properly when he'd followed her into the house. Clearing his throat, he hoped he wouldn't make a complete ass of himself now in the attempt. "Aye, Maggie, it's me. Have you, um, fared well while I've been away?"

"Well enough."

The sound of her soft voice was almost his undoing. When he could catch his breath, he ventured a few more words. "And the youngers?"

"They're well, too." Her voice held a whispery quality, as if she weren't quite certain he hadn't come to do her harm. "They've grown some, even though it's not been quite a month."

"Isaac looked taller. Looked ready to to take me on, in fact." The minute the words left his tongue, he regretted them. He'd do better not to remind her of his latest blunder. "Maggie, I'm sorry," he blurted, "I thought—that is, I didn't know—"

"You thought Gid was one of the men who helped murder Jedd."

Wordlessly he nodded. That wasn't precisely what he'd thought, but it would do for now. "He's all right—that is, I didn't break his jaw. Leastwise, he was able to explain a few things."

"You went back to the house? I searched everywhere for you."

Cabe's gaze played hungrily over her flushed cheeks, her grape-stained lips and her windblown hair. Borrowing courage, he stepped closer, holding her gaze by force of sheer will so that she wouldn't notice his agitation and be frightened of him. "That's, um, a new gown you're wearing, isn't it?"

The color in her cheeks heightened and she ducked her face to study her purple fingertips. "I reckon I'd best get back and set the bread to baking. Would you like pickled beef, too, or will bread and beans suit you well enough?"

"What I'd like is to talk some before we go back. That is, if you aren't—I mean, if you don't . . ." Frustration beat at him. Gathering his courage, he approached her, not stopping until he was so close that the toe of his moccasin brushed against her skirt. "Damn all, Maggie!" he burst out.

As if his words had been hailstones, Maggie shrank from him, and Cabe's courage fled. She hated him. Was it any wonder? She'd known naught but brutality from his hands from the very first. He, a man who deplored cruelty in any form, had berated her and mistreated her, just one more in a long line of such men, he feared.

With a sinking heart, he recalled that first day in his cabin when he'd caught a glimpse of her scarred and bruised back. God, even now it sickened him to think of it! After first sending Isaac from the room, Gideon had told him something of their earlier life, blaming himself for not staying on to protect his mother and sister. He'd been afraid of his own temper after being provoked into a fight that had nearly killed his stepbrother.

Cautiously Cabe lowered himself to the ground beside Maggie, taking care not to touch her. He took a deep breath and blurted out what had to be said. "Maggie, I'll not blame you if you never want to hear my name spoke again, for I've used you shamefully, even to hurting someone you love, and him hardly able to stand, much less fight. It's no comfort to you, I know, but I do heartily regret my misdeeds. I can truthfully swear that I'll never knowingly hurt you again."

There. He'd said what had to be said. The rest was up to her, now that she knew how he felt about her.

He waited.

And waited.

"Well?" he barked when his patience ran out.

Maggie slanted him a wary look. "Well . . . what?"

"Well, don't you have anything to say?"

"I—I'm not certain what you're wanting to hear."

Drawing his knees up, feet braced apart, he turned toward her, eyes blazing. "Damn all, Maggie, I just poured out my heart to you! Can't you at least tell me if you will or you won't? I know I'm not much. My temper's foul, as well you know, and I'm gone a good part of the time, but I can change. I'm not a rich man, Maggie, but I'll always provide for you. My ways are rough, and God knows, my tongue is, too, for I'm a seaman, and it's a rough life. If now and then I come down too hard on a body, I mean no disrespect. A man learns to be forceful when the lives of his crew depend on him. But I vow to care for you, Maggie, as tenderly as ever a man cared for any woman."

Maggie had not drawn a breath since he'd begun speaking. Her lips were parted, her eyes wide, and she felt the fragile moment shimmering around her like the lightning that flashed out over the water. If he had touched her just then, she would have likely flown into a thousand pieces.

"Maggie? Did you hear anything I said? What I'm trying to make you understand is that I'll always cherish you. That is, if—if you'll have me."

Slowly Maggie allowed the words to sink in. She was afraid to believe what she'd just heard, afraid to reach out to him— even afraid to move for fear he would vanish and she'd be left with the same old empty arms and empty dreams.

Cabe sighed heavily. Moving with a woodenness that was totally alien to his usual masculine grace, he got to his feet and turned to go. His eyes were shadowed with pain in a face grown suddenly bleak.

As if suddenly released from a spell, Maggie jumped up and grabbed at his sleeve. "Wait!"

Guardedly he turned back, not trusting himself to speak again.

And she couldn't. Or at least, she wouldn't. While he watched, she opened her mouth and closed it twice, her eyes pleading with him for—for what?

Hope began to stir inside him. "Maggie?"

And then her words spilled out as she clung to his arm, gripping it with surprisingly strong fingers. "Cabe, did you mean it? Do you really want me? *Me?*" There was fear and hope and wonder in her tremulous voice.

"Want you! God help me, woman, haven't I just told you so? Didn't I—oh, hell, come here! There's a better way to show you how much I want you."

His arms crushed her for only an instant, then eased enough so that she could breathe. His lips devoured hers for only a moment, too, then grew tender and gentle as he made love to her mouth, telling her beyond all doubt that he wanted her, that more than wanting her, he loved her.

Maggie never knew when her feet left the ground, never heard the thunder, nor saw the lightning coursing toward the water offshore. The thunder of her heart drowned out the storm, and the lightning that streaked through her body at his touch was more powerful than anything the heavens could send down.

Finally he held her away long enough to loosen her gown and draw it over her head. Maggie, her shift and petticoat pressed against her body by the wind, stood trembling before him as he whipped off his shirt and tossed it onto the ground. Stepping out of his moccasins, he peeled his trousers down over his hips and stood naked before her, and she stared at him in awe.

"A man don't feel comfortable baring himself before a woman, and she still clothed, Maggie. He feels...naked. Humble."

Maggie allowed her gaze to wander over him, spanning the admirable breadth of his shoulders, the remarkable depth of his chest, following the tapering line of his hips and lingering on that fascinating place of dark magic that she'd seen only once before.

And then her eyes rose to meet him, and what she found there told her more clearly than words that he was offering himself to her. He had bared himself deliberately, giving her the power to accept or reject him. For a man as proud as Cabel Rawson, there could be no greater admission of love.

She began to smile. "Humble?" she teased gently, stepping closer to place her hand in his. "Lord, there's nothing humble about you, leastwise, nothing that I can see."

As if he'd been holding himself erect by sheer force of will, Cabe relaxed. His lips curled in a wry smile and he lifted her hand to his lips. "All the same, woman, I'd feel better if you weren't wearing so da—so bloody many—" he sighed in exasperation "—so *very* many clothes."

He stroked the sides of her fingers, exploring the soft crevices between them, and then his thumb began to stroke the pad at the base of her thumb, slipping off now and then to venture into the hollow of her palm.

Maggie's breathing grew ragged. A film of sweat beaded her upper lip. "Cabel, I can't think when you do that."

"I'm wooing you, Maggie."

"Oh, is that what it is?" Her voice was unsteady, barely more than a whisper.

"I owe you your wooing, dearling, for the first time I took you, it was—"

She placed a finger over his lips, stopping the flow of words. "There was no other time, Cabel. It begins today. It begins now. Right here in this wild place, with the wind and the water and the trees overhead."

"You deserve better." He gathered her to him, stroking her back and gently easing her shift down over her shoulders. "I'll give you silks and fine laces, and a horse and cart of your own, and a chair with cushions for your back, and—"

"There's only one thing I want from you, Cabel, and that's your love. I never really believed in it before, but—oh, glory, what are you doing?"

Having bared her breasts for his delectation, Cabe paused long enough to smile up at her, vulnerable in his openness. "I'm loving you, dearling, the best way I know how. If I'm not pleasing you, then best tell me now, while I'm still capable of reason."

When she made no reply save a gasp of pleasure as his tongue circled her nipple, he went to work on the ties that held her petticoat, his fingers clumsy in their haste.

Boldly Maggie slid her hands over the satin strength of his shoulders to the place where the hair grew in crisp flat curls on his chest. As her petticoat crumpled silently to the ground, she found what she'd been seeking.

"Saints in heaven, woman, you're making me daft," Cabe groaned as she stroked his nipples. His mouth found hers and he crushed her to him, and somehow they were on the ground surrounded by the heady fragrance of resinous pine straw, ripening grapes and pungent salt marshes.

"God, how I want you," he whispered, his voice thick with emotion. As if it were a treasure more precious than gold, he cradled her soft breasts, caressing them until their peaks hard ened against his palm. Taking care to be gentle, he suckled her until she was twisting helplessly in his arms. "I need you so— Maggie, please . . ."

Beyond speech, she could only lie there and allow the glory to wash over her. He kissed her eyes, her nose, murmuring broken words in that heathen tongue of his that she didn't even try to understand. His lips traced the line of her throat, crested her breasts and smoothed their way over the soft plateau beneath.

"So beautiful. *Wisto roosomme*—my soft little fawn. How I love you. How I want you," he murmured between kisses. "Don't let me hurt you, Maggie. I'd cut out my heart before I wounded you again."

"Hush! Never speak of hurting." Drawing her knees up, she curled around him. His arms tightened around her body so that they were twined together, all hungry, seeking hands and mouths on warm, tingling flesh, "I only know that I want you to touch me—to take away this awful craving, for I don't know how to make it stop."

At her words, his eyes kindled with a fire that threatened to consume her. And then his mouth took hers once more, twisting to break the seal of her lips, plunging, taking, conquering a willing captive.

He loved her mouth, by turns gentle and forceful, until she was writhing beneath him, aching for a fulfillment that was still denied her.

Nor were his hands idle. He stroked down her belly, brushing softly against the nest of curls, while she circled the flat of her palm over the tiny hard points of his nipples. She found his shaft and clasped it, and he shuddered.

"Woman, if you would see me carry this thing through to a proud end, then you'd best unhand me, or I vow I'll finish the race and leave you far behind."

"But I like to touch you." The words were muffled against his throat, and she tasted the salt of his skin with the tip of her tongue.

"Then touch me with this." His fingers sought out the passage and found it damp and swollen with readiness. "There's much I would teach you, loveling, if you'll let me."

Not waiting, he mounted her, taking care not to press his weight on her small body, for the earth was rough beneath her back. First the floor, he thought, and then the ground . . . he would have given her the finest beds, the softest sheets.

And then he thought no more, for he had come home. She clasped him tightly, and he reined in his eagerness, for this time he would give her her own taste of heaven first.

Using all his considerable skill, Cabel took her gently where he was certain she had never been before. The moment he felt her begin to shudder beneath him, her breath coming in startled little gasps, he began to stroke furiously, and together they were caught up in a tidal wave of ecstasy. As the waves receded he held her tenderly, murmuring incoherent words of love, words he had never uttered to another woman. Dream words.

Long afterward they lay twined together, damp and exhausted, while unheeded, a sharp wind blew across their bodies. A flurry of red creeper leaves rained down on them as lightning split the skies. They neither knew nor cared.

"You're cold, dearling. I'd best get you dressed and take you home."

"We won't be able to—that is, I reckon it wouldn't be proper . . ."

Cabe knew what she was trying to say. It had been on his mind, too. "We've a guest, Maggie. Your brother might have something to say if I was to climb into your bed, and us not wed."

"Oh." Her doleful look was too much for him, and Cabe swung her up in his arms and buried his face in her throat. "Ah, my sweet Maggie, I fear I'll not be doing much sailing for many a day."

"I've heard tell there's Anglicans a-plenty up in Virginia. Do you ever sail up that way?"

"I reckon it could be arranged. But I thought you weren't partial to sailing."

Wriggling to the ground, Maggie proceeded to finish dressing, though in truth, she was much more interested in watching Cabe step into his buckskin trousers and slide his bronzed arms into his white linen shirt. "I can tolerate some," she allowed.

"As long as there's good cause?" Cabe teased.

"As long as there's good cause," Maggie agreed, her grin every bit as teasing as his. And when he caught her up in his arms for one last embrace before they headed down to the house, the 'good cause' threatened to spring out of control all over again.

Long after the others were asleep, and Maggie had exclaimed over her precious hoard of rose slips and decided where each one would go, Cabe and Maggie sat talking. "Dearling, if you'd told me about your brother, it would have saved me many an hour of agony."

"So many times I wanted to tell you, but I was afraid to. With all the bankers vowing to see every pirate on the Atlantic hang, I didn't dare speak out, even though I knew Gid wasn't truly one of them."

"I don't wonder you found it hard to give your trust." Over a supper of Isaac's oysters and fresh baked bread, the four of them had talked of Jedd's family and the McNairs. Gid had been offered a place with Jeremiah at the boat yard, but he'd claimed to have plans of his own, something involving a woman at Ocracoke.

"You'll never have to fear anyone again, Maggie," Cabe reassured her for the third time in as many hours. "Gideon might have other plans, but as for me, I've a notion to go to work for Jeremiah and leave the sailing to—"

"You'll do no such thing! Cabel Rawson, it's a seafaring man I fell in love with, and it's a seafaring man I'll wed. I only ask three things of you."

"Ask for the moon, and I'll fetch it for you."

"I'd like to see if I can abide on the water for more than an hour without getting sick—"

"Done! Dearling, I'll have Jere build a bed big enough for both of us in my cabin, and I'll show you green islands abounding in all manner of birds and flowers, and waters so clear you can see ten fathoms down!"

"Not so fast. Maybe I'll go out in Gid's sail skiff a time or two first, and then we'll see. Then there's the preacher. If it's all the same to you, I'd as lief have a real Anglican say the words over us, with Sara and Gid and the youngers and—"

"The whole da—the whole bloody—oh, hell, Maggie, invite the world!"

"And last of all, when the babies start to come—you do want babies, don't you?" It took only the fire that leaped in his eyes to assure her on that point. "Well, I want to name our first daughter Jane, after my mother, and Anne, after yours."

"Love, you can name as many babies as you want to, and I'll do my best to provide for them."

"Well, first you have to provide the babies," she said in her most practical tone.

Strangling, he stood and raked back his hair. "Woman, if you expect to sleep alone until we can lay hands on a preacher, you'd best mind your tongue."

Maggie blew out the candle and inhaled the sweet fragrance of bayberry and beeswax. "Gid snores something awful. Like as not you won't get a bit of sleep tonight."

She felt his hands on her shoulders and smiled into the warm, familiar darkness. When he spoke, his breath stirred her hair on her cheek. "Then I reckon I'd best set out for the *Bridget*. It won't be the first time I've slept on board to try and keep from going crazy a-thinking about you sleeping on the other side of that wall."

"Set one foot out that door, Cabel Rawson, and I'll break your oars over your wicked head," Maggie purred. As she stood and slipped her arm about his waist, she had a feeling that Jedd would understand.

Cracka mast, pecka meal, one aig. At last, the winds had turned in her favor.

* * * * *

COMING NEXT MONTH

#25 SO SWEET A SIN—Brooke Hastings

Fiery Sophie Stoddard would be governed by no man. So
when her uncle, the Earl of Wynbourne, entrusted her care
to merchant Edward Holt for the voyage to America, the
handsome Puritan was sorely tested. But as British
sabotage beset the Colonies, Sophie proved a rewarding
ally to the patriotic Edward, as well as an irresistible
temptation.

#26 SEIZE THE FIRE—Patricia Potter

Young widow April Manning winced at the army's cruel
treatment of their stoic prisoner, MacKenzie. In her heart
she knew the half-breed scout was innocent of the
atrocities he'd allegedly committed. But her intuition was
tested to the limit when MacKenzie took April and her
small son hostage to escape his executioners. Did the flash
of fire in his eyes signal honor or danger?

You'll flip . . . your pages won't!
Read paperbacks *hands-free* with

Book Mate • I

The perfect "mate" for all your romance paperbacks

Traveling • Vacationing • At Work • In Bed • Studying • Cooking • Eating

Perfect size for all standard paperbacks, this wonderful invention makes reading a pure pleasure! Ingenious design holds paperback books OPEN and FLAT so even wind can't ruffle pages — leaves your hands free to do other things. Reinforced, wipe-clean vinyl-covered holder flexes to let you turn pages without undoing the strap . . . supports paperbacks so well, they have the strength of hardcovers!

Pages turn WITHOUT opening the strap

SEE-THROUGH STRAP

Reinforced back stays flat

Built in bookmark

BOOK MARK

BACK COVER HOLDING STRIP

10 x 7¼ opened
Snaps closed for easy carrying, too

Coming in June...

Harlequin Presents...

PENNY JORDAN

a reason for being

We invite you to join us in celebrating Harlequin's
40th Anniversary with this very special book we
selected to publish worldwide.

While you read this story, millions of women in 100
countries will be reading it, too.

A Reason for Being by Penny Jordan is being
published in June in the Presents series in 19
languages around the world. Join women around
the world in helping us to celebrate 40 years of
romance.

Penny Jordan's *A Reason for Being* is Presents June
title #1180. Look for it wherever paperbacks are
sold.